ISLAND OF SECRETS

DIANE DEMETRE

LUMINOSITY PUBLISHING LLP

ISLAND OF SECRETS

Copyright © October 2018 DIANE DEMETRE

ISBN: 978-1-9993066-1-8

Cover Art by Poppy Designs

DEDICATION

For all those who believe in the power of love to cross time and space. Welcome home.

*Wherever a human being goes, there is a challenge.
Be the best man you can, and your gods will look with
favor upon you.*

— James A. Michener, *Hawaii*

PART ONE

1973

CECILIA

CHAPTER ONE

For a day that had started out so right, she had no idea how it went so horribly wrong. She'd rather be struck blind, than dumb. But no. Like the mute village idiot, Cecilia stared in disbelief at the scene playing out in front of her. Right there. In broad daylight. *This can't be happening.* Yet it was. She wasn't imagining it. Her skin crawled. The tiny hairs on the back of her neck jabbed like cactus needles, torturing her to say something, anything. But, how could she? The moisture in her mouth had evaporated, instead replaced by a desiccated salt lake. In this, her hour of need, her traitorous body abandoned her.

Infuriated, she looked away. The morning sunlight glittered across the rolling waves, and she wondered how in the most beautiful and romantic place on earth, her world could fall apart right in front of her eyes. Literally. But she would not embarrass herself. No. She would not rant and rave. Instead, she remembered what her mother had drilled into her from an early age. "Cecilia, a woman must remain dignified no matter the circumstance. Only then can she achieve great things." And as much as she'd distanced herself from her controlling, protective parents over the past five years, some of her Pacific Heights' upbringing remained. But more than her upper-class background, she would not lose her cool in front of the Brotherhood — the small band of free-loving, pot-smoking, flower-power hippies with whom she'd spent the last month living an alternative lifestyle. *No, this will not break me. I am more than this.* With jaw set and lips pursed, Cecilia silently repeated her self-love mantra as she glowered at the horizon.

Decision made, she folded her legs beneath her and sprang up with the force of a freed jack-in-the-box. God, she hated those toys. They had scared the hell out of her when she was a child. Even accompanied by a loud *harrumph*, her animated impersonation of one of those hideous little dolls had little effect on those beside her. With a determined push, she slid her sunglasses high on her nose to hide the threatening tears. She reached down and tugged her sarong around her bikini-clad body, then hefted her fringed leather tote bag onto her shoulder. Inside amassed all her meager worldly possessions. Another pair of sandals, some colorful skirts, pants and blouses she'd bought from second-hand shops, a collection of shell-and-bead jewelry, a few basic toiletries and the remainder of her cash. Her parents would be mortified to know how she was living. But as she'd informed them when she'd left, it was her life, not theirs.

"Hey, Cecilia, where're you off to, babe?" Tony's lilting voice drawled up toward her as if disembodied.

At least he seemed to care. Although stoned most of the time, he displayed more compassion than Michael — the Brotherhood of Love's tall, gorgeous, love-you-forever-babe guru. All of this was Michael's doing. All of this was Michael's fault.

A couple of months ago, she'd met him at one of the gay-rights and freedom-of-speech rallies in their hometown of San Francisco. Like a feather floating on a breeze, he had epitomized the personal freedom and transcendental life she sought. A talented busker, he had serenaded her into his bed with his honey-toned voice. On a double mattress on the floor in the basement of his parents' brownstone, they had made love, day after day, night after night. With pledges of everlasting love, their life had consisted of endless sex, blissful sleep and deep conversations about how they would change the world. All nourished by liberal lashings of his drug of choice.

"Come on, Cecilia," he'd crooned, his voice raspy from too much Acapulco Gold. "Come with me and the gang to Maui. We can make love, smoke pot, surf some sick waves and make beautiful music together. We'll be the Brotherhood of Love, living, loving and hanging out together. We'll be the first of a new world order."

Loose and warm from sex, she'd lounged in his arms, a reefer between her fingers, falling in love with him and his Hawaiian dream.

In her rare moments of lucidity, she'd voiced her concerns about leaving San Francisco. "But, Michael, I want a singing career. Here in San Fran—"

Ignoring her dreams, he'd sprung to his feet and sung Simon and Garfunkel's "Cecilia" in her honor. He'd wailed and danced naked in front of her, begging down on his knees, stealing her heart and aspirations. Beguiled, she'd cast aside the last remnants of common sense and followed him across the ocean to the Magic Isle. Now, all she wanted to do was get the hell out of Maui's idyllic paradise.

Naïve. That's what she'd been. To think Michael would not share his lean, tanned and highly sexed body with any other girl was sheer stupidity on Cecilia's part. But this was too much. This time he'd gone too far. Screwing a Hawaiian girl who was a mere adolescent, under a towel on the beach, right beside her was unforgivable. She wanted to wrap her hands around his talented larynx and throttle him. But no, her mother's training prevailed. Cecilia jutted her chin high, disregarded the rhythmic action under the towel and forced a strained smile. She chose her words in the vernacular of the Brotherhood of Love and gave Tony a disparaging look. "Hey, man, this place bums me out. I'm off."

When she turned to leave, Michael rolled off his lunchtime conquest with the languor of a well-sated lion. "Hey, Cecilia, what's up? Don't go, babe."

"Dude, that's cold." Tony finally registered the cause of Cecilia's unexpected departure, before closing his eyes and falling unconscious in the midday sun.

"Forget it, Michael. This isn't my scene anymore. You dig?" She glared balefully at him and hoped the fury behind her sunglasses found its mark.

Michael frowned, shrugged his shoulders and joined Tony in a marijuana stupor, while the stupid girl sniggered in triumph.

Gritting her teeth, Cecilia shuffled a turn and stumbled up the beach in a hasty retreat. She tripped over the folds of her sarong and cursed the sand's clutches. With each fumbled step her heart pounded a war cry, while around her the island lifted its resplendent face to the bluest of blue skies on the fairest of days. But for Cecilia, nature's glorious display dissolved, replaced instead by her anger, humiliation and hurt. The whole world had turned against her. It laughed at her indignant immaturity with its age-old wisdom. The normally gentle and welcome ocean breeze whipped her hair across her tear-streaked cheeks. Fine, hot sand slipped through her sandals and stung her feet which made her escape more frustrating. Even the sun turned spiteful and nipped at her torso's fair skin. She stumbled again and hissed a curse. The sound of the barreling waves mocked her until they drove her from their sandy domain and into human territory. Finally, on the sidewalk, she stopped and caught her breath. Although soft sobs rattled in her throat, she swallowed them into her soul. *No time to feel sorry for yourself.* She tossed her head, sending her golden locks in a cascade behind her shoulders. *This will not break me. I am more than this.*

After wiggling the hot sand from between her toes, she tightened her sarong with a sharp tug of the knot. She scanned the main street of Kahului's seaside shopping precinct, which only made her angrier. Carefree couples and families drifted along, obviously living far happier lives than hers. Shrill-voiced children pleaded with their patient parents and were swiftly rewarded with whatever they wanted. Why wasn't her life like that? Simply ask for it, and it's yours. But she wasn't a child any longer. "You've made your bed, now you must lie in it, Cecilia," is what her mother used to say. She groaned at the memory. In her purse was some cash, but not enough to get back to San Francisco. Having made a personal promise never to ask her parents for help or money, she was on her own.

God, what a fool I've been. Unable to think clearly under the sweltering August sun, she needed a cold drink and time to consider her options, limited though they were. With head held high, she strode off down the sidewalk, dodging a sea of sunburnt tourists happily licking ice-creams and slurping sodas.

* * * *

"What can I get for you, honey?" The familiar, dulcet tones of Billy's Beach House's owner pulled Cecilia from her reverie. Propped on a rickety, handmade timber stool, she turned toward the voice.

"Just a Coke, thanks, Mary." Running her eyes over the middle-aged woman, she inclined her head and grinned. "New mumu, Mary?"

Clothed in a colorful dress of vibrant orange-and-red hibiscus flowers, Mary smiled a gigantic grin which nearly split her face in two. "Yes, I bought it from Lilian at the markets. She does lovely sewing, don't you think?" Mary executed a twirl and the cotton fabric filled with air like a fluttering parachute.

Cecilia thought she resembled a plump candy packaged in a bright wrapper. "You look wonderful, Mary. It's a very pretty dress." She glanced past the proprietress and nodded at the handful of tables bursting with local and mainland tourists taking advantage of the beach, sun, and surf during the summer vacation. "And business seems to be good, too?"

"Yes. We make money for a little while. Then they go away. But they always come back. I'll get your Coke."

Mary bustled off, and Cecilia returned to her sightless gazing out the window; although it couldn't really be called a window. Most of the café's sidewall that faced the main street opened upward, cantilevered on a couple of old planks of timber. If it rained, water poured in and drenched everything. If they shut it, the café turned into a sauna, broiling everyone inside like pot roast. Mary said she preferred to be soaked than stewed, hence the wall remained propped open. Billy's Beach House was one of the few remaining properties still untouched by the city's new town plan. In its original condition, and with its somewhat unconventional charm and rich history, Billy's stood in silent protest against man's progress. Much like her, the café remained steadfast against the establishment. Cecilia loved it for that.

Mary returned and placed the icy bottle of soda on the weathered counter. "Are you okay, honey?" She rested her doughy hand on Cecilia's thin shoulder, its weight and warmth comforting.

"I guess so. Why do you ask?"

"Because you're usually here with your friends and today you're alone. Sometimes, when a young woman comes in alone and stares off into space, she has boy trouble."

Cecilia fiddled with her soda. "Yes. Boy trouble is what you could say. Michael and I have broken up. I've left the Brotherhood."

"Good. Those people were beneath you. You are far too smart for them. Lazy, good-for-nothings in my opinion."

Cecilia giggled at the ferocity of Mary's assessment. "You sound like my mother."

"I would very much like to meet your mother. She sounds like a wise woman." Mary chuckled long and deep, obviously pleased with the comparison. "Look at you, you have gone to skin and bone since I met you." Cecilia glanced down at her once well-proportioned body, which now resembled that of a pre-pubescent teenager. Where had her womanhood gone? "You need to get some meat back on your body, get healthy and be happy."

"Yes, you're right. All of the above."

"So, what are you going to do?"

"I have no idea. I don't have enough money to get back to the mainland. Besides, I think Maui's worked its magic on me, and I'd like to stay here a while. Find myself a job, save some money. But I don't want to run into the Brotherhood, if you get my drift?" She cocked an eyebrow at the older woman, who nodded in understanding. "I can sing. Maybe there's a job going somewhere for a singer?"

Mary scratched her chin. "The hotels don't want American singers. They want Hawaiian performers for their shows."

"Well, I have to do something. I need a job, a place to live and a life to call my own without a man screwing things up."

"Ah, you possess the passion of the goddess Pele. She is the goddess of fire, lightning, wind, and volcanoes. She is the creator of the Hawaiian Islands." Mary flung her arms wide before folding them across her watermelon-shaped bosom. She tilted her head and regarded Cecilia closely. "You are young, strong and pretty. But more than this, you're smart and kind. You're passionate like Pele. I know what you must do." Waving a finger in the air, Mary looked like an evangelical preacher. "My brother is driving across the island this afternoon. You can go with him."

"Go with him where?"

"To Kaanapali, of course." Mary's bushy brow lifted in surprise at Cecilia's ignorance.

"But where is Kaanapali?"

"It's a long way from here to the east." She raised her arm and pointed in the direction.

"But why on earth would I go there?"

"Because that is where every goddess begins her journey of self-discovery. Now, finish your Coke and come with me." She marched away in full command.

Cecilia downed her drink, grabbed her tote bag and scampered behind her. *Another rash decision. Off to who knows where based on the direction of an eccentric Hawaiian woman. Cecilia Freemont, you are crazy.* Despite the absurdity of the situation, her mouth curved upward. At least this time, she wasn't following her lover's pipedream. She was following a goddess's journey. Tickled by the thought, she quickened her pace.

CHAPTER TWO

Joseph whistled a merry tune as they bumped along in his old Ford truck. Because of an overindulgence of food, his hefty frame was squashed behind the steering wheel, leaving him little room to maneuver. Every time he turned the wheel, he had to breathe in, and Cecilia suppressed a smirk. This afternoon, when Mary lumbered Cecilia on him just before departing, he'd showed no signs of annoyance. Like his sister, he possessed an easy-going, happy disposition matched by a twinkle in his eyes. Although he didn't speak much, he occasionally glanced over, a friendly grin lighting his round face. *A man of few words.* Cecilia reciprocated his smile. The companionable silence suited her. It gave her time to think. Not one to dwell on the past, she decided that coming to Maui with Michael had not been a mistake. Rather, it had been another adventure she'd willingly chosen. Despite, or more correctly, because of the episode on the beach today, she now forged ahead in a new direction, literally and figuratively. *I'm swearing off men for a while. They're nothing but trouble. Time for me.* A short, sharp nod affirmed her thoughts. She'd grown used to unexpected events changing her life and being with Joseph in his old pickup driving across the Magic Isle was one of the better ones. Filled with promise, a new, unknown future beckoned. Instinctively, her foot tapped along in time with his whistling, while she nestled back in the flaking vinyl bench seat.

For as far as she could see, acres of tall, green sugar cane painted a moving foreground against the mountain ranges and deep valleys beyond. Millions of thick cane stems swayed and moved in unison like schools of fish, in sync with the distant ocean waves. Cecilia had never seen so many shades of green before — emerald, olive, moss, pistachio, forest, and pea. She couldn't think of enough colors to name all the greens painted on this landscape's palette. Raw and primitive, the magnitude of nature's beauty was at once overwhelming and comforting. Everything about this place resonated to an almost mystical rhythm. *Maybe that's why it's called the Magic Isle?* Although they'd passed the sugarcane factory, puffing its plumes of thick, white smoke a few miles back, the dense, pungent smell of sugar lingered in the humid afternoon air filling the cabin.

"How long will it take to get to Kaanapali, Joseph?"

"An hour, maybe two. But we will be there before dark."

"Thanks." Another hour or two suited her just fine. More time to think.

Leaving the island's inland green palette behind, the road curved around McGregor's Point, where the sparkling blue tones of the ocean greeted them. The narrow thoroughfare, at times only wide enough for one vehicle to pass, wound its way around the volcanic rock crags launching upward to their right., The mountains towered over their journey, a sense of foreboding oozing from their mighty presence. With the intense, sapphire blue of the Pacific Ocean to their left, Cecilia felt like she was caught between the devil and the deep blue sea. A silly saying her mother used to quote whenever a tough decision had to be made. A faint chill skittered up her spine. She chased away the random memory and hoped it was not a premonition of things to come.

* * * *

True to his word, Joseph delivered them to Kaanapali just before sunset. Cecilia slid from the truck cabin and flexed her shoulders to release the stiffness of the long trip.

"Follow me." He strode in big, plodding steps toward the ocean with Cecilia scampering behind. Within moments, they stood on the crest of a pristine white beach, and she breathed crisp, salty air into her lungs. "Kaanapali is beautiful." Her gaze traveled along the vast beach, before stopping on a tall cliff of rugged volcanic rock jutting out from the shore. "Joseph, what are those men doing?"

"They're testing their spiritual strength and courage by diving off Puu Kekaa, Black Rock. King Kahekili, who ruled over Maui and Oahu, performed many dives in his royal life, including this one. Now, young men come to Black Rock to dive and prove themselves."

Silhouetted in the fading golden light, Black Rock imposed itself on the sunset, daring the new-age warriors to leap from its precipice and survive. With enormous force, the men launched themselves from the peak of the rock high above the ocean. For a split second, they hung in midair, before plummeting like fishing birds into the frothy waves roiling at its base.

"It looks very dangerous. Have you done it?"

"Yes. When I was a young man."

"You are very brave, then."

"Each of us is brave in our own way. Many would think you are brave. You are a pretty, young woman on an adventure alone. You too are brave, Cecilia." A fatherly smile graced his face.

"My parents think I'm silly and irresponsible. But I'm twenty-five years old. I've got to get out in the world and experience it for myself. What do you think?" She stared up at the gentle, giant Hawaiian and waited.

He shifted his gaze to the ocean. For a few moments, the eternal lapping of the waves interrupted by the triumphant splash of the divers was the only sound to be heard. After quiet deliberation, and with his attention fixed on the horizon, he began, "I was around your age when I dived off Puu Kekaa. When I climbed the rock, I was scared. When I stood on the edge, I was even more scared. But when I leaped off the rock, I flew through the air for a split second before my body dived into the water. In that instant, I felt like I was flying . . . like a bird." He lifted his hand in demonstration. "My soul took flight from my body, and I was free. I have never forgotten that feeling."

Cecilia noticed a blissful expression settle on his face. She wondered if she too could dive off Black Rock. "That freedom must have been magic."

Joseph's scrutiny of the horizon where his past seemed to reside returned to her. "It was. Many years before I jumped, my grandfather said to me, 'Freedom from that which burdens us is how we find God.' That is how I felt. Unburdened." He held her in his intense gaze. "You are on a quest to find God, Cecilia."

She frowned. "Well, I never thought of it that way. I don't even know if I believe in God. But I do believe in living life to the fullest and in following my heart."

"Following your heart is how you find God." His face lifted in a jubilant smile. "Now come. It's time to visit my family, eat and rest before tomorrow." He turned and headed for the truck.

"But what is actually happening tomorrow?" She hurried beside him as the last streaks of deep orange washed the sky.

He slowed to a stop and faced her, a faint look of surprise creasing his forehead. "Tomorrow you will start your quest to find God."

* * * *

A better night's sleep Cecilia had not experienced in weeks. Though the kapok mattress on the floor of Joseph's parents' shack was lumpy and uncomfortable, she'd fallen into a dead sleep and woke invigorated. After a breakfast of fresh fruit and coconut water, they set off once more.

"So where to, Joseph?" She looked forward to spending more time with her Hawaiian mentor, listening to his youthful adventures and learning from his wisdom.

"I'm going back to town. But I'll be dropping you off at Lahaina Harbor. From there you will catch the boat."

"A boat?" She squirmed, disappointed. "A boat to where?"

"To Harbor Island. My friend Smith will take you across. He goes weekly with supplies. If you don't want to stay, he will bring you back in a week's time."

"But . . ." The cold chill of rising panic prickled her skin. The idea of adventure excited her, but her well-instilled common sense drew back on the reins. No one except Mary, Joseph, and this Smith character knew where she was. Her parents would deem this exploit as reckless behavior that could get her into trouble, or worse, killed. She sucked in a lungful of air. If anything did go wrong, she'd just disappear forever. "I'm not so sure about this." She disliked the hesitant, childish whine in her voice even more than the idea of going on a boat.

"Why not wait until we get to Lahaina Harbor and meet Smith before you decide? I've got to drive through there anyway. You don't have to go if you don't want to." He offered a reassuring smile. "But, remember what I said last night about diving off Black Rock when I was your age?"

"Which part was that?"

"That I was scared when I climbed up the rock and more scared when I stood on the ledge." He glanced away from the road and winked at her.

"Yes, I remember." She nodded, piecing together his meaning.

"You are climbing up, Cecilia. You have every right to feel scared." He inclined his head, stuck his arm out the window and began to whistle a new tune. The mid-morning's heat warmed the cabin and slowly melted her apprehensions. She decided to take his advice and wait.

* * * *

The pickup slowed to a standstill on the dock. Tied to the solid wharf bobbed a timber boat that had seen better days. In fact, the timeworn vessel looked as if a large wave would shatter it as decisively as Joseph's fist slamming a peanut shell. Determined to keep an open mind, Cecilia swallowed her rising anxiety. From the boat emerged a Hawaiian man who unfolded his tall, stick body like a praying mantis. His face sported a lop-sided grin, and his ropey arms waved in big arcs as they approached. He reminded her of the skinny comedian in the duo of Laurel and Hardy. She sneaked a sideways glance at Joseph and giggled. He made the perfect Hardy to Smith's Laurel. In vivid, floral shirts and ragamuffin shorts, they made an absurd, amusing pair.

"Aloha, Smith." Joseph threw his arms in the air.

"Aloha, Joseph." The men clasped each other in a bear hug, clapping a brutish welcome.

"Smith, this is Cecilia." Joseph stepped aside, motioning her forward.

"Hello, Smith."

"Aloha, Cecilia. So, I am to take you to Harbor Island?" He swiveled his head and pointed into the distance.

"Well . . ." The shape of an island was barely visible atop the shimmer of the sea. "I'm not so sure if Harbor Island is the place for me."

"The owners of the island are looking for someone to help manage their house and family." Smith tapped his finger to his nose as if divulging an important secret. "They are good people. See. This is their boat I drive." With pride, he nodded toward the old cruiser.

"Are you sure this boat will make the trip? It looks like it'll fall apart at the first breath of wind." She eyed the vessel, noting the non-existent varnish, the peeling letters of its namesake, *Harbor Island*, and its all-around dilapidated, unseaworthy condition.

"Don't you worry, Miss. The boat will get us there. Besides, Mr. Reginald is having a new boat built even as we speak — another thirty-six-foot pine cruiser. Lovely, she will be. Just like this one was, many years ago, when she was new."

Both men fell silent, their gazes fixed on her. She looked from one expectant face to the other. "Are you sure they're looking for someone?"

"Yes. They are looking for an American housekeeper, not Hawaiian. Although you are young, you may get the job. But you must understand, Miss, Harbor Island does not have all the luxuries of Maui. It is primitive compared to what you are used to, but everyone there is free to live as they choose, as long as they respect the island and don't hurt each other."

Free to live as they choose. Her face brightened at the thought of an unencumbered lifestyle — exactly what had motivated her to drop out of college all those years ago, leave home and come to Maui with Michael in the first place. That, and a small ache in her heart at the thought of being part of a family who needed her, stirred unexpected longing. She'd done some babysitting before leaving college, which she'd found rewarding, and by the parents' account, she'd also been good at it. Besides, if she didn't like it, she could be back in Maui next week. She had nothing to lose.

"Well, I came here looking for a new world. I guess I can go to Harbor Island to see if it exists there." She wavered, but only for a moment. "Okay, Smith. I'm in. Let's go." She turned to Joseph and took his hand. "Thank you, Joseph. And thank Mary for me."

"You are welcome, Cecilia." He shared a smile.

"I'm sure we'll see each other again."

"You are young and at the beginning of your life. I am old and near the end. Remember, be brave, leap, and let your soul take flight. Good luck on your quest. Aloha, Cecilia."

She watched his big, brown eyes sparkle. Probably with the same thrill he'd felt when he had leaped off Black Rock all those years ago. Stretching up, she did her best to embrace his massive frame. "Goodbye, Joseph. Take care. And thanks for inspiring me to leap. I will never forget you." The tremble of emotion in her voice surprised her. She'd known Joseph for not quite a day, yet the impact he'd made on her had changed her somehow. She reached out to Smith, who helped her off the wharf and into the boat. Onboard, she squeezed between crates of flour, sugar and other supplies, and tucked her tote bag safely beside her. Smith nodded to Joseph to untie the ropes.

"Aloha, Joseph," he called, steering the boat from the wharf.

"Aloha." Joseph's baritone voice called across the rippling waves of Lahaina Harbor.

Cecilia looked back and waved. While the sun cut dazzling diamonds on the wave tips, the calm, green waters of the harbor transformed into the mighty blue waves of the open sea. Filled with renewed excitement, she turned her face away from Joseph and her past, and toward Harbor Island and her new future.

CHAPTER THREE

Tucked between the dozens of crates stacked high in the back of the boat, Cecilia settled in for the journey, relieved that she was not obliged to make conversation. While Smith stood at the helm, she held firm to her wide-brimmed straw hat and lifted her face to the sun, soaking up its morning glow. Yesterday's sunburn still tinged her upper body in a rosy hue, but today's choice of a long-sleeved cheesecloth top and drawstring pants protected her without being stifling. Squawking seagulls circled overhead on the lookout for possible snacks, and she wished she had some bread to help them on their own journey from island to island. *Harbor Island* chugged further into open seas, riding the rolling waves.

Today was magnificent — still and clear. It was a perfect boating day, but Cecilia's stomach begged to differ. What with the big, black plumes of diesel smoke coughing out from the old engine and the increasing pitch of the waves, she began to feel decidedly green. The further the vessel ventured into the deep blue ocean, the more she thought her breakfast would make a reappearance. She closed her eyes briefly and then thought better of it.

"Come into the cabin with me!" yelled Smith, waving her from the back deck.

Grabbing whatever was steady and in reach, she hauled herself up next to the skipper.

"I'm not feeling so good, Smith." The taste of saliva slime coated her mouth.

"Have you not been on the ocean before?"

"No. This is my first time." With her stomach churning, she understood what the saying "all at sea" meant.

"Stand up, keep your eyes on the horizon and hold on." Smith tapped the dashboard in front of them. "If you need to be sick, here use this." He passed her a brown paper bag. "Keep it open in your hand, just in case."

She took the bag with meek thanks, determined not to use it.

"Today is a good, smooth day on the sea. You will get used to it, if you come back and forth to the island a lot."

Smith's upbeat attitude didn't help. Instead, it intensified her sea sickness until she was no longer able to swallow her breakfast, and she launched her face into the bag. "Argh!"

"Good, you will feel better now," assured Smith, who waited until she'd finished. "Here, give me the bag." Extending his sinewy arm, he clasped the bag and disposed of it in a bin.

"How embarrassing." She wiped an unsteady hand across her mouth, thankful for Smith's preparedness. Lifting her long hair, she let the sea breeze cool her clammy neck.

"It takes time to get your sea legs. Have a sip of water. Not too much." He handed her a tin cup of water, and she took a tentative sip. "Good. Eyes on the horizon. We will be there soon."

"Thank you. I feel better now," she said, although she wasn't too sure. She hoped he had more paper bags — just in case.

Land loomed up like a stupendous monster draped in a singular mountainous mantle of luxurious green foliage. A sweeping crescent bay spanned the entire length of the island, creating a near-perfect semi-circle where the ocean's waters sliced into its shore. From the air, Cecilia suspected that Harbor Island resembled the curved shape of an orange segment after a bite had been taken from the juicy pulp. From the boat, it resembled a multilayered party cake. The island's harbor, beach, jungle, cliffs, and sky sat atop each other in tiers of azure, gold, juniper, chocolate and cerulean in a delicious combination.

Once in the bay's protected waters, she stepped gingerly out of the cabin and edged along the bow of the boat. With her face exposed to the breeze, she leaned on the guardrail, and her heart skipped a beat. A more enchanting place she could not imagine.

All around her, transparent, lime-green waters glistened like an enormous vat of precious stones. She peered into its shallow depths and watched striped, tropical fish dart in all directions without collision. The water was so clear, she could even see a lone hermit crab trudging on its lone quest on the sand below. No longer nauseous, she wanted to dive in and join him.

Harbor Island changed direction and headed toward the far left-hand side of the expansive bay. Tucked near an exposed rock groin teetered a rickety jetty, one far less sturdy than the wharf in Lahaina Harbor. Hewn tree trunks which supported the sun-stripped gangway emerged from the water at uneven perpendicular angles. She suspected one strong wave would dislodge the entire structure, but by the looks of it, neither strong waves nor winds penetrated the shelter of the harbor. The long-standing jetty had stood the test of time, as evidenced by the hoary barnacles and lichen that made the pylons their home.

At the sound of playful whooping, she lifted her head to see a couple of coffee-colored young men jogging toward the jetty. Their maturing muscles flexed under a gloss of perspiration and rippled with pride in the sunlight.

"Throw them the rope at your feet," hollered Smith, pointing to a coil of rope on the bow.

Cecilia nodded. Smith grazed the boat alongside the jetty, and she tossed the rope, hoping her strength would get it far enough.

"Aloha," one of the young Hawaiians called as he caught the rope, sunshine beaming from his face.

"Aloha," she called back, exchanging a wide smile.

Within minutes, the boys tied off the boat and hoisted the first boxes of provisions onto their strong, young shoulders. She cast a furtive glance at each of their virile bodies and flinched. *None of that*, she scolded. *You're off men, remember*. Clutching her tote bag over her shoulder, she accepted Smith's hand to disembark onto the jetty. "Thank you so much for bringing me here safely."

"You are welcome, Miss. Now, if you follow where Andrew and Jacob are walking up the path, it will lead you to the Local Store. Ask for Beatrice and tell her you're here for the housekeeper's job with Mrs. Reginald. She will help you. Aloha." He cracked a smile, then leaped back onboard to continue unloading.

Shoving her straw hat on top of her head, she set off in search of the Local Store. Andrew and Jacob set a brisk pace, so with a swing of her arms, she double-timed to keep them in view. As she marched on, it became apparent that not finding the Local Store would be nigh on impossible. With the harbor to her right and a massive, jungle-cloaked mountain to her left, the path led in only one direction without detour. Flushed and damp, she crested a small hillock and spied a neat row of colorful shopfronts, into which Andrew and Jacob disappeared. She'd noticed the peculiar buildings from the boat, and now as she slowed her pace, she saw a truck parked on a curved dirt road in front of them. *The Esplanade*, she mused with a giggle.

She strolled along the adjacent dirt pavement and officially entered what she suspected was the main street of Harbor Island. Three timber buildings faced onto the road, the first of which was Smith's Repairs — Cars, Trucks & Boats. She stopped to stare at the hand-painted sign. "Well, I know who owns this business," she said aloud with a chuckle. "A man of many trades is our

Smith." Empty except for piles of tools and engine parts strewn on the floor and counters, the run-down garage was open to anyone who wished to enter. It seemed security wasn't necessary on Harbor Island.

She clucked in amusement and strolled to the next building. Little more than the size of a large room, its windowless walls consisted of wooden planks lashed together with vine, teetering precariously under a slanting, dilapidated tin roof. The sign out the front proclaimed it was the Ladies Markets. Cecilia thought it was aptly named when she heard tittering women's voices spilling out the doors. On peering inside, she saw a dozen or more Hawaiian women sewing on old Singer sewing machines, their feet trundling the foot pedals. Swathes of brightly colored fabric furled beside them as they created mountains of clothing.

"Aloha," called Cecilia over the chatter and noise.

"Aloha." The voices chimed a greeting, eyes curious as to the newcomer, but not interested enough to be disturbed from their work. Faces down, they resumed their dressmaking. With another amused cluck, Cecilia continued her mission.

The third building with its canary-yellow façade and cherry-red door proved to be her destination — the Local Store. She pushed open the door, and a bell tinkled, telegraphing her arrival. "Aloha. Is anyone here?" Rows of rough, timber shelves displayed an assortment of tinned and packaged foods, many dusty from being on display too long. A mountain of tinned spam and huge bags of white rice balanced on the front counter, confirming they were the dietary staples of the island. Kites and other cheap toys hung from the ceiling, while scattered on the counter in front of the antiquated cash register lay sugary candies and gum. *At just the right height for children to pester their mothers to buy.* With fond nostalgia, she remembered how she used to do the same thing to her mother.

"Aloha," came a clipped voice. Its owner, a buxom woman, with a piggy nose and beady eyes, entered from a back room through a green plastic-beaded curtain. Her caramel-colored skin indicated she possessed mixed parentage, which gave her the unusual Caucasian features, while her full figure displayed the fortitude of her Hawaiian heritage. "How may I help you?"

"I've just come over with Smith. He told me to ask for Beatrice about . . ."

Before she finished, a mighty scowl deepened the woman's brow. "Where is he? He's been away for three days now. Wait until I get my hands on him." Like a whirling dervish, she dashed past Cecilia and rushed out to the sidewalk. Fisting her hands in the air, she yelled toward the jetty. "Smith, you get your sorry bag of bones up here!" Her tirade continued in both native and English languages, which only added to her dramatic performance. Stifling a laugh behind her hand, Cecilia tried hard to be polite. Nevertheless, her hysteria bubbled over when she realized the woman looked like the Duchess from *Alice in Wonderland*.

Slamming back into the store, the woman pointed an angry finger at her and snorted. "Stop that. Who are you? And what do you want?"

"I'm terribly sorry." Cecilia did her best to be serious. "I'm looking for Beatrice. Smith told me she can help me with the housekeeping job for Mrs. Reginald."

Like a cat with a mouse, the woman circled Cecilia, her eyes raking her from head to toe. She sniffed, leaned closer, then snarled, "I'm Beatrice."

"Oh, hello, Beatrice. I'm Cecilia." She stopped herself from bobbing a curtsey and prayed for mercy.

Knuckling her hands on her broad beam hips, Beatrice cocked a brow. "Why do you think you can do the job for Mrs. Reginald? What would a young, silly girl like you know about running a household or caring for a family?"

Cecilia stuck her chin high and met Beatrice's cynical stare. "Well, I did lots of babysitting when I was at college. I had to do household chores growing up, and I also helped my nan when she got sick. I cooked, cleaned and even bathed her. I may look young, but I'm strong, smart and am not afraid of work." With a firm nod, she finished her impromptu job interview while Beatrice chortled sarcastically.

The bell on the door tinkled, and Cecilia turned, hoping to see Smith, who might save her from his irate wife.

"Beatrice, what are you doing? Not scaring another visitor away?" The velvety voice belonged to a young, curvaceous woman with waist-length ebony hair. "Hello. I'm Victoria Reginald."

"I'm Cecilia Freemont. I'm here about the housekeeper job."

"You? You can't possibly be applying for the job. How old are you?"

"I'm twenty-five and very capable of doing the job—"

"Oh, I don't mean that. I mean you're only five years older than me. What are doing applying for a housekeeping job here? Didn't you go to college? You could be traveling around Europe with a boyfriend or something more exciting than coming here?" A look of disbelief widened Victoria's dark, almond-shaped eyes.

"Well, this is exciting to me. I want to be a professional singer, but that hasn't panned out . . . yet. My parents sent me to college, but I dropped out. I got sick of reading about other people's adventures, so I decided to have some of my own. I marched, protested and partied pretty hard in San Francisco." She threw this in to impress the younger girl with her worldliness. "Then I came to Maui with a boyfriend who turned out to be a jerk. And now, here I am — on Harbor Island hoping to escape boyfriends, the establishment and live a life of my choosing."

"I take my hat off to you, Cecilia Freemont. My parents would disown me if I tried anything like that."

"Mine probably will if I don't return soon. But the seventies are our times, right?"

"I'd like to believe that—"

"I know they are. So, I have to give it my best shot." Cecilia restrained herself from thrusting her fist in the air like a true feminist.

"Well, I think you're crazy wanting to live here, away from all mod cons. But, it's your choice. I'll take you to meet Mom." With a twitch of her lips, she turned back to the shop owner and wagged her finger. "Beatrice, just because Smith makes you angry doesn't mean you can frighten the visitors. Okay?"

"Okay, Miss Vickie." With downturned mouth, Beatrice appeared duly chastised.

"Now, once your sons have unloaded everything, will you send our supplies to the house, please?"

"Yes, Miss Vickie." An obliging smile replaced Beatrice's hangdog expression.

"And take an extra bag of rice for yourself and Smith." Victoria reached out and patted the older woman's hand.

"Thank you, Miss Vickie. Thank you." Beatrice turned and scurried back into the storeroom where, in a loud, gruff voice she instructed Andrew and Jacob on the correct stacking of the provisions.

"I've got the truck outside. I'll drive you up to the house. Do you have any luggage?" Victoria led the way from the store.

"No. This is it." Cecilia tapped her tote bag. "I learned to travel light when I left home. Being able to go where I want, when I want, means I can't tie myself to possessions. I only carry what I need."

"I'm not sure I could do that. I took so much stuff with me when I went to college that when I come home now for vacation, I have to carry it back and forth." She stopped at the 1962 blue Chevrolet truck, the only vehicle on the street. "This is it. The old Chevy. Jump in."

Cecilia dragged open the heavy door, which grumbled at being dislodged, and clambered in. She stared at Victoria as she inserted the keys in the ignition. "I thought the job for your family included looking after children? You certainly don't need looking after. Do you have younger brothers or sisters?"

The V8 engine labored to life. Victoria engaged the clutch, grated it into gear and eased the beast along the street. "There's only me and my younger brother, Richard. He's eighteen and starting his freshman year at college shortly. We all call him Dickie." She flashed a lame smile. "Yeah, I know. Vickie and Dickie. Awful, isn't it." Cecilia nodded in sympathetic agreement. "But only Beatrice calls me Vickie."

"Why's that?"

"She was my nursemaid when I was born. She helped raise me. To her, I've always been Miss Vickie. She really is sweet, you know. She just pretends to be a mean old woman."

"Well, she does a good job at it," snorted Cecilia.

"Just don't get on her bad side."

"How do I not do that?"

"I'm not too sure come to think of it." Victoria's melodic and carefree laughter was infectious, and Cecilia joined in the joke.

Turning her attention to the landscape crawling past them, Cecilia gave an audible sigh. "Harbor Island feels like it's caught in a time warp — like it doesn't belong in the twentieth century."

"I guess I don't appreciate it enough because I grew up here. But you're right. It is pretty special. Whether you get the job or not, I can show you around while you wait to go back to Maui with Smith, if you like?"

"Gee, that would be terrific. Thanks."

As the Chevy circled the arc of the bay, Cecilia stuck her head out the window like a dog taking in the sights.

The harbor's calm waters provided a safe haven for the handful of day-tripper yachts moored offshore. She could just make out semi-clad bodies lazing on the decks and worshipping the sun. No one strolled along the miles of gleaming white beach, or played in the pristine waters at its shore, except for a group of boisterous native children. Virtually deserted, the island listed on the Pacific Ocean. Like a dream, it floated in time and space. It was what Cecilia imagined paradise to look like. Only when the road inclined and began snaking through a tangle of foliage did she draw her attention back from the sparkling harbor.

Victoria crunched the Chevy down into low gear. "It's just up here," she said.

"It's a helluva walk from the village."

"For us maybe, but the locals are used to it. They seem to be able to walk all day."

"Well, if I end up staying, I better get used to it, too."

Cecilia's emphatic nod set Victoria laughing again. "Oh, Cecilia, I do hope you get the job. We could all use some of your optimism around here." Her eyes crinkled at the corners.

"If I stay, we'll have to go into PT training. What's this hill called anyway?"

"Harbor Hill. Not very original, but there you go." Victoria shrugged.

"Simple and to the point. I like it. Miss Vickie, you and I will learn to walk Harbor Hill." This time, Cecilia led the chorus of laughter in the truck, while they planned their fitness regime.

On reaching the top of the ridge, Cecilia drew a long breath. Below them sprawled at least an acre of manicured green lawn, bordered by well-tended gardens of hibiscus, tropical shrubs and plumeria trees. Dotted on this lush canvas lazed an impressive collection of six wooden, thatched-roof bungalows. Open verandas circumnavigated each bungalow which was connected to the other by covered breezeways. The whole complex resembled the architectural symmetry of a beehive. Every piece off-set the other and all fanned out from the great pavilion in the center.

"This is it. The Reginald residence of Harbor Island," said Victoria, a hint of pride in her voice.

"Wow. This is amazing. Who designed this place?"

"My father did. He's an architect by profession, hence why Dickie and I must go to college. After he inherited the island from his father, he tore down the original house and built this." She stopped the truck on the crest of the driveway and indicated to her right. "That's my bedroom bungalow over there. That's Dickie's bungalow on the other side. The kitchen, great pavilion, and family room are there in the center. Behind is my parents' bungalow and the other two bungalows are for guests or relatives. Then there's the pool and entertainment area behind that again."

"It's enormous. It's like a private resort."

"That's exactly what it is. We have staff, of course, who look after it all — gardeners, groundsmen, housemaids, cleaners, and cooks — but we need a housekeeper to look after the staff. That's where you come in. Are you up to it?" She lifted a brow. "You may think this is paradise, but it's no different to anywhere else."

"It's not what I expected. I thought the job was for a normal housekeeper. You know, like someone who tends to the household chores and babysits children, that sort of thing." Cecilia blinked. She wondered if the idyllic scene shimmering in front of her was a mirage and would disappear on their approach.

"Oh, no. It's much bigger than that." Amused pity lifted Victoria's lips. "Anyway, you're here now. Why don't you meet Mother and Father? See if this is what you want to do?"

Cecilia swallowed hard. "Yes, why not?" Her voice lacked confidence.

"Cecilia, one day you will bite off more than you can chew," her mother had threatened whenever her only daughter strode out of their palatial home on some egalitarian mission. Now, for the first time, she thought her mother might have been right.

* * * *

The first thing she noticed after alighting the Chevy was the number of staff working on the property. Cecilia stopped counting at five outdoor male staff only because she stubbed her toe on the flagstone steps of the great pavilion. "Shit," she hissed.

Victoria grabbed her arm and whispered in an urgent voice, "You mustn't swear. Father is dreadfully religious, and he won't abide swearing. Okay?"

"Yeah. Yeah. Okay, sorry." Rubbing her toe, she wondered if the loss of sensation in her toe was more or less painful than the loss of her freedom of speech. But as Cecilia's gaze traveled upward to the striking, vaulted roof of the great pavilion, both hurts faded. Hung under the lintel and tickled by the afternoon breeze, curtains of white gossamer cloth fluttered over open doorways, teasing anyone who dared enter to do so without breaking their rhythm. Catching the tempo, the girls slipped through the billowing fabric into the huge, open gabled pavilion.

Contemporary furniture, decorated with plump, colorful cushions had been placed strategically in the cavernous space, so no matter which view anyone wanted, a sofa awaited them. And the view was breathtaking. Like a cherry perched on an ice-cream soda, the Reginald residence sat high atop Harbor Hill surveying its domain. To the east, the ocean skidded into the horizon, interrupted only by the protective coral reef rounding the bay. The north and south views included the furthest tips of the island, with their cliffs sweeping around the harbor, barricading it against the unrelenting domination of the Pacific Ocean and the trade winds. Behind them and to the west, the sleeping jungle towered, staking its unassailable claim on that side of the island. Speechless, Cecilia wandered like an early explorer discovering a new land, trying to comprehend how the rest of the world didn't know about such a place.

"Father. Mother. I have someone here about the housekeeping job," called Victoria, as she strolled toward the back of the great pavilion. She gestured to Cecilia to follow. "They're probably in the kitchen. Come through."

"I'm not so sure about this. I thought this job . . . I mean I thought I'd just be helping out." Before Cecilia finished her excuses, a tall, stern-faced man with a meticulously combed crop of silver hair appeared from behind the matting partition. Rigid in bearing and with lips pursed in a tight line, he strode into the room as its elder sovereign. The vibrant blues of his shirt and dazzling white of his trousers did little to lighten his overbearing presence. *He's king of the castle around here.* Cecilia recalled how her father puffed himself up in a similar manner to impress visitors. Beside him trotted his exact opposite — a cheerful, moon-faced Hawaiian woman of much younger years, with a smile that brightened even his shadow. Cut short, her jet-black hair kinked in a modern hairstyle to match her neatly pressed shift of pea-green cotton. Possessing the same exotic features as Victoria, this woman had to be her mother.

"Cecilia, this is my father, Percy Reginald and my mother, Leilani."

"Very nice to meet you, Mr. Reginald." With the decorum and respect, she'd been taught, Cecilia stepped forward, offering her hand. For her efforts, she received a thorough once-over that concluded in a curt nod.

Mrs. Reginald rescued her hand. "How lovely to meet you, Cecilia. Won't you sit down?" She gestured to one of the many sofas. Everyone waited for Victoria's father to be seated before Mrs. Reginald indicated who should sit where.

"Iced tea please, Loretta." Mrs. Reginald waved a diminutive hand in the air. From the corner of her eye, Cecilia noticed a woman scurry away like a mouse down a hole.

"You'll have to excuse how I look," said Cecilia. "I just got off the boat, and I unexpectedly met Victoria in the Local Store. She was kind enough to drive me up here to meet you. I haven't had time to freshen up."

"That's quite all right, dear. Victoria, please take Cecilia to the guest bathroom so she can at least wash her face and hands."

"Yes, Mother. Follow me." Victoria nodded in the direction and led the way. Once out of earshot, she gave a short laugh. "Don't mind Father. He's always like that. I've never known him to be anything but terse. You'll get used to it."

"Do you think so?" She was doubtful.

"Don't worry. His bark is worse than his bite."

Cecilia hoped so.

Tucked to one side of the great pavilion was a pretty powder room filled with fresh, sweet-smelling flowers. "Here you go. I'll wait here while you freshen up. Use the towels. Loretta will come in after and clean up." She eased the door closed.

Wheeling to face the mirror, Cecilia caught sight of a startled, disheveled young woman. "If you want a chance at this job, you better shape up," she said aloud. She fumbled her brush from her tote bag and dragged it viciously through her sun-streaked hair before strangling it into a ponytail.

I'm not sure about working for Mr. Reginald. He's a real grouch. But I need the money, whatever it pays. Mrs. Reginald seems sweet. Besides, I like Victoria, a lot. It would be nice to have a girlfriend to talk to, even if it was only when she came back from college on vacation.

She turned on the faucet and rubbed the journey from her face, neck, and hands. An invigorating polish from the fluffy towel brightened her appearance, but still, she looked like a street urchin. She had no mascara to highlight her green eyes, the best feature she'd inherited from her mother, or lip gloss to moisten her sundried lips. With no good clothes or decent shoes and dressed in cheesecloth, she felt more like a smelly cheese than an intelligent young woman about to start a new career. She tutted at her reflection. "Well, I'll just have to win them over with my witty repartee." She squared her shoulders and opened the door. "Okay. I'm ready for the lion's den."

They linked arms and strode back into the great pavilion. Before coming into view of Victoria's parents, they released their gesture of solidarity, then slipped into their assigned seats and waited. Loretta had set the table with four tall glasses brimming with tea, in which chipped ice melted at a feverish speed.

"Please, Cecilia, have some tea." Only after Mrs. Reginald took the first sip did Cecilia and Victoria follow suit. Meanwhile, Mr. Reginald remained still, eyes fixed on their guest.

"So, young lady, tell me a little about yourself and your family."

"My name is Cecilia Freemont. I'm an only child. I grew up in Pacific Heights, San Francisco. You may have heard of my father, John Freemont. He's the deputy mayor of the city."

Mr. Reginald was stony-faced. "Perhaps I've seen his name in the newspapers from the mainland. But what takes you away from your prestigious family and brings you here to the islands?"

"Well, sir, I wanted to experience life rather than read about it in books. I went to college for a while to study to be a teacher—"

"That's what I'm studying at college, too," Victoria piped in, beaming a smile.

"Victoria, don't interrupt." Mr. Reginald's voice was as cold as his steely glance. "Go on, Cecilia."

Surprised at his unexpected reprimand of Victoria, she stumbled on. "I . . . ah . . . I wanted to experience life rather than read about it in books. One thing led to another, and I ended up in Maui, hoping to start a new life. Mary from Billy's Beach House thought I should apply for the housekeeping job here. Her brother, Joseph drove me to Lahaina Harbor where I met Smith, who also thought I'd be good for the job, and he brought me over here this morning."

"He did now, did he?" Mrs. Reginald's lips lifted in a sweet smile.

"How old are you?" Mr. Reginald leaned forward to retrieve his iced tea. Like a magician, Loretta appeared and flicked a napkin across his lap, so condensation wouldn't drip on his trousers.

"I'm twenty-five, sir. But I'm very reliable, a quick learner and good with people."

"Would your parents agree with your self-assessment?"

"You'd have to ask them, sir."

"I suspect your parents are not in agreement with your gallivanting all over America on some liberal, feminist adventure?" His tone hardened, and his eyes narrowed with obvious disdain.

"My parents view my actions as silly and irresponsible. However, I am an adult and as such can make my own choices." Doing her best not to sound disrespectful, she coated her answer with a fine layer of feminine wile.

"Would you like some more tea?" asked Victoria, her voice light and bubbly.

"No thanks. I'm fine." The brief interlude gave Cecilia time to breathe. Something she'd not done since the beginning of Mr. Reginald's interrogation.

"Why would you, a pretty, smart twenty-five-year-old want to take on this job?" asked Mrs. Reginald as she reclined in her wingback chair.

"To be very honest, Mrs. Reginald, I'm not quite sure what the job entails. I just heard about it. And because I've nearly run out of money and everyone else thought it would be a good job for me, I followed their advice." She heard Mr. Reginald cluck his tongue in disapproval.

Ignoring him, Mrs. Reginald explained, "We have staff that maintain the residence and provide for us. Up until now, it has been my job to manage them, organize their rosters, ensure the work is done to our standards and keep an eye on them. Victoria used to help me before she went off to college a couple of years ago. Dickie took over from her for the last couple of years, but now he's off to college as well. So, I need to find someone to be my second-in-charge."

"I'm sure I could do that, Mrs. Reginald." Cecilia brightened at the prospect of working with her.

"But, young lady, there is one glaring problem which you do not seem to register," interjected Mr. Reginald. All eyes turned to him, awaiting the important fact. "You are too young. The staff will not respect someone of your age."

"But, Father. They respected me."

"Well, of course they did. You are my daughter," snorted Mr. Reginald.

"But, Percy, we've been looking for someone to take this role for months now. Every day, I get more tired. I need someone to help me, and I have a feeling Cecilia will be able to earn the respect of the staff. I know she is young, much younger than we expected, but she is smart and keen. I think she could be a good fit for us."

Mrs. Reginald impressed Cecilia. She admired the woman's ability to state her case with logic and passion.

"Please, Father. Give Cecilia a chance."

"Percy, I need someone now." Humble demand and desperate entreaty rang in Mrs. Reginald's voice.

In a last-ditch effort, Cecilia joined the feminine chorus. "Mr. Reginald, I am willing to work the first week with no pay. If you don't think I'm the right person for the job, I'll leave."

"But you don't even know if there is any pay. Or what it is. Or whether it will be enough to sustain you," he taunted, skepticism in his eyes.

"As I said, I'm willing to work as housekeeper for one week. After that, we can discuss the other details." She steeled her jaw, wondering if she'd pushed too far.

Mr. Reginald's gaze shifted from his wife to his daughter and finally to Cecilia. "Let me state, I am not happy with this arrangement." Turning to his wife, he softened. "But for you, my dear, I am willing to concede." He reverted to Cecilia in his business-like manner. "I will meet with you after your first week's employment to discuss your performance and possible future here on Harbor Island." Rising to his feet, Mr. Reginald indicated that the meeting was over. He departed in grand fashion, Cecilia and Victoria jiggled with delight, and Mrs. Reginald smirked over her iced tea.

CHAPTER FOUR

"Welcome, Cecilia. It's good to have you with us." Mrs. Reginald walked over and pressed a soft kiss to her cheeks. "Victoria will help you settle in. Tomorrow she will orientate you to the island, and the next day we begin in earnest. I will see you later this evening for dinner. Aloha." Petite and gracious, Mrs. Reginald drifted outside into the grounds.

"Oh, this is wonderful," said Victoria. "I can't believe that Father actually agreed. What a time we'll have whenever I'm home on vacation."

"It looks like I'm in, at least for a week. Lead on." A huge smile creased Cecilia's face. For the first time since coming to Maui, she felt like she belonged. She and Victoria chatted about her good fortune as they cut across the pavilion in a westerly direction and headed toward the blanketing green of the jungle one hundred feet ahead.

"Where are we going?"

"I'm taking you to where you'll stay while you're working here. You can't stay in the staff quarters if you're the housekeeper. You'll stay by yourself in your own quarters."

Surprise lit Cecilia's face. "Really? I get to live in my own place?"

"Of course. Here we are." At the edge of the property, Victoria stopped and pointed up toward the jungle canopy. "There. See it? That's the roof of Hill Cottage. That's where you'll live. Come on."

Chiseled into the volcanic cliff side, a staircase of gently sloping steps inclined upward under a shadowy corridor of well-maintained foliage. On either side of the hewn stairs, strangling vines, age-old trees, thorny shrubs, feathery ferns and hundreds of other plants tried to invade the passageway.

"The staff have their work cut out for them here," said Cecilia, amazed with the constant effort it took to prevent the jungle from reclaiming its natural birthright.

"Yes, but they've done it for so long, and Mom has such a tight schedule, it really is maintenance rather than a major slash and burn."

The air was cool, crisp and fresh on their short climb through the jungle to the top. Cecilia counted twenty-six treads before she stepped back into daylight. After the dimness of the jungle corridor, she blinked while her eyes readjusted to the sun's brilliance. When her vision finally sharpened, she caught her breath.

Topped with a white-washed roof, a quaint timber cottage that resembled an oversized candy box shimmered under the blistering midday sun. With its matching white-washed casement window frames and sills, the brave, little building rebuffed the sun's assault. So, too did the five painted wooden stairs that led up to the narrow veranda that hugged the front of the housekeeper's quarters. Every railing, post, and frame, including the front door, gleamed vivid white, while the body of the cottage looked freshly painted in the palest shade of lavender. The same color as her mother's prized hydrangeas. Across the front façade of the cottage grew a neat garden of tropical flowers and orchids that bloomed in an outrageous display of sultry purples, innocent pinks, and dazzling yellows. A hand-carved sign — Hill Cottage — hung over the front-door mantle, lest anyone be confused as to where they were.

"Oh, Victoria," she gasped, her hand touching her heart.

"Pretty, isn't it?"

"It's more than pretty. It's perfect."

"Come on. I'll show you inside." She scampered up the stairs while Cecilia strolled behind, trailing her hand over the glossy white handrail.

Once on the veranda, she sidled in beside Victoria and turned. Set on the island's highest summit, Hill Cottage stood sentinel to all it surveyed. Like a seabird, Cecilia hovered over the island and the Reginald's residence below. She'd never experienced such a sight. Nervous excitement tickled her stomach, and she wondered if that was what the young men diving off Black Rock experienced when they reached the top. Mesmerized by the one-hundred-and-eighty-degree view, she gazed outwards past the glassy waters of Harbor Island to the furthest ends of the earth. "Amazing. Simply amazing," she said, breathless, not from the climb, but from the majesty of the panorama.

"Come inside. You've got plenty of time to gaze at the view later." Grabbing her hand, Victoria tugged her to the door.

Cecilia stepped inside and scanned the small interior through moist, happy eyes. Like long sticks of lilac musk candy, the interior tongue-and-groove timber walls were painted the same lavender and looked good enough to eat. Short white lacy curtains fluttered over the windows determined to free themselves on the gusty afternoon breeze.

"My father built this cottage and every piece of furniture in here." Greying pieces of twisted driftwood formed an assortment of commonplace furniture. However, the furniture was anything but commonplace. Extraordinary workmanship had crafted and turned every piece until it looked more like art rather than furniture. A solid dining table and four matching, yet subtly different chairs, sat dead center in the cottage. Directly to the left was a kitchenette complete with a two-burner stove, a small fridge, three overhead cupboards, and an L-shaped timber counter. Opposite, a two-person sofa brimmed with thick purple cushions, and two armchairs nestled under corner windows. In the back corner, a three-quarter bunk bed with matching side tables were tucked away from the glare, while on the opposite wall stood two timber wardrobes, doors flung open awaiting its next inhabitant's belongings. "Father lived in Hill Cottage when he was a young man before he inherited the island. After that, Hill Cottage was turned into staff quarters by Mom when she married him. She thought it was time he gave up his bachelor pad and stayed in the main residence."

Cecilia wandered into the heart of the cottage and dumped her tote bag on the table. "It's terrific." Her eyes roamed the space once more. "But where's the bathroom?"

"It's a bathhouse, outside." Victoria headed to the rear door of the cottage. "Here." She opened the door and pointed to a timber shed. "Come on."

They walked along the short gravel pathway, and Cecilia's apprehensions grew. Her outdoor bathroom was no bigger than the size of a powder room. Under its roofline, a fifteen-inch grate of fine steel mesh connected the walls to the ceiling. With no windows and only one door, it resembled a prison cell, not a bathroom. "There's a pit toilet in there, and a shower and basin with running water. Not very modern, I'm afraid, but the boys come each week to make sure the pit is hygienic and to keep the snakes away."

"Snakes!"

"It is the jungle, you know," reminded Victoria. Leaning forward, Cecilia peered into the bathhouse. Due to the heat in the cramped, under-ventilated space, an unpleasant smell hung heavy in the air. "I know it smells a bit right now, but it will get better once you start using it. Loretta cleans it every day. Just don't leave the door open. Otherwise, the creepy-crawlies will pay you a visit."

"But what if I want to go to the toilet during the night?"

"I wouldn't if I were you. At night, use the pot under the bed and empty it into the toilet when you get up."

"Oh, goodness." She shook her head. "Everyone warned me about it being rough, but I wasn't expecting a smelly bathhouse, snakes and other things crawling over me at night."

"You'll get used to it." Victoria shrugged, then linked Cecilia's arm, and they walked back into the cottage. "After a while, it becomes second nature. Now, at night, before you get into bed, untie the mosquito net from the hooks on the wall. Climb in and make sure the netting comes all the way around you and over the bed." Victoria demonstrated by flicking the net, so the side splits overlapped. "Then tuck it into the side of the bed so the rats can't get in."

"Rats?"

"Don't worry, we only get rats if there's food left out. So, make sure you clean up after yourself every day. You can't afford to be lazy, messy or dirty when you live next to the jungle. And you can't possibly sleep with the windows closed, the heat is stifling. Leave the windows open and use your mosquito net. That way you won't lie awake all night wondering what's going to creep over your face."

Cecilia scuttled back to the safety of the armchairs. Sagging into one, she moaned. "Creepy-crawlies, snakes, rats . . . I had no idea."

"Most people think island living is so much fun, but it's really hard work." Victoria dropped into the other armchair and patted her arm. "But you'll be fine. If you made it this far, you'll get used to living on Harbor Island in no time. Father always says cleanliness is next to godliness, and in the jungle, it's true."

"Hey, Vic, are you here?" A young, masculine voice drifted into the cottage before its owner appeared.

"In here, Dickie." Victoria headed toward the doorway.

Cecilia inhaled a deep breath and rose from the chair to welcome her first visitor. After all, this was her home, at least for the time being. Despite the initial shock of four-, six- or eight-legged unwanted visitors, she intended to make the most of her new life. How bad could it be?

Beside Victoria stood an imposing young man; at least six feet tall, broad-shouldered and square of jaw like his father, almond-eyed and caramel-skinned like his sister, and he possessed the same enchanting smile as his mother.

"Hi. You must be the new housekeeper. I'm Dickie." He offered his hand, which elicited a tingle up Cecilia's arm when they touched.

"I'm Cecilia. Good to meet you, Dickie." She reclaimed her hand and rubbed away the sensation.

"Welcome to Harbor Island, or as I like to call it, the madhouse." He exchanged a conspiratorial grin with Victoria, who nudged him in the ribs. "So, what do you think of Hill Cottage? Pretty place, isn't it?" A tempered version of his father, Dickie wandered into the cottage, as if gracing it with his presence.

"Yes, it is," said Cecilia, admiring his trim, muscular body, before scolding herself silently for doing so.

"And what do you think of Mother and Father?" He spun a slow turn, a cheeky smile lifting his lips.

"Well, I can't really say. I just met them."

"Well played, CiCi. You don't mind if I call you CiCi?" Innocent mischief flickered across his face.

"Ah . . . no."

Victoria pushed in front of him. "You'll have to excuse my brother, Cecilia."

"Why? What have I done?" He frowned at her.

"Really, Dickie. Don't you think you're being just a little rude? Walking into Cecilia's quarters, questioning her about our parents and then deciding on a nickname for her? Sometimes, I wonder if you've inherited too much of Father's traits and not enough of Mother's."

"It's okay." Cecilia raised a conciliatory hand. "It doesn't bother me. Besides, I had a good school friend who used to call me CiCi." She exchanged a furtive smirk with Dickie. "Tell me, why do you call it the madhouse?" She pulled out a kitchen chair, nodding for them to join her.

"I think it's because we're so removed from the rest of the world. Father acts like a lay preacher most of the time. I'm sure he thinks it's his purpose to convert the locals rather than employ and educate them. Wait for Sunday. Along with the rest of us, you'll be required in the great pavilion to listen to his Sunday sermon."

She shot an anxious glance at Victoria, who nodded. "He's right. Every Sunday, Father punishes us with one of his lengthy sermons. They are truly awful." Both she and Dickie groaned in unison.

"For the other six days of the week, nothing much changes. Like mice in a cage, we all go around and around doing the same chores, traveling the same road, living and speaking with the same people. That's why I call it the madhouse."

"But Harbor Island is so beautiful," insisted Cecilia. "It can't be as bad as you make out."

"But nothing changes. It's the same old, same old. I'm hoping now that you're here, things will liven up a little. At least, Vic and I will have some company our own age before we go to college."

"I know Victoria is studying to be a teacher. What are you going to study, Dickie?"

"Much to Father's dismay, I'm going to study environmental science, rather than architecture like all the previous Reginald men before me."

"Father thinks environmental science is a waste of time." Victoria rolled her eyes.

Impersonating his father, Dickie straightened in his chair and declared, "You need to know how to build, mend and fix things, not how to understand nature. Nature looks after itself. Man must do the same." His excellent mimicry had both Cecilia and Victoria doubled over giggling.

"Seems your dad and mine have a lot in common," said Cecilia, wiping laughter from her eyes.

"And what would that be? They're both obstinate and narrow-minded?" His tone hardened.

"Dickie, stop it," hushed Victoria.

"Father doesn't understand that unless we protect Harbor Island and start to implement some long-term conservation strategies, this place won't sustain itself over the coming hundred years. Building more shit is not the way." The vehemence with which he spoke inspired Cecilia. For an eighteen-year-old, he displayed a wisdom and maturity beyond his years.

"I agree with you," she said, enthralled by his passion. "If we don't take affirmative action and change how we live, the planet won't survive what we're doing to it. Goodness knows what sort of mess it'll be in by the time we're old."

"Good for you, CiCi. You understand. It's up to us to make a difference."

Waving her hands in the air, Victoria interjected, "Okay, you two. I agree we need to do whatever we can to save Harbor Island and the planet, but for now, let's take one step at a time." After casting her brother an icy sideways glance, she turned back to Cecilia. "Since you're not starting work tomorrow, would you like the grand tour of the island? Dickie and I can show you around, introduce you to the people in town, those sorts of things."

"Yes, please. But I need to get myself some more clothes. Maybe we can go to the Ladies Markets as well?"

"Done." Victoria nodded. "We'll make a day of it. Come on, Dickie. Let Cecilia settle in and get washed up before dinner."

Rising from his chair, he struck his hand toward her. "Really pleased you're here, CiCi. I look forward to talking with you more."

"Me too." She shared an intimate smile with him, wondering if the glint in his eye and extra-tight squeeze of her hand relayed only an intellectual compatibility.

"I'll send Loretta up with some food and supplies. Then when you're ready, come down, and we'll see what Mom's got planned. I'm so happy to have you here, Cecilia. I just know you'll fit in." Bending forward, Victoria kissed her cheek. "Aloha."

"Aloha." Watching sister and brother amble down the steps of Hill Cottage, a warm glow nestled in Cecilia's heart.

* * * *

After Loretta had stacked her fridge and cupboards with enough food to feed a family of four, Cecilia sat alone on the veranda, gazing out into the distance with her legs stretched in front of her on the railing. That her life had turned around in just over twenty-four hours thrilled her more than she had expected. She recalled Joseph's advice about being afraid on the climb, about disregarding the fear and climbing anyway. And she'd done exactly that. Now, perched on top of the world in Hill Cottage, she was about to leap into a new opportunity. Despite Dickie's opinion of it being the madhouse, she decided she would make her own assessment about Harbor Island over the coming week.

The balmy afternoon breeze drifted up from the harbor to caress her face. She closed her eyes, enjoying its tender touch. But she knew her stalling of the inevitable must come to an end. *I better get in and shower before it gets dark.* Unsavory as her first experience of the bathhouse had been, there was no other option. She dragged her weary body up from the rattan chair and trudged inside the cottage and collected the fluffy purple towel Loretta had laid in the shape of a flower on her bed. From the wardrobe, she selected a burnt-orange gypsy skirt and blouse, hoping the sharp color would give her more energy.

Once outside she walked the fifteen or so steps to the bathhouse, opened the wooden door and peered inside. This time the foul smell was replaced by the sweet fragrance of plumeria flowers scattered in coconut shells throughout the small room. Little bottles of shampoo, soap and other toiletries perched on the basin, as did a face cloth and hand towel. Every corner had been swept and cleaned of lurking dirt and insect carcasses. Even the pit toilet lid was firmly secured with a large rock. *Dear Loretta. She misses nothing.*

Cecilia locked the door behind her and placed her bath towel on the basin. After peeling off her clothes, she checked her shoulders, pleased to see her sunburn had changed to a golden tan. Instead of rushing her shower for fear of unwelcome visitors, she delighted in the warm stream of water, lathering her skin and hair. To have her own private bathroom was a luxury she'd missed since leaving home. One she took full advantage of now. With eyes closed, she allowed the grime of the events and journey that had brought her to Harbor Island wash away. A sense of dreamy languor enveloped her body as she slowly rinsed, toweled and dressed. In fact, her initiation of the bathhouse left her relaxed and rejuvenated. Ensuring all was in place and the door closed behind her, she exited and ambled along the short, rock-bordered path back to the cottage. Fresh and recharged, she returned to the veranda to finger-dry her hair in the afternoon breeze. Aside from the chirrup of a few birds, the peaceful spell of Hill Cottage was unbroken. She ruffled her long curls and settled in to savor the quiet. But her solitude was short-lived. A movement in the garden below caught her attention.

She leaned over the railing. "Dickie, what are you doing?"

"I thought I'd escort you down to dinner. Sorry if I startled you." Flashing a disarming smile, he bounded up the stairs and leaned against one of the veranda's posts.

"That's kind of you, but I can come down when my hair dries. It'll take a while yet." When his mouth turned down at the sides, she ceased fluffing her hair and faced him. "What is it? What's the matter?"

Dickie lowered his eyes. "Oh . . . It doesn't matter." His feet shuffled.

"It's okay. You obviously came here for something?" she said, in a reassuring voice. "Go on. I'm listening." Cecilia watched the young man struggle with his decision.

After a few moments, he lifted his head, and she met his troubled gaze. "Okay, then. Can I ask you something?"

"Of course." With a vague air of concern, she folded into one of the chairs and motioned him to the other. She watched his eyes roam her face, his expression fraught with uncertainty.

"Have you ever been happy, CiCi? Really happy?"

"Now, that's an odd question."

"But tell me, have you ever been really happy? And how do you know when you're happy?"

Brushing damp hair from her shoulders, she sat upright and considered. "For me, I feel really happy when I sing. That's why I want to be a professional singer."

"So, what are doing here? Why aren't you off singing and being really happy?"

It was a good question. One she had asked herself many times over the past few years. "Sometimes, life doesn't always work out the way you intended. You've got to make a few adjustments along the way. I'm here because I need the money to get back to San Francisco. Then I'll sing professionally. I'm only twenty-five, you know. I've got lots of time yet."

"Do you think we can run out of time to be happy?"

She frowned. "I don't understand what you mean."

"Well, do you think there's some unknown deadline in our lives that if we haven't been really happy by then, we never get the chance again? That it's all too late?"

"No, of course not. We can be happy any time in our lives. Happiness isn't a commodity we deplete or run out of. It's not like the planet." She watched him consider her answer and sigh. "What about you, Dickie? How do you know when you're really happy?"

A long pause stretched between them. While he stared off to nowhere, she studied him with stealthy glances. Fashionably long, thick black hair framed the striking planes of his maturing face. Dickie appeared blessed with good genetics; his well-cut nose, cheekbones, and jaw predicted the emergence of a very handsome man in years to come. Unlike many boys his age, his body was hard and muscled, probably from the physical chores required of him on the property. His smooth, coffee-colored skin, further darkened from the sun, contrasted against his white T-shirt and khaki shorts. Perplexed, passionate and purposeful, he reminded her of the extraordinary young men leading the civil rights and environmental movements on the mainland; at once inspired and a little forsaken. A small muscle flinched in his jaw, and she wondered if he'd forgotten her question.

She prompted, "Dickie, how do you know when you're really happy?"

He half turned toward her, sadness shadowing his face. "I don't know, CiCi. I don't think I've ever been happy. Not really happy. And certainly not yet."

CHAPTER FIVE

After Dickie's sad revelation of never being happy, that night's dinner had been a strange and strained affair. While the Reginald family chatted, Cecilia sat at the dinner table a little shell-shocked. Making polite conversation, complimenting the food and ensuring she showed the respect a prospective new employee would to their employer, exhausted her. Straight after dinner, she excused herself and with her newly appointed night-time escort, Bartholomew, by her side, she trudged up the stairs to Hill Cottage, pleased to return to her sanctuary.

"So, Bartholomew, how long have you worked here?"

"Nearly forty years, Miss. I worked here for the former Mr. Reginald and then when he died, I worked on for this Mr. Reginald."

Studying the Hawaiian's face in the moonlight, she would have guessed his age much younger. "And what is your job here? Aside from being my escort at night." She shot him a grateful grin.

"I help Mr. Reginald mostly. Doing carpentry jobs here and on the shops. He taught me how to use the tools, to build and repair things."

"I see. You're an important man if Mr. Reginald puts his trust in you?"

"Maybe, Miss. I just do what I'm told." His voice quieted, giving her the impression that he was uncomfortable talking about his employer.

"Are you married, Bartholomew?"

"Yes, Miss. Me and Loretta are married."

"Oh, your wife is wonderful. I watched Loretta work in the main house. She stocked Hill Cottage for me today and cleaned my bathhouse so beautifully. You're a lucky man."

"Yes, Miss." A blinding smile split the dark canvas of his face.

"Do you and Loretta have children?"

"No, God did not bless us with children." As quickly as it had appeared, his smile vanished.

"Oh, I'm sorry, Bartholomew."

When they reached the front door of Hill Cottage, he turned to her. "Here you go, Miss. Would you like me to check inside?"

"You mean for snakes and rats and things?" A breath trembled between her lips.

"If you like, I can have a look around for you."

"Yes, please." From the doorway, she watched him circumnavigate her one-room cottage, checking in corners, under furniture, and behind wardrobes.

"Better you close the windows at night, Miss." He pulled shut the old casement windows, twisting their latches into place.

"But Victoria said to leave them open otherwise I'll get too hot."

"Better to get too hot than to let strange things in."

"Yes, I suppose you're right." She shuddered.

"I will come up tomorrow and put some screens over your windows, Miss. The bedroom windows on the other bungalows have it. Then you can leave your windows open. But still use your mosquito net at night, even with the screens. Okay?"

"Thank you, Bartholomew. That would be terrific. I will."

"Very good, Miss. Good night." A slight frown creased his forehead as he waited.

"Good night and thank you." He turned to leave and then stopped. "What is it, Bartholomew?"

Motioning her to the door, he drew her attention to the old-fashioned lock. "Loretta put the key in the lock today, Miss. See?" His bony finger pointed to the antique skeleton key resting in the mortise lock. "Lock the door after me, Miss." His dark, piercing eyes drilled into hers. She blinked a few times. Tiny pinpricks of gooseflesh nibbled the back of her neck. She rubbed them away.

"Thank you, Bartholomew. I will lock the door. Good night." She held the door open, and Bartholomew disappeared into the dark.

In one swift movement, Cecilia closed and locked the door. She leaned against it and pushed the nudging anxiety from her mind. With a determined flick of her hair, she inhaled sharply and focused on her new home. In the pale light of the bedside lamps, the cottage's loveliness glowed. She gazed around the room and studied every shadow, shape, and angle cast by its furniture and furnishings, familiarizing herself with her new home. She strolled to each window, checking the locks and drawing the curtains. At the back door, she noticed it was locked. Not something she did before leaving this evening, so Bartholomew must have locked it when he checked the cottage. She reminded herself that it was a sweet, little cottage, but Bartholomew's insistence on locking the door unsettled her. If the shops in the main street had no security and everyone lived in harmony on the island, why did Hill Cottage have locks on the door?

"Stop it," she said aloud, as she moved toward her bed. "You're being over-dramatic. You locked your doors back home, so why shouldn't you lock them here."

Having given herself a good talking-to, she undressed and crawled naked under the sheets. Even their cool comfort did little to cure the aching tiredness in her body. When her hands pressed her weary muscles, she realized she'd become way too thin. Mary was right. She needed to get healthy. Put some meat on her bones and muscles on her limbs. But for now, she needed to relax. She reached over and grabbed one of the *Glamour* magazines Loretta had left on her bedside table. Then she tucked in the mosquito net with meticulous care, just as Victoria had shown her. She flopped back onto her pillows to read, but before she'd finished the introduction to The Best New Fall Looks, she crashed into a deep sleep.

A rustling sound stirred Cecilia awake. Her fingers hung limply on the magazine, and a soft glow filled the cottage from her bedside lamp. *Scratch, scratch, scratch.* Something was outside, on the veranda. Her breath clutched in her chest, as did her fingers on the magazine. Silence. A long silence. *For goodness sake, it's just rats running across the veranda. They can't get in. Everything's closed and locked.* Just as her chest relaxed, she stiffened at a new sound. *Scrape, scrape. Scrape, scrape.* This time on the windowsill. Her body stiffened, either unwilling or unable to move. With her hearing on high alert, she listened for something else. What else? She dared not think what else it could be, except rats. She prayed it was rats.

Thud!

She launched bolt upright in bed and clenched the damp sheet to her chest. Perspiration ran down her back and arms. More rustling, moving away from the cottage. Then nothing. She forced herself to breathe. A few minutes more. Still nothing. Her shoulders dropped, but only a little. Another five minutes. Nothing again. She slumped. *You're going to have to get used to the sounds of the jungle if you're going to work here.* She slithered back under the sheets and lay down. Reaching her hand through the mosquito net, she switched off the bedside lamp and cast the room into an array of shadows. The moonlight peeped through the gaps in the overlapping curtains, like welcome visitors adding silvery shafts of security. Even if Bartholomew put screens on her windows tomorrow, she wasn't convinced she'd ever sleep with them open. When her heartbeat returned to normal, she closed her eyes. But sleep visited her only in fits and starts. It wasn't until the first golden tinge of dawn offered its protection that she allowed herself to fall into the deep death of sleep.

Tap, tap, tap. Then a little louder. *Tap, tap, tap.* "Cecilia, are you awake?" A woman's voice drifted into her consciousness. Who was that? Where was she? As if waking from a big night on the hooch with Michael, Cecilia finally came to, groggy and confused. The mosquito net swam into focus, and she pushed upright in bed.

"It's me, Victoria. Are you ready?" the voice shouted.

Flailing through the netting, Cecilia stumbled out of bed and toward the door, clutching a sheet to cover her nakedness.

Bleary-eyed, she flung the door open. "Sorry. I slept in. Give me a minute." She pulled on her panties, a pair of white cheesecloth pants and a pale-blue drawstring top. "What time is it?"

"Nine o'clock. You missed breakfast."

"Damn. I really need to eat more. Is there somewhere we can get food?"

Victoria laughed. "No fast food on this island. But don't worry, I had Loretta put a picnic lunch together for us, and she added a breakfast sandwich for you."

"She's a treasure." Cecilia dragged her fingers through her uncombed hair in a lame effort to tame the delinquent cowlicks before lashing it in a hair band.

"Do you have a bikini or something? You better bring it."

"Got it," said Cecilia, shoving the pieces into her tote bag and throwing a towel over her shoulder. Hat and sunglasses in hand, she sported a cheeky smirk. "I'm ready."

"Okay. Let's go."

At the front door, Cecilia hesitated, wondering if she should lock it.

"What's the matter?"

"I had the strangest night." She became serious. "When Bartholomew walked me home, he insisted on locking all the windows even though I told him you said to leave them open. He also insisted I locked the door when he left. Then during the night there were all these rustling and scratching noises. To be honest, it scared me."

"It's probably just rats and other night-time creatures scurrying around outside. I did warn you."

"That's what I told myself. And then there was this almighty thud." Deciding not to lock the cottage, she turned and trotted down the cottage stairs beside Victoria.

"It was probably a coconut falling off a tree. They do that. Sometimes the boys miss cutting them down in time." She paused, looking around. "There it is, on the ground." Victoria pointed to the offender — an enormous yellow shell a few feet away. "See. A coconut. That'll be the thud you heard."

"I suppose so. But it scared the hell out of me. I didn't really get any sleep after that. That's why I slept in." Like an awkward child retelling a silly nightmare, Cecilia blushed.

"That's okay. Night noises take a bit of getting used to. Dickie and I grew up with them, so we don't notice them." Unconcerned, Victoria pranced down the hewn-rock staircase.

Cecilia pressed on. "Can we go and see Bartholomew before we leave? He promised he'd put some screens on my windows today, like you have on your bungalows."

"Sure. He's on morning tea. We'll catch him before he goes back to work."

Dashing past the great pavilion, Cecilia glimpsed Dickie running toward them. "Hey, where are you two off to? Aren't we going to town?"

"Sure, but we have to see Bartholomew first. Come on." Waving him to join them, Victoria jogged off in the direction of the staff quarters.

Down a steep slope and obscured from public view behind the pool and entertainment area, hid a village of dilapidated shacks. Not one solitary building looked sturdy enough to withstand a fierce wind or torrential downpour. Interconnecting dirt pathways snaked between the decrepit dwellings, while washing hung on the strung lines under the wizened plumeria trees. Drifts of brown-tinted, decaying leaves sheeted the ground, creating the perfect breeding place for all sorts of insects and spiders. Grubby children scampered around like refuse dogs, digging and scratching in the dirt. Poverty and despair pervaded the air, jolting Cecilia's sensibilities. "Is this where the staff live?" she whispered.

"Yes. This is the staff quarters," said Dickie in an apologetic tone.

"But isn't your father an architect? Can't he build them something better than this?" She had difficulty in suppressing the seething injustice in her gut.

"Don't get me started, CiCi. Both Vic and I have pleaded with Father to do something about their living conditions." Exchanging a look of desperation with his sister, he shook his head in obvious frustration.

"But what does your mother say? She can't possibly approve of this." Cecilia threw her arm toward the squalor in front of them.

"Ever since they married, Mom has battled with him to tear this place down and rebuild it. But some of the staff say they're happy and don't want their homes destroyed."

"You are kidding me, right?" Cecilia gaped in disbelief.

"Father said that unless there is a consensus of all the families living here, he won't take any action." The sarcasm in Dickie's voice and the muscle flinching in his jaw showed his disgust at the situation.

"Please, Cecilia . . . Dickie and Father often come to verbal blows over it."

"But I don't understand how in 1973 this type of inequality exists, particularly when your father obviously has the money and the means to change the lives of his staff." Realizing the audacity of her criticism, she bit her lip. "I'm sorry. I shouldn't have said that. It's none of my business."

Victoria rubbed Cecilia's shoulder. "It's okay. We feel the same way. So does Mom. But even in the short time you've been here, you can see that Father rules this place with an iron rod. What he says goes."

"Not for long, though." Dickie clenched his fists to match the mounting tension in his jaw.

"Please, Dickie," soothed Victoria with a soft touch to his forearm. She forced a smile. "Come on, let's find Bartholomew." Setting off down the slope, she led the way into the village. Grimy-faced children ran to meet her, their soiled hands outstretched for sweets. "Sorry. Not today." Victoria waved her empty hands in the air. With little pouts, the kids turned on their heels and returned to their squalid play.

"Miss Victoria, Mr. Dickie, what are you doing here?" Loretta scurried out from an open, slanting doorway, rubbing her hands on an apron. She wore an expression of worry, and Cecilia suspected mild embarrassment. Dressed in her mumu of bright blues and greens, she smelled of jasmine and coconut oil. With her tight curls reefed into a snug bun and a pink-and-yellow plumeria flower tucked behind her left ear, Loretta appeared the quintessential Hawaiian woman.

"Is Bartholomew here?" asked Victoria in a sweet voice.

Nodding, Loretta rushed back through the doorway and called for her husband. In a matter of moments, he appeared, his brow lifted in surprise.

"What has happened? Is something wrong?"

"No, no, Bartholomew. Miss Cecilia wanted to talk to you about the screens for her windows before we went sightseeing around the island."

His serious gaze narrowed on Cecilia. "Is everything all right, Miss Cecilia?"

"Well, to be honest, I didn't sleep well last night. There were lots of noises outside."

"What sort of noises, Miss?" He and Loretta traded worried glances, twisting their mouths in a grim line.

"Lots of scratching and scraping, rustling too, and a thud." Watching closely, she studied husband and wife but saw no other exchange between them.

"It was just a coconut falling out of the trees. You need to get the boys to check the trees there today, Bartholomew," instructed Victoria.

Bartholomew shifted his attention. "Yes, Miss Victoria. I will."

Cecilia licked her lips and hesitated before asking, "Are the screens strong, Bartholomew?"

Before the conversation diverted to anyone else's opinion, he pinned her with his heavy-lidded eyes. "Strong enough to keep a big animal out, Miss Cecilia."

"But we don't have big animals on the island," clucked Victoria.

"No, Miss Victoria, we don't." Returning his attention to Cecilia, he continued, "I will get the screens on today, Miss Cecilia." He offered a polite smile and turned back into his shack.

"Thank you," she called after him.

Loretta nodded primly and followed her husband inside.

"What was all that about?" Dickie scratched his head as they began the climb away from the staff quarters.

"I just wanted to make sure Bartholomew installs the screens today while we're out," explained Cecilia. But the odd interplay between him and Loretta prickled her skin. She had the distinct feeling that something else was going on. Maybe she was overreacting. She was known to enjoy a good conspiracy theory and had spent hours debating JFK's assassination with her friends, thoroughly engrossed in the clandestine elements of the tragedy. Perhaps she was too eager to find some secret scheme afoot here on the island. In the end, she chose for the mundane and decided that living in the jungle would take some getting used to. Nevertheless, she remained uneasy about leaving her windows open at night.

CHAPTER SIX

Squeezed between Victoria, who drove, and Dickie on the other end of the bench seat, Cecilia chomped on her breakfast sandwich as they jostled along in the Chevy. On their way down the steep, bumpy Harbor Hill Road, Victoria pulled over a few times to give a ride to the locals walking into town. With the open rear cargo bed full of happy, chatting passengers, the old truck trundled along, providing much-needed respite from the hot journey.

"Hey, look." Dickie pointed to the beach coming into full view as they turned into The Esplanade. "We've got visitors."

From a couple of yachts moored in the harbor, a dozen or so people had come ashore. Settled on the beach, they lazed, played games and bathed, enjoying the serenity of the island.

"So, what happens after they've gone?" asked Cecilia.

"What do you mean?"

"Well, the beach is so perfectly maintained. There's no rubbish, or food scraps or anything. I bet visitors don't clean up after themselves all the time?"

"You're right," said Victoria. "At the end of each day, a team of groundsmen go over the beach, collecting rubbish and raking the sand."

Cecilia frowned and looked at each of them to check whether they were joking. "Rake the sand?"

"I know it sounds absurd," said Dickie, exchanging a smile. "But it's our family's role to support the local families here. So, we employ as many as we can in whatever jobs we can. Raking the beach is one of them. Believe me, the groundsmen who do it enjoy it. It's easier than many of the other jobs. And because no one supervises them, they take a lot longer than they should. They're a cheeky lot." He shook his head and chuckled at their staff's cunningness.

"I have no doubt Mom will send you down to check up on them once you settle into the housekeeper role," said Victoria.

Cecilia scratched her head. "Raking the beach. Now I've heard everything."

Even at only ten o'clock in the morning and with the truck windows wound down, cool air proved elusive. The warm breeze wafted up from the harbor and swirled in the cabin, creating pools of invisible heat. Shafts of sunlight pierced the windscreen and increased the cabin temperature until the towel on the bench seat turned damp beneath Cecilia's thighs.

The Chevy slowed to a stop. Victoria switched off the engine and slid out of the cabin. "Okay. Let's go into the Ladies Markets first and organize some more clothes for you."

Cecilia shuffled across the seat after Victoria and then looked back at Dickie. "You coming?"

"Nah, I'll wait here I think. Maybe take a stroll on the beach. Just don't be too long. Okay?"

"Okay," Cecilia and Victoria replied in unison.

* * * *

The sound of trundle sewing machines busy at work reverberated in the Ladies Markets. Louder still was the chatter and laughter of women's voices as they created items to sell, either to residents on the island, or visitors from the boats. Lined up in two rows, about a dozen machines droned away in the stifling heat in the ramshackle shop. Small towels draped around the women's necks in lame efforts to soak up the sweat from their toil. Bypassing the toweling blockade, perspiration escaped into evaporating puddles on the bare floorboards and gave off an odor of damp flesh unsuccessfully masked by coconut oil. Despite the difficult working conditions, portable racks of artfully-made clothes hung behind each dressmaker, displaying their creator's skills and talents. It was retail shopping at its primitive best.

Seated in the middle of one of the rows worked a mountain of a woman. On seeing Victoria, she erupted from her chair, arms outstretched. "Aloha. Aloha, Miss Victoria."

"Aloha, Martha." Consumed in the woman's bosom, Victoria visibly grimaced at the warm, clammy welcome.

Breaking free of the dressmaker's embrace, she turned to Cecilia. "This is Martha. She makes my island clothes. She's very good." The large-boned woman with a megawatt smile towered over them. Adorned in a white cotton mumu, hand-painted with pink-and-yellow plumeria flowers, she filled the space behind her Singer sewing machine like a psychedelic painting in a modern art gallery.

"Pleased to meet you, Martha, I'm Cecilia." She snapped out her hand, so as not to be consumed in Martha's embrace, but the dressmaker hugged her just the same. Although Cecilia wiggled away, she thought better of wiping the transferred perspiration from her bare arms. That would be impolite. Instead, she traded a laughing smile with the enthusiastic dressmaker.

With a flourish of her arm, Martha presented her clothes hanging on the rack behind her. "What you want in clothes? I make everything good."

"How about you make Miss Cecilia three pairs of long cotton pants like the ones you make me, three matching tops, two dresses and four pairs of shorts and matching tops." Victoria winced. "Sorry, Cecilia. I thought I'd get you started with what I've found the best and then you can come down and organize other items. Is that okay?"

"Sure. Sounds good." With a tilt of her head, she tugged Victoria to one side out of earshot. "But how much will all that cost? I don't have much money until I get the housekeeper job and that's not a certainty yet."

"Don't worry about the money. I'm sure you'll get the job. The clothes you buy from the Ladies Markets are paid for out of your uniform allowance. No need to worry about money here."

Cecilia's face brightened. "Really?"

Victoria nodded. "Now, go pick the colors you want for each of the pieces."

Within fifteen minutes, Cecilia had picked the fabrics, colors and had her measurements taken by a very efficient Martha. "These be ready tomorrow afternoon, Miss Cecilia."

"Wow. That's fast. Thanks, Martha. I'll come and collect them, then. Aloha."

The deal made, they strolled back outside into the fresh air. An idea popped into Cecilia's head, and she paused for a moment. Here she was on a private island, living in her own quarters and not required to pay for clothes or food or supplies. Added to that, she was about to start a job for which she would be paid. She'd gone from nothing to a whole lot of something in a matter of days.

"Can I ask you a personal question?" She turned to her new friend.

"Sure."

"Where does the money come from to pay for everything? To keep all these people in work? It must cost your family a fortune."

"Most of it is inherited money that came from mining on the other side of the island years ago. It's been wisely invested and luckily hasn't run out. It's Father's job to keep it that way, so Harbor Island is secured for the rest of our lives."

"Oh, I see. It's a big responsibility." She marveled at the size of the fortune the Reginalds must have amassed to support such a mammoth venture as Harbor Island.

"Certainly is. I think that's why Father is so cranky all the time. It falls on his shoulders to keep Harbor Island profitable and never have to sell it."

The shriek of a woman's voice sliced the air. "Smith, where are you? You're nothing but..." Beatrice's barreling figure charged toward them. Arms waving and spittle popping in the air, she cursed an assortment of expletives listing her husband's shortcomings.

On closer approach, she tempered her language and nodded. "Morning, Miss Vickie, morning, Miss...?"

"Miss Cecilia," prompted Victoria. "Whatever is the matter now, Beatrice?"

"Smith is what is the matter," she snorted. "He in his workshop."

"Okay. Let's go there together and see if we can't sort this out." Keeping Beatrice at bay, Victoria wheeled to their right and led the way into the workshop. "Smith, are you in here?"

Smith's attention lifted from the handiwork on his bench. "Aloha, Miss Victoria. Miss Cecilia." His fleshy lips tugged upward into a lopsided smile. It was obvious that no matter how much Beatrice berated him, it had little effect.

"What are you working on?" asked Victoria, peering over his shoulder.

"I'm doing some work for Bartholomew. I'm making the window screens for Hill Cottage."

Cecilia studied the finished screens resting against Smith's bench. "Goodness. Things happen fast around here."

"Yes, Miss Cecilia. As soon as you arrive, I start the screens."

She inclined her head and frowned. "But why would you do that?"

"Ah, because... um..." The atmosphere in the workshop transformed from prickling with heat to prickling with tension.

"Yes, Smith, why would you do that?" asked Victoria, surprise in her voice.

Beatrice edged in beside him. In a conciliatory manner, she patted his shoulder. "Smith a good judge of character. As soon as he meet Miss Cecilia, he's sure she will get the housekeeper job. So, he begins to make the screens for Hill Cottage. Keep out the insects and such like."

Cecilia fixed Beatrice with a suspicious stare. *There's something odd going on here.*

While Smith steered the conversation with Victoria to maintenance on the Chevy, Cecilia eased Beatrice to one side. "Tell me, Beatrice, you and Loretta are good friends, yes?"

"Yes, Miss." She stared down at her fidgeting fingers.

"And Smith and Bartholomew are good friends, too?"

"Yes, Miss." More fidgeting.

"What's going on at Hill Cottage?" Beatrice's head snapped upward, her eyes round as saucers. "Is there something you all know that I should know?"

"Oh no, Miss." She shook her head so hard, her tight curls resembled springy strands of licorice.

"Are you sure? You're all concerned about these screens and making sure I keep my windows and doors locked at night."

Beatrice's face flushed hot. Her hand flew to her throat and then scraped across her lips. "I don't know what you mean, Miss."

If Cecilia needed any further confirmation that something suspicious was going on at Hill Cottage, Beatrice's unconvincing performance of innocence was it. "There is something going on, and I want to know what it is."

Unable to escape, the store owner looked around, trying to catch her husband's attention. "I don't know anything, Miss."

"Tell me, Beatrice. What is it?" Cecilia did her best to persuade the shop owner to tell her, but she was losing her patience.

Desperation raced across Beatrice's face. "Please, Miss. I don't know anything."

"What are you afraid of? Am I in danger at Hill Cottage?"

"Oh, Miss. No, you're not in danger once the screens go up." Beatrice quivered like a cornered mouse.

Exasperated, Cecilia puffed out a breath. "Very well, Beatrice, but as the new housekeeper, I have a right to know what's going on. One way or the other, I will find out." Beatrice bobbed and scurried over to her husband, where she clung to his side. Every now and then, she'd glance up at Cecilia, then revert to the conversation.

While Victoria and Smith continued talking, and Beatrice feigned interest in their discussion about mechanics, Cecilia wandered outside. This morning's guarded reactions from Bartholomew and Loretta at the staff quarters, and now Smith and particularly Beatrice's peculiar behavior confirmed Cecilia's initial suspicions. There was something going on. She was sure of it. None of them wanted to give her a straight answer about Hill Cottage. She'd hoped in the light of day, her night-time fears would be dispelled, but after speaking with Beatrice, she was more unsettled than ever. Victoria seemed oblivious to whatever the staff suspected or knew. And although Dickie had confided in her last night about his unhappiness, Cecilia didn't know him well enough to discuss her concerns. Perhaps Dickie was right. The whole place was a madhouse.

Once more, she found herself gazing out over the ocean's vastness to where it met the vertical edge of the world. She thought of Joseph and how he'd been drawn to ocean-gazing when he'd considered his answers to her questions. Likewise, the horizon had become her secret solace. It represented stability and dependability. The horizon never wavered. It was always there, reminding her that life could be smooth and steady. Now, as she concentrated on the thin line of blue on blue, she prayed its steadfastness would also bring answers to what was going on at Hill Cottage.

* * * *

By the time she and Victoria returned, Dickie was tapping his fingers on the wheel. "Come on, you two. Let's go." He cranked the engine over, and before Victoria closed the passenger door, he pulled away in a dust cloud.

"Go easy, Dickie," she snapped. "You drive like an idiot."

"Yeah, yeah. You take too long. It's hot, and I want to get to Rainbow Falls."

Over the next hour, he drove them deeper inland on a narrow, pot-holed dirt road. The Chevy rattled along at a reduced speed, sometimes as slow as a crawl. Because no work crews maintained the road in this part of the island, any encroaching branches were snapped off by the truck as it passed by. The screeching sound of branch on steel set Cecilia's teeth on edge. Nevertheless, there was one advantage in the time-consuming trip — the cooling effect of the jungle through which they drove. Since the sun rarely penetrated the canopy, the heat in the Chevy dropped to a bearable temperature. Wedged between brother and sister, Cecilia settled back and enjoyed the ride, despite the occasional screech.

Dickie steered with one hand on the wheel, while his other arm crooked out the window. She thought he epitomized the young-man-most-likely-to-succeed image. Confident, intelligent and charismatic were the words she suspected his college lecturers would use to describe him.

He flashed a smile and slanted her a glance. "This road was cut through the island at the turn of the century. It leads all the way across to the old Reginald mines on the other side."

Victoria took up the family history. "That's where the Reginald wealth I was telling you about came from — gem mining — obsidian, peridot, and black coral, mainly for jewelry. It was big business. But the mines were shut down years ago and the money invested."

"But how did your family end up owning Harbor Island in the first place?" Cecilia asked.

"It goes way back." Victoria counted on her fingers. "Our great-great-great-grandfather Reginald bought the island in 1852 from the local Hawaiian king."

"Really? I didn't know that was possible."

"Oh, you haven't been able to do that for years. But back then, just before the new land division came into effect across all the islands, the king of this district decided to sell Harbor Island, and he pocketed the money," said Victoria.

"For how much?"

"Seven and a half thousand dollars," interjected Dickie, his lips tight.

Cecilia whistled long and slow. "Is that all?"

"I guess back then it was a lot of money to the king." Victoria sighed. "All the Reginald men have been savvy businessmen. The deal was obviously good for the king, and our great-great-great-grandfather, but maybe not so good for the native Hawaiians caught in the middle."

"What do you mean?" But from what Cecilia had seen that morning at the staff quarters, she suspected she knew the answer.

"Well, when Great-great-great-grandfather bought the island it came with the population of local natives. It was up to him to make sure their way of life would be sustained. That was part of the deal with the king. Father never talks much about that period of our family history, because I think he's ashamed."

"Of what?"

"They turned them into slaves," hissed Dickie, an unforgiving tone in his voice.

Victoria hushed him. "We don't know that for sure. It's all just gossip on the local grapevine. Anyway, over the generations, the Reginald men who inherited Harbor Island have tried to do better — to give jobs, better living conditions and education to the local families wherever they can."

"So how many families are there still living here?"

"Probably about twenty or so, I think. Most of them either run their own little businesses, like Smith and Beatrice, and the others work for us."

"And what about your mother? She's Hawaiian, isn't she?"

"Yes, Mom's maiden name was Kaiwi. The Kaiwi family were on the island since our family bought it. Because Mom showed such promise, my Father's parents paid to send her to college for three years to get an education. After Father's parents died in a car crash, and he inherited the island, Mom returned. She took the job of housekeeper, helping Father run the property. It was her way of repaying the opportunity his parents had given her, as well as helping the local families. They fell in love, got married and here we are, Dickie and me — half Reginald and half Kaiwi."

"Yes, half master and half slave," spat Dickie, a shadow passing over his face.

"Stop it, Dickie. It's not that bad," begged Victoria.

"To me it is. I don't fit into the Reginald men's mold. I'm nothing like Father at all. There's too much Kaiwi running through my veins. I can tell you things will change when I inherit the island." He fisted his hands on the wheel.

Cecilia shot a confused look at Victoria. "But what about you? Don't you inherit the island as well?"

Victoria gave a sad shrug. "Only the male children can inherit Harbor Island."

"What! That's so unfair and sexist," said Cecilia, not hiding her indignation. "You deserve your share in the inheritance."

"I agree," said Dickie. "It's fundamentalist Christian thinking at its most archaic. Only men inherit, unless of course there were no sons. But that's never happened. There's always been a male child born. Believe me, there's no way Father will break with tradition on this."

"But don't you get anything at all?" Cecilia stared hard at Victoria, who merely offered a lame smile.

"Don't worry about Vic. I'll look after her." Dickie's mouth stretched in a wide grin as he glanced across at his sister.

"Aw, shucks, little brother. How sweet of you," she teased.

Still surprised by the inequality, Cecilia continued, "So you get nothing in the will." She swiveled from Victoria to Dickie. "And you inherit the lot and have to stay here for the rest of your life?"

"That's it in a nutshell," he said, sounding quite upbeat despite the fact that his life had been planned out for him since birth. "I look at it this way, CiCi. It's my duty to help the staff and locals here. Until I inherit the island, I have no power in how the island is managed or how the residents live or what happens to them."

"It's true. Dickie is like a royal prince. Until the king dies, he has to bide his time."

"But when Father dies, and I inherit, I can actually do some good here. Hopefully, Mom will outlive him, so together we can make Harbor Island a better place for everyone."

"Well, I have to give it to you, Dickie. You're one helluva a young man."

"When Dickie marries and has a family, he can change the inheritance ruling, so all his kids can inherit equally, if he chooses."

"That's a while off yet." He chuckled. "For now, we're here at Rainbow Falls. Everyone out."

* * * *

Cecilia splashed around on her back, entranced by the colors captured in the waterfall spray. Sparkling mountain water suffused with sunbeams thundered from the ledge a hundred feet above, fracturing into endless rainbow arches before smashing into the bottomless lagoon in which they swam. No matter how many times she'd watched this awesome spectacle over the past few hours, she still wasn't tired of it. "Now, I understand why it's called Rainbow Falls. If the rest of the world knew this place existed, it'd be filled with tourists."

"Exactly what we don't want." Dickie swam closer and flipped over onto his back to admire the same view. "I hope you end up getting the housekeeper job, CiCi." He grinned at her.

"I hope so, too. Harbor Island is like heaven on earth."

"It can be. One day, when I own it, it will be."

"I'm sure you'll do a terrific job. And with your environmental science degree, the island will be saved for generations to come."

"That's the plan." His eyes drifted, as if looking toward a happier future. Paddling closer, he added, "I expect you'll be long gone by then. Off on the mainland with a big singing career."

"That's the plan." She held his dark gaze.

In the vortex of crashing water, pristine jungle and a lagoon so clear you could see the bottom, their hands brushed, sending ripples up her arms. He ran a finger along her forearm so delicately she quivered at its touch.

"I have a feeling I will miss you when you go, CiCi."

"Me too," she whispered, her lips tilting in a soft smile.

The blast of the truck horn broke the moment. "Come on, you two. Time to go." Propped on the running board, Victoria waved them over.

In a cheeky challenge, Cecilia tweaked his chin. "Race you to the edge." Her arm flew overhead, taking the first stroke.

"Damn." Dickie slammed headlong into the water, his strong arms pulling forward. Before she reached the edge, he stood there, his hand outstretched to help her out of the lagoon. She met his burning gaze and pretended not to notice it. But when he clasped her hand, a bolt of energy raced up her arm. Unlike her, Dickie didn't feign indifference. He noticed. Oh, yes, he noticed.

* * * *

The beach-raking crew was already on duty by the time the Chevy drove along The Esplanade.

"There. See." Dickie pointed out the groundsmen with metal rakes, leveling the beach and collecting rubbish. "Let's stop, Vic, and see if they're about finished. We'll give them a lift home."

She pulled the truck along the road a little further, and they got out.

"Hey, fellas, you finished yet?" Striding down the sandy slope to the work crew, Dickie wore the mantle of would-be-king well.

A chorus of "Yes, Mr. Dickie" greeted him as he slapped hands with the workers.

Standing beside Victoria on the road, Cecilia folded her arms, admiring his easygoing way with the staff. "He is quite something your younger brother, isn't he?"

"Yes. He is. You can see how he and Father clash, though. Dickie is progressive in his thinking, whereas Father is so traditional. It's going to get worse as Dickie gets older."

"It's the same with me and my parents. They just can't see how they need to change with the times. That's why I left home. Poor Dickie's stuck here. I'm not sure I could do it."

"I know I couldn't. That's why I'm not concerned about not inheriting. I want to finish college, teach, get married and start my own family. I'll help Dickie whenever he needs, but I don't want to spend the rest of my life on Harbor Island. Come on. Let's join them."

With the sun setting behind them and the harbor stretching before them, Cecilia wondered if she could spend her life here. Above, vivid strokes of orange speared the sky and tinged the cottony undersides of the clouds in a golden wash. At her feet, the ivory white beach surrendered to the vast ocean as it dashed to-and-fro, its waters shimmering in every shade of blue. She sighed. As tempting as it was, she doubted she could stay here forever. She needed more. Harbor Island, in all its pristine glory, was at once seductive and yet symptomatic of the battles being waged by her generation to save the world. A dichotomy, this picture-postcard-perfect landmass represented a traveler's grand adventure and an activist's vision to make a difference. Lucky for the island that Dickie was the heir apparent.

"Look what I found," he hollered as he strode up the beach.

"What on earth...?" Victoria blinked at his companion. "Where did you find that?"

"Down on the beach. Obviously, left here by one of the day-trippers we saw this morning, either on purpose, or accidentally, though I don't know how."

"Oh, he's beautiful." Cecilia raced down the sand and dropped to her knees to hug the golden retriever, who returned her affection with wet, sloppy kisses.

"It's a she. She's got a name tag, but no owner information. Her name's Lucy." Dickie ruffled the dog's honey-colored ears.

"But what are you going to do with her?" Victoria joined them, concern in her voice. "I don't think Father will let you keep her. You know how he is about animals at the house."

Dickie sprang to his feet, facing her. "Damn him. She's either been forgotten or abandoned. I'm not leaving her here."

Still rubbing the dog's back, Cecilia looked up. "She's not a puppy. Maybe she's been trained. At least if she's obedient, your father mightn't mind so much?"

"Good idea, CiCi. Come on, girl. Come on, Lucy. Show us what you can do." He ran to the water's edge with Lucy close behind him. He collected a piece of driftwood and hurled it into the water. "Go fetch, girl."

The dog bounded in after it, clasped the stick between her teeth, swam out and dropped it at his feet. A happier dog Cecilia had not seen in a long time.

"Okay, girl. Sit. Stay." Dickie held up his hand and backed away. "Stay." He moved further away. "Sta–a–ay." He turned his back on the dog and walked toward Cecilia and Victoria. The dog's tail thumped and swished arcs of sand. She was desperate to break position and play, but she obeyed and remained riveted on her bottom, her eyes fixed on her new master.

"You're right, CiCi," Dickie whispered. "She's been trained." Striding back to the dog, he released her with a swing of his arm. "Okay, Lucy." On cue, she bounded toward him, knocking him backward onto the sand with happy doggy kisses.

Cecilia glanced at Victoria. "What do you think? Will your father allow her to stay?"

"I hope so, for Dickie's sake. He's wanted a dog since he was little, but Father never allowed him to have one."

"But what will happen to Lucy if your father says no?"

"He'll get one of the men to kill her. She'll be clubbed to death."

Cecilia stumbled in the sand. "He couldn't possibly do that to his son. Or to a dog for that matter, surely?" Horror cracked in her voice.

"As I said yesterday, you may think this is paradise, but it's no different to anywhere else. In some ways, life is crueler here. It's sad, but that's the way it is."

"Oh, God. That's terrible." Tears pricked her eyes at the thought of such a heinous act being carried out on such a loving dog. Watching Dickie and Lucy roll in the sand together tore at her heart.

Victoria clasped her hand. "Don't worry too much about it. I know Dickie, and despite everything, he usually gets his way. He has Mom on his side. I think he has a good chance to win this battle with Father." Raising her voice, she called, "Come on, Dickie. We need to get everyone home. Come on, boys, bring your tools and jump in the truck."

Needing no further encouragement, the work crew hurled their equipment into the rear cargo bed and then jumped in, obviously delighted not to have to hike up Harbor Hill with their gear.

Dickie tapped the cargo tray a couple of times, coaxing the dog. "Come on, Lucy. Get in." She leaped in and propped herself amid the staff, who laughed at her happy disposition.

Victoria started the Chevy as Dickie climbed in. "You ready?"

"Yeah. Drive on, Vic." His face lit with an incandescent smile.

"I don't mean are you ready for the drive, I mean are you ready for the showdown with Father over Lucy?" Her face foretold the gravity of the situation.

He scowled and gritted his teeth. "Oh yes, Vic. I'm ready for Father. Drive on."

With only the burble of the V8 engine filling the cabin, she put the truck into gear and drove off. Not a word was exchanged as the Chevy climbed Harbor Hill. With Dickie spoiling for a scene and the truck chugging up the road, Cecilia was reminded of Joseph's words about jumping off Black Rock. *Be brave, leap, and let your soul take flight.* As she steeled herself for the confrontation between Dickie and his father, a strong, determined hand squeezed her thigh. Without looking at him, she nodded and squeezed Dickie's hand, pledging silent allegiance to his cause. No one was clubbing Lucy, not on her watch.

CHAPTER SEVEN

As chance would have it, or more likely a stroke of bad luck, Mr. Reginald stood on the side of the driveway instructing a gardener in the correct technique of pruning. Impatient with his student, he tugged at the gardener's arm, demonstrating the correct place to cut. *Not the best mood for him to be in*, thought Cecilia, noting the ominous scowl creasing his brow. At the sound of the Chevy, he lifted his head and pointed to where he wanted Victoria to park. As the truck passed him, he returned the secateurs to the gardener and ambled over.

"Hello, Father." With an extra-sweet smile, Victoria leaped out and scurried over to kiss his cheek. "I spoke to Smith this morning about servicing the Chevy, and he can do it tomorrow. I can take it down if you like?" By the askance look she shot Cecilia and Dickie, it was obvious she was wooing her father into a better mood to receive the news about Lucy.

He wrapped his arm around his daughter's waist and smiled down at her. "That was good of you, Victoria. Tomorrow, you say? I'll check and see if your mother needs it for anything. Otherwise, you can take it down."

"Hi, Father." Dickie approached from the other side of the truck, while Cecilia hung back, not wanting to intrude.

"Everything go well? The boys do the beach properly?"

"Yes, Father. The crew worked well. The beach looks spotless."

"Excellent. And I see you have our prospective housekeeper with you. Come out, girl. Don't hide behind the truck." He waved his hand, motioning Cecilia forward. She did as instructed. "I hear Victoria and Dickie took you to Rainbow Falls today."

"Yes. It's really wonderful." Trying hard to please, she shot him a sunny smile.

"It is spectacular, isn't it? Now, it's nearly time for dinner. You all better freshen up."

Dickie straightened and stepped in front of him. "Father, I found something on the beach today that I want to show you."

Mr. Reginald stopped and regarded his son. "What is it?"

Dickie whistled a short, sharp note. "Lucy. Here, girl." The dog rushed to his side. "Sit," he instructed, and Lucy obeyed. Dickie looked at his father. "She's been left behind accidentally or dumped on purpose. She's an older dog, and she's well trained. Maybe her owners will return, but in the meantime, I'll look after her. She'll be with me and not get in the way. If no one claims her, I'd like to keep her. Please, Father. Please."

Motionless, Mr. Reginald slanted his gaze down at the dog, pursing his lips as if swallowing a bitter pill. With beguiling innocent eyes, Lucy looked up at the man who held her fate in his hands, unaware of the life-or-death situation. Shifting his gaze between the hopeful expressions of Victoria and Dickie, Mr. Reginald scratched the back of his neck. For a moment, Cecilia thought he might relent, but he was such a hard man to read. She was as ignorant of Lucy's pending fate as the dog itself.

"I don't think this is a good idea, Dickie." The flat, dismissive tone in his response sent chills up Cecilia's spine.

Dickie's chin jutted forward, and his hands clenched into fists at his side. "And why is that, Father? Why is my caring for an abandoned, well-trained dog, not a good idea?"

"For a start, there's food."

"Take it out of my allowance."

"Where will it sleep?"

"With me, in my bungalow. She won't disturb anyone else."

"Who will clean up after it?"

"I will. None of the staff will have to do anything. I'll do it all."

Mr. Reginald's mouth twitched in a cynical smirk. "But, Dickie, you leave here in just over a week's time to go to college. Who will look after your dog then?"

Both Victoria and Dickie deflated a little as the realization dawned.

"I will, Mr. Reginald." Cecilia squared her shoulders and stepped forward, emboldened by the horrible alternative. "I'll look after Lucy while they're at college. After all, isn't that the job of a housekeeper? To manage the household in the best manner for all the family."

"CiCi, that's a terrific idea!" cried Victoria, erupting with delight.

"Of course. It can be part of CiCi's job to look after Lucy when I'm not here." A grateful smile accompanied Dickie's sideways glance, which Cecilia accepted with a nod.

"But she hasn't got the job yet." Mr. Reginald pointed out the obvious flaw in their plan.

"But can't we give Lucy a reprieve until CiCi finishes her trial? Then, if she keeps the job, she can look after Lucy if no one comes for her. Everyone will know within the week. Please, Father."

"I think it has merit." Mrs. Reginald's even voice joined the conversation. All eyes turned toward the great pavilion as she appeared from behind the fluttering curtains. Within moments, she stood beside her husband. "Please, Percy. Give Dickie a chance. Let him prove he is responsible, in his own way."

Mr. Reginald lifted his chin and paused. Narrowing his eyes, he regarded Lucy, still seated beside Dickie. "Very well." He nailed Cecilia in a frosty stare. "If you pass the trial and become housekeeper, Dickie can keep his dog. But it will be up to you, young lady, to make sure it behaves itself, care for it and clean up after it while he's away."

"You have my word, Mr. Reginald." Cecilia nearly saluted.

"I won't let you down, Father." Striking his hand forward, Dickie waited to shake hands.

Mr. Reginald accepted his offer and shook. "Mark my words. If your dog gets itself into any trouble, you know the outcome."

A silent pall settled over everyone. "Yes, Father, I do." But just as Mr. Reginald released his grip, Dickie held firm, drawing his father a little closer. Through gnashed teeth, he whispered, "One day this island will be mine and all who live here, men, women, children, and animals will be equal. You mark my words, Father."

Mr. Reginald's face turned ashen and ugly. Dickie pinned him a contemptuous glare, before relinquishing his grip and striding off. "Come on, Lucy. With me." The dog sprang up and galloped beside her new master.

"I mean it, Dickie. Keep that dog under control." Mr. Reginald's threat missed its mark. Dickie was already out of earshot or at least pretended to be.

"Come on, Percy." Mrs. Reginald hooked her arm through her husband's, and with Victoria on her other side, guided the three of them into the great pavilion. Alone on the driveway, Cecilia breathed a sigh of relief. *Another showdown at the madhouse.* Victoria had been right. Island life was not at all what Cecilia had expected. She peered down at her sandaled feet and paused. Today, she'd made a stand. She'd been brave and leaped to Dickie's defense to save Lucy's life. A blithe vitality effervesced in her limbs and tickled a smile to her face. Joseph was right. Her soul took flight, even if just for a moment.

* * * *

In the sultry stillness of late evening, Loretta served coffee, iced tea, and cookies as everyone relaxed on the sofas in the great pavilion after dinner. Outside, Lucy lay on the step nearest Dickie, watching him with love-struck eyes. Cecilia and Victoria exchanged fond smiles at the doggie display, while Dickie gestured for Lucy to remain where she was with a surreptitious wave of his hand if she moved closer to join him. Discussion waned, and Cecilia longed to go to bed. But no matter where she looked, she couldn't see Bartholomew. She wondered who would escort her to Hill Cottage in his absence.

"So, Cecilia, Victoria and Dickie tell me you sing?" Mr. Reginald reclined in his chair, casual interest gracing his severe face.

"Yes, Mr. Reginald. I do."

"Are you any good?" A taunting smirk lifted his thin lips while he sipped his coffee.

"My singing teacher thought I showed promise."

"You can hold a tune, then?" He grinned.

"Yes. I can hold a tune." She grinned back.

"Good. You can lead the singing on Sunday when I give my sermon."

"What a super idea, Father," agreed Victoria.

"Oh, yes, please. Do sing for us, CiCi," urged Dickie.

"But I–I don't know any hymns," she stammered, aghast at the request.

"That's quite all right, Cecilia. I assume you can read music?"

"Yes, sir, I can." *Damn.* She admitted to it before even thinking.

"Well, I have the sheet music for the hymns, some old records, and a record player. You can practice tomorrow after you finish your first day with Leilani. You'll have plenty of time to be in fine voice by Sunday morning."

"Oh, I can't wait to hear you sing," cheered Victoria.

"Me too," chimed in Dickie.

"You don't mind, do you?" Mrs. Reginald leaned forward and patted her knee.

"Oh, no. No. Of course not. Happy to help." A sinking feeling dropped like a rock in her stomach. She hated hymns. She used to sing them in church when she was a little girl — boring, repetitive dirges with no scope for personal expression. Now, she was expected to stand up and lead everyone in the wretched tunes. She stifled a groan and forced a weak smile.

"Dickie, will you walk Cecilia to the cottage? Bartholomew's not on tonight." Mrs. Reginald signaled Loretta to clear away the service.

"Yes, Mom. Come on, Lucy. Let's go. Good night, everyone." As he rose, Lucy sprang to his side, and they waited while Cecilia bade her good nights.

Scampering beside him, Lucy sure-footed each step as they strolled across the property. Once out of earshot, he shared an intimate smile with Cecilia. "Thank you for standing up with me today. Without you and Mom, I doubt whether Father would have relented so easily."

"That's fine. I couldn't let anything happen to her. Besides, when you and Victoria go to college, Lucy will be good company for me. In fact, I'm going to like having her sleep with me in the cottage."

They climbed up the rock staircase to Hill Cottage with Lucy sniffing and snorting at the new smells along the way. Once on the veranda, Dickie pointed to the windows. "Look, your screens are on. Good job too."

Cecilia stepped up to the window and pushed on the screen, testing its strength and fit. "Yes. They're strong, just as Bartholomew promised. That makes me feel better." Before opening the front door, she turned to Dickie. "Would you mind looking inside for me? Just to make sure I've no unwanted visitors. Bartholomew did it for me last night."

"Sure. Not a problem." He went inside, followed by Lucy, who sniffed in all the corners as if on the same mission. "All clear," he said, returning to join her at the front door.

"Thanks." Her hands fidgeted, and she hesitated.

"What is it?" The rich timbre in his voice comforted her.

"I'm not sure."

"Do you want me and Lucy to stay for a while?"

Yes. Yes. Yes. "No. It's fine. I just have to get used to things that go bump in the night."

He leaned forward and clasped her shoulders in a warm, reassuring grip. "You don't have to be scared, CiCi. You're safe."

Struggling not to bury her head in his chest and hold him close for protection, she locked eyes with him. "Are you sure?"

"Of course, I'm sure. You can even leave your windows open now that the screens are on. In you go. Get a good night's sleep. Don't forget. Tomorrow starts at eight o'clock. You don't want to be late on your first day. See you in the morning."

She mumbled goodnight and went inside and locked the door.

"Come on, Lucy. Time for bed."

As the sound of their feet faded into the night, she rushed to the back door and checked it was locked. Despite the screens, she locked each window and pulled the curtains closed. After stripping off, she hurled herself into bed and tucked in the mosquito net. *Stupid, stupid girl.* "How are you possibly going to stay here if you act like this every night?" she said aloud. She slipped under the sheets and stared at the lilac rafters on the lilac ceiling, which met the lilac walls. Lilac was supposed to be a calming, soothing color. She didn't feel calm, and she was not soothed. Her hand reached out to turn off the bedside lamp, but before she closed her eyes, she shoved another pillow over her head. At least tonight she wouldn't hear whatever might be lurking outside trying to get in.

CHAPTER EIGHT

Cecilia awoke after an uninterrupted night's sleep and wondered why she'd overreacted the night before. Victoria had been right. The jungle and its noises just took a little getting used to. Freshly bathed and breakfasted, she now sat in Mrs. Reginald's office, doing her best to learn the intricate details of managing the property. Rosters, meal breaks, staff meals, cleaning, grounds, stock and laundry checklists; Mrs. Reginald ran the entire property like a military operation.

"And please call me Leilani, not Mrs. Reginald."

"I'm not sure I can do that, Mrs. Reginald," blundered Cecilia, uncomfortable with the familiarity using her employer's first name implied.

"Nonsense. You cannot possibly be my housekeeper and earn the respect of the staff if you call me what they do. Cecilia, you and I are a team now. We each call the other by our first names, or I'm sorry, I don't think this job is for you." She placed her pen on the desk, determination creasing her brow.

"Very well . . . Leilani," she stammered. "You're the boss."

Triumph graced Mrs. Reginald's face. "Good. Now, we're ready for you to officially meet the staff and do an inspection of the property. Bring that clipboard and pen with you, plus the rosters and checklists. This will take us most of the day." Sliding back her chair, she bent forward and collected her sunglasses and a large-brimmed hat. "You'll need both of these if you're going to be outside on the property for any length of time."

"Oh, I have sunglasses and a hat, except I left them in the cottage."

"Well run and get them. I'll meet you on the driveway. We'll start from there."

Filled with excitement, Cecilia dashed through the great pavilion and hurtled headlong into the path of Mr. Reginald. "Go steady, girl. This is a house, not a speed track."

Propping on her heels, she skidded to a stop, puffing. "I'm sorry, Mr. Reginald. I need to get my hat and sunglasses before I can do the property inspection with Leilani."

"Who?" His voice sounded like a wrathful god.

"I mean, Mrs. Reginald." Then praying she wouldn't incur more fury, she added, "It was at your wife's request I call her Leilani, sir."

He snorted and turned up his nose as if smelling an unpleasant odor. "Well, just go steady in future. There's no need to run unless there's an emergency." With a sharp wag of his gnarled finger, he turned on his heel and marched off. Contrite, Cecilia scampered from the pavilion at a brisk walk. Once out of sight, she raced up the stairs, into Hill Cottage and grabbed her sunglasses and straw hat. As she strode back onto the veranda, her scalp tingled with tiny pinpricks of anticipation. *This is my time. I can do this.*

* * * *

Mrs. Reginald glanced at her watch. "My, look at the time. It's four o'clock already. That's the end of the day for us and the daytime staff."

Surprise washed over Cecilia's face. The day had sped by in a flurry of activity. What with meeting the staff whose names her memory had mostly forgotten, she had learned many tasks and taken copious notes. The pages fluttering in the breeze on her clipboard, reminded her of what being housekeeper at the Reginald residence entailed.

"I think you did well today, Cecilia," said Mrs. Reginald as she strolled across the lawn. "Come sit with me." She headed toward two white Adirondack chairs under a nearby plumeria tree. Small grey-and-white birds with striking red crests chirped a bright melodic welcome and then flew off to take up residence elsewhere. In heavy clusters of velvety petals, the tree's vibrant white-and-saffron flowers secreted the summery fragrance of frangipani. Not a fallen petal lay on the ground, a testament to the meticulous care with which the gardeners worked. Mrs. Reginald gestured to the other chair as she folded into hers.

Cecilia settled with a soft sigh. "Thank you, Leilani. It's been a terrific day. Being housekeeper is a big job. I hope I don't disappoint you."

Mrs. Reginald tilted her head and narrowed her eyes. "Why are you here, Cecilia? Really?"

"Because Mary, Joseph, and Smith thought I'd be good for the job."

"Maybe they thought the job would be good for you?" A twinkle danced in her dark, exotic eyes.

"Maybe. But I'm pleased I came."

"But what is it you really want to do with your life? Working here on Harbor Island is certainly not the dream of a young woman."

"I want to be a professional singer. That's my dream, but I need to save up enough money to get back home to San Francisco. Working here will hopefully get me there."

Flints of ice doused the warmth in Mrs. Reginald's eyes. "So, I'm going to spend all my time training you up, and once you have enough money, you're going to flit back to the mainland? And what about the promise you made to Dickie to look after Lucy when he goes to college?"

"Oh, I don't mean to sound ungrateful and selfish. It's just that . . ." Her mouth twisted as she searched for the right words. "I guess I've been moving from place to place for so long, I'm always thinking of where to next." *That's not right, either.* "Even though my dream is to sing, I've fallen in love with Maui and Harbor Island.

Being here, working with you and Victoria and Dickie, I guess I want to follow my dream of singing, but at the same time . . . Oh, I don't know what I'm trying to say." She dragged a hand across her forehead, trying to rub the confusion from her mind.

Mrs. Reginald softened. "I understand. Knowing which direction to take in life can be confusing. What about your parents? I've no doubt they'd send you the money to fly back to San Francisco to follow your dream if that's what you want to do. They must want you home, especially since you're their only child."

Cecilia hadn't thought of her parents since she boarded *Harbor Island* with Smith. "Yes, Mom would send money, but I don't want to ask. I'll just look like a failure if I ask for money. It'll confirm everything Dad said to me when I left. No, I can't ask for their help. It's up to me to support myself."

Mrs. Reginald's thumbs tapped together in her lap. "Did you tell your parents you were coming here? Do they at least know you're safe?"

Cecilia bit her lip. "No, on both counts." A twinge of guilt plucked at her heart.

"Well, let's go into my office right now. You can call them, tell them where you are and that you're okay. They must be worried sick about you." With that, Mrs. Reginald rose and headed toward the office. Beside her, Cecilia remained silent. Despite their differing views on the world and how to live in it, she loved her parents. At times, she even missed them, particularly her mother. Although overbearing, her mother only wanted the best for her. Cecilia knew that. She hoped they would be happy about her news of finding a job.

* * * *

"Oh, darling, are you sure you want to stay?" Relief and concern flooded Helen Freemont's voice. "You know I would happily send you the money to come home."

"No, Mom." She clenched her jaw, remembering why she kept contact with her parents to a minimum. "Thank you for the offer, but I'm going to work on Harbor Island for a while. It's beautiful here, and Mrs. Reginald thinks I can do the job. I just rang to let you know I'm okay and give you the address, so you can write me if you like."

"Of course, I'll write," whined her mother. "Do you think Mrs. Reginald would mind if I had the phone number as well, in case of an emergency?"

"I'll ask her and call you back tomorrow. I'm sure she wouldn't mind. But, Mom . . .?"

"Yes, darling?"

"Don't ring unless it is an emergency, okay? Mrs. Reginald is my employer, not a call service. You understand?"

"Of course, Cecilia. I don't know why you're so touchy at times. Your father and I only want the best for you. You've always been so independent, wanting to do things your way, even as a little girl, you—"

Cecilia rolled her eyes. "Mom," she interrupted. "I have to go. I'll call you tomorrow. Say hello to Dad for me." Shame bit her tongue. "I'm sorry. I really want to stay here and do well, okay? I love you and Dad. Talk tomorrow."

After hanging up, she rubbed the heels of her hands into her eyes. Why did it always end that way? Why couldn't she be less defensive? But then again, why couldn't her parents allow her to live her life without being so damn judgmental? Right at that moment, the thought of returning to San Francisco and pursuing her singing career was far less appealing than staying on Harbor Island. Besides, she couldn't let Dickie down after promising to look after Lucy. Her singing career would just have to wait a little longer. *What's a couple more years in the scheme of things?*

* * * *

"Hello." The sound of a man's voice made her jump. "May I come in?" Not waiting for permission, Mr. Reginald strode through the doorway of Hill Cottage.

Cecilia bent to collect the spoon she'd dropped on the floor. She tried to hide the surprise but suspected she'd failed. "Of course, Mr. Reginald. Come in. I'm just cooking myself some dinner." She stuck the spoon back into the bubbling pot and stirred vigorously.

He looked over her shoulder. "Aren't you joining us for dinner tonight?" His breath skimmed the top of her head.

She flinched and stepped sideways. "No. After everything I learned today, I need to go over my notes and get an early night."

"I brought you these as promised." He placed a record player, some vinyl records, and sheet music onto the kitchen table. "Well, come closer, girl, so you can see better."

She edged into his personal space. Her skin prickled at being so close to him. As he shuffled through the sheet music, explaining the order of the hymns for tomorrow's service, she ignored her uneasiness and listened. To be publicly humiliated at the service for not getting the songs in the correct order would be too much to bear. Straightening to his full height, he looked down his nose with his usual haughty demeanor. "I expect you in the great pavilion by eight-thirty in good voice. I want to hear you sing the hymns before I commence the nine o'clock service. Agreed?"

"Yes, Mr. Reginald. I will practice this evening and be there on time. I won't let you down, sir."

"Good. Your participation and performance will go a long way in your securing the housekeeper job." He unexpectedly traded his customary aloofness for a warm, magnanimous smile. For an instant, she saw the man Leilani must have fallen in love with. The man whose charm Dickie had inherited. He turned to leave, but instead of heading to the door he detoured to the windows. "I see Bartholomew has put up your screens."

"Yes. He did." She trembled but didn't know why.

He brushed his hand against the screens, tested their strength and paused. Without warning, he resumed his normal gruffness. "Good idea. You never know what's lurking around in the jungle at night." He stiffened, and within three strides he exited the cottage and headed down the stairs with the same stealth as he had arrived.

Cecilia shivered as she watched him disappear into the jungle corridor. *He gives me the creeps. Maybe I should lock my doors and windows before dark?* She swept the thought away and returned inside. Back at the table, she sat down and drew an unsteady breath. She needed to focus on tomorrow, not on Mr. Reginald. She flicked through the sheet music. Fortunately, she remembered singing these hymns as a little girl, so it shouldn't be too hard. After deciding to rehearse after dinner, she returned to her stove.

"Hi, Cecilia, can we come in? I've got your clothes from Martha." Victoria and Dickie wandered into the cottage, their arms loaded with bundles of brown-paper-wrapped clothes.

"Sure. Thanks for getting this for me. I forgot all about it what with my first day on the job." She rushed to greet them and offload the clothing parcels.

"What are you cooking?" Dickie swiped a finger in the pot bubbling on the gas burner.

"Some chili beans. They're hot," she warned.

He licked his finger quickly to stop the heat burn, only to discover the chili burned worse. "Whoa. That is hot."

"Dad used to cook really hot chili when I was growing up. I guess I got used to it." She spooned a large bowlful and placed it on the driftwood table. Beside it, she laid another two spoons. "You can have some with me if you like."

Dickie held his hands up in defense. "Pass."

"No thanks. I think I'll wait for dinner," said Victoria, eyeing the bowl with suspicion. "So, did you enjoy your first day with Mom?"

Cecilia blew on a spoonful of beans and waited for them to cool a little. "I did. This place is huge, and the work your mother does is enormous. She's a remarkable woman."

"We think so. Dickie and I would have both gone mad if it was just us and Father. He can be quite tyrannical in case you haven't noticed." They laughed at the obvious. "But Mom makes everything easy. I knew you'd get on well with her."

"Are you going to stay, CiCi?" asked Dickie, stirring a spoon in the chili beans.

"Dickie, either eat some or leave it alone," said Victoria.

Cecilia smiled at the sibling antics before her, then ate a mouthful of chili and licked its bite from her lips. "To answer your question, Dickie, I hope I'm good enough for the job because I would like to stay, at least for a while. Time will tell, I guess."

Victoria spied the record player and music. "I see you have everything to practice the hymns for tomorrow?"

"Yes, your father just brought it. You must have passed him on the stairs on your way up."

"No. We didn't see him," said Dickie.

"That's odd." Cecilia swallowed another spicy mouthful. "Is Lucy with you?" She craned her neck, looking outside.

"Yeah. She's sitting on the veranda. Why? What's wrong?"

"Oh, nothing. It must be the witching hour. I'm just a bit spooked as the sun sets." She lifted another spoonful of beans toward them. "You sure you won't try my chili?" Tiny beads of perspiration dotted her flushed face.

Victoria held up her hands and shook her head. "No thanks. If your dinner is doing that to you, imagine what would happen to us. We'd explode."

"Wow. You've nearly eaten all of it." Dickie stared at the near-empty bowl.

"I've got too thin since being in Maui. I need to put on some weight and get healthy. Otherwise, I'll never be able to do all the running around the housekeeper needs to do here." Scraping the last from the bowl, she managed a final swallow. "Okay, you two. You better go as I've got lots of work to do. I'll see you in the morning."

The three of them sauntered to the door, chatting and teasing each other.

"Remember what I told you about this place, CiCi?"

"What's that, Dickie?" She rolled her eyes and giggled.

"Tomorrow you'll see Father in full flight as the lay preacher." Dickie struck a righteous pose, his voice mimicking his father's. "As I said, it's a madhouse." His melodramatic laughter filled the cottage.

"Go on, get out and let me practice." She flipped a hand at them, and with Lucy prancing beside them, brother and sister strolled down the stairs and disappeared.

* * * *

To sing, even though it was only dull, traditional church hymns, filled Cecilia with unrestrained joy. It had been a while since she'd tested her voice, but it responded with perfect pitch and solid control. Perhaps the time off had been a disguised blessing. Having given her vocal chords a rest, they'd returned stronger and better than ever and reminded her how much she loved to sing and how good she actually was at it. By the time she packed up the record player and decided to study her housekeeper's notes, night had enveloped Hill Cottage. She'd been singing with the doors closed and windows open, but now that dusk's indigo had turned to inky darkness, she decided to lock up. Undertaking her nightly ritual of securing the windows, she groaned but ignored the source of her discomfort. Again, another stab. This time one that would not be denied. *Damn those chili beans. I need to go to the toilet.*

With no other option in her current condition, she scrambled to the back door. Unlocking and opening it, she peered out into the blackness. *I need a torch.* Then she remembered Loretta saying she left a torch in one of the cupboards. She rummaged through the kitchen cupboards, found it and flicked it on. At the back door, she bit her lip as her stomach clenched. She needed to go, now. Shining light on the short pathway, she strained her eyes, checking to see it was clear of snakes and rats. Once sure there were none, she stepped out, closed the door behind her and scampered to the bathhouse. Inside, she locked the door, switched on the light and found relief just in time. She decided to take chili beans off her menu from now on. Moments passed, and still, her stomach moaned. No matter how conscientious the boys were, sitting atop an open pit latrine with the night closing in around her, she struggled not to imagine slithering, crawling things below. As quickly as she could, she finished the task, cleaned herself and shut the lid. *Ugh.* She shuddered as she soaped and scrubbed her hands repeatedly. Thrusting long curls of damp hair off her face, she turned to leave, torch in hand. *Scrape, scrape, scrape.* She froze. The sound was on the outside of the door. Prickling on high alert, her flesh commando-crawled over her body. *Oh, God. Not again.* Her heart pounded so loudly it sounded like a timpani drum in her ears. Whatever was outside sounded a lot bigger than a rat or small animal.

"Lucy, is that you? Dickie, are you out there?"

Silence followed, and she let out a tense breath. Then the scraping resumed — this time higher up the door in a more insistent and frenetic fashion. She backed away, terrified that whatever it was would soon build enough momentum to crash through the timber door. *Oh, God. I'm trapped.*

"Help! Help! Someone help me." Although convinced no one would hear her, she still shouted with the power she'd unleashed in her singing practice and hoped that whatever it was would run away. "Help! Help! Someone help me."

Up the door the scratching continued, growing louder and more relentless to match her voice. With eyes riveted at the steel-mesh grate between wall and ceiling, she stared wide-eyed at the spot she expected the animal to appear. Then everything stopped. She could have sworn she heard running feet, but she was so unraveled, she—

"Miss Cecilia, are you all right?" It was a man's voice.

"Who is it?" she demanded.

"It's me, Bartholomew, Miss Cecilia."

"What are doing out there, Bartholomew?"

"I was doing my late-night rounds, and I heard you calling."

"But you're not rostered on tonight. Mrs. Reginald said so."

"Robert was supposed to do the late-night rounds, but he is sick. So I take his place. Come out, Miss Cecilia. I'm here now."

With extreme caution, she stepped to the door and turned the key. She peeked out and shone the torch in Bartholomew's face, blinding him in case he tried to snatch her.

Blinking madly and waving his hands, he shuffled backward. "Miss Cecilia, I'm here to help you. Come outside."

Tentatively, she took his hand and swallowed the lump of lead wedged in her throat. Together they walked to the back door of the cottage, where she passed the threshold, and he remained outside.

"Thank you, Bartholomew." She was still unsure whether he had saved her or scared her.

"Miss Cecilia, you must stay in the cottage at night."

She dragged in a deep breath. "Now listen to me, Bartholomew. I don't know what is going on around here, but I'm going to get to the bottom of it. Whatever was scratching at the bathhouse door was not a small animal. Even you admitted to the screens being able to keep out a big animal. Yet Victoria says there are no big animals. Tell me, Bartholomew, what is prowling around the jungle up here at Hill Cottage? Tell me!" The shriek in her voice ricocheted into the night, tearing at the stillness and her vocal chords. Hands knuckled on hips, she tapped her foot in demand of an answer. He gazed at his shuffling feet, his lips pursed. An interminable silence stretched between them, but still she waited.

Finally, he lifted his forlorn face. "Miss Cecilia, we have an old saying here on Harbor Island. Never share a secret unless you want it known by all. You are safe, Miss Cecilia. Aloha." Not waiting for a response, the old Hawaiian turned and dissolved into the night.

"For goodness sake." She slammed the door and locked it. "These people will drive me crazy. Dickie is right. This place is a madhouse." She stormed to the sink, boiled some water and made a cup of hot honey water to soothe her throat. "Now I've strained my voice."

At the table, she dropped into a chair and sipped her honey water. She tried forcing herself to forget about the incident at the bathhouse. But it was no use. Her mind wandered back time and again to the recent nighttime happenings. None of the Hawaiians were going to tell her anything. That was obvious. Whatever was going on at Harbor Island, and more specifically at Hill Cottage was not general knowledge, but a secret the Hawaiians knew. She slammed her empty mug on the table. She would not be intimidated like this any longer. Somehow, she would have to outsmart them and find out for herself.

CHAPTER NINE

"Goddamn it." Shoving the mosquito net from her face, Cecilia tumbled out of bed, later than she wanted. "Another night with not enough sleep," she grumbled. Bleary-eyed, she slipped on some clothes and shuffled to the bathhouse. A small amount of hazy sunshine filtered through the grate which did nothing to enhance her reflection. After wringing out a wet face cloth, she rubbed her face as if scrubbing graffiti from a wall. She managed to remove a fine layer of skin, but not the tiredness. "Now, I look like an overcooked beet." Irritated, she jabbed the toothbrush into her mouth. The peppermint taste delivered a much-needed kick.

Back inside the cottage and with more sips of honey hot water, she executed a careful vocal warm-up. Overstretching her voice now would be disastrous for singing the hymns in an hour's time. Once satisfied that her voice was ready, she dressed for the service. *Conservative and ladylike.* With only two options, she reached for the more subdued of the dresses Martha had sewn for her — a cotton shift of soft lemon-drop yellow dotted with tiny white plumeria flowers. She tugged it on and puffed the frothy short sleeves high on her shoulders. Using some baby oil, she rubbed it into her tan leather sandals before slipping them on. As she brushed and finger-curled her long hair, she wandered onto the veranda. Her spirits lifted. Buttery sunlight stretched and slanted through the jungle and cut shimmering shapes on the veranda. She breathed in the calm solitude and counted to ten. It was a pre-performance ritual to steady her nerves that she'd learned from her singing teacher. To the right of the cottage, a massive plumeria tree blossomed, offering its fresh fragrance to the morning. *Perfect.* She picked a bunch of flowers, dashed back inside and pinned them center front on her straw hat. Pushing the freshly adorned hat on her head and with sheet music in hand, she figured her appearance was befitting of a parishioner, considering her limited circumstances. Radiant, she strode out of the cottage and closed the front door behind her. It was a glorious morning. Just the type of Sunday to be singing hymns of glory. She trotted down the stairs towards the jungle corridor, its subtle scent calling her. Although nervousness nagged in her stomach, she did her best to ignore it. Instead, in her mind, she repeated her mantra. *I am more than this. This will not break me.* This time, she believed it.

* * * *

"Good morning, Mr. Reginald," said Cecilia, as he directed the staff where he wanted the chairs placed for the day's sermon. He spun around, his eyes raking her with an imperious look. She hoped he approved of her Sunday-best clothes.

"Good morning, Cecilia. Are you ready?"

Clinging the sheet music to her chest, she nodded. "Yes, sir. I am."

"Good. Well, let me hear you. Stand there in front of where the congregation will sit." He pointed further up the rows toward a lectern. "Go on, then. I'll sit here and make sure I can hear you." He lowered his tall frame into a fold-out chair and crossed his arms.

Cecilia prepared herself. She spread the sheet music on the lectern and pitched the opening note in her mind. She swallowed, drew in a deep breath and—

"Mr. Reginald, Mr. Reginald, come quick. Mrs. Reginald has fallen, sir. Maybe broke her leg, sir." Loretta rushed past Cecilia on her way to the master. "Please, sir, come quick."

Mr. Reginald launched from his chair, his face a mask of anguish. "Where Loretta? Where?"

"Staff quarters, sir. Hurry." Loretta headed to the back of the great pavilion.

With a fling of her arm, Cecilia threw off her hat and joined the rescue. From the corner of her eye, she noticed Dickie and Lucy jogging toward the pavilion. "Hey, what's wrong?"

"It's your mother. She's had a fall at the staff quarters. Come on."

By the time they arrived, worried staff hovered over Mrs. Reginald, who lay groaning on the ground. Many of the women sniffled into their hankies, while the men swayed, murmuring and shaking their heads.

"Stand aside," roared Mr. Reginald, pushing them out of the way. He dropped to his knees and reached out to his wife. She lay prostrate on a corner of the dirt path where it turned sharply downhill. With teeth clenched, she grimaced. "Oh, Percy, I slipped coming down with medicine for one of the children. I heard an awful crack in my ankle, but I don't think it's broken. Just terribly sprained. I can't stand." Pain dragged at her face and tears pooled in her eyes.

"Dickie, go get the stretcher from the office. Cecilia, go organize some ice packs. Where's Victoria?"

"I go find her, sir," called Loretta.

Leaving the melee behind, the three of them fled back up the pathway. "I thought you told me this place didn't change much. Just the same old, same old?" puffed Cecilia, running stride for stride beside Dickie and Lucy, while Loretta lumbered behind.

He laughed. "Well, it was until you got here."

"Ha-ha. In the short time I've been here, nothing's stayed the same for even a day." She poked her tongue at him. When they hit the plateau, they veered off in different directions, and each went in search of their assignment.

* * * *

With Mr. Reginald hollering instructions, six men carried Mrs. Reginald up from the staff quarters on the stretcher. Under threat of losing their jobs if anyone dropped her, they eased her up the slope and settled her into the guest bedroom directly behind Victoria's bungalow. With its timber-louvered sliding doors stacked open to reveal a wide circling patio, the bungalow looked out onto fragrant gardens and verdant lawn.

"Are you comfortable?" Victoria fussed over her mother like a wet-nurse, fluffing the pillows behind her head.

"Yes, yes, Victoria, I'm fine. The ice packs have helped, as have the painkillers you gave me." Mrs. Reginald reached out a hand and beckoned. "Cecilia, Dickie, come closer."

"Are you sure you're okay? Do you want us to send for a doctor?" Dickie asked, taking his mother's hand.

"Let's wait and see. I'll have to rest and keep my ankle strapped and iced. If it's no better in a few days, you can call a doctor over. But I think I've just badly sprained it. Victoria, you'll have to be my nursemaid and help me to the bathroom for a while."

"Of course. I'll make sure Loretta checks on you regularly as well." Propped on the side of the bed, Victoria stroked her mother's other hand.

"Well, Cecilia." Mrs. Reginald fixed her in a steady gaze. "This means you're running the place."

"Mrs. Reginald, I can't." Cecilia's eyes widened at the mere thought.

"What did you call me?" Even though she angled a haughty eyebrow, amusement played on Mrs. Reginald's face.

"I mean, Leilani. I can't run the residence yet. I've only done one day with you. There's so much I don't know."

"Nonsense." She waved her delicate hand in a dismissive fashion. "Dickie can help. He knows how it all works."

"Sure, CiCi. What with you, me and Vic, you'll be running this place within the week." His confident exuberance in her capabilities quelled some of Cecilia's anxiety.

"Cecilia, I'm depending on you. Victoria and Dickie will be leaving for college in just over a week's time. There's no way I'll be well enough to be up and about by then. I need you."

Three expectant faces corralled Cecilia into making a decision. Whether she thought herself capable of doing the job, current circumstances had thrust it upon her. "But what about what Mr. Reginald said about my week's probation?"

With a flick of her hand, Mrs. Reginald halted her objection. "Everything has changed. Either you want the job, or you don't. I need someone now. No probation. No trial. Now. And I need a commitment that you'll stay on here for at least a year. As I said, I'm not going to go to all this effort and have you flitting off on another adventure when you get bored." Mrs. Reginald shuffled upright in the bed, her small figure exuding a commanding strength of will. "If this doesn't suit you, I will accept your decision. I will arrange for Smith to take you back to Lahaina Harbor tomorrow. The choice is yours. But unfortunately, my accident has hastened the time in which you can make it."

The energy in the bungalow sizzled. Even the red-crested cardinals in the towering breadfruit trees outside stopped their merry trill. With a sideways glance, Cecilia spied a couple of groundsmen pretending to rake leaves, but who were obviously eavesdropping on the drama unfolding in the bungalow. Managing these people would test her patience and powers of persuasion. While the groundsmen feigned work, her gaze traveled back to Leilani, Victoria, Dickie and finally to Lucy. Leilani's ultimatum reminded her of her parents' unreasonable demands, and yet she'd grown attached to the Reginald family in this short time. She'd come to enjoy living and working in the madhouse. *But to commit to one whole year?* What about her quest for freedom and adventure? The last time she had committed to anything or anyone on her quest, it had been to Michael and the Brotherhood, and look how that had turned out.

"Cecilia . . ." Mrs. Reginald's voice softened. "I remember you said when you first arrived here, you wanted to have adventures of your own rather than just reading about other people's adventures in books."

Cecilia nodded.

"I'm offering you an adventure — to work on Harbor Island as our housekeeper. Give me one year, and I promise you will have a marvelous adventure here. One you will be able to write your own book about."

"Please, Cecilia." Victoria rushed over and clasped her hands. "Dickie and I will be home during vacations. We can help out then. Please stay."

"Come on, CiCi. You promised to look after Lucy." All eyes turned to the dog whose tail wagged madly in response to being the center of attention. "You promised."

Despite the noises in the night, Mr. Reginald's strange and unpredictable behavior or the staff's self-imposed silence over some island secret, the promise of Harbor Island's adventure proved too great. "All right. I'll take the job. For one year. After that, we'll see what happens."

"Excellent," said Mrs. Reginald. A cheer erupted in the bungalow and outside from the eavesdropping staff. "Now, leave it to me to break the news to Percy. Hurry along. You don't want to be late for the service."

"What? There's still going to be a service?" Shock strangled Cecilia's throat.

"Of course. Nothing stops Father's Sunday sermon," giggled Victoria.

"Not even Mom's sprained ankle," added Dickie, giving his sister a wink.

"So, after all this, I'm expected to sing the hymns now?"

"Well, you wanted an adventure. Here's the first of many to come. Now off you go. I look forward to hearing your beautiful voice from here." Breaking into laughter, Mrs. Reginald shooed them from her room, as Cecilia hummed some warm-up scales.

* * * *

With all the morning's commotion, the service now ran over two hours late. The staff sat perched in prim rows in the great pavilion, fanning themselves. As added evidence of the escalating heat, the fresh bunch of flowers Cecilia had pinned on her hat that morning had wilted. Her pretty lemon dress, now splattered with ugly brown marks, no longer shone with bright vitality. She gazed at the fine layer of dirt coating her feet and huffed. She looked a bedraggled mess. Not someone to be singing the hymns.

"And now, I call upon Cecilia to lead us in our first hymn, 'All Creatures of Our God and King'." Mr. Reginald nodded at her and vacated his place at the lectern-cum-pulpit.

With the required reverence she'd learned as a young church-going girl, Cecilia walked over. Beneath the long curls trailing down her back trickled an uncomfortable stream of perspiration on its course to her buttocks. Like an ice-cream, she melted under the heat and the pressure.

With a quick fidget of her sheet music and a smile, she silently pitched and prayed her voice would not let her down. "All creatures of our God and king, lift up your voices and with us sing. Alleluia! Alleluia! . . ." Clear, fluting notes pierced the hot dullness of the service. Heads snapped up with faces stretched in white-toothed grins. Even Mr. Reginald sat agape and blinked at her. Emboldened, she opened her voice for the next lines. "Thou burning sun with golden beam, thou silver moon with softer gleam."

Obviously inspired, Bartholomew shot to his feet and joined his baritone voice with Cecilia's lyric soprano on the next alleluias. She cast him a grateful wink. Up jumped Loretta, and Albert, and Robert, and Elsie and then all the staff sang out in worship. Their participation carried her to new confidence. With lungs bursting, she raised her voice to the rafters of the great pavilion. By the time the hymn finished, her body buzzed. A rush of euphoria flooded her senses. Triumphant, she opened her eyes, returning from the ecstasy of singing. Only then did she hear the thunderous applause. She spied Victoria and Dickie clapping wildly. They were seated beside their father, who by the look on his face, was both overwhelmed and disgruntled by her performance. Could it be he was jealous of her singing?

Clearing his throat, he returned to the lectern and resumed in dramatic manner. "And now today's lesson. It is taken from Luke 10:25–37, the parable of the Good Samaritan. This is a most apt lesson for today considering what has befallen Mrs. Reginald this morning..." While Mr. Reginald droned on, the congregation once more fell into the drudgery of listening to him wax lyrical on the Bible's message. It wasn't until twenty minutes later, when he introduced Cecilia once more to lead them all in the second hymn, that the congregation rediscovered their interest in the Sunday service.

By the close of the final hymn, the Reginald residence resonated to a blend of voices she'd not heard before. Like a celestial choir, a joyous harmony rose high into the vaulted ceiling. Even after the end of the service, a chorus of "Praise the Lord, praise the Lord, let the people rejoice . . ." continued in the great pavilion while the staff rearranged the chairs.

Victoria rushed up and hugged Cecilia tight. "My goodness. What a songbird you are!"

"Wow, CiCi. I've never heard anything like it." Dickie cast around for his father, and after spying him directing staff, he added in a whisper, "I expect the staff were worshipping you rather than God."

"Stop it. Both of you. I'm just happy my voice didn't let me down." She sighed and pulled the straw hat off her head. She picked off the shriveled flowers and gave her hair a vigorous ruffle. The great pavilion was a hive of activity with staff moving furniture and setting trestle tables with linen. "What's happening now?"

"It happens after the service each week. The staff join us for Sunday lunch. Come on, we'll show you how it works." Dickie grabbed her hand and tugged her toward Loretta, who was busily setting paper plates and cups. Once more, the smile he shared sparkled with intimacy, and she sensed a deeper connection forming between them. A part of her was pleased he'd be leaving soon. Having decided to stay on Harbor Island, she didn't need any further complications with a young man — a much younger man who would be king.

CHAPTER TEN

By the time that week rolled into the next, Cecilia was exhausted. The task of managing the massive property was made even harder because of the short lead time to learn everything before Victoria and Dickie left for college. But with their help, she acquired a basic understanding of most things. Each of the staff took on a new perspective as she put names to faces, and more importantly, personalities. Due to her Sunday singing performance, they'd given her a nickname — *leo o ka anela*, voice of an angel. Though to her face they called her Miss Cecilia, it became common knowledge that *leo o ka anela* was what they called her amongst themselves. And contrary to Mr. Reginald's initial misgivings, the staff respected her. She suspected more because of her talent rather than her position. But that was good enough, at least for the moment. Over time, she would earn their trust and respect.

Ordering supplies, paying invoices and financial record keeping were still beyond her grasp, but Leilani agreed to manage the administrative work if Cecilia had operations and logistics under control.

Another Sunday, another service, another praising of God had come and gone, and she, Dickie, Victoria, and Lucy lazed on the veranda of Hill Cottage watching the sky prepare for its command performance. Overhead, murky grey clouds hung like overripe, pendulous fruit in the darkening sky. The unmistakable smell of impending rain kicked up dirt in her nostrils and pasted an earthy tang on her tongue. Off in the distance, heavy mists of rain moved in across the harbor, creeping toward them like a thief.

"I love watching storms roll in from this veranda." Pushed back in a rattan chair and legs propped on the railing, Dickie gazed at the distant display as it approached the island. Lucy's head nudged over his thighs for more attention, and he chuckled. "Don't be scared, Lucy. Storms won't hurt you." He reassured her with a gentle stroke along her smooth, glossy snout.

"I can't believe how much this place changes when the weather turns. It's even more magnificent, more primal." Sitting side-saddle on the railing, Cecilia watched the wind tease the waves.

"Mom used to say the storms made meringue tips on the harbor. See." Victoria pointed to the white peaks being whipped on top of the water. "I'm going to miss this place when we leave tomorrow. I always do."

"I will too. But it's my first time away. I'm excited and scared at the same time."

"It's just like Joseph said about diving off Black Rock on Kaanapali Beach."

"We know about Black Rock back on Maui, but who's Joseph?" asked Victoria.

Cecilia told them the story of Joseph leaping off the edge of Black Rock and the sense of freedom he'd experienced. "I'm sure once you're at college, Dickie you'll feel free."

Lucy whimpered. "Don't worry, girl. CiCi will look after you. I'll be back soon." He kissed Lucy's head and received a big, wet lick in return. "I'm so happy you're staying, CiCi. I know Lucy will be safe with you around."

"And I'll be safe with Lucy around."

"Are you still scared by the noises at night?" asked Victoria.

"Actually, over the past week, I haven't heard a thing. Either I'm too tired or whatever it was hasn't returned. But having Lucy sleep up here with me will be great. I'm so pleased no one claimed her. I'm sure she'll be a terrific guard dog."

"She is. She'll keep you safe from the things that go bump in the night," Dickie teased.

"I don't care if you think I'm imagining things. But there was someone here when I first arrived." She scowled at him and huffed.

"Anyway, you'll feel safer with Lucy here once we go. I will miss you, Cecilia." Victoria wrapped her arm around Cecilia's shoulder. "Even though it's only been a week since you arrived, you're like the big sister I always wanted."

Cecilia returned the hug. "Me too. Funny how things work out."

"And what about me? Where do I fit in?" Dickie sprang up to join in the group hug. "I'll miss you as well, CiCi." He wrapped his arms around Cecilia and his sister and squeezed tight.

A knot tightened in her heart. Tomorrow she would be all alone, without Victoria's pragmatic efficiency and Dickie's forthright optimism. "I'll miss you two more." She leaned back from the embrace and glanced from sister to brother, wishing time would stand still.

* * * *

On the island's rickety jetty with Lucy by her side, Cecilia handed Victoria's gym bag down to where she stood on the aft deck of the cruiser. Stacked beside her were an assortment of suitcases and boxes Smith had sorted to ballast the boat.

"We'll see you soon for the Christmas vacation. Take care," said Victoria. Her mouth pulled in a wide smile. With her exquisite face, Cecilia knew Victoria would have the college boys in a panic, desperate for her attention.

"Bye, CiCi," called Dickie as he stood beside his sister. "And, Lucy, you look after her, you hear." The dog tilted her head at her master's instruction and strained at the leash to jump onboard.

"Quiet, girl. It's just you and me for a while," cooed Cecilia, sympathizing with the dog. She also wanted to jump in the boat with them. With Smith behind the wheel, the old pine cruiser pushed away from its mooring and set course for deeper waters.

"Bye, have fun! Try not to get into too much trouble, Dickie. And don't come home engaged, Victoria." With one hand waving goodbye and the other patting Lucy's head, Cecilia struggled to sound upbeat. Her eyes burned hot with suppressed tears. Even when she'd left home, she hadn't experienced this sort of sadness.

"Bye. Bye." Brother and sister waved furiously as the boat motored further into the harbor.

"Love you!" hollered Cecilia, straining on tiptoe.

"Love you too." It was Dickie's voice she heard drift back to her. Unsure as to whether Victoria vouched the same as her brother, she realized it was his pledge that held greater power. A little piece of her heart skittered out to the boat and pasted itself to his chest. Despite her best intentions, she had grown more than fond of Richard Reginald.

When they turned around and joined Smith in the cruiser cabin, Cecilia decided not to feel sorry for herself. It was time to start her new life with Lucy. "Come on, girl. We have work to do." Until confident Lucy would obey her instructions, she kept her leashed. The last thing she wanted was for the dog to take off and never return. Together they walked from the jetty and back up the dirt track toward The Esplanade. Pointy-leafed pandanus trees edged the path on the beach side, their roots holding firm to the sand. Hundreds of their waxy, pine-nut-fruit segments lay discarded, having been nibbled open overnight by the hermit crabs.

Intoxicated by the fresh smells, Lucy pulled at her lead, desperate to explore. "Once we do some training together, I'll bring you down the beach to play in the afternoon, but not today. Come on." With a soft tug, Cecilia encouraged Lucy to keep in step and before long the dog tread obediently in time.

They strolled by Smith's workshop. As usual, he'd left it open, his tools and equipment scattered everywhere while he skippered the boat across to Lahaina. Cecilia chuckled. None of the locals seemed to care too much about their worldly possessions. Instead, they sought out ways to enjoy their life, hard as it may be. Unlike the white man, whose possessions consumed most of his thoughts and actions, they made time to enjoy their meager share.

"There's a lot we could all learn here, Lucy," she said, half expecting the dog to respond as they walked along.

Making a quick stop at the Ladies Markets, she stuck her head in with a loud shout. "Aloha, ladies!"

A merry chorus of "Aloha, Miss Cecilia" and "*leo o ka anela*" resonated from the industrious dressmakers. Some discarded their sewing and shuffled out to greet her. Babbling excitedly about her singing and how they were going to come to this week's service, Martha's effusive voice led the contingent. "Miss Cecilia, we all be there this Sunday to hear you sing." If Martha's smile widened any more, Cecilia thought the dressmaker's face would split.

"That is so sweet of you. Thank you. I'm sure Mr. Reginald will be delighted to have you all at his service."

"*Pfft*. We not interested in the service. We want to hear you sing." Accompanied by much head nodding and trill chatter, the ladies made their intentions clear.

"Even so, you must listen to Mr. Reginald's sermon. He puts a lot of effort into the Sunday service." The last thing she needed was for him to think she was upstaging him and ban her from the service.

"Yes, Miss. We understand." Martha leaned closer and added, "But we really come to hear you sing." Amid bellowing laughter, the ladies moved back into the shop, their hips swaying from side to side.

In front of the Local Store, Cecilia turned to the dog. "Right, Lucy. You wait here. I've got to get some supplies from Beatrice. Stay." She presented her palm close to Lucy's face. On the command, Lucy plonked her bottom on the dirt sidewalk and settled down next to the store's red door.

Before Cecilia got more than a few feet inside, Beatrice was upon her, alerted by the tinkling of the bell. "Aloha, Miss Cecilia. Miss Vickie and Mr. Dickie get away okay with Smith?" She wiped her hands on her patterned apron.

"Yes, they did. I'm sad to see them go, though." Her mouth drooped in disappointment.

"They be back soon. You have much to do as housekeeper, helping Mrs. Reginald run the property."

"That's true. I expect I'll be too busy to miss them."

"And Mr. Reginald?" With a distinct drop in her tone, Beatrice's eyes narrowed.

"What do you mean?"

"How is he about you being housekeeper? And singing in his service?"

"Well, it was his idea I lead the hymns. He hasn't said for me to stop. And as far as the housekeeper job, he hasn't said anything about that, either. So . . ."

Beatrice nudged closer. "You just stay out of his way, Miss Cecilia."

"Whatever do you mean?"

Beatrice cringed. She began rearranging stock on the shelves, and an awkward silence filled the store.

Cecilia fumed. "If you have something to say, come out and say it. But it better not be silly local gossip. Well?" Hands on hips, she nailed Beatrice with a chilly stare.

"I'm sorry, Miss Cecilia." Beatrice dropped her head.

Cecilia blew out a pent-up breath. Playing hardball would not get her what she wanted. She knew this from working with the staff at the Reginald residence. If she tried pushing them to complete a task, they just went slower. But if she promised them a reward, they usually complied. It was the carrot or the stick analogy. Cecilia changed her approach to a more conciliatory one. "Beatrice, what is it you want to tell me? I know there's something. Please tell me."

"It's just you are a fine young woman. Mr. Reginald can be a hard taskmaster. Just stay out of his way." She turned and scuttled back to the counter. "What can I get you?"

Cecilia was gobsmacked. Because of Beatrice's refusal to elaborate, she had no other option but to pretend nothing had happened. She ordered more supplies and watched Beatrice fuss around with the paperwork. But the tension between them sizzled. It became obvious that no matter how much she pleaded, cajoled or threatened, Cecilia would never unearth the secret that the staff was hell-bent on keeping from her.

* * * *

While Leilani hobbled on her crutches along the pathway, Cecilia hovered beside her, concerned and circumspect. Inching along the outside wall of the bungalow, they did their best to evade the sheets of water cascading down from the pitched tin roof. The tropical evening deluge carved trenches in the ground, making a slippery moat around the walkways that linked the bungalows and the great pavilion. Despite their efforts to escape, they were no match for the driving rain which plagued their every step. Lucy hung back. Terrified of the lightning that streaked between the clouds in the darkening sky, she huddled in the doorway, unwilling to follow.

"Are you sure you're all right, Leilani? I really think it's too wet. Please be careful."

"Of course, I'm all right. Don't worry so much."

"Loretta could bring your dinner to the bungalow rather than you coming to the great pavilion." If Mrs. Reginald tripped, there was no way Cecilia was strong enough to catch her. Despite the chilling rain, her skin broke into a hot sweat. It became clear that when Mrs. Reginald got her mind set on anything, managing the risk became someone else's responsibility — in this case, hers.

"Cecilia, it's been over a week, and I must get used to using these damn things. Rain, hail or shine." Doggedly, Mrs. Reginald pushed forward on her crutches. One step, two steps and then, she skidded, lost her balance and ricocheted into Cecilia's arms. They teetered for a moment like marionette dolls with slack strings. Cecilia faltered, but as her shoulder slammed the wall, she gave an almighty shove and stabilized them both.

"Please, Leilani, I insist you come back to your bungalow. If we both injure ourselves, who will run the property then?"

"Oh, all right," she snapped, her voice tinged with a clap of frustration.

Cecilia pivoted carefully and steered her back along the pathway. Without interval, the driving rain spilled from the gutters and splashed their already soaked feet and legs. After edging their way back, they arrived wet and relieved. Still seated in the threshold of the bungalow's doorway, Lucy thumped her tail, delighted at their return.

"Now, you sit here, and I'll fetch Loretta. She can come and get you some dry clothes and organize dinner. Okay?" Cecilia settled Mrs. Reginald into an armchair, stacked her crutches to one side and closed the louvered sliding doors.

"Yes, yes. Go get Loretta." With a wave, she dismissed Cecilia. "But before you go . . ." She beckoned her back, and her manner softened. "You've done an admirable job this past week, and I know you will continue to do so even though Victoria and Dickie have left. You make a fine housekeeper. Thank you." The curt petulance gone, Mrs. Reginald's gentle face shimmered in the soft lamplight of the bungalow.

"Thank you, Leilani. Here, let me put this blanket on you." She lifted Mrs. Reginald's sprained ankle onto a footrest and wrapped her in a navy cotton blanket. As she tucked in the blanket and made her employer comfortable, she toyed with the idea of broaching the topic that had bothered her since her arrival on the island. "Do you mind if I ask you something?"

"Of course, whatever you like."

"When I first got here, Bartholomew insisted I keep my cottage windows and doors locked, even though Victoria said it wasn't necessary. Bartholomew said he'd arrange for screens to be put on the cottage windows the next day. Then that night, I could've sworn there was someone outside my cottage, making noises. And then a couple of nights after that when I went to the bathhouse, there *was* someone there, scratching at the door. To be honest, I don't know what to make of it all. But it's got me a little scared." Throughout her monologue, she scrutinized Mrs. Reginald's face, for any telltale signs of recognition or understanding, but she was poker-faced.

"And what do you think it was, Cecilia?"

"I have no idea. I thought you might know what's going on."

"I guess it's probably rats or small jungle animals running around." She tilted her head, her face pulled in a flat smile.

"But I'm sure it's not."

"Why?"

"Because I think Bartholomew and Loretta know more than they're letting on." Her gaze drifted, and she stared out the window at the storm. "And then there's the peculiar way Smith and Beatrice reacted when I found him making the screens. He'd started making them the day I arrived on the island. Way before he even knew I was staying. Doesn't that strike you as being odd?" She wheeled back to find Mrs. Reginald sitting ramrod straight, her face pale as if she'd seen a ghost. "What? What is it?" Cecilia rushed over and clasped Mrs. Reginald's hand. Cold, so cold. Her delicate fingers trembled. Cecilia rubbed them fiercely. "Leilani, what is it?"

After a moment, Mrs. Reginald traded the momentary look of shock for her customary serene composure. "Rats, my dear. I'm sure it's just rats. Now, you run along and find Loretta for me. Take Lucy with you. And I'll see you in the morning."

Cecilia blinked, but knew she'd been royally dismissed. *Rats, my ass.* "Come on, Lucy. With me." She snapped her fingers and strode to the door.

"Watch where you're going, girl." The familiar chilling tones of Mr. Reginald's voice skimmed over her head, and she sprang to attention before bumping into him. "Sorry, Mr. Reginald. I'm just off to find Loretta. Leilani is having dinner in here tonight. Do you want me to have Loretta also serve you here, sir?"

"Yes, thank you. Be sure you get that dog out of here. It smells." He growled down at Lucy, who cowered at his tone.

"Yes, sir, good night." With a quick backward glance, she noticed Mrs. Reginald looking troubled. Something about her reminded Cecilia of a friend of her mother's, Robyn Forsyth. Mrs. Forsyth's husband was an alcoholic — a terrible man who treated her badly, but she stayed married to him. Mrs. Reginald wore the same expression as Mrs. Forsyth — that of a long-suffering wife. The proverbial bells and whistled clanged in Cecilia's mind. *She knows. Damn it, she knows. The staff know. The locals know. Everyone knows what's going on here except me.*

CHAPTER ELEVEN

Over time, Cecilia found a sustainable rhythm and settled into her new role as housekeeper. Her days filled with endless tasks, most of which, she enjoyed. It was only those that required disciplining staff for not performing their duties correctly, which disturbed her. Having not discovered the secret behind the nighttime noises at her cottage, she worried if the staff were involved. If so, scolding them might only aggravate the situation. So, she tried her utmost to keep everyone happy as best as she could. Wherever possible, she forfeited her disciplinary responsibility to Mrs. Reginald, who never questioned her reluctance in the matter. Although walking unaided, Mrs. Reginald lost some of her mobility and retreated into her office most days to do the administrative work, leaving Cecilia to physically manage the estate. After that evening when she'd confided in Mrs. Reginald, an unspoken distance grew between them. Feeling more like an employee than ever before, Cecilia spent most of her free time up in Hill Cottage, taking her meals there and practicing her singing for Sunday's service.

As the weeks turned into months, her savior from loneliness became Lucy. With the faithful golden retriever by her side every night, the nocturnal episodes never returned, and she found sleep a wonderful respite to the busyness of her days. Fast friends, she and Lucy hung out together every moment, with the dog attentive to her every command. As promised, each afternoon when she finished her shift, she took Lucy to play on the beach.

Sitting side by side on the warm sand, Cecilia hugged the dog's damp neck. "What am I going to do about you, Lucy? You've been the best friend ever." She exhaled a heavy sigh. "I'm going to leave Harbor Island in the not-too-distant future, you know. I've saved my money, and I've nearly got enough to get back to the mainland."

Lucy tilted her furry face upward and dragged her tongue across Cecilia's cheek. Laughing, she hugged the dog tighter. "I'm going to miss you, girl. But until Victoria and Dickie come back, I won't leave you here alone. Dickie and I will have to work out what's going to happen to you before I finish working here." A seagull fluttered down to the water's edge and picked at the sand. "Look, Lucy. Bird."

Lucy barked and charged full throttle down the beach and jumped in the air at the flying nemesis. On instinct, she vaulted into the waves, following its flight path. "Come on, Lucy. Time to go," shouted Cecilia. The dog splashed a half-turn and then bounded out onto the beach. After a full body shake, which splattered sticky sand over Cecilia, the dog trotted beside her new master. As they stepped lively up the beach, Cecilia regarded the furrowed sand before her. She shook her head in amusement and giggled. *Raking the beach?*

Behind the wheel of the Chevy and with Lucy propped in the rear cargo tray, she drove home. The old truck trundled up Harbor Hill, weaving its way in and out of the shadows cast by the setting sun and the towering spine of mountains. Alongside the road trudged Loretta, a hand-woven bag of groceries in each hand. Cecilia steered the truck beside her and nodded for her to jump in.

"Thank you, Miss Cecilia." She threw the bags onto the seat between them and then scrambled into the cabin.

"You're late today, Loretta. Is everything all right?" She put the truck in gear and spun the wheels on the loose stones.

"Yes, Miss. I cook something special tonight for Beatrice's birthday." A layer of perspiration glossed Loretta's skin as she huffed and puffed.

"That's so sweet of you. What are you cooking?"

"Luau chicken wings. Beatrice loves my chicken wings." A proud smile lit Loretta's flushed face.

"Sounds wonderful. Maybe you can teach me how to cook them?" She shot a hopeful glance at her panting passenger.

"Maybe . . . But, Miss Cecilia, whatever you eat now is working. You fatter than before. Look like real woman now." Grinning with mischief, Loretta air-gestured the shape of a curvaceous woman.

"Yes. I was too thin when I arrived. I've been cooking and eating better. All that running around on the property has helped. I've got more muscle, which is good."

"Yes, Miss Cecilia. You pretty woman. You need to be strong, have lots of energy to be housekeeper."

"So, how old is Beatrice if you don't mind me asking?"

"She be fifty, Miss Cecilia."

"Really? She looks much younger than that."

"She be here on Harbor Island a long time, Miss."

"Beatrice is mixed race, isn't she?"

Loretta fell silent. Her cheery expression eclipsed, not by the shadows of the looming ranges, but obviously by the topic of conversation. The Chevy crested the hill and Cecilia slowed to a stop. She turned to her passenger.

"What is it, Loretta? What have I said?"

Loretta shook her head; her lips pursed so tight Cecilia thought it would take a specialized dental instrument to prize them open.

"Loretta, what is it?" she coaxed, hopeful of an answer.

Quicker than expected, Loretta opened the passenger door and thudded to the ground. She reached over and collected her bags in one deft movement. "Thank you for the ride, Miss Cecilia. I show you how to cook chicken wings some other time." She turned and trotted down the hill. The normally congenial Hawaiian left no doubt as to her haste to escape.

"Seriously! What has got everyone so spooked around here?" She slammed the Chevy into gear and drove onward.

With a loud crunch, Cecilia brought the truck to an abrupt stop on the gravel driveway. Still annoyed by Loretta's behavior, she let Lucy out and then returned to collect her beach gear from the cabin. Fumbling, she tried to jam the towels into the bag, but instead dropped everything on the ground. "Shit."

"Excuse me, none of that language around here, young lady."

God, where did he come from? Like a menacing phantom from hell, Mr. Reginald materialized before her. His demeanor typified that of an old-world undertaker rather than the owner of a glorious tropical island.

She bit her tongue. *I don't have time for this shit.* "Sorry, Mr. Reginald," she managed, swallowing the frustration rising in her throat.

"Let me make myself very clear, Cecilia," he cautioned, wagging a bony finger at her. "You may be the housekeeper, but you must still abide by my rules. We will not tolerate cursing and cussing here at the Reginald residence."

Her temper strained at his holier-than-thou reprimand. "I'm sorry, sir. It won't happen again." She forced a compliant smile and bent to collect her things from the ground. On hearing him huff, she breathed a sigh of relief and watched his feet swivel on the gravel and march away. "Stupid old prick," she muttered.

"Here. What are you doing, you wretched dog."

Cecilia snapped upright and scanned the grounds. She spied Lucy digging like a demented groundhog in one of the newly planted gardens. The groundsmen had spent the past week replacing shrubs and orchids in the garden, and now Lucy was hurling them between her legs.

"Lucy, stop that!" screamed Cecilia. She dropped her gear, and at breakneck speed sprinted toward the dog. Like a slow-motion movie reel, Mr. Reginald stepped out in long strides before her, his fists pumping the air. Without breaking stride, he leaned down and clutched at something. When he rose, he wielded a long-handled, post-hole shovel that one of the groundsmen had forgotten.

"Lucy, no!" Terror clawed at Cecilia. Her vision blurred, and she pumped her legs harder, trying to outrun her employer and protect Lucy. Just as Mr. Reginald skidded in beside the unsuspecting dog, he bellowed and raised the shovel high overhead. Lucy looked up and cowered. Lungs bursting, Cecilia hurled her body into the air. With an almighty thud, she tackled him to the ground, winding them both. At the same time, she heard another voice screech.

"Percy!"

Cecilia gulped a lungful of air and scrambled off his crumpled body. She glared down at him, hatred raging in her heart. "What the fuck is wrong with you?" She spat the words with as much venom as she could muster. Not interested in anything the wretched man had to say, she snapped a turn and found Lucy hunched in fright under the only shrub she hadn't uprooted. Cecilia edged toward the quaking dog. "Come on, girl. It's all right. Come on, Lucy." She kneeled, opened her arms, and Lucy slinked in to safety.

"Percy, get up. Get up this instance."

Cecilia watched Mrs. Reginald standing over the prone figure of her husband, hands on hips, her face twisted in a mask of fury.

Mr. Reginald clambered to his feet and brushed himself off, his chin stuck high. When he opened his mouth to speak, Mrs. Reginald stopped him short. "What on earth do you think you were doing? Going to club our son's dog?"

"I was going to teach it not to dig up my gardens." His tone was unrepentant.

"Well, let me teach you something about dogs, Percy Reginald. They say you can't teach an old dog new tricks." She leaned menacingly into him, her eyes flashing like flints of stone. "So, I suggest you leave Lucy alone and try learning new tricks yourself. Do I make myself clear?"

He met her challenge with an icy blast from his pale-blue eyes. His thin lips twitched, and a vein throbbed in his neck. Both faced off. Neither refused to surrender.

Cecilia watched the ferocious interplay between husband and wife and bristled. She hugged Lucy close and was relieved no other staff were present to witness the scene. Nevertheless, knowing the island grapevine, this family drama would burn down the lines of gossip like an uncontained bushfire.

In a deliberate gesture, Mr. Reginald ran his fingers through his silver hair, combing it into place. He then stroked his chin and tugged at his shirt. Without breaking eye contact, he nodded at his wife. Lifting his head in Cecilia's direction, he barked, "Keep that dog under control. If you can't, you will be fired." He leaned closer to Mrs. Reginald and hissed, "Satisfied?"

She mirrored his sarcastic grin, held her ground, but didn't answer. With a final growl, he marched off toward the great pavilion.

At the sight of his retreating back, Cecilia released her grip on Lucy. She exhaled a trembling breath and collapsed backward on the grass with the dog huddled beside her. "How could such a beautiful place produce such violence," she wondered aloud.

"Every place has its troubles," said Mrs. Reginald as she struggled to sit on the lawn beside her.

Cecilia pushed upright and helped her down. "I'm so sorry, Leilani. I shouldn't have said those things to Mr. Reginald, but he made me so mad. I thought he was going to kill Lucy. I couldn't forgive myself if anything happened to her. Dickie would never forgive me." A flood of tears washed her eyes, which she tried to stem.

"There, there, my dear." Mrs. Reginald wrapped an arm around her shoulders, rocking back and forth. "Everything will be all right. There's no need to be scared. Percy won't bother you, I promise, or Lucy for that matter."

Cecilia pulled out of the hug and stared at her. "I know you're all not telling me something, and I guess I'm just going to have to live with that. But do you mean it? There's nothing to be scared of?"

"I can guarantee you, there's nothing to be scared of." Mrs. Reginald kissed her forehead. "Now, let's put all this behind us. You and Lucy go up to the cottage. Get a good night's sleep, and I'll see you in the morning."

"But what do I say to Mr. Reginald? How am I supposed to act from now on?"

"Act as if nothing happened. I can promise you that's how he will act. The Reginald men are very good at pretending nothing happened. Now go."

Exhausted, Cecilia wiped her cheeks and climbed to her feet. "Here, let me help you up."

"No, thank you. I'm just going to sit here a little longer and enjoy the last of the sunset." Her face lifted in a smile. She looked triumphant, like the victor of a hard-fought battle.

Cecilia called Lucy to her side. "Good night, Leilani." A rush of relief propelled her toward the great pavilion. With brisk steps, she made their way along the path and up the twenty-six stairs hewn through the jungle corridor to Hill Cottage.

Once on the veranda, she sighed and faced the harbor, Lucy beside her. A veil of mauve darkness draped itself across the vista, signaling night's imminent return. Dancing on the wave points, the last glimmer of light made the most of the dying day. Again, the horizon became her solace, the place to ponder her life, her choices, her actions, and emotions. Moments passed. While the dark of night claimed the landscape, she whispered, "Come home, Dickie. We miss you. Come home." Only then did the hot burn choking her throat yield to the hiccupping sobs of her loneliness.

CHAPTER TWELVE

Excitement reigned. Cecilia shifted her weight from one foot to the other, unable to stand still. "Everything is ready, Leilani. Even Lucy is freshly bathed." On cue, a whiff of plumeria shampoo wafted up from Lucy's glossy body as her tail beat a brisk, happy beat.

"Excellent, Cecilia. Excellent." Mrs. Reginald tapped her fingertips together in a miniature clap.

The entire household assembled nearby. All equally keen to welcome Mr. Dickie and Miss Victoria home for the Christmas vacation.

"Here they come." Cecilia pointed to the Chevy as it crested the hill and her face burst with unrestrained joy.

A beaming Victoria sat propped between Mr. Reginald at the wheel, and Dickie. Her hands waved non-stop in swift, short arcs while she bounced up and down on the bench seat. Hanging out of the passenger window, Dickie whooped and hollered like a cowboy. "We're home! We're home!"

The staff rushed to the truck and escorted it down the driveway, calling "Aloha" and clapping hands.

Once stopped, the Chevy doors flew open, spewing forth Dickie and Victoria, who all but fell over themselves and each other.

"Mom!" cried Victoria, running to embrace her mother.

For an instant, Cecilia stiffened. She wondered if she'd been overly optimistic with the welcome she hoped to receive.

"CiCi. Lucy. My two favorite girls. Come on." With his arms outstretched, Dickie waited. Lucy galloped in a beeline and found his embrace first and nearly bowled him over. After drowning him in wet, sloppy kisses, she shuffled next to his leg, panting in excitement. Rising to his full height, he locked eyes with Cecilia. A glimmer of a smile twitched her lips, which he returned. *He's changed.* His features bore more strength, his frame more bulk and his presence more power. *He's a man, now.*

"CiCi, don't I get a hug?"

As much as she wanted to rush into his arms, she restrained herself. "Of course, you do," she quipped. "But maybe you should meet me halfway?" With a hearty chuckle, he strode forward and encircled her in his arms. In one strong lift she was off the ground and being spun in circles, his face buried in her belly. She dug into his muscled shoulders while the world whirled past. Lightheaded, she threw her head back and squealed. "Enough, Dickie! Enough. Put me down."

"Aren't you pleased to see me?" he teased, lowering her to the ground.

"Of course, I am, but you're not the only one who's come home." Reaching out, she caught Victoria's hand. "I'm so happy you're home. We've missed you. Both of you." She dragged Dickie in with her other arm and hugged them to her, while Lucy scampered around the group hug, nuzzling her way in.

"All right, everyone, back to work. Loretta, Bartholomew, take their bags to their bungalows, please." Mrs. Reginald gave a short, sharp clap and the staff dispersed to their duties. Linking arms with her children, she smiled from one to the other. "Now, time for lunch and for you both to tell us how you went at college." She stepped off toward the great pavilion.

Looking back over his shoulder, Dickie frowned. "You're coming too, aren't you, CiCi?"

"Of course, she is," said his mother. "Now, come inside and let's catch up on all your news."

* * * *

With Christmas Day not far away, a festive mood infused the Reginald residence. Unlike other places further north, the daytime temperature remained sultry, making every day a good day for fun, sun, and sodas. In anticipation of her friends' return from college, Cecilia had stocked her cottage's modest fridge with a selection of fizzy drinks. Now, lounging at Hill Cottage, she thrilled at playing host.

"Here we go. Three ice-cold sodas." She handed a bottle each to Victoria and Dickie before sitting atop the railing with hers.

As the sun descended behind the cottage in its mid-afternoon arc, its golden light glanced off the distant waves in checkerboard patterns. Even Lucy seemed hypnotized by the incessant ebb and flow of the shimmering tide in the harbor.

"CiCi, you were right." With his hand resting on Lucy's adoring head, Dickie propped his legs on the cottage's railing and gazed out to the harbor.

"Right about what?" She swung her leg in lazy circles.

"About college."

"Sorry, Dickie, I don't understand." She frowned.

"Neither do I," said Victoria, after taking another mouthful of soda.

"Before we left, you said I'd find freedom at college. And I have. For the first time, I feel like I belong, like I have a future. Environmental science and I are a great fit." He lifted his bottle toward CiCi. "Cheers."

"That's good to hear." She saluted back before gulping a mouthful of her Coke. "Does that mean you're happy?"

"Maybe a little too early to tell, but I'm sure happiness is in my future." His mouth stretched in a hopeful grin, and Cecilia explained to his sister the previous conversation she'd had with him about happiness.

"So, how's everything been here for you as housekeeper?" asked Victoria, reclining in the other rattan chair on the veranda.

"Actually, it's been okay. The staff have been pretty good. Your mom has been terrific and—"

"And has Father been an ass?" Dickie slurped on his soda while scrutinizing her from the corner of his eye.

"Just the usual," said Cecilia with a shrug. She decided not to tell Dickie about the episode with Lucy digging up the garden just yet. She'd pick a better time over the coming weeks.

"Are you still singing the hymns at service?" asked Victoria.

"Yes. And everyone comes from near and far. I think your father is pissed off because they're not coming to hear his sermon. But what can I do? They all stand up and sing their lungs out with me. It's great fun, really. I'll be singing the hymns for Christmas Day service, which to be honest, I'm looking forward to."

"Marvelous," said Dickie. "With you singing, the service will be worth going to for once."

"Listen, you two. I'm going to go and unpack. I'll catch you for dinner." Victoria walked over and kissed Cecilia's cheek. "It's good to be home, but it's even better that you're here. Thanks for taking on the job. See you at dinner?"

"Sure. See you then."

"Don't be late for dinner, Dickie. You know how Father is." Tossing a wave, she drifted down the stairs and into the jungle corridor.

The whooshing of wings from a small flock of spotted dove flying overhead signaled evening's arrival. "I love this place," whispered Dickie. "And now I know for sure that my destiny is here."

"That's wonderful to hear. I know you'll do great things for the island when you inherit."

Lowering his feet from the railing, he placed his bottle beside him. He leaned forward, rested his elbows on his thighs and stared hard at Cecilia. "I had time to think about a lot of things when I was at college."

"Well, that's one of the advantages of getting out of the home . . . time to think and ponder life." Her skin tingled under the intense scrutiny of his dark-chocolate eyes.

"Can I ask you something?"

"Sure."

"It's about sex . . ." He paused. "I don't have anyone to talk to. I can't talk to Victoria and definitely not Mom. And you know Father." He screwed up his face in disdain. "So, I was hoping you might be able to . . ."

She gnawed her lip. "What about talking to your male friends at college? Did you try talking to them?"

"No way. They'd all laugh at me if they knew."

"Knew what?"

"I'm a virgin."

Cecilia's hand fluttered in her lap. It wanted to fly to her cheek in surprise, but she held it tight with the other. "There's nothing wrong with being a virgin. Your time will come, I'm sure."

"But you're not a virgin, are you, CiCi?"

"No, I'm not." Her lips tilted in a soft smile.

"That's why I wanted to talk to you. You know things." Hope glittered in his eyes.

"About what specifically?"

He rose to his feet and walked over. He clasped her hands, his face clouded in a flurry of emotions. "About all of it . . . About how to kiss properly, how to touch, what it feels like, everything."

The more he spoke, the more her hands flamed. Heat rushed up her arms, blushing her neck and face. "You just sort of start and the rest takes care of itself." He paled and looked away. "Dickie, what is it? You're trying to say something. Go on. You know you can ask me."

He released her hands and moved beside her, facing the harbor. Tension closed around them like an impending thunderstorm. Cecilia could tell he was confused, hurting. She slithered off the railing and stroked his shoulder. He looked so alone and forlorn.

"Dickie, what is it? What's bothering you?"

In the silence, she studied his profile, and was struck by the anguish etched on his young face. His hands white-knuckled the railing, and he chewed at his cheek. She waited, knowing he needed time. Finally, he turned his head and spoke. "I'm not sure, but I might be gay or bisexual."

Cecilia only just managed not to stumble at the body blow he had just delivered. *Oh, no*, her heart cried out. She drew a steadying breath and regrouped. "And why do you think that?"

"Because I'm equally attracted to good-looking men and beautiful women, like you." He enfolded her hand and smiled. She held tight for a moment, determined to store this sweet memory away for later. Suddenly, the storm of emotion broke. He shoved back from the railing and began pacing the veranda like a caged tiger. "It's all so fucked up. Really it is. I enjoyed college, but I felt so isolated. The classes and study were easy, but not the social side of things. Stuck out here all these years, I haven't had a lot of friends or parties or things. But there, at college. It's like one big buffet. I'm ashamed to say, I found myself looking at my classmates in the showers. You know, down there." He glanced at his crotch. "Other times, I found myself ogling some girl's breasts and wondering what it would be like to bury myself in them. I tell you, CiCi, I'm so confused. I'm driving myself crazy."

She stepped in front of him, reached up and shook his shoulders. "Dickie, stop it. What you're talking about is normal. You haven't experienced sex yet, so that's all you see around you — particularly at college. Besides, whether you like girls, boys or both, what does it matter? You'll work it out."

His handsome features contorted with heartbreak. "But I want to like only girls. I don't want to be gay or have urges toward men. Imagine what Father would do." He grimaced. "I want to fall in love with a wonderful woman, get married and have children so they can inherit Harbor Island."

"Maybe you're thinking too much about all this. Maybe you should just let things take their course." Her thumb stroked the line of his square, shaven jaw. A shudder registered deep in her body. She'd not had sex in months, and until Dickie returned, she'd not realized how much she needed it. Now, as she stood there in front of him, her body hungered to show him how much love a man and a woman could share. "Listen, you're home for vacation. Relax, unwind. The three of us will hang out and have some fun, like we did before you left. See how you feel then?" Grabbing his hands, she tugged his arms in a playful gesture.

Holding firm, he wrapped his arms around Cecilia's waist and pulled her closer to him. He gazed down and tipped his forehead to hers. "I think you're wonderful, CiCi."

Crushed against his body, Cecilia had no doubt about his sexual attraction at that moment. With his growing excitement pushing against her belly, she used every ounce of willpower not to grind against him in response. "And I think you're wonderful, too, Dickie. Now, what do you say we go down to dinner?"

"Can we finish our talk another time?" he purred, his warm breath stroking her eyelashes.

"Let's just let see what happens." Worried her pounding heart and surging body heat would betray her, she wiggled out of his embrace and straightened her clothes.

Adjusting his crotch, he blushed. "See what you do to me?"

The feeling's mutual. And the ache in her groin thrummed.

CHAPTER THIRTEEN

"I cannot believe you're not coming home for Christmas. Your mother is beside herself." Cecilia's father's voice dripped with disappointment and disapproval. "You didn't even have the courtesy to call to tell us instead of writing it in your letter. Really, Cecilia, it's obvious to me this Reginald family means more to you than your own flesh and blood."

"Dad, I'm sorry." She sighed. "But I'm working here. I can't take any holidays yet. Whether I wanted to come home or not, I can't. You should understand out of everyone. As deputy mayor, you're forever grousing about dependable staff. Well, here I am being dependable for my employer. I thought you'd be proud of me for finally settling down in one place with a good job. I know it's not what you or Mom expected, but I'm doing well, and I'm saving money."

Her father huffed. "All I know is that your mother is very upset."

There it is, the guilt card. "I'm sorry, Dad. But I won't be home for Christmas."

"When will you be home, then?"

She knew that tone only too well. His temper would soon flare. "To be honest, I don't know. I've committed to staying here for one year. So, I may not be home until September next year." She flinched and waited for the tirade.

Instead, a long, silent pause ensued. In a deep, modulated voice, her father began, "Let me make myself very clear here, Cecilia. If you don't come home and visit your mother before next September, you won't be welcome in this house ever again. I find your attitude reprehensible and disrespectful considering everything your mother and I have sacrificed to give you the best life we possibly could. We paid for you to go to college, but no, you simply dropped out to go gallivanting around with all sorts of hippies. Then you wind up on some island, being a housekeeper, of all things. This is not the life we planned for our daughter."

"I understand how upset you are that I haven't turned into the daughter you wanted. Imagine how I feel to constantly disappoint you both." Hurt turned into anger. "But this is my life. It's no use my pretending to be someone that I'm not, just to please you. I'm sorry, Dad. I'll be home when I'm home, and if you leave me standing on the front doorstep, then so be it."

Not another word did her father say. The cold, hard slam of the phone receiver from his end severed the call. She placed the receiver gently in its cradle and stared at it. She knew how obstinate her father could be, and she also knew her mother rarely stood up to his irrational decisions. She would never be welcomed home again. In fact, she didn't even have a home now, as far as her father was concerned — not unless she returned to San Francisco before next September. *What have I done?*

* * * *

At the end of her shift, Cecilia escaped the property unnoticed and headed to the solitude of the beach. She needed time to think. With her trusty straw hat and sunglasses blocking the glare of the winter's afternoon sun, she ambled down the slope lost in her thoughts.

"Hey, CiCi, want a lift?" Dickie called, bringing the Chevy to a halt beside her.

"Yeah, okay. I was just going down for a swim." She opened the door and climbed in. On spying his naked chest, she tried not to stare. He was only wearing a pair of blue board shorts and sunglasses. He could have passed for one of those young fashion models in the Studio 54 jean ads. Tall, tanned and lean muscled, he possessed an intoxicating beauty due to his mixed heritage. She had no doubt Dickie was equally attractive to men and women.

"I've got Lucy in the back. We thought we'd hit the waves." He spun the wheels and drove off, a megawatt smile lighting his face. "So, how was your day at the madhouse?"

"Pretty good. No major stuff-ups, so that's a blessing. We've got everything organized for the Christmas service and lunch. I'll be happy when that's over, and we can all have a day or two off."

Once on The Esplanade, he parked the Chevy and shoved the keys into the visor. "Come on. The water looks magic." He leaped out of the cabin and released Lucy from the rear cargo tray. After bolting down the sand at top speed, she stretched out in midair and belly-flopped onto the crashing waves. Barking and biting the water, she paddled in circles, crazy with delight, while Cecilia and Dickie wandered down the beach. "Thanks for taking care of her while I was away. It really means a lot."

"It was my pleasure. But to be honest, I miss having her with me now that you're back." She pressed her lips in a sulk.

"How about I have her during the day while you're working, and she can stay with you in the cottage at night?"

"Do you mean it? That would be great. Thanks." She flung her arms around his neck in a tight hug.

Lifting her off the sand, he wrapped her legs around his hips and crushed her body to his. For a moment, she enjoyed being suspended in his arms and feeling his heartbeat under his naked chest. Energy sparked between them, but Cecilia tried to quash it.

"You better put me down, Dickie. You know what the local grapevine is like around here." She scrambled to the sand and dropped her bag.

"You're right. Even though we can't see them, there'll be pairs of spying eyes watching everything.

Come on. Let's join Lucy." He slipped off his flip-flops and raced toward the water.

Cecilia undressed down to her beige crochet bikini, knotted her hair on top of her head and hurried after him. He dived into the water and spun around. Their eyes met, and his steamy gaze sent shivers over her body, leaving her physically and emotionally exposed. Unraveled, she scampered into the water and crashed through the waves. She needed to turn down the heat between them. Otherwise, there was no telling what might happen. She knew a topic which was certain to dampen his charm. "Dickie," she called, splashing around out of arm's reach, "you asked how I got on with your father while you were away. Well, there was an incident involving Lucy. She was digging in the garden, and because I didn't notice her before your father, he took off to stop her." She winced at the memory.

"Tell me. What did he do? What happened?" Dickie paddled closer as the gentle waves eddied around them.

"He was going to hit her with a shovel, but I tackled him to the ground. Your mother was there shouting at him, and they had a huge argument afterward. But it worked out all right. Lucy didn't get hurt, and since then, she's clung to my side. And your father's given both of us a wide berth. I'm so sorry." Tears moistened her eyes at how close Mr. Reginald came to killing Lucy.

"Oh, CiCi. You saved Lucy. You have nothing to be sorry for. My father is a violent man. I'm not sure whether it's because his father was cruel to him or that when his parents were killed in a car crash, he resented being left the responsibility of Harbor Island while he was still young. I don't know. But he uses violence to get his way. You saved Lucy, and that's all that matters." He swam up to her and pressed a kiss to her cheek. "I would have loved to see your flying tackle, though. I bet that surprised him." Dickie's eyes twinkled.

"It did. Then I yelled what the fuck was wrong with him. I'm not sure what shocked him more, the tackle or the swearing." She giggled and swam away.

"Well, just as well you're here. Lucy's a lucky dog, and I'm a lucky man." Floating on his back, he paddled in circles.

"Yes. I guess so." She took a breath and slipped under the waves, not daring to discuss the matter of her not being there forever.

* * * *

On Christmas Eve, Loretta set the main dining table for the Reginalds' dinner in the best of their festive finery. Scarlet linen contrasted snowy-white porcelain plates at each of the five dinner settings, while a row of baskets brimming with artificial red poinsettia and white lilies dotted the center row of the table. Draped in glittering decorations and paper chains, the great pavilion burst with unabashed merriment. An artificial Christmas tree stood in pride of place in one corner, its multicolored lights twinkling on and off, with a faded, hand-carved nativity scene wedged in front of it.

"The table looks beautiful, Loretta." Sweeping her discerning eye over the preparations one last time, a radiant Victoria turned to the staff. "Well done, everyone. You can all finish up now and spend Christmas Eve with your families. See you tomorrow for the service." She tapped Cecilia's shoulder as she straightened a wayward spoon. "Come on. Let's go for a stroll before the others arrive."

Linking arms, they wandered across the great pavilion. "I've really come to love this place," said Cecilia. "I don't know how, but it just gets more beautiful." Exchanging smiles, they eased through the gossamer curtains and strolled out onto the manicured lawns.

"You've done a terrific job," said Victoria, surveying the property. "The gardens and grounds look spectacular. Mom says you've been a godsend to her while her ankle recovered. And all the staff love you as well. I hear they call you *leo o ka anela* because you have the voice of an angel. How sweet."

"Surprisingly enough, I love singing the hymns. It's given me a chance to develop my voice."

"I can't wait to hear you sing the Christmas hymns tomorrow."

They reached the white Adirondack chairs, and Victoria nodded for them both to sit down. "So, what are you going to do, Cecilia?" she asked, a serious tone in her voice.

"About what?"

"About Harbor Island? About your job as housekeeper?"

"Well, I promised your mother I'd stay for a year, but that's caused all sorts of drama with my father."

"What do you mean?"

She told her about her father's ultimatum.

"That's awful."

"He doesn't care that I've made a promise to work here for a year, or that I'm happy doing the housekeeper job. He's just being a pain in the ass about it." An angry frown lined her brow.

"I don't know what it is about fathers, but they can be so unreasonable."

"You're right on that point." Cecilia folded her arms with a huff.

"What are you going to do?"

"What can I do? Once I leave here, that's it. I don't want to be banned from my home, but I can't break my promise to your mother. And—"

"And then there's Dickie?" Victoria completed Cecilia's thought.

She sighed. "Yes, and then there's Dickie."

"You know he's quite smitten with you. A college-boy crush, first love, that kind of thing."

Cecilia dropped her head in her hands and moaned. "Has he said something?"

"Oh, no, Dickie doesn't go around confiding his feelings to anyone. But I know what I see, and he's infatuated with you."

"It's all so messy. I promised him I'd look after Lucy, but I can't stay here for the next three years while he's away." She paused. Her head hurt from too much thinking, and her body ached from the worry she shouldered. "Victoria, you're the only person I can talk to and trust. What should I do?"

"I don't know. The life I've mapped out for myself is much simpler than yours. Finish college, get a job as a teacher, find a man, settle down and raise a family. I don't have your big dreams of adventure and visions of stardom."

"Big dreams and visions aren't all they're cracked up to be." She pouted and tapped her fingertips on the chair. While the mauve-tinged shadows of late afternoon stretched and slanted across the freshly mown lawn, they mulled over their thoughts.

Victoria shuffled her chair closer. "I know this sounds really odd, but I've often wondered if Dickie is confused, you know, sexually."

Cecilia frowned at her. "Why would you think that?"

"Oh, I don't know. It's just a feeling I've had ever since he was young. He's never said anything about it, but—"

"Have you ever said any of this to your mother?"

"I did speak about it once with her, but she shut me down quick smart. She said if Father ever thought Dickie might be queer, he'd disinherit him straight away."

"Oh, God. That's terrible. Poor Dickie." She paused. "But if you think he's gay why would he be infatuated with me?"

"Well, that's what I mean by being confused. He knows Father would disinherit him if he found out. What can he do? He's got to keep it secret — at least until Father dies. I think Dickie's got a crush on you because he doesn't want to be gay. Besides, you're the first girl who's shown him any real affection or attention, even if it is platonic." Victoria angled her a look. "Or is it platonic? I know you're seven years older than him, but do you have feelings for Dickie? Real feelings?"

This was the very question Cecilia refrained from exploring in the quiet of night, when she lay staring at the ceiling. "Oh, Victoria, you talk about Dickie being confused. I'm confused too. I'm very attracted to him, but there's so much else I want to do in my life. And besides, he's just on the brink of exploring his life, his future. What good would it be if I allowed myself to fall in love with him, if it turns out he really prefers men? No. It would never work." She shook her head, determined to maintain the status quo with Dickie, despite the growing attraction.

"Mom always said you can't control who you fall in love with." Her mouth curled in a sympathetic smile.

"Regardless of what your mother says, I can't risk breaking Dickie's heart or mine with a casual romance. I've had my share of jumping in and out of bed with men who make and then break promises. The next time I fall in love, I want it to be with a man who really loves me."

"You mean, a man who loves you forever?"

"Yes. A man who loves me forever."

CHAPTER FOURTEEN

"Hark the herald angels sing, glory to the newborn King . . ." The entire congregation held the final note of the last hymn of the Christmas service before erupting into raucous clapping and celebration.

"Merry Christmas, everyone," proclaimed Mr. Reginald, looking uncharacteristically happy.

"Merry Christmas," said Mrs. Reginald as she strolled through the crowd, shaking hands and kissing cheeks.

Cecilia and Victoria traded greetings and kisses, before moving to other chatting groups of staff and locals. Feeling his hand slip into hers, Cecilia turned to Dickie. "Merry Christmas, Dickie." She stretched up to press a quick kiss to his cheek.

"Merry Christmas, CiCi. Here, I have a present for you." From behind his back, he offered her a package wrapped in colorful Christmas paper. "Come over here and open it." Still holding her hand, he pulled her to one of the sofas tucked in the back corner on the far side of the great pavilion. "Come on. Sit down and open it." She settled into the sofa beside him.

"Oh, you shouldn't have." She plucked open the tape and peeled back the paper. "I haven't got anything for you."

"That's okay. There's nowhere here for you to buy anything. But I wanted to give you something you'd really like and use." A big, fat grin spread across his face as he watched the wrapping paper unfurl.

"Oh, Dickie, this is the best present anyone has ever given me." In her lap lay a dozen or more records.

"They're the top-selling songs on the mainland. I thought you could practice to them rather than Father's boring hymns all the time."

Titles such as "Killing me Softly", "Delta Dawn", "The Morning After" and many other hits sung by well-known female artists lay in her lap. "Thank you, thank you." Tiny tears pricked her eyes, and she blinked them away.

"Don't cry, CiCi. I didn't mean to make you cry."

"I'm crying because you gave me such a thoughtful gift. You really are the sweetest young man. Really you are." She cupped his face, but before she could pull away from the platonic kiss, his mouth claimed hers. She lingered, though she knew she shouldn't. But he tasted so sweet and forbidden. Within moments, she melted into the tentative kiss and invited his tongue to entwine with hers. Exploration turned to demand, and his full moist lips pressed harder against hers, craving more. And she responded. Offering her mouth up to his, wanting to be devoured, to be taken, and to be loved, she succumbed. Their hot breath mingled, synchronizing their inhale and exhale to become one. One couple, one pair, one love.

Raised voices from the other side of the great pavilion broke the spell. Cecilia recoiled and wiped his passion from her lips. She glanced around and shuddered, wondering if anyone had seen. "Dickie, wipe your lips," she instructed in a whisper. He obeyed.

"CiCi, come with me tomorrow. Let's go to Rainbow Falls. Alone. Please?"

She didn't know what to say. This was not supposed to have happened. She stalled for time by folding the wrapping paper over the records in her lap in slow, deliberate movements. "I'm not sure that's a good idea." As much as her body and heart ached for him, her rational mind screamed danger.

"Don't say no. Not yet. Think about it overnight. Okay?"

"Okay. I'll think about it overnight. Now, we better get back before we're missed."

She prepared to stand, but he caught her hand. "Please, CiCi. Help me become a man. A man to be proud of."

"My poor Dickie, you don't need me to help you become a man. You already are. One I'm very proud to know and love." Still trembling from the encounter, she stood and smiled down into his expectant face. Her heart fluttered, and she wondered if she'd made the right decision in not going home for Christmas.

* * * *

With Lucy by her side, Cecilia threw her beach bag over her shoulder. She shoved her hat on her head and looked down at the dog. "Last chance, Lucy. What do you think?" Beating her tail on the floorboards next to the cottage's kitchen table, Lucy wiggled her approval.

Last night, Cecilia had anguished over whether to go to Rainbow Falls today with Dickie. Despite it being a new moon, she and Lucy had braved the dark and sat outside on the veranda around midnight. With no moonlight, she had marveled at the billions of stars pasted in the velvety black sky. Like a carpet of diamonds, the luminescent pinpricks of light had glittered for anyone fortunate enough to see them. She and Lucy had enjoyed the overhead light show together in the silky stillness. *If I'm supposed to go to Rainbow Falls, send me a sign.* Not normally superstitious or particularly religious, she'd surprised herself by her silent request to the heavens. Then as if on cue, a shooting star had jetted in an arc across the sky, extinguishing its fireball run over Rainbow Falls. "Well, girl. It looks like we're off to Rainbow Falls in the morning," she'd said with a rub to Lucy's head.

Now, with the dog by her side, she closed the front door behind them and paused, looking out across the harbor. From somewhere in her subconscious, she remembered the conversation she'd had with Joseph all those months ago about freedom and her quest to find God. And she had told him she didn't know if she believed in God, only following her heart.

She blew out a shuddering breath. "I guess it's time to follow my heart and see where it leads. No point procrastinating when you're on a freedom quest." Side by side, they trotted down the veranda stairs and through the jungle corridor — two intrepid explorers off on their next adventure. When they arrived at the bottom of the stairs, Lucy bolted. There, against the Chevy leaned Dickie, arms folded and long legs crossed casually at the ankles. The dog bounded toward him, and he squatted down to welcome her with a good-morning rub. By the time he finished, Cecilia stood in front of him. He took her bag, relief written across his face.

"How did you know I'd come?" she asked.

"I didn't."

"So, how long have you been standing here?"

"About an hour."

"And how long would you have waited?"

"All day." His face broke into an enchanting smile.

Bemused, she shook her head. "If you're this persistent with everything else in your life, you'll go far, that's for sure."

"I'm hoping to go far today." A cheeky curl tipped his lips.

* * * *

Like a movie director racking lenses on a tight shot, Rainbow Falls drew closer. The distant tangle of foliage cascading over the rock faces sharpened until the outlines of leaves and branches became visible. Abandoned on the lagoon's edge over thousands of years, clusters of rocks distinguished themselves more clearly as ledges, boulders, and fractures, each telling their own story in time. Overhead, the jungle canopy draped like a billowy green curtain protecting this place from the outside world. The only prying eyes were those of the animals and birds, eager to spy but not be seen. Like a great masterpiece, nothing compared to the power and majesty of the waterfall in the center of the image. Unyielding and unstoppable, its life force rushed to its death in the lagoon, while the seven colors of the rainbow danced on the mist.

Dickie guided the Chevy to the lagoon's edge and shut off the engine. He grew still, his hands resting on the steering wheel. Surrounded by the deafening sound of the water spearing down a narrow gorge and hurtling off the cliff, the mundane surrendered to the sublime. He reached over and clasped Cecilia's hand with a gentle squeeze. "Whatever happens, CiCi, promise me one thing." He inclined his head, his gaze fixed and steady.

"What's that?"

"Promise me you'll never forget me or Harbor Island."

"Of course, I won't. How could I?"

A tender smile chased away the anxiety in his face. "Let's grab Lucy and have a swim."

While Lucy wasted no time leaping into the water, she and Dickie laid out a rug, unpacked a picnic lunch and undressed down to their swimmers. Balancing on the rocky edge of the lagoon, she stepped into the icy water with a shiver. Her toes curled in fright and gooseflesh prickled her skin.

"Swim around for a while. You'll warm up," he called, stroking to the waterfall and back. She joined him on the next lap, her body acclimatizing to the chill. After a few minutes, they paddled in a delicious languor of timelessness. Closing her eyes, she delighted in the gentle water spray falling on her face.

Warm, soft lips pressed a kiss to her shoulder. A bolt of pleasure flashed through her body, but she suppressed its insistence for more. Coming upright, she paddled around to face him. "Dickie, I don't think a casual romance is a good idea, for either of us."

"Who said anything about a casual romance?" He hesitated. "I think I'm in love with you." The sincerity in his tone made her heart flutter.

"You may love me like I love you, but I don't think either of us is in love with each other. We haven't spent enough time together to be in love. And not only that, as my mother would say, you're too young." Keeping her tone light, she explained the difficulties of the situation as best she could, while respecting his feelings.

"Well, I don't care what your mother says."

"Of course, you don't, and neither do I. But . . ." She became serious. "Dickie, regardless of how we feel right at this moment, there is one thing I know for certain."

"What's that?"

"I have to follow my dream of being a singer. I can't stay here at Harbor Island. I promised Leilani one year, and that's the most I can give. Even now, my parents are so upset they may disown me if I don't come home before next September. So, what good is talking about love?"

His face fell. "But what about me? What about Lucy?" He cast his eyes to the contented golden retriever drying off in the sun. "What's going to happen when you leave?"

"You're going to have to entrust Lucy into someone else's care. I'm sure your mother will look after her. And as I said, your father steers clear of us now, so I doubt he'll be a problem. Dickie, you're embarking on a wonderful new stage of your life. You're going to fall in and out of love many times before you find the right one."

"But what if the right one is you, CiCi? What then?" Clutching her hand, he stroked to the side of the lagoon, where they could both stand.

"Then you'll find me when the time is right, and we'll be together."

He gathered her to him in a tight embrace. For a long moment, she clung to his cool body, not daring to let go. The ache was back, but it wasn't the ache in her groin that bothered her. It was the dull ache clotting her heart. What if he was right? What if they were meant to be together? Dickie may well be sexually confused, but she'd become emotionally confused over this young man.

Still holding her tight, he whispered, "I guess you're right. There is a lot for me to learn and experience yet. And you've got to follow your dream like I've got to do my duty here. We both have our own lives to explore, and they go in different directions. I was just hoping you could have been part of my life now. Not somewhere in the future."

Standing in the clear waters of the lagoon and cocooned from the everyday world, her senses blurred. She tilted her face and met his love-struck gaze. As the water crashed, drowning out everything but their desire, she found herself surrendering. "Maybe I *can* be part of your life now." She broke free of his embrace, and taking his hand, urged him out of the water. Across the soft ferns and mosses at the water's edge and onto the wild grass, she led him to the picnic rug. There, she folded to the ground and reached up for him to join her. Warmed from the sun, the rug toasted their bare, damp skin as they reclined beside each other, sharing an intimate silence. They gazed into each other's eyes and their fingers intertwined in an unspoken mating ritual. Without the bruising urgency of insatiable lust, a sense of oneness bonded them. "You stop me if you want," she purred. Tracing her fingers over his toned, buff chest, she murmured a seductive sound.

"Oh, CiCi, I don't think I'm ever going to want you to stop."

"Very well, then. Just lie back and relax."

With a breathy moan, he lay down and closed his eyes. Sprawled on the rug, he looked like a young god — the architecture of his physique cut well-proportioned mountains and valleys across his body. Cecilia admired his beauty while a part of her warned that this was not a good idea. But her affection for Dickie had grown into love. A love where fools rush in and do irrational things. From somewhere inside her, an impulsive voice urged her on. As her hands explored the ridges of his chest and the taut muscles of his stomach, she noted his willingness and responsiveness to her touch. Like Harbor Island itself, he was one of nature's best-kept secrets. In the spell of the midday sun, he entwined her heart like a thorny vine and captured her in his grip; as did his lips when he pulled her toward him. She immersed herself in the latent promise of his mouth and yielded to the desires she'd ignored these past months. She crushed her body against him, and he responded, hot and hard.

With hungry urgency, she took charge. She peeled off her bikini in slow, provocative movements, her hands trailing over her ripe body and breasts. Bending over, she rubbed her nipples in lazy circles against his thighs, while her teeth nipped at his prickling flesh. When she finally shrugged off his swimmers, releasing his impressive erection, he heaved a breath. She purred. The cat that got the cream. Like sweet torture, her skillful hands and mouth devoured him, bringing him to total submission. He moaned and gasped on every deliberate stroke, setting her heart pounding. Untiringly, she rode the ebb and flow of his agonized delight, her body salivating for satisfaction. Then, with bodies primed and senses heightened, she straddled him. He needed no further encouragement. She inserted him into the welcoming warmth of her body, easing herself further down until she consumed him.

"Oh, CiCi . . ." he groaned, a look of bliss on his face.

Leaning forward, she drove him deeper. "You are no longer a virgin, my love."

For one long, lightheaded moment, their gazes locked, and her groin tightened. She set a slow and steady tempo, grinding up and down on his pelvis.

Abandoning himself to her expertise, he closed his eyes. Lost in the moment, he growled deep and long in the curve of her neck, his voice reverberating through her being. Until, in a crushing embrace, he emptied himself, yowling like a lone wolf in the wilderness. She clung tight to him. For she knew. She knew this exquisite, enchanting encounter would be their first and last. She gave a sad sigh. Another little piece of her heart broke free, and she stamped it into this place, into this man. She blinked away the tears of ill-fated love. She rolled off and propped on her elbow beside him, toying with his luxurious black hair. "So how do you feel?" she whispered.

"Like I'm flying." He sighed.

"Good."

As if awakening from a wonderful dream, his eyelids fluttered open. In a long, languid movement, he rolled onto his side and faced her. "But what about you? That mustn't have been much fun for you, I'm sure."

"Sometimes, the best love-making is when you give and not receive. Today was your day. If nothing else, you can always look back on the day you lost your virginity and smile because it was with me."

He wrapped his arms around her and pulled her beside him. They lay together for some time, not speaking. Nestled into his shoulder, she breathed in his sweet smell of sex and sweat. Around them the jungle continued in its never-ending quest to grow, enfolding them in its protection. She yearned to stay in this time, with him. She also yearned to be satisfied — but she knew. Even at her age, she'd had enough lovers to know. A heterosexual man would have touched her, tweaked her breasts, grabbed her sweet spot and taken her. He wouldn't have been able to keep his hands off her. But not Dickie. Her feminine form held little consequence to him. He had no interest in exploring or pleasuring her. Instead, he wanted to cuddle, love and cherish her. He may no longer be a virgin, but it would be men who would slake his carnal lust in the future. Although selfishly disappointed, she knew that in time, Dickie would come to accept his homosexuality. Theirs would never be a love to last forever.

CHAPTER FIFTEEN

The following week passed without fanfare. Whenever she finished work, Cecilia met up with Victoria and Dickie. Walks and swims on the beach with Lucy, hanging out at Hill Cottage or trips into town filled their spare time together. Neither she nor Dickie broached the topic of their sexual liaison at Rainbow Falls. For Cecilia, it became part of her history, tender yet painful. But it had been her choice, and Dickie would always hold a special place in her heart. More than she wanted to admit.

To celebrate Victoria and Dickie's last night on Harbor Island before they returned to college, Cecilia offered to cook a special dinner for the three of them. Alone at Hill Cottage, Dickie stood next to her as she cooked some nacho beans on her little stove.

She was about to add her favorite ingredient when he peeked over her shoulder. "Not too much chili. Vic and I aren't used to it."

"Don't worry, I'll be kind," she promised and replaced the chili bottle on the shelf.

As she stirred the bean mix, he gently placed his hands on her shoulders. "You have been more than kind to me, CiCi. About what happened at Rainbow Falls—"

She reached up and pressed her index finger to his lips. "Shh. You don't have to say anything."

"But I do. I've been thinking a lot about it. And I've realized something."

Without a word, she inclined her head and waited.

"I so wanted to make you feel good, but . . ." Obvious shame and confusion creased his brow.

"But?"

"But although I love you, I'm not attracted enough to you to—"

"I know. I know. It's okay." She flicked a few strands of his thick black hair from his forehead, admiring his intoxicating good looks.

"But it's not okay, CiCi. I'm so sorry. Not just for you, but for me, too. What will my life be like now? I can never get married or have a family. I'm going to have to live a secret life, at least until Mom and Father die. I can't even tell Vic." Distraught, he pulled out a kitchen chair and slumped into it, his head in his hands.

She sat beside him and tilted his chin upward. "Listen to me. Firstly, you can tell Victoria anything. I suggest you tell her. She already suspected you were gay since you were young, so it won't come as a surprise to her." He opened his mouth to speak, but she rushed on. "And yes, you will have to keep this a secret from your father. But once he dies, I'm sure your mother will be able to accept the news. She won't have to contend with her husband then. Her focus has always been you and Victoria. She wants you to inherit Harbor Island and fulfill your vision. She will support you. I have no doubt about it. And as far as sex is concerned, you're just going to have to work that out for yourself. You're not the only gay man in America. Once you get back to college, you'll find friends, who like you, lead a secret sexual life. Just be careful and don't get yourself beaten up or arrested. Okay?"

"Thank you, CiCi. I don't know what I would have done without you helping me through all this. I do love you, you know."

"I know. And I love you, too. But as a couple, we're just not meant to be." She hugged him tightly, not wanting to let go. Together, they sucked in a unified breath, loving each other one more time. Her sad heart battered against her ribs, but she needed to keep a brave face. She stood up and pulled him to his feet. "Now, help me finish setting up before Victoria arrives."

"Will you sing one of those songs from the records I gave you while we set the table?"

"Sure." She leafed through the lyrics in her head. "This song sung by Maureen McGovern is perfect, considering everything that's happened. Go sit over there, and I'll sing it for you." She pushed him toward the sofa under the window and then took her position center stage in the cottage. Swaying to the music in her mind, she serenaded him on there being a morning after, just outside the storm. That with love, they'll escape the darkness and that it's not too late. Looking past him to the harbor in the distance, she poured herself into the performance. Hope edged her voice while she struggled with the tide of tears brimming in her eyes. Another piece of her heart fluttered toward him. It made its way to her fateful love, and she lost control. There, from his red-rimmed eyes streamed tiny rivulets of tears. She flew to him, and she threw herself onto his lap, and he held her close. Encircled in each other's arms, they cried and grieved for the love and the life they could never share together.

* * * *

Once more, Cecilia found herself on Harbor Island's jetty saying farewell, with Lucy by her side. "See you in your spring break," she called, waving madly. The boat gleamed. Delivered just before Christmas, the new thirty-six-foot pine cruiser with its hand-crafted polished timber and detailed paintwork motored away with barely a sound. Smith's permanent megawatt smile summed up his delight in the new craft.

"See you then," yelled Victoria, before joining Smith inside the cabin, leaving Dickie alone on the aft deck. Dressed in cream trousers and a blue polo shirt, he matched the paintwork palette of *Harbor Island II*. Both stylish and elegant, he and the boat suited each other well. They exuded sophisticated charm and power. With a slow wave of his arm, he called, "Bye, Lucy. Bye, CiCi. See you in spring." A melancholy smile graced his face.

"Goodbye, Dickie." Cecilia ruffled Lucy's ear as she perched beside her, a forlorn look on her furry face. "See you in the spring." But as she called her promise, something deep within her stirred, telling her she would be gone by then.

* * * *

"Aloha, Miss Cecilia." Beatrice's normally pinched face opened wide when Cecilia appeared in the Local Store.

"Aloha, Beatrice. I've come for our supplies, please."

"They are ready. I will get the boys to load your tuck." Moving behind the counter, Beatrice stuck her head into the back room and hollered, "Andrew, Jacob. Load Miss Cecilia's truck." On her return, she employed a dust cloth to the countertop. "Everything good at the Reginald residence, Miss?" she asked as she cleaned industriously.

"Oh yes, Beatrice. Thank you. We all miss Victoria and Dickie, though."

"Yes, it been how long now?"

"They've been gone just over two months. Poor Lucy misses Dickie. They used to play every day. Now with me working, she just mopes around until I get off work in the afternoons. But aside from that, all is good."

"It is good Lucy is with you at the cottage at night. She good guard dog." Beatrice nodded, obviously satisfied with the dog's permanent sleeping arrangement.

Too tired to question Beatrice about her pointed remark, Cecilia redirected. "And how are you, Smith and the family doing?"

"Smith much happier now Mr. Reginald give him new boat. Each week Smith go back and forth to Lahaina Harbor for supplies. Make him happy when he is on the sea in a good boat."

Rubbing her forehead, Cecilia suddenly felt faint. She reached out to the counter for balance and moaned.

"Miss Cecilia, what is wrong? Here, I get chair." Beatrice dropped her dust cloth and scurried a chair around for Cecilia to sit on. "I get you some water, Miss Cecilia." Moments later she returned with a cloudy-looking glass half filled with water.

Cecilia declined the offer. "I'm all right, really I am. Just a little dizzy."

Beatrice pushed her face close to Cecilia's and stared hard. "You open them eyes. Let Beatrice see."

Although reluctant, Cecilia lifted her head and allowed Beatrice to study her eyes. They traded a grave stare in the silence. "See I'm fine, Beatrice. Just a little dizzy."

Beatrice snorted. Rising to full height, she knuckled her hands on her hips while her mouth set in a grim line of concern. "No, Miss. You are not fine. Beatrice knows. We go see Loretta. She good with medicine. We go now." She assisted Cecilia to her feet and guided her outside to the truck. "You okay to drive?"

"Yes, I'm fine. Really, Beatrice, you don't have to come with me—"

"I come. We go." She waited until Cecilia slid in behind the wheel and then heaved up into the passenger seat. Not a word was spoken during the short journey back to the residence, but Cecilia's discomfort grew.

* * * *

With her feet on the sofa in Hill Cottage, she leaned back and rested her head on the pillow Beatrice had placed there before rushing off to find Loretta. The pounding of feet on the veranda stairs indicated her arrival. Beatrice and Loretta rushed into the cottage, both taking positions beside her prone body.

Leaning forward, Loretta took Cecilia's hand and patted it in a motherly fashion.

"You two must stop worrying. I'm fine," she assured.

Loretta nodded to Beatrice to bring over a couple of chairs on which they took up residence.

"Miss Cecilia, you know I say when you arrive you need to eat more?" said Loretta, a respectful tone in her voice.

"Yes, Loretta. I remember." Cecilia didn't feel like any chit-chat.

"You take Loretta's advice, and you get curvy. Now, you put on too much weight, Miss Cecilia." Without permission, Loretta touched her belly, and she flinched. "You pregnant, Miss Cecilia."

"What?" Her thoughts skittered. "Don't be silly. Now you better get back to work. Off you go." Cecilia launched from the sofa and pointed to the door. She staggered and only just managed to swallow the nausea rising in her throat.

"We sorry, Miss Cecilia."

"Yes, we sorry, Miss."

Amid their whining apologies, another bout of lightheadedness struck, and Cecilia collapsed into Loretta's arms. The women hauled her back to the sofa, chattering furiously. The last thing she remembered was the two of them patting her clammy hands and clucking like wet-nurses.

Eventually, the lilac walls of Hill Cottage swam back into focus, and Cecilia stirred. As instructed, Beatrice and Loretta had left, but on her head lay a cold pack and beside her a lukewarm cup of tea. Though their considerate actions tempered her indignation, they did nothing to quell the sinking feeling in her stomach. It was time.

* * * *

"Leilani, can I see you for a minute, please?"

"Of course, Cecilia, come in." Leilani closed the office door behind them. "Take a seat."

Cecilia folded into the chair, cupped her hands in her lap and licked her lips. Her gaze swept the small room. A room where she had learned so much, a room where she'd grown from a brash newcomer into a respected young woman. Her heart clutched. "I have some bad news. I cannot see out my contract. I'd like to tender my resignation today. I have to leave as soon as you allow me."

Shock pulled at Mrs. Reginald's face. "But, Cecilia, why ever for? You are doing so well at the job, and I thought we had an understanding that you would stay for a year?"

"I simply can't stay, Leilani. Please don't ask me why. I just can't."

Mrs. Reginald pushed out of her chair and paced to the window. She gripped the ledge, and stared outside, her body rigid and tense. Without turning, she said, "Did my husband touch you?"

Cecilia gasped. Mrs. Reginald turned sharply and pinned her with a steely stare. "Did Percy touch you?"

"No, of course not. Why would you say that?"

Visibly relieved by her answer, Mrs. Reginald returned to her chair and clasped Cecilia's hands. "I'm sorry, but I had to ask." She bowed her head as if in silent prayer.

"Leilani, I know something's been going on here since I arrived, but no one will tell me what it is. You need to tell me now. Please."

Mrs. Reginald hesitated. "Very well," she said with a nod. "But then you will tell me your reason for having to leave us so suddenly." At her employer's insistence, Cecilia agreed to the hard bargain.

Mrs. Reginald leaned back in her chair, her eyes fixed on Cecilia. "Percy grew up in the early 1900s, in a fanatical, fundamentalist Christian home. Through fire-and-brimstone lectures and regular beatings, my husband learned the wicked side of faith. In many ways, when his parents were killed in a car crash when Percy was only a young man, it came as a blessing. But it also unleashed the belligerence his father had whipped into him. Percy became his father, perpetrating his violence on the locals — particularly the women." She cast an uncomfortable look at Cecilia. "He believed all the local women were at his beck and call. They were for his pleasure, and if they refused, he raped them."

A ragged breath escaped Cecilia's mouth.

"He would call them to Hill Cottage where he lived and take advantage of them there. Most of this disgusting behavior happened before I was born. I'm twenty years younger than my husband, you know. But my family vowed to put an end to his abuse. And that would be me. I was raised to become his wife, to know his secrets and as such protect the women on Harbor Island."

"But this is terrible on so many levels. Aside from the crimes he committed on women, how could you marry a man who did those things? How could you have sex with him? How could you—"

Mrs. Reginald raised her hand halting the questions. "Cecilia, you don't understand. It wasn't about me. It was about the good for our community. Long before my time, in the kingdom of Hawaii, human and animal sacrifice was commonplace. It was performed as a way to appease wrathful gods. When the Reginald family bought this island in 1852, the local community's isolation from the rest of Hawaii meant they retained their old ways and religion. To a certain extent, the Reginald men became like gods, to be worshipped and feared. You must remember, my forebears were innocent people. They had no rights, and no one to protect them. I was born in 1922 and raised to be the sacrifice, metaphorically speaking, to appease Percy and protect our people. My role was to become a Reginald by marrying him, bear and raise children, and in doing so, change the future. And as strange as all this sounds, by the time I grew up and returned from college, and supported Percy in the housekeeper role, he'd stopped these crimes against my people."

"My God, you're amazing. You're the original feminist." Cecilia shook her head at the enormous sacrifice Mrs. Reginald had made. A sacrifice beyond imagination. Her mind began to piece together the strange events on Harbor Island since she arrived. "So, was it Mr. Reginald trying to get into my cottage when I first came here? Was he the cause of the noises in the night?"

Mrs. Reginald shook her head. "Oh no. He's seventy years of age and far too old to have any of those urges. Besides, as a God-fearing man, he still struggles to face his past demons. His gruff bravado belies a tormented soul."

Cecilia frowned. "Then what was making all the noises?"

"It was the staff."

"The staff?"

"Yes. I had no idea until I investigated further. Beatrice, Loretta, and their husbands were so concerned for your welfare, that they thought by scaring you to stay in your cottage at night, to keep your windows locked and install screens, you'd be safe in case Percy went on one of his old nightly prowls. The poor dears remember those awful days, many years ago, when Percy terrorized women. Even though their actions were misguided, they were only trying to protect you."

"They scared the hell out of me," growled Cecilia.

"Once I got to the bottom of it, I put a stop to it immediately. As I said, they are a simple, loving people and they try their best to protect the innocent in whatever way they can. When I discovered all this, I also made sure Percy stayed clear of you as much as possible, so the staff could see there'd be no return to the horrors of the past. Try to forgive them. You see, Percy is Beatrice's father."

"What?" Cecilia's hand flew to her cheek.

"He raped Beatrice's mother about fifty years ago. And Beatrice is the result of that terrible act. Poor Beatrice."

"Does she know?"

"Yes, as does most of the community. It's awful for her. She's angry and bitter because of it. But I make sure she and her family are well cared for. They will want for nothing for generations to come."

"Do Victoria and Dickie know any of this?"

"Heavens, no. They must never know. They find their father's puritanical behavior offensive enough as it is without knowing any of this. No, this secret must go to your grave with you, Cecilia. I'm only telling you this because you have demonstrated to me your trustworthiness. You must never tell anyone any of this. Agreed?"

She nodded. "So, does Mr. Reginald know that you know all this?"

"Oh, yes. Over time, I have used my knowledge to keep him in check — to reduce his acts of violence, like what nearly happened with Lucy, and to ensure the inheritance of Harbor Island goes to its rightful heir, my darling Dickie."

Cecilia rubbed at the needles pricking the back of her neck. "I knew this place had secrets, but what you've just told me is unbelievable."

"Every place, even paradise, has its secrets. Harbor Island is no different." Her face hardened. "Now, I have confided in you, and you must tell me why you have to leave us." Mrs. Reginald arched a brow. It was obvious she would not be stalled any longer.

Cecilia dragged in a nervous breath and held her employer's gaze. "I'm pregnant, Leilani. Dickie and I slept together, just once, and now I'm pregnant."

Mrs. Reginald's face fell. She looked like the life had been knocked out of her. "Are you sure?"

"I haven't had my period for over two months. Beatrice and Loretta guessed it when I got dizzy today. They tended to me at Hill Cottage, and there was no doubt in their minds. And to be honest, there's no doubt in mine." Cecilia wanted to close her eyes and pretend this was all a bad dream. But she knew it wasn't. Just as her mother had predicted, she had bitten off more than she could chew and now she had to live with the consequences.

A heavy silence descended on the office, its weight squeezing the air from the small room.

"I see." Mrs. Reginald's voice sounded cold, almost distant. It carried no hint of emotion. Cool, calm and collected she remained poised in her chair, obviously too shocked to speak.

"I'm so sorry, Leilani. The last thing I want to do is ruin Dickie's right to his inheritance. I love him too much to put that in jeopardy."

"But you don't love him enough to stay and marry him?" A hint of judgment laced her words. It was the poison on the tip of the arrow piercing Cecilia's heart.

"I can't marry him, Leilani. Dickie is gay." Any air left in the room was sucked away. Cecilia caught her breath as she watched a pained expression flicker across Mrs. Reginald's face.

"Go on," whispered Mrs. Reginald, a fine edge of sorrow in voice.

"He was going to tell you when Mr. Reginald dies, but considering the circumstances, I think you have a right to know now. I don't want you thinking that I'm just running away. I know it looks like that because that's what I've always done in my past when things got too tough. But I'm not. Our brief love-making proved to Dickie he really preferred men. There's no future here for me. Or for Dickie, if I stay. In fact, if I stay, it will only make matters worse. I'm so sorry." The emotion tickling her throat gathered momentum. She tried to stem the flow of tears and swallow the sobs. On both accounts, she failed.

"Thank you for telling me the truth, and all of the truth. I know how you feel about Dickie, and I can see in his eyes how he feels about you. I understand only too well how life can deliver a cruel blow to the best of us. I don't expect you to stay and live in a sham of a marriage. Times for that are over."

Cecilia accepted the handkerchief from Mrs. Reginald's trembling hand.

"But what about Dickie? Where are his rights in all of this? He is the father, after all."

"Oh, Leilani, I've struggled over this for weeks. Imagine what would happen if he knew. He's such an honorable young man. He'd want to stand up to his father and marry me. It would all end in pieces — disinheritance, a doomed marriage, an unhappy baby. No, I can't tell him. His destiny is here, on Harbor Island, following in his mother's footsteps. Like you, he has an inherent sense of duty to this island, and nothing must be allowed to stand in his way. Not me. Not a baby. Nothing."

"So, what do you plan on doing?" Mrs. Reginald's face pinched at the thought of the ugly reality.

"I'll go back to the mainland to have the baby and then I'll put it up for adoption. There's no way I can raise a child on my own, and there's no way my mother or father will have anything to do with me if they know I'm pregnant. After the adoption, I'll just have to get on with my life. I'm so sorry. I wish it could all be different."

Long moments passed while Cecilia's broken heart cleaved open with despair. She swallowed the endless tide of grief and took comfort in the expression on Mrs. Reginald's face. An expression of pure grit. She had experienced more pain than Cecilia could ever imagine. Meeting the older woman's determined gaze, Cecilia balled the handkerchief in her hand and composed herself. It was her turn to be strong.

"In Hawaiian, we call this *'a'ohe lanakila*. A situation, where no matter what choice you make, the outcome is painful. Although I hate the thought of losing my first grandchild, I agree with you, there is little alternative. Above all else, Harbor Island is what is at stake here. Dickie's legacy must come first." Cecilia sighed. Momentary relief washed over her. Mrs. Reginald's compassion and understanding made the terrible situation somehow more bearable. "Despite everything that's happened, I knew the moment I met you, you were the right person for the housekeeper's job. You have had Harbor Island's best interest in your heart from the start. I would have been very proud to have called you my daughter." A breath hitched in Mrs. Reginald's chest. "What are you going to tell Dickie and Victoria?"

"I'm not sure yet, probably about having to go home because of my parents. I'll write them a long letter each when I get back to the mainland."

"You know Dickie will be heartbroken, don't you?"

"I know, but so am I. We can be heartbroken together across the two thousand miles of ocean which separate us. But, there's no other way."

"I understand." A dark cloud of resignation passed across Mrs. Reginald's face.

"Will you look after Lucy? Make sure she's cared for, taken to the beach. I'm so upset about leaving her. Dickie gave her to me, and now I'm just abandoning her." Cecilia's voice broke, and she buried her face into the handkerchief.

"I will personally look after Lucy. Every afternoon, we will go to the beach, and I will send you prayers of comfort and kindness from Harbor Island."

"Oh, Leilani, I'm so upset. I'm about to give birth to a tiny baby, your grandchild, who we'll never know or hold. I'm just going to give that baby away forever. Oh, God, what am I to do?"

Mrs. Reginald clucked her teeth. "Cecilia, look at me."

Cecilia wiped her face with the damp handkerchief and straightened in the chair.

"As women, we make tough choices all the time. You chose to leave the world most young people live in and instead you chose adventure. And as I promised, you have had the biggest adventure of your life here on Harbor Island. Now, you choose to go off to other adventures. Some will be hard, some easy. Maybe one day, you'll make your dreams come true and become a professional singer. But through it all, your courage, resilience, and resourcefulness will grow. You will love and be loved. I believe you are destined to succeed, Cecilia Freemont. You are a woman who will achieve great things."

"Thank you, Leilani. And when I do, it will be because of everything you have taught me."

"Now, you must write to me. There is no need for you to go through all this alone. You must also call me 'collect' whenever you want to talk. You are my son's first true love, and I would like for us to stay in contact, if you like."

"Oh, yes, please. That would be wonderful."

Mrs. Reginald walked to the safe and withdrew a wad of cash. "You will take this with you. To help pay for expenses and to get you started on your new life. Do not refuse. I would view that as an insult to me, my son and my grandchild." She slanted a stern look at Cecilia, who smiled gratefully and accepted the money. "When would you like me to arrange with Smith to take you to Lahaina?"

"I'll work out this week and leave Sunday, if that's all right with you?"

"Of course, it is. I will miss you terribly." The waver in Mrs. Reginald's voice broke the tense atmosphere, and Cecilia flew into her arms, crying.

"Me too, Leilani. I love you."

"And I you, my dear daughter." They held each other close for a long time until Mrs. Reginald resumed her regal posture with a sniff. "Don't worry about what the staff will think or say, or Percy for that matter. I will handle everything. I'll make sure Beatrice, Loretta, and their husbands are silenced. No one will ever know the truth of your leaving. Like the other secrets of Harbor Island, it will remain buried forever. Now go, take Lucy to the cottage and have a good cry. I know I will. Aloha, *leo o ka anela.*"

Pursing her lips in a tight grimace, Cecilia nodded her thanks once more through blurred vision. She opened the office door and turned, emotion choking her words. "Aloha, Leilani."

But Mrs. Reginald didn't reply. She stood facing the window with her head in her hands, her body shuddering.

CHAPTER SIXTEEN

"Goodbye, Mr. Reginald. It's been a pleasure working here and singing in your services. Whether you believe it or not, I have listened to your sermons, and I might keep going to church when I get home." Cecilia struck out her hand, which to her surprise, the old man accepted.

"Despite our conflicting views on some matters, Cecilia, you have proven to be a sterling housekeeper. I know my wife and the staff will miss you. It's a shame your parents need you urgently back home. But family comes first. We understand."

She managed a meek smile before turning her attention to Mrs. Reginald. With no words left to say, she merely shook her head and hugged Leilani tight. "Thank you."

"Be strong, my dear. Be strong."

Bending down, Cecilia turned her affection to Lucy. Clearly, the dog sensed a change. She was confused and unsettled, her normally playful expression was replaced by a sorrowful look. Over the past nights, Cecilia had spent many hours explaining to her furry friend the reasons as to why she had to leave, but now, at crunch time, she disintegrated into tears. "Oh, Lucy, I'm going to miss you, girl." Muffled by the retriever's golden fleece, she sobbed her goodbyes. After a few moments, she struggled to her feet and wiped her eyes. She looked past Mr. and Mrs. Reginald who stood beside her on the jetty, to the crowd of staff milling on the path behind. Handkerchiefs dabbed eyes and waved in the harbor's afternoon breeze. "Goodbye, everyone. I'm going to miss you all," she cried, her heart shuddering in her chest. "You be good now." With a sniff, she strode to the edge of the jetty where Smith helped her down into the cruiser. He'd already packed two boxes filled with clothes and gifts she received as farewell presents onto the boat. Now, as she handed him her old tote bag, she noticed tears glistening in his eyes. "Not you too, Smith?"

"Sorry, Miss Cecilia. But me and Beatrice going to miss you. You be so good for the island, for the staff, for the family." Looking away, he swiped his cheeks and walked into the half-cabin to begin cast-off.

The engine rumbled to life and Smith's eldest son, Andrew, cast off the ropes from the jetty, while Cecilia sat on the aft seat. Shoving on her sunglasses and straw hat, she disguised some of the emotion but couldn't totally hide it. *Harbor Island II* pulled out from the ramshackle jetty, setting a slow course across the harbor. Just over seven months ago, she came to the island with a young woman's fantasies of adventure. She'd arrived seeking independence and freedom from her previous life. Filled with determination and dreams, she'd launched into a new job, a new family and a new life. Now, as she returned to Maui and then to the mainland, she took stock of what that desire for adventure had cost her. Instinctively, her hand went to her belly. *So, this was your adventure, Cecilia. To fall in love and then lose love?*

From the shore drifted a lilting melody sung by a familiar blend of voices she'd heard many times in the Sunday service.

She rose and stuck her head in the cabin. "What are they singing, Smith?"

"It's a traditional song of farewell. It wishes you love and success on your travels with the hope that one day you will return."

She moved to the guide rail, clasping both hands to her breaking heart. The crystal waters of the bay lapped against the gleaming hull of the boat as Smith steered it toward the reef break. Memories flooded back to the day she arrived and her embarrassment at being so seasick, how Beatrice had interrogated her in the Local Store and how she'd been saved by Victoria, her new best friend. A nostalgic smile tipped her lips as the ghosts of her recent past revisited. Watching the people she'd grown to love raise their voices in goodbye, she ignored the hot tears streaking her cheeks.

"I hope one day to return too," she said aloud, with another touch to her belly.

With mournful voices raised and arms waving white handkerchiefs, they sent her on her way. She would not forget these wonderful people or this place, or the soulful melody which was now etched into her memory.

Not until they became tiny specks on the shore did Cecilia finally sit down. Smith turned and waited for her instruction. She nodded, and he pushed forward on the throttle. Bright and new, *Harbor Island II* cut through the ocean waves. Long accustomed to the rolling and pitching of the waves, she no longer felt squeamish. She'd matured. For neither the ocean nor life's challenges held sway over her. Like *Harbor Island II* forging toward Lahaina, Cecilia was unstoppable in her purpose. Once more she turned away from the past. With jaw set, she faced into the stinging, salty wind, her chin lifted high, and like the cruiser, powered into her future. *This will not break me. I am more than this.*

END OF PART ONE

PART TWO

2017

TINA

CHAPTER SEVENTEEN

In contrast to the solemn reason for her visit, the magical mosaic of color tinged everything with its vibrancy. Around her, the ocean shimmered in shifting bands of luminescence as if overflowing with brilliant-cut sapphires. In the near distance, the beach's powdery white sand sparkled under the sun's blinding glare. While further behind the coastline grew the jungle, a dripping backdrop of rich, succulent green. Harbor Island reminded her of a giant Hawaiian goddess, its outstretched shores welcoming everyone into her comforting bosom.

Tina Templeton leaned over the ferry's railing and inhaled a bracing breath of sharp, salty air. The smell unlocked distant memories, transporting her back through long-forgotten years. Back to when she had come here during the summer school holidays when she was a young girl. What wonderful times she'd had then. *My happy place* was how she'd described it to her envious friends every time she had left Australia. Recalling the youthful enthusiasm that had inspired her those decades ago, she realized it had been some time since she'd felt that happy.

Her gaze drifted down from the approaching island, and she couldn't help but smile. Impudent dolphins played in the bow wave with reckless abandon, taunting her to join them. Snorting and laughing, they frolicked without a care in the world. Unlike Tina, their family pod rejoiced in the invigorating Pacific Ocean, while her family traveled individually over these waters on a more somber mission. Nearing the coral reef, the ferry slowed, navigating the deepest channel through which to enter the harbor without destroying the colonies of coral polyps. The skipper maneuvered the ferry skillfully and gave all onboard a unique view of the breathtaking ecosystem living under the crystal-clear waters. Tina turned her face into the gentle wind and reveled in its familiar touch. The shattered house of cards that was her life fluttered in the breeze's comforting caress. A sense of home awakened within her. Perhaps here, she would be happy again. Perhaps here, she could rebuild her life.

As always, waiting for her on the wharf was Uncle Dickie's housekeeper of over forty years. Andrew had been here even before Tina. A mainstay of his employer's household and life, Andrew's love for, and loyalty to, Uncle Dickie never wavered. About twenty years older than Tina, Andrew was in his late fifties and still possessed a strong, fit physique. Although his wiry hair had lost some of its Polynesian curl and had faded grey at his temples, the warmth and sincerity in his eyes remained the same. Normally, he greeted her with an expansive, welcoming smile and a long-arcing wave, but not today.

The small ferry pulled alongside the concrete wharf, scraping the tall cement pylons. A couple of ferrymen jumped down, tied off and then secured the gangway for the day-trippers. Being Friday, only a few dozen die-hard tourists were onboard. Parents with impatient children, couples seeking some secluded place for a romantic tryst, or artists with their easels venturing over to practice their painting, disembarked like a gaggle of clucking geese. Tina hung back, waiting for them to leave. Her gaze roamed the small dock as more fond memories tiptoed back. On the other side of the wharf stood the old boathouse, where Uncle Dickie kept his cruiser. Perched on top of a craggy outcrop, it was constructed of unpainted timber with a rough concrete slipway sloping into the harbor. The boathouse and its surrounds had been a favorite hiding place when she and her brother had played hide-and-seek down on the beach during their holidays here. But the best times were when she got older, and Uncle Dickie took her out in the boat. Together they'd circumnavigate the island, with him teaching her how to drive. She loved being in charge of the cruiser. As captain behind the wheel, she'd motor through the waves while her uncle delivered his passionate conservation message. He'd educated her on the island's unique environment, the integral relationship between fauna and flora, and how the nesting egret and sea turtle populations must be protected for future generations.

A whistle from one of the ferrymen pulled her from the past, shooing away her happy memories. It was time to disembark. Over her shoulder hung a duffel bag, packed with a few clothes, bathing suit, loafers, sandals, and toiletries. Knowing she could buy island wear from the Ladies Markets, she traveled light. In figure-hugging white capri pants, her athletic legs strode down the gangplank and up the wharf toward Andrew. Her breath hitched. The closer she drew, the more grief she noticed etched in his face. Behind her sunglasses, tears welled in her eyes, but she managed a brave smile. "Hello, Andrew. It's good to see you again."

"And it is good to see you, Tina. Please let me take your bag." Andrew's strong arm unburdened her shoulder. "The truck is just over here in the car park." He nodded in the direction of Harbor Island's only public car park, barely large enough to fit six cars. Not that anyone aside from those living on the island could bring vehicles across. The ferry was for pedestrian traffic only. That had been Uncle Dickie's stipulation when he'd negotiated with the Maui Visitors Bureau to allow a daily service to and from Maui to Harbor Island.

Arriving at the truck, Andrew threw her bag in the back and opened the door.

"How old is the Chevy now, Andrew?" She lifted her sunglasses to study the weather-worn Silverado, a melancholy smile twitching her lips.

"Going on twenty years." He traded a smile with her. "You know Dickie. He never liked to waste money on upgrading the property truck too often."

They shared a nostalgic chuckle over Uncle Dickie's thrift and clambered into the Chevy and set off.

The truck burbled slowly along The Esplanade with Andrew giving commentary. "Not much has changed since you were here last. Suzie Lin still owns the souvenir shop." He pointed to the garish shopfront closest to the wharf side of the street. Each vertical weatherboard plank dazzled a different color of the rainbow, giving the shopfront the appearance of being made from giant candy sticks. Brightly colored necklaces, picture frames, mugs, ashtrays and an assortment of other knick-knacks crammed the shop window. Crisscrossed over the door's threshold two large withered pandanus branches drooped, hardened by years of salt and sea spray.

Tina giggled. "Is Suzie as crazy as ever?"

"Crazier. Now, she's taken to concocting some sort of Hawaiian love potions." He sniggered under his breath.

"But she's not even indigenous Hawaiian, she's Chinese Hawaiian."

"Yes, but the tourists buy from her, and it subsidizes her living."

"What did Uncle Dickie say about her making and selling potions?"

"He gave her the native ingredients to make sure she didn't accidentally poison anyone. You know your uncle. Give someone a fish, and you feed them for a day. Teach them to fish, and you feed them for a lifetime."

As Andrew recited the philosophy by which her uncle managed Harbor Island, Tina swallowed hard. Although she hadn't seen Uncle Dickie for a few years, she loved him more than she had realized.

"Marty and Pat Henderson still run the Local Store, and they do whatever they can to help and support the local families." He nodded to the shop with the red door, in front of which half a dozen local children squatted on the pavement. Their laughing mouths and tongues worked overtime trying to eat their popsicles before they melted.

"Yes, I remember Marty and Pat. They never had any children, right?"

"No. But they've acted like pseudo parents to lots of the local kids. Most afternoons, they give the kids a free popsicle each. See?"

"And judging by their faces, they're a great hit, too."

Andrew tooted the horn and waved at the man strolling along the pavement. "Hey, Jacob. Look who I've got."

"Is that Tina?"

Leaning across the seat, she yelled past Andrew, "Hi, Jacob. See you up at the house."

"Sure will," he called with a wave. He turned and strode up to the lone petrol bowser rooted on the pavement in front of his mechanic's workshop.

"Did Jacob ever find a wife?"

"No, he's too much like Dad was, too absorbed in his workshop and engines. Anyway, after growing up with Mom shouting at us every minute of the day, neither of us was very keen on living with a woman. He stayed single and as for me . . ." Glints of copper flashed in his dark eyes.

"Yes, I know. You swing the other way." She reached across and slapped his forearm. Gripping tight for an instant, she added, "It's good to see you again, Andrew."

"And you too."

They drove on in the silence of mixed emotions — glad to be reunited and sad at what it had taken to bring them together again.

When the Chevy crested the hill, Andrew slowed to a stop at the top of the driveway. The view of the Reginald residence never failed to impress her. A massive, sprawling estate plucked from the pages of a

James A. Michener novel, it epitomized everything beautiful about the Hawaiian Islands. With its half a dozen bungalows, interconnecting pathways, and sumptuous gardens, it exemplified nature and man working in harmony.

She licked her lips and shot Andrew an anxious stare. "Who else has arrived?"

"Your stepmother and Sebastien are here. They arrived together yesterday."

"Who else?"

"Alan Rosenbaum, the lawyer is here. He motored over on his own boat this morning. "And there's one other. She'll be here when Jacob brings her over later."

"Who's that?"

"That's not for me to say. Alan's looking after everything. Come on. Let's get you settled in." Andrew drove the Chevy down the driveway and stopped on the gravel turning circle at the end. "I've got you set up in your usual bedroom bungalow, just here on the right. I'll take your bag in for you. Victoria and Sebastien are waiting in the great pavilion."

"Thanks, Andrew." Tina slid from the cabin, her white-sneakered feet touching down with a crunch. Giving her spiky, platinum-blonde hair a quick finger comb, she smirked in satisfaction. She'd cut off her hair in an act of defiance when she and David had divorced nearly a year ago. He had never liked women with short hair because they "weren't feminine enough". When she finally had enough of his macho ways and threw him out, followed by his precious Armani suits, she had stomped into the bathroom and hacked off her glossy honey-blonde tresses. Of course, she'd made a terrible mess of it. Not at all like in the movies when the heroines cut their hair, and it looked fashionista fabulous. Unfortunately, it took a couple of months before her hairdresser could salvage it into this sassy haircut, which she loved. And it proved perfect for traveling. A finger comb and voila!

She gave a sharp tuck of her red-and-white check blouse into her pants and squared her shoulders. Holding her head high, she walked up the steps surrounding the great pavilion and pushed through the gossamer curtains. Seated on one of the many sofas sat her stepmother and half-brother.

On seeing her, Victoria rose and stretched out her arms. "Oh, Tina I'm so pleased you made it. Really, I am." Normally, no one would ever think her stepmother was sixty-four years of age. Blessed by an exotic Hawaiian beauty, Victoria had barely been touched by the passage of time, but today those years had taken up a long-overdue residence on her face.

Tina's composure faltered somewhat, but she wrestled back control and strode into Victoria's arms. She'd been a loving step-mom to Tina since she was three years old. She'd married her widowed father not long after her mother had died. Over the years, it had been Victoria's counsel Tina had sought, particularly since her father's death two years ago. Without her support, Tina suspected she might never have summoned the courage to kick David out, despite his philandering. "How are you holding up, Vickie?"

"I don't think it's hit me yet. Not really. I can't believe Dickie's gone. He was only sixty-two. That's far too young." A rush of tears filled her eyes, and she dropped her head into her tissue-filled hands.

"Come on. Sit down." Tina assisted Victoria to sit down beside her on the sofa. She glanced to her right and nodded at her brother. "Hi, Seb, how are you doing?"

"I'm okay. You?" Like their father, Sebastien was a strong mountain of a man. But unlike Tina who'd inherited her mother's fair skin, fine features, and slender build, Sebastien had inherited Victoria's striking Hawaiian ancestry, giving him an almost godlike aura. Despite the obvious genetic differences, she and Sebastien were both tall of stature, stubborn by nature and determined to get their own way. Like any older sister and younger brother, they'd endured the normal sibling rivalry, which for Tina had toughened her to succeed as a woman in the man's world of television journalism, while Sebastien, still only thirty-two, was making his mark in property development.

On the sofa with Victoria propped in the middle of her two children, they sat in an awkward silence for a few moments, holding hands.

Tina leaned forward a little. "I'm sorry I couldn't make the funeral and cremation. I just couldn't get a flight here in time." Uncle Dickie's sudden death happened when she was returning from an overseas assignment. Caught in Denpasar airport in Bali, she couldn't change or divert flights no matter how much she's tried. Instead, she had to fly back to Sydney as scheduled and then fly to Hawaii. All of it had added days to the trip.

"That's all right, darling. None of us were prepared. I still expect him to walk through the curtains and say, 'Hey, Vic, want to go down to the beach?'" Burying her face in balls of twisted tissues, she sobbed as Tina and Sebastien rubbed sympathy circles on her shoulders.

"There, there, Mom. It'll be all right." Sebastien's big hand gripped his mother's shoulder.

"I know it will. It's just such a shock, that's all." Victoria rubbed her inflamed nose, sniffed and composed herself.

"I've brought you some iced tea." Andrew placed a tray of three ice-filled glasses on the coffee table.

"Andrew, you shouldn't be waiting on us. Sit with us. Please." Victoria extended her hand to a nearby armchair.

"Thank you." Andrew's red-rimmed eyes told of his own sorrow. "Poor Dickie, he'd just finished organizing the last of the garden clean-up and was packing away the tools with the groundsmen. He never let anyone do a job he wasn't prepared to do himself." A wistful smile trembled on his lips.

"He was always like that, even when he was young. No one was greater or lesser than. So, egalitarian was our Dickie." Victoria's face softened as she shared the memory.

"All I heard was the staff screaming and yelling. By the time I got to him, he was falling unconscious. I tried, but it was no good. There was nothing any of us could have done out here. Even if we were on Maui, unless we got him to emergency fast, he still would have died. The doctor said he died of sudden cardiac arrest." Andrew shook his head. "I've devoted over forty years of my life to that man. I'm not sure what I'm going to do without him." The pool of tears swimming in his eyes breached his lower lids and streamed down his cheeks. He swiped them with the back of his hand, but it did little to stem their flow.

"Oh, Andrew. I'm so sorry." Victoria rushed over, and they took comfort in each other for a few moments. She forced a thin smile and looked at her children. "Listen, why don't we all have a rest? Freshen up. Alan Rosenbaum wants to meet us all here at three o'clock for the reading of the Will."

"Good idea, Mom," said Sebastien. "I'll see everyone then." He rose and strode toward the back of the great pavilion in the direction of his bungalow. Even when he was a boy, he'd never been someone who showed his emotions. Tina suspected Uncle Dickie's untimely death applied salt to the yet unclosed wounds from their father's death only two years before. Ever since Dirk had died, Sebastien had retreated further in on himself. He'd become sullen, less communicative and quick to anger. No matter how Tina had tried to penetrate his defenses, she'd failed. His quick exit now reinforced her concerns over his emotional state.

"Tina?"

Directing a grateful smile at her stepmother, she stood and stretched. "I know I could definitely use a shower and a lie-down."

"Very good." Victoria nodded. "Come on, Andrew. You and I will go for a short walk around the gardens. See you at three, Tina."

Victoria and Andrew linked arms and exited one way, while Tina exited another, across the cool flagstone floor, through the curtains, and down the steps. She paused for a moment and scanned the Reginald residence. *Funny how life works out.* Here she was standing in a place she'd never have known had her father not married Victoria Reginald back in 1984. In that one ceremony, Tina had gotten a new mother, a new uncle, a new brother a few years later and a new future. Unlike many children whose parents remarry and their lives spiral into misery, hers had blossomed in the newly acquired family. She'd been one of the lucky ones.

A spasm clenched in her shoulders and chased away her fond musings. She'd just done back-to-back international flights, and her body screamed for rest. Strolling along the pathway to her bungalow, she breathed the fragrant smells of summer and sensed Uncle Dickie's presence all around her. From the garden flanking the pathway, delicate trails of vibrant dendrobium orchids caught her eye. *Uncle Dickie's favorite.* With numerous fuchsia-and-white flowers on each pea-green stem, they floated in dozens of suspended sprays.

See, Tina, they're too pretty to pick. Some things in life are so unique, we can only marvel at their perfection from a distance. Uncle Dickie had repeated this to her time and again, allowing her to gently cup the fragile stem of waxy orchids in her hand, careful not to bruise them. Now as she stooped to touch them, her hand hovered. Big, fat teardrops fell on the precious petals, and she pulled away. She dared not damage them, even with her tears. *From a distance . . .* The same as Uncle Dickie was now — from a distance.

Clogged with emotion, her nerves jangled. The best she could hope for was to freshen up, lie on the bed and meditate. Trudging to her bungalow, she knew sleep wouldn't visit her until much later, unlike her uncle, who walked beside her every step of the way.

CHAPTER EIGHTEEN

Tina jolted upright in bed. Confused as to the basics of time, place and circumstance, she shook her head. Her mind spun, trying to find traction. Everything slammed into focus when she grabbed her phone. *Shit, it's nearly three o'clock.* Dragging her legs into a pair of black trousers and shrugging on a ruffled black-and-white polka-dot silk blouse, she stepped into her black pumps. In the bathroom, she hurriedly speared her hair and swiped on some lipstick and blush. Frowning, she scrutinized her reflection and came up short. *Damn it. It'll have to do.* She barreled out of the bungalow and along the pathway to the great pavilion, where she took the steps two at a time. She sneaked in through the curtains, hoping not to draw attention. But as she appeared, forlorn faces turned to her as indication she'd failed. Mourning friends and staff milled around her, offering their sympathies.

"Tina, over here." With a slight scowl, Victoria waved her closer.

Even at thirty-eight years of age, she cringed. Her step-mom detested tardiness and today was the worst day she could have chosen not to be punctual.

Edging closer, she whispered, "I'm so sorry I'm late. I . . ."

Victoria squeezed her hand. "It's all right. We're still waiting on one other. Here, let me introduce you to Alan Rosenbaum."

She drifted beside Sebastien and Victoria, who introduced her to Uncle Dickie's lawyer. Not listening to the conversation, she glanced at the faces of friends from the town and staff she'd known many years before. Standing in solemn groups, the consensus of expression was one of incredulity. Uncle Dickie's death had taken everyone by surprise.

Crunching gravel quietened the hushed conversations as all eyes turned to the Chevy stopping outside the great pavilion. With the curtains fluttering, the onlookers only glimpsed the person Jacob helped down from the truck. Deft-footed, a woman walked up the steps and waited. In one flowing movement, she pulled aside the curtains. There was a gasp from those who knew her, and then the room stood still. Petite and immaculately groomed, she wore a rainbow-colored Camilla caftan sprinkled with crystals that matched those studded on her designer sandals. Under an enormous purple picture hat curled her long, golden hair, which cascaded over her shoulders. Her glamorous appearance seemed incongruent to the occasion, but there was no mistaking the sadness in her well-proportioned face. Hidden behind delicate sunglasses, her eyes were unreadable, but her posture spoke of a woman of substance; confident, in control and comfortable in her own skin. A sweet smile graced her glossed lips as she stepped into the great pavilion. The mourners parted like the Red Sea and chatted behind their hands as she glided toward Victoria. The two women faced off, fixing each other in a long, steady gaze.

"Victoria," said the woman in a soft, lilting voice.

"Cecilia. Thank you for coming." Victoria gathered her in a tight hug. They clung to each other for a long moment, obviously finding solace in the embrace. Finally, Victoria began the introductions. "Tina, Sebastien. This is Cecilia Freemont, a dear friend of mine and Dickie's. We go back a long, long time."

"Hello, Cecilia." Tina offered her hand, as did Sebastien.

"Lovely to meet you both. I've known your mother for many years, and she's kept me informed of what wonderful children you've been to her and your father, and of course, to your Uncle Dickie."

Before Tina had a chance to reply, Alan Rosenbaum cleared his throat. "Now that Ms. Freemont has arrived, if everyone would take their seats please for the reading of the Will." When the shuffling of feet and scraping of chairs finally settled, he continued, "Ladies and gentlemen, I will not read the entire document as this is a private matter for the immediate family." He nodded to the five of them seated in the front row. "However, I can confirm this is the last Will and Testament of Richard (Dickie) Reginald. He requested I read this specific section of the will today before all of you gathered here."

After adjusting his glasses, he projected his solemn voice through the great pavilion. "Regarding the land estate of Harbor Island, I leave this in its entirety to be shared equally between my niece, Tina Templeton and my nephew, Sebastien Templeton . . ." An audible gasp escaped Tina's mouth. ". . . on the proviso that they manage the island with the same commitment to protect its environment and its people as I have done during my stewardship." Tina was stunned. She shot a frown at Victoria whose mouth creased in a half-smile. *She knew.* Leaning forward, she looked at Sebastien. Pale-faced he stared back at her, shook his head and shrugged. *He's as surprised as I am.*

"In the matter of Andrew Smith, eldest son of Beatrice and Smith (both deceased), Harbor Island's long-term housekeeper and my devoted companion, I bequeath him the one acre of land on which stands his private home. He is no longer required to perform any duties on the island, unless he so chooses. His current financial remuneration is to be paid by Harbor Island for the rest of his natural life. On his death, his property will revert once more to the estate of Harbor Island." Soft sobbing fluttered up from Andrew, who slouched next to Tina. She patted his knee, and he clutched her hand in a tight squeeze.

"In the matter of my sister, Victoria Templeton (nee Reginald), I bequeath one million dollars." The whole room inhaled. Muffled voices rose and fell while Alan waited. "And Dickie asked me to say this directly to you, Victoria. To the best older sister a man could have, I promised I'd look after you, and I always keep my promises. I love you."

Victoria dissolved into tears.

"Finally, in the matter of Cecilia Freemont. Again, these are the words he specifically wanted me to say to you. My wonderful CiCi. You taught me how to fly, you taught me about being a man, about love and duty, and most of all, about being true to myself. I have missed you all these years, CiCi. I loved you then, and I always have." A chorus of soft moans and sniffles resonated in the great pavilion. Tina glanced sideways but couldn't see Cecilia's face. It was conveniently hidden by the enormous brim of her picture hat. But she did notice that the delicate hand which lifted a dainty handkerchief to her face, trembled. "For you, CiCi, I bequeath Hill Cottage. It is yours for the rest of your natural life, after which it will revert back to the estate of Harbor Island."

Excited whispers swirled around the great pavilion, while in the front row Andrew, Tina, Victoria, Cecilia, and Sebastien sat in stunned silence and stared into space. For Tina, she stared into another new, unexpected future. When she was young, and her father married into the Reginald family, her life changed in dramatic ways. Today, on inheriting the Reginald estate, she sensed a change of cataclysmic proportions taking place.

The lawyer removed his glasses and placed them on the table in front of him. Shuffling his papers, he allowed those present to chat among themselves for a few moments. "If I may have your attention please." He tapped his pen on the table until silence prevailed. "There are a few conditions to the aforementioned bequests which I will discuss with the interested parties in private. There are also some other minor bequests to people here today. I will speak to each of you before you leave this afternoon. That concludes the official reading of the will. Thank you all for coming. Victoria has informed me they will be serving refreshments here in the great pavilion to celebrate Dickie's life, and you are all welcome to stay."

Shell-shocked, Tina remained seated, while the animated whispers from the mourners behind the front row continued. Only when Victoria stood and approached Alan Rosenbaum did the tense atmosphere dissipate, giving rise to louder conversations. Sliding across into his mother's seat beside Tina, Sebastien said, "God. He left us the entire estate. Can you believe it?"

"I can't even believe Uncle Dickie is dead, let alone leaving us the island. Oh, Seb, this is too much—"

"I know. But we'll have to start thinking about it over the next day or two. We'll need a strategy and business plan moving forward. Harbor Island won't wait for us to procrastinate."

She pursed her lips. It was obvious her younger brother had wasted no time coming to terms with the great behemoth they'd inherited. He was already formulating plans for the island's future. That wild gleam in his eyes he always got when he started a new project proved it. But this was not a project. This was Harbor Island, and Uncle Dickie had left it to their care and protection.

"Alan would like to see us for a few moments." Victoria motioned to Tina, Sebastien, Andrew, and Cecilia to join her. Leaving the staff to set up for afternoon tea, they walked to Uncle Dickie's office. Subdued and speechless, each wore an expression of disbelief. Once inside, Alan closed the door. Victoria and Cecilia sat in the only two chairs available, while Tina and the men remained standing.

"I need to advise you of the conditions Dickie has placed upon his will bequests. For those of you who have received property or estate bequests, if, at any time, you are arrested or convicted of a criminal act, your bequest will be rescinded. The estate or property will be reclaimed immediately, and you will vacate said property or estate. Therefore, although you have received these property or estate bequests, they will remain in the name of Harbor Island, securing them always to the proprietary limited company."

"So, Tina and I never own Harbor Island?" asked Sebastien, looking peeved.

"Legally, not at this time. You've inherited a half share each of the estate, with certain provisos of how it must be managed. On fulfilling those provisos and over a specified time, you'll become the sole directors of the estate's proprietary limited company. Eventually, this will then pass onto your children or beneficiaries at the time of your death. As Dickie's lawyer, it's my ongoing duty to ensure his will is executed as per his wishes. I'm here to help you all through this process."

"Thank you, Alan. I'm sure no one will have trouble staying on the right side of the law or in complying with Dickie's wishes," said Victoria, rising royally from her chair. She stood beside the lawyer and addressed the group. "Dickie's will is a lot to digest, and I'm sure you'll have many questions. But now isn't the right time to be discussing business. I suggest we all go back to the great pavilion and celebrate my brother's life and his achievements. Tomorrow we'll scatter the ashes as he wished. After which, we can get down to the business of securing Harbor Island for the future generations to come." Flourishing her arm toward the door, she closed the conversation. They filed out like dutiful schoolchildren and wandered back to the other mourners enjoying afternoon refreshments.

"I'm so pleased to finally meet you, Tina." Cecilia Freemont removed her sunglasses and fell in step beside her. From beneath the brim of her hat, a pair of glittering green eyes looked up at her.

Tina's first impression of the woman was that she was kind. Though the vague air of mystery surrounding her tickled Tina's journalistic curiosity. "Thank you, Cecilia. I'm sorry, but Vickie never mentioned you. Since you were so close, and obviously Uncle Dickie thought the world of you, I wonder why they never said anything to Seb or me?" They reached the refreshment table, and Tina offered to pour a cup of tea for Cecilia, which she accepted.

"Time has a funny way of transforming friendships. I'm sure you've lived enough of life to know that." She raised a sculpted blonde eyebrow. "There are some friends you may not see for years, and yet, when you meet up again, you pick up where you left off. Victoria, Dickie and I were like that."

"Still, it's strange that neither of them mentioned you all these years." After passing her some biscuits, Tina helped herself. Realizing she hadn't eaten for sixteen hours, she devoured the first biscuit within moments.

"Victoria tells me you've been the daughter she always wanted."

"Vickie is a very special lady. She's been the best step-mom. And what about Uncle Dickie leaving her the million dollars?"

"It doesn't surprise me one bit. Dickie always said he'd look after his sister, and he did. Your uncle was a man of his word." Her eyes blurred with pooling tears. Blinking, she set her cup and saucer on the table and dabbed at them with her handkerchief.

"I'm sorry, Cecilia. Forgive me. Would you like to sit down?"

"No, my dear. I think I'll just go for a walk in the gardens alone. Reminisce for a while on the wonderful times we had together. I'll see you a little later on." She slid on her sunglasses and floated across the great pavilion.

"Who is she?" Sebastien sidled next to Tina.

"To be honest, I have no idea. But she was terribly close to Vickie and Uncle Dickie. Don't you think it's odd that we've never heard of her before?"

Sebastien shrugged. "Maybe. But Mom and Uncle Dickie had a really close bond. Maybe Cecilia was part of that. Who knows?" Another shrug. "Anyway, knowing you, Tina Templeton, investigative reporter, you'll find out the truth." He snorted and gave her a cheeky grin.

"Oh, very funny, Seb." She nudged his ribs. "But you're right. I will get to the bottom of this." She frowned as she watched the mystery woman disappear through the curtains. "I guess we better go mingle and help Vickie. Come on." Linking her arm through his, she steered them into the crowd.

CHAPTER NINETEEN

At the end of Uncle Dickie's wake, people drifted away, offering final condolences with their goodbyes. With dusk encroaching, Andrew drove the last of the mourners back to town, while Victoria and Tina helped the staff clean up. Sebastien retreated to his bungalow to check emails, while Cecilia ventured back to the garden to rest on one of the white Adirondack chairs under the plumeria tree.

"Thank goodness that's over." Victoria sighed and gathered the last of the side plates.

Tina reached over and clasped her hands. "Come on. Leave that. The staff can finish off. Why don't you sit down for a minute?" She guided her to a comfy sofa and dragged over a couple of footstools on which to hoist their legs.

"Oh, that's better. It's not until you get your feet up that you realize how much they hurt." A grateful smile graced Victoria's face, and she leaned back into the sofa with a long stretch.

"I agree. Nothing like getting your legs horizontal." Tina exchanged a smile with her step-mom and gave her hand an affectionate squeeze. "It's all very strange, I must say. Uncle Dickie leaving Harbor Island to Seb and me. I take it you knew all about it?"

Victoria angled a glance at her and grinned. "Yes. Dickie discussed it with me many times. I thought it was a good idea. But of course, no one expected it all to happen this soon. But it is what it is." She shrugged.

"Inheriting the island certainly throws our lives into disarray. I mean, are we supposed to live here now? I doubt Seb will want to do that. And to be honest, I don't know if I do either."

"Dickie knew that asking you both to manage the island was a big call, but there was no one else young enough, strong enough or smart enough to do it. Since he never had any children of his own, you were his heirs. He so wanted to keep Harbor Island in the family. Now, it passes from the Reginald to the Templeton name." Pride spread across her face. "Dickie loved you, regardless of whether you were blood or not. Remember how he used to put it?"

"Just because you're not blood, doesn't mean you're not loved." Tina recalled her uncle with deep affection.

"And that's why he wanted you and Sebastien to have equal shares in the estate."

"But you know as well as I do, and I'm sure Uncle Dickie knew, Seb and I have conflicting views on most things. Finding common ground on managing the island will not be easy." She rubbed at the creases on her forehead.

"Yes. Dickie was well aware of that. His whole life he was duty-bound to this island, and he hoped at least one of you would feel the same. I know it won't be easy."

"But what he's really done is given two dogs one bone."

"Indeed, he has." Victoria patted her knee.

For a few moments, Tina pondered the situation. Aside from the obvious difficulty of her and Seb finding any consensus on a stewardship strategy, the issue of on-site management further complicated the matter. Without consistent and committed hands-on leadership, the future looked shaky for Harbor Island. "Maybe Andrew will manage everything when Seb and I can't be here?"

"Perhaps," said Victoria, sounding unconvinced.

"You are no help at all," Tina scolded in a playful tone. "This isn't going to be straightforward."

"I know. But you're stubborn, passionate and opinionated — and you love a challenge. Look at what you've already achieved in your life. Award-winning investigative journalist, traveling the world on dangerous assignments, reporting on places and situations most people would avoid. Managing Harbor Island will be a cake-walk for you." She reached over, squeezed Tina's leg and winked.

"Well, if that's the case, you better tell me about Cecilia Freemont. Who is she and why have you kept your friendship a secret all these years?" Tina swiveled in her chair to face Victoria, intent on getting the answers she sought.

"If you want to find out about Cecilia I suggest you ask her."

Tina narrowed her eyes in demand of an answer.

"Very well," Victoria conceded. "Cecilia Freemont was a well-known nightclub singer in America for many years. She played the cabaret circuit, released some records and made quite a name for herself. We met over four decades ago when she came here to be the housekeeper. And we've been friends ever since, although we don't often see each other." With a firm nod, Victoria stared her down, signaling that was the most she would divulge.

"She must have been good." Tina used her best nonchalant tone.

"She was. A real talent."

"And she never married?" she coaxed, digging a little deeper.

"Right. That's it." Victoria threw up her hands. "You're still the craftiest person I've met. I am not one of your informants on speed dial. If you want to know more about Cecilia, you'll have to ask her yourself." She pushed to her feet and gave a heavy sigh. "I'm off to bed." Melancholy shadowed her face. "I missed your father so much today. Time to meet him in my dreams."

Tina stood. "Forgive me, Vickie. Today must have brought back lots of sad memories. I miss Dad too."

"I know. We all do. Now, why don't you go and help Cecilia up to Hill Cottage? I think she's still sitting outside." Victoria pressed a kiss to her cheek. "I'll see you in the morning."

"Good night, Vickie. Thanks for the chat."

"You're welcome." After a quick hug, she turned and walked away. One of the female staff who Tina hadn't met, ran to escort Victoria to her bungalow.

Even this simple act of devotion illustrated the responsibility she and Seb had just inherited. *All these people who depended on Uncle Dickie and Harbor Island for their livelihood are now going to depend on Seb and me.* She shuddered at the thought.

Outside, the fading light tinged the property in a honey-colored haze. Rather than vivid and vibrant, nature's colors waned to softer, muted tones. Like a mother cuddling her child, readying the little one for sleep, dusk cradled the property in its protective embrace. She strolled over to where Cecilia sat, legs extended on the spongy grass, head reclining on the back of the chair. On her approach, Tina strained to see whether Cecilia had fallen asleep. With her large-brimmed hat resting in her lap, she looked a picture of composed, island elegance. Pausing for a moment, Tina studied the fine structure of the older woman's face: high cheekbones, pert nose, and cupid-bow lips. In her younger days, Cecilia would have been described as a pretty girl. Now obviously in her sixth or seventh decade, her prettiness hadn't diminished, only matured.

Cecilia turned her head, a gentle smile lighting her face. "Tina, will you help me up." She lifted her delicate hand and waited for assistance. "I used to love sitting out here with Leilani. We'd talk and chat about so many things. She was a great woman, your grandmother."

"I was only thirteen when she died. I don't remember her much, but from what I understand, I think Uncle Dickie took after her a lot. I would have liked to have known her longer."

"Yes. Dickie was very close to his mother. She adored him. But everyone adored your uncle. He was an easy man to love. Come. Will you help me up the stairs to Hill Cottage, my dear?"

"Of course." Tina ushered her across the lawn. "What about your bags?"

"Andrew's already taken them up. I remember him as a young man of fifteen when he and his brother Jacob tied off the boat the first day I arrived here. Who would have thought he and Dickie would have formed such a long-lasting relationship?"

"It's obvious Uncle Dickie thought the world of you, too, since he left you Hill Cottage. Do you think you'll move here to live?"

"I have no idea. I have my friends and my life in San Francisco. I'm sixty-nine years old. I'm not sure I want to move all the way out here. But Harbor Island has always held a special place in my heart. We'll see."

On reaching the bottom of the steps leading to Hill Cottage, Cecilia stopped. "The last time I walked these steps, I was a young woman of twenty-five. Dickie and I used to race each other to the top. We had such fun back then." A sad nostalgia shrouded her. "Oh, how I've missed him."

Tina watched the tiny tears trickle down the older woman's face, and she sniffled back her own emotion. "Me too. I miss him."

Cecilia straightened. "Well, at least the steps are all cemented and level now. They even have a handrail. That makes it easier for an old woman like me." Looking up, she flashed a humble smile.

"I don't think there's anything old about you at all."

"Thank you, my dear." She stepped onto the first stair. "And if I'm not mistaken, there are twenty-six stairs. He's a wicked man, your uncle, leaving me Hill Cottage." Mischief flickered across her finely-lined face. Matching the older woman's ironic smile, Tina escorted her through the jungle corridor up to the quaint lavender cottage high on the hill.

* * * *

Although Tina had been back and forth occasionally to the island over the past decade, the last time she'd swum in the unspoiled waters of the harbor had been nine years ago, just before she and David had married. Full of youthful romanticism, she'd brought him over to meet Uncle Dickie, eager for her uncle's approval. But he'd not been that impressed with her choice of prospective husband. "He's not smart enough for you, Tina. You deserve someone with more intellect and ambition," he'd said. *Uncle Dickie had been right.* But she'd been goo-goo-eyed over David, entranced by his suave personality and good looks. *How silly and immature I was then.* Still, the marriage had been fun at the beginning, until David became resentful of her career, the travel it entailed and her growing celebrity status. But the one thing Uncle Dickie had insisted she do, since she was so hell-bent on marrying the gorgeous stockbroker, was to keep her prenuptial estate separate. And she had followed his advice. With her little unit in Sydney now worth over two million dollars and her investment portfolio worth more, when Tina had quit the marriage, she had retained a strong financial position. On the divorce settlement, she had accepted an equal share without surrendering her prior private assets. Now, she'd need every ounce of her uncle's financial savvy to generate the future wealth Harbor Island required.

"Tina," called Sebastien, jolting her from her thoughts. "Mom's about to start."

She hurried down to join the group at the water's edge. From north to south, the beach traced the harbor in a near perfect semi-circle of flawless, crystallized quartz. Because of Uncle Dickie's conservation and maintenance efforts, its condition remained unspoiled. As the cool, fine sand slid between her toes like ribbons of silk, she longed for more time to appreciate it. With the sun still waking, the harbor languished; a sleeping giant rousing for another day's work and play. The waves stirred the beach and revived it with their never-ending rhythm, while discordant seagulls squawked and circled overhead, their beady eyes looking for breakfast. Tina glanced back over her shoulder. Lined along The Esplanade, dozens of staff and friends watched on, respectful of Uncle Dickie's last wish. Only the immediate family, Andrew, and Cecilia were to be present for this final goodbye. But still, the rest came to stand sentinel.

Ankle-deep in the chilly harbor waters, Victoria gripped the urn close to her heart. "It was Dickie's wish for his ashes to be cast into the harbor, and for the five of us to be present." She acknowledged each of them with a grateful smile. "Andrew, I'll let you swim out and scatter them after I read this small tribute Dickie wrote:

"My ship has sailed, but do not mourn for me. I leave with the wind in my sails, the sun on my face and the moon to guide me. Some may say I have gone, but I have merely left this glorious harbor. I embark on a new adventure, across a vast unknown ocean to a new port. You may be saying farewell, but there are others who are welcoming me. I live on and will return one day and welcome you to join me."

Each of them lingered, misty-eyed and gazed out to sea, lost in their own thoughts. After a few minutes, Andrew claimed the urn and strode out through the waves. Once through the small, early-morning breakers, he side-stroked into the swell and spent a quiet moment alone. He lifted the urn and upended it. Then, the outgoing tide swept Uncle Dickie's ashes toward the reef. Tina clutched Victoria's hand as she stared across the harbor watching the imaginary ship set sail. A gentle peace settled on her as a similarly gentle breeze caressed her neck. *He is gone. He is gone.* Behind her, voices sang a forlorn melody, which drifted down the beach. She turned and saw the staff, arms and handkerchiefs waving, as they sang a Hawaiian farewell to their employer and for many, a good friend.

In unexpected harmony, another voice joined in. Cecilia launched herself vocally onto the breeze, her hands clasped across her heart. That such a petite body possessed such a powerful, melodic and emotive voice brought fresh tears to Tina's eyes. Tiny prickles of gooseflesh chased each other all over her body, and a deep sadness claimed her. The sheer emotion Cecilia expressed when she sang rented Tina's heart. By the time Andrew returned and rose from the shallow waters, the song dissipated on some unspoken cue and nature's symphony reigned supreme once more in the harbor.

Forcing a stiff smile, Victoria held firm to Tina and clasped Sebastien's hand. "Now, we look to the future. We have a lot to do, and it's time to start." In determined strides, she began to march up the beach, Tina and Sebastien beside her and Andrew following close behind with the empty urn. Casting a backward glance, Tina watched Cecilia standing at the water's edge.

Wrapped in a dress of sunshiny yellows and lemons, she looked so small and alone. Like a child forgotten on the beach, she gazed out to sea as the wind played with the golden curls trailing down her back. Slowly, she stepped further into knee-deep water, the hem of her dress swirling around her like cotton candy. She tilted her head and removed the cluster of plumeria flowers tucked behind her ear. She paused and kissed the soft petals before offering them to the waiting waves. After a few moments, her tiny floral tribute found the current and was carried out to the reef. Cecilia remained in the waves, a solitary figure staring wistfully out to sea.

Tina watched and waited. *She may look small and alone, but she knew love here at Harbor Island.* She felt certain of that.

CHAPTER TWENTY

The next morning, and in an attempt to brighten everyone's spirits, Tina invited Victoria, Sebastien, Andrew, and Cecilia to join her at the Harbor Island diner. They gathered at a cozy table, tucked under a window with a sweeping view of the harbor. Its outlook had the desired effect. Light-hearted chit-chat replaced the previous day's sad conversation.

"So much has changed since I was here over forty years ago. Dickie always had a grand vision for Harbor Island. It's wonderful to see he achieved it," said Cecilia, in between sipping the foam off her cappuccino.

"Yes, he certainly did." Victoria waved over two young women with bright smiles and fresh faces. "These are the owners of the diner, Melody and Veronica Poppenpeck. Their mother was Hawaiian, hence their beauty." The sisters giggled. "And their father was an English sailor." Victoria introduced the women, giving everyone a quick family history. Tina figured they were not much younger than her. Strong, fit and obviously educated, they'd turned an ordinary diner into a smart establishment situated on The Esplanade with magnificent harbor views. Painted in a palette of blues, offset by shabby-chic white tables and chairs, the diner exuded an upbeat, friendly atmosphere. Though it served only basic food for breakfast and lunch, the place bustled. About eight locals perched at the counter, resembling birds roosting on an electric power line, while bronzed yachties occupied the tables, hoeing their way through plates of hot pancakes and syrup.

"What made you want to open up a diner?" Sebastien switched on his usual playboy charm. Tina rolled her eyes and watched her brother make a move on the girls. She looked away in annoyance, and Cecilia caught her eye and grinned.

"Oh, it was Dickie's idea, really." Dressed in short shorts and a cut-away white singlet, Melody's toned body rippled with corded muscles. "He wanted us to stay on the island after we graduated our hospitality training. So, he helped us with a deposit and the construction of the diner. We're still paying him back." Scowling, Veronica jabbed her sister in the ribs. "Oops, sorry. We're still paying *you* back." Melody nodded in deference to the two new owners.

"Well, I'll come down over the next few days, and we can discuss this outstanding loan. See what we can do about it." Sebastien's sly grin reminded Tina of the big, bad wolf in the fairy tale.

Giggling, Melody and Veronica returned to the service counter. Before Tina had a chance to admonish her brother for his blatant display of sexism, a familiar voice crooned beside her ear.

"Well, if it isn't Tina Templeton."

Startled, she inclined her head upward and studied the craggy-faced man leaning over her, looking like another wolf. Finding confirmation in his piercing pale-blue eyes, salt-and-pepper hair, tanned skin, and athletic physique, she managed a polite smile. "Rod Fischer."

"At your pleasure. I heard you were back. Sorry I couldn't make the wake yesterday, but I had some work that couldn't wait. Geez, it's good to see you." He squeezed her shoulders, and she flinched. Not waiting for an invitation, he seconded a nearby chair and squashed in next to Tina.

She shuffled her chair over, making sure to avoid eye contact. "Ah, Rod, you know Andrew and Vickie, of course. This is my brother, Seb, who you probably haven't seen for a while."

"How're you doing, Seb?" Rod reached across the table and pumped Sebastien's hand in three brisk beats.

"Pretty good thanks, Rod."

"And this is Cecilia Freemont, a friend of Uncle Dickie's and Vickie's." She flourished a hand in Cecilia's direction.

"Pleased to meet you, ma'am."

"And you, young man." She didn't offer her hand. Tina suspected she didn't want to be caught in his boisterous grip. Although blessed with above-average good looks and a charming smile, Rod could be boorish at times. And this one was of them.

"And what is it you do here on the island, Rod?" asked Cecilia in a sweet, old-lady kind of way.

"Oh, I've been here since I was about sixteen." He tossed a cheeky glance at Tina. "Dickie hired my dad to do a lot of the construction work in town, and I came over with him. Dad died a few years ago, but I stayed on. You know how it is. Harbor Island gets in your blood." Like a politician trying too hard to win over his constituents, Rod chortled stiffly.

Cecilia asked again, "But what is it you do on the island, Rod?"

"I'm a bit of a jack-of-all-trades, actually. I work on the bigger projects of road, wharf and building construction and maintenance. And whenever the tourists are here, I keep an eye on them to make sure they don't do any damage around the place."

"You're a bit like a park ranger, then?" She raised her brow.

"Yeah, I guess you could say that." He rubbed his bristled chin.

"You must know every inch of the island if Dickie entrusted you to protect it."

"I guess so. I hadn't thought of it like that before. But after all these years, I guess I do." He turned to Victoria, his tone hushed. "Sorry to hear about your brother, Victoria. Dickie was a good man."

"Thank you, Rod. Yes, he was."

Brightening once more, he grinned at Tina and Sebastien. "I hear you two have inherited the island." He whistled long and low. "I hope there's still a job for me?" Again, the stilted guffaw.

"I wouldn't worry about anything at the moment, Rod. Harbor Island will maintain the status quo until Seb and I go over everything." This time Tina answered before her brother had the chance. This joint ownership promised to be a tussle of wills.

A prickly silence fell on the family, which Rod either missed or ignored. Instead, he stared at Tina, happiness pasted on his face.

"Does anyone want anything else?" Melody sashayed over, batting her eyelashes and directing a naughty smile at Sebastien.

"No thanks, Melody. That's all for now." Andrew's mouth twitched a grimace, and he stared at her, hard. Without another word, she cleared the crockery quick smart.

Rod scanned the group with the look of an excited puppy. "I've got an idea. Why don't you all come down to the boathouse? Dickie replaced the cruiser last year, and she's a beauty. After all, she's part of the assets of the island and your inheritance." He winked at Tina.

"Why not?" Sebastien rose godlike from the table. "I'll walk down with you. Andrew can drive the ladies."

Tina shook her head. Cecilia leaned over and whispered into her ear, "By the look on Rod's face, he'd much prefer to walk down with you to the boathouse."

"Probably," Tina groaned, her mouth compressing in annoyance. "We were teenage lovers, and I don't think he's ever gotten over it."

"He's never gotten over you, that's for sure." A mischievous smile lit Cecilia's face.

Narrowing her gaze on the older woman, Tina chuckled. "Now, I understand why Uncle Dickie loved you so much. You're as astute and quick-witted as he was."

Inclining her head, Cecilia grinned like the Cheshire cat while offering her hand to Tina for assistance.

* * * *

"It is a beauty." Tina ran her hand over the gleaming white surface of the hull of *Harbor Island V*. Spanning most of the thirty-six feet, a polished toffee-colored timber cabin housed the wheelhouse and snug sleeping quarters below, leaving a small aft deck for passengers. In dry dock, the vessel was flanked by a timber gantry adjacent to the forward, port and starboard sides of the cruiser. No gantry enclosed the stern. It faced the boathouse's huge barn doors, which when opened, gave the boat access down the concrete slipway into the harbor. "Simply beautiful."

"She certainly is," said Sebastien. "Mom, have you seen this boat before?"

"No. But it's the same make of boat as all the others Dickie had. And the same as our father had. It's become a bit of a tradition since 1974 to replace each boat with the latest model and keep *Harbor Island* as its namesake. They're hand-built, well-crafted vessels." She turned to Andrew and added, "I remember how much your father enjoyed driving these boats, especially when the new one arrived."

"Yes. He was meticulous when it came to looking after them. Jacob and I did the heavy lifting while Dad got all the easy jobs." A good-natured chuckle accompanied the memory.

"Yes, I remember Smith yelling at you boys to tie off the boat or unpack provisions," said Cecilia.

"Well, this one looks hardly used. How many times did Uncle Dickie take her out?" Tina leaned over to inspect the underside of the hull.

"Maybe half a dozen times since he'd had her."

"What's happened with her over the past year, then?" On tiptoe, Sebastien tried to peer over the side rail.

"Not a lot. I've taken her out a few times to run the engine. But aside from that, she's not been used much at all."

"Well, we'll have to change that," declared Tina, hoisting herself into the boat in one bounding leap.

"Be careful, Tina," said Victoria, a hint of concern in her voice.

"Oh, Vickie, don't worry about me. I've parachuted out of planes, repelled down cliffs and gone on recon missions with the SAS guys. Besides, Uncle Dickie taught me how to skipper these cruisers years ago. I know my way around a timid thirty-six-footer." Ignoring the blinking faces of those standing on the gantry, she turned and strode into the cabin to study the instrumentation. Within moments, Rod hovered beside her, answering her questions. After a few minutes of crash instruction, she paced back to the aft deck. "I'm going to take her out. Who wants to come?"

"I'm in." Sebastien hoisted himself onto the boat. "Come on, Mom. You'll love it. It's the perfect time of day before it gets too hot."

Victoria exchanged an impish grin with Cecilia and shrugged. "Do you remember what Dickie used to say? The madhouse?"

"I most certainly do." Cecilia giggled like a school girl.

"We're in," called Victoria. "Help Cecilia and me onboard."

"Go around the back, Vickie. Andrew can give you a shove up. Seb, go help them."

"Aye, aye, Captain." Sebastien saluted in mock obedience. "Give that woman anything she can take charge of, and she will," he muttered.

"I heard that," she called over her shoulder. "Okay, Rod. Walk me through this. How long's it been since the engine kicked over?"

"I started the engine last month, and the batteries are charged. But you're gonna want to kick her over now before we hit the water."

Tina opened the compartment to the left of the helm and thrust in her hand. On finding what she sought, a radiant smile lit her face. She retrieved a shabby blue-and-white cap with Harbor Island emblazoned on the front of it. Chugging it on her head, she turned to her passengers. "I was hoping Uncle Dickie still kept his cap in the same place. He used to always wear this whenever we went out. When I captained the boat, I got to wear it." She poked her tongue at Sebastien. "See. I am the rightful captain."

"Yeah, yeah, yeah," he said with a roll of his eyes.

Resuming her duty, Tina turned the key in the ignition and the diesel engine kicked over. Letting it run for about thirty seconds, she raised her voice to be heard. "She's purring like a kitten, Rod." She reversed the key and shut it off. "Now what?"

He passed her a hand-held remote control. "Everything is operated from this one device. No need for any manual labor." As he showed her how it worked, she studied the control and repeated each button's functionality to herself.

"Got it." She paced to the others milling on the aft deck. "Okay, everyone. Grab a seat. It'll take a minute or two to lower the boat and then we're off."

"Are you sure you know what you're doing?" Sebastien flashed a sarcastic sneer.

"I've had a boat license for years, but if you don't think I'm capable of skippering this vessel, you don't have to come with us. You can go back to the diner and flirt with the Bobbsey Twins if you like." She chuckled and shot him a challenging stare, while the others sniggered at her caustic humor.

"It's not me I'm thinking about. What about Mom and Cecilia?"

"Seriously?" asked Tina, bemused.

"I have every confidence that she knows what she's doing," interjected Victoria.

"And I second that. Sail on, Captain," cheered Cecilia, waving her hand in the air.

Andrew chose not to comment, but the irony creasing his face demonstrated his vote of confidence in Tina.

"Okay, then. No more bagging the captain, otherwise, she'll order her first mate to chuck you overboard." She scowled at Sebastien before striding back into the wheelhouse.

"Let's do it, Rod." She cast him a cautionary look, signaling she wouldn't tolerate a sexual innuendo from him.

With the flick of a button, she opened the huge, double barn doors behind them. She expected to hear lots of wear-and-tear groaning from the salt-rusted hinges, but they were noiseless. "Boy, you must have them greased up?"

He nodded. "Yeah. Much better with lots of lube."

On seeing the salacious look on his face, she shook her head. "Seriously, Rod. You need to get a life and stop thinking about the past. We had a brief teenage love affair for a month."

"I know, but—"

"But nothing. It's been over for twenty years. The end." She punched the bottom right button, and the electric winch whirred into action. The launching trolley which carried the one-ton vessel began a slow, effortless descent down the slipway toward the waves. A rush of excitement coursed through her veins as a glorious, sun-kissed day beckoned. When the stern drifted in the water, she turned over the engine. *Harbor Island V* came to life. Obeying her skillful touch, the cruiser wheeled. She thrust it into forward, and the cruiser slipped through the jewel-bright blue waves at a moderate pace.

"I know it's high tide, Rod, but where's the deepest channel to get out through the reef?"

He pointed to starboard, just off-center. "There. See?"

She steered in the general direction, checking with her depth-finder and GPS. Funny how after all these years, the skills she'd learned from Uncle Dickie flooded back. Reflecting on how much time she'd spent on her school vacations cruising around the island with her uncle, she realized it had been Dickie who had unreservedly nurtured her love for adventure. Unlike her parents whose anxiety stifled some of her daring-do characteristics, Uncle Dickie had encouraged her to take calculated risks and leap into life with gusto. In her uncle, she'd found a soul mate. No wonder the other men in her life had fallen short. On some level, she probably had compared them to her intelligent, resourceful and inspirational uncle. He'd been a hard act to follow.

As her confidence grew, she pushed forward on the throttle, increasing speed. Cruising through the channel toward the reef, she inhaled a long breath. The smell of salt tickled the tiny hairs in her nostrils as its taste seasoned her tongue. Being on the water nourished her soul. She wished she'd visited Harbor Island more often over the past years. Perhaps she would have handled life's challenges with more compassion if she had? One thing she knew for sure, being on the water cleared her mind and liberated her emotions. Here she felt free and alive.

Glancing back at the passengers, she shouted, "Everyone okay?" A duet of happy voices, a begrudging smile from Sebastien and a thumbs-up from Andrew confirmed all was ship-shape. "Okay. Hold on. I'm going to cut through these waves and go out in deeper water.

Let me know if anyone feels seasick, and I'll slow down. Hang on."

Giving it more throttle, she unleashed the engine's horsepower, and the cruiser launched. Heading due east beyond the semi-circular reef, *Harbor Island V* set off on its first mission under the control of its new owner. *Thank you, Uncle Dickie, thank you.* Unexpectedly, tears pricked her eyes as she steered the boat into the mid-morning sun. *I will make you proud, I promise.* A torrent of emotions poured over her. She wanted to cry, to laugh, to jump up and down like a kid who'd just received the best-ever Christmas present. Overcome with elation, she thrust the throttle forward a little more and then, with both hands gripping on the wheel, she banked the cruiser in a wide arc bearing north. Giving it more power, she hooked the boat tighter, slicing into the waves. Foamy water flashed up the hull, its spray sending the passengers into gales of laughter. In the distance, she spotted a pod of dolphins. If only they were closer, they would ride the white-water wash chasing the cruiser. She grew happier by the moment.

"Where are we heading?" Gripping the backs of their chairs, Sebastien balanced between her and Rod.

"Around the island. Since we're the new owners, I figure we should have a look at what we just inherited." Inclining her head, she gazed up into her younger brother's handsome face, with her own stretched wide in a jubilant smile.

"Well, that's one plan of yours I'll agree with." He winked at her. "Motor on, Captain."

In no time, the cruiser breached the northernmost corner of land and arced to the west. Navigating the sweeping rear side of the island, she steered one hundred feet offshore and slowed down to ten knots. "Rod, will you take the helm for a while?"

"Sure." He rose from his seat and took the wheel.

"Thanks." She gathered everyone to the port side of the vessel. "This north-western side of the island was

Uncle Dickie's favorite. In his opinion, it has the most stunning stretch of untouched beach anywhere in the world. It runs in a sweeping crescent shape for miles. He named it Origin Beach. The only way anyone can get to it is by boat. And you've got to be a damned fine skipper not to come aground on the reef hidden under those small breakers." She pointed to a border of frothy foam lacing across the top of the water about ten feet closer to shore than their current course.

"Dickie talked about an old quarry. Where's that from here?" asked Cecilia, holding up her hand to block the sun's glare.

"That's further inland."

"But couldn't you trek from the quarry out to this stretch of beach?"

Tina laughed. "Only if you're SAS or a Navy Seal. It's treacherous jungle. Deadly to most people. Easier to come in by boat. Look there. That's what I was hoping for." She pointed to a section of bleached sand, stretching out like an airline runway about half a mile long. Where the jungle spilled onto the sand, dozens of monolithic marbles of volcanic rock lay as if discarded by giant children.

"What are we looking at?" asked Victoria, straining her head forward.

"Can you see those wide furrows going up the beach? They look like someone's driven a tractor over the sand." Wagging her finger in front of Victoria's face, she drew imaginary lines to match those on the beach.

Victoria squinted. "Yes. I see them now."

"They're the tracks of green sea turtles. It's nesting season. They've been coming to this part of the island for decades to lay their eggs in the sand, away from human interference."

"There are hundreds of them," said Sebastien, a hint of awe in his voice.

"There used to be more," interjected Andrew. "Dickie and I came here every nesting season. He called it the Origin Project because it was where the origin of life for the sea turtles began. I've kept observational data on the number of tracks each year for the past forty years. We recorded everything we could and compared each subsequent year against the previous years, hoping to ensure the turtle population's longevity. Out of all the projects Dickie managed, this was his favorite. He wanted the turtles to have a safe breeding ground for generations to come."

"I remember Dickie telling me about it," said Victoria.

"And how is the Origin Project going?" asked Cecilia, her eyes glued to the shoreline.

"Over the past few years, we've witnessed a decrease in tracks on this stretch of beach, or at least that's what it looks like. We only observe. We never go ashore, but Dickie thought something was wrong. Either we're losing more sea turtles in the oceans due to pollution, or they've chosen not to come back to the island." He shook his head, obviously confused and disappointed.

"But why would they choose not to come back since they've been doing it for generations?" asked Cecilia.

"Because they know it's not safe."

"But how could that be?" Tina's eyes narrowed on Andrew as concern fired her synapses.

"That's what he wanted to investigate more this season — to find out why the number of nesting females is decreasing. But now that he's gone, that's not going to happen." Andrew hung his head and fidgeted with his hands.

Tina dragged a hand across her chin. It was a trait both she and Sebastien had inherited from their father. Not terribly feminine, Victoria often reminded her, but neither was Tina when she was on a case. And the vanishing turtle population piqued her journalistic instinct.

She reached over and patted Andrew's twisting hands. "Don't you worry. We'll sort it out one way or the other. I'll make sure Uncle Dickie's wishes are fulfilled."

"And what about me?" demanded Sebastien, his tone indignant.

"And you too, Seb. Of course. We'll both sort it out." Hurriedly, she tried to undo the unintentional slur she'd made at her brother.

Sebastien glared daggers at her, turned on his heel and joined Rod in the cabin.

"Really, Tina, you will have to learn more diplomacy," warned Victoria.

"He needs to grow up, Vickie. If he's going to pout every time I don't include him, then that's his problem. We don't have time for petty disputes and tantrums." She bit her lip to curb the rest of her opinion.

"Sebastien is your brother and partner. You two need to find a way to work together. Both of you will have to temper your language, learn to listen and negotiate. Those are the skills your Uncle Dickie possessed in barrow loads. And they're the ones you'll both need to employ if Harbor Island is to succeed." Rarely did Victoria voice her opinion with such vehemence, but Tina knew her stepmother was correct. She and Sebastien needed to be more conciliatory with each other.

"You're right," she conceded. "I'll go sort it out with him." She turned heel, to soothe her brother's wounded pride. But inside she knew that what Victoria had said yesterday was wrong. Owning Harbor Island with Seb was not going to be a cake-walk.

CHAPTER TWENTY-ONE

Over the next week, the island resumed its usual rhythm. Cashed-up day-trippers came and went either on the ferry or their own boats, the stores in town conducted their everyday business, and the newly named Templeton staff continued in their duties on the property with Andrew overseeing as housekeeper. Unwilling to retire, he resumed his role, advising that he needed to work to keep his mind and hands busy, now that Dickie had died.

For Tina and Sebastien, Andrew's insistence on working proved a blessing. It freed them to spend time in the office together, poring over the business accounts, spreadsheets, and investments.

"My God, this is a huge business." Tina leaned her elbows on the desk and speared her fingers through her hair.

"Yeah. Uncle Dickie sure made some shrewd investments through the years. But by the look of the accounts, the return hasn't been as good of late as it was. We've got an enormous payroll to support if we're going to keep all these people employed." He shook his head and mirrored Tina's look of concern.

"I know. And I can't see any way of reducing expenditure except terminating some of the staff." She winced at the thought of it.

"Agreed."

"We can't do that. That would be too awful."

"I know, but tough decisions have to be made if we want to keep Harbor Island operating at all."

"There has to be another way." She shoved back from the chair and paced around the office. Shelves filled with year-dated folders, rosters, invoicing and suppliers lined three walls, challenging her to solve the problem. She peered out the window and watched the cheery faces of the groundsmen as they maintained the exquisite gardens. Every one of them oblivious to the dilemma the new owners faced. "We hold their livelihood in our hands. And their families. We can't simply do a slash and burn in the business and cast them adrift." She spun back to face Sebastien. "It isn't right."

"Let's go back to business basics one-on-one. If you can't cut expenses, then you have to increase revenue. So, if we're not going to cut staff, we have to find a way to increase the island's revenue to pay them. If we're lucky, and we encounter no catastrophe, this place will survive maybe another five years based on the current state of the business. To keep the business profitable, we need to look at other ways, aside from investments and the meager fee we get from the ferry and store leases."

"No wonder Uncle Dickie died of a massive cardiac arrest. He must have been worried sick over the future." She slumped down into her chair.

"Who knows?" He shrugged. "Maybe he'd already found a solution and died before he had a chance to implement it. All I know is we're going to have to sort this out fast. Five years may sound like a long time, but we're currently on the wrong side of the bell graph heading down a steep slope."

"I know. It's decision time." She traded a worried look with her brother. She knew only too well how fickle investments could be since the American financial crisis in 2008. Recovery had been torturously slow, and most economists agreed that the world had changed forever. Tough times lay ahead for Harbor Island and especially for the both of them, who bore the responsibility for its future.

"What are you going to do, Seb?" She leaned forward and rested her arms on her thighs.

"What do you mean?"

"Well, are you going back to Australia or do you intend staying here, or what?"

He shook his head. "I have no idea. What about you?"

"I have no idea as well. I'm owed a few months' leave, so I'm going to use all that now and stay here. See if we can't get this sorted out." Her eyes raced over the spreadsheets scattered on the desk.

"I've got some property deals going on back home I should be there for, but I can probably stay a while."

A grateful smile chased away her seriousness. "Terrific. I'm sure we'll work it out. Between you, me and Vickie, there has to be a way."

"You're going to tell Mom?" He scowled.

"Why not? She knows this place better than anyone. I figure she'll make a great sounding board. And she's not stupid, you know."

"I don't mean that. I just didn't want her worrying about this sort of stuff."

"Listen, Seb, this is Vickie's childhood home. It was as much hers as Uncle Dickie's. She has a right to know what's going on. Anyway, I'm no good at keeping secrets. I have to confide in her."

"Okay. But if it were up to me, I'd keep her out of it. At least until we come up with a solution." His lips pursed, displaying his uneasiness. He fiddled with the ring on his pinkie finger. A gesture he rarely did, but Tina knew it well enough to know a battle could be imminent.

"Three heads are better than two. Let's use her brain capital and see what she has to offer." She tried her best to lead him with tact and logic.

The shadow passed from his face. "Okay." But his agreement sounded tentative.

"Thanks. I'm calling it quits for the day. I do my best thinking when my mind is elsewhere. I'm going to wander around the gardens for a while before dinner." She rose from the chair and stretched.

"Me too. I think I'll drive down into town and grab a coffee." He rose and tugged at the crotch of his jeans. A wicked gleam played in his eyes.

"I don't care what you do, Seb. But just keep it in your pants." She gave an askance glance down. "You can't go around screwing Melody, Veronica or any of these women. Okay?" She wagged a threatening finger at him.

"But Melody is old enough to make her own decisions." Annoyance rumbled in his voice.

"That's not the point. The point is you're her financier, some might say, employer. In this day and age, it could be construed as sexual harassment. If she brought a case against you, you'd lose. Then where would you be? Remember what Alan Rosenbaum said about the conditions in the will?" She drew a quick breath. "At any time, if you're arrested or convicted of a criminal act, you'll lose your inheritance. And the damage it could cause to Harbor Island would be irreparable." Her voice sounded sharp. "Keep it in your pants, Seb."

Sebastien pouted. "Yeah, yeah, yeah. But it won't be easy." He avoided her steely stare.

Tina softened. "You're a handsome man, Seb. I'm sure there are plenty of tourists on offer, flaunting themselves on the beach. It'll be easy for you." Sporting a persuasive smile, she waited until the tension passed and he lifted his gaze. "Come on. Don't sulk."

"I hear you," he grumbled, although his surly appearance remained.

"Good." With a motherly cluck of her tongue, she linked arms with him, and they traipsed from the office.

* * * *

"Hey, you two," called Tina as she strolled toward the veranda steps of Hill Cottage.

"Hello, Tina. Come join us," welcomed Cecilia with a wave.

"Yes, darling, come tell us what you and Sebastien are up to," said Victoria. Perched in beige rattan chairs, she and Cecilia reclined like regal residents of Hill Cottage. Because the day's heat had not yet surrendered to a balmy evening, both women sipped tall glasses of iced tea and fluttered hand-woven pandanus fans to cool their faces. Tina took her time climbing the stairs, so she could study the tableau in which the women starred. It epitomized chic island living, without any effort or vanity on their part. *Probably take a magazine a couple of days to get that shot*, she mused, a smile twitching her lips.

"There's more tea in the fridge inside. Help yourself," offered Cecilia.

"Thanks. I will." As Tina strolled into the cottage, she called back over her shoulder, "I must say, you two look like you've set up residence here. People will start calling you the Duchesses of Hill Cottage." She heard them titter from the veranda as she opened the fridge door. It had been some time since she'd seen Victoria look so relaxed. Obviously, she and Cecilia shared a special friendship, one that transcended time and circumstance. Being career-minded and a bit of a loner, Tina hadn't experienced that type of close female friendship before. She'd invested so much in her career, she'd had little time or energy for anyone else. At least, that's the pitiful excuse David had given her to justify his sexual dalliances. Despite his unwelcome opinion, the relationship Victoria and Cecilia shared made her envious. She hoped that one day she would find a BFF like they had found in each other. *Not much chance of that here.* She shook her head and shooed the cynical thought from her mind. *For goodness sake, I'm starting to think like Seb. Positive, be more positive, Tina.* She returned with a dripping glass of iced tea.

"Despite what's brought us together, I'm really enjoying catching up with Cecilia after all these years." Victoria raised her glass to her long-time friend.

"Me too. It's wonderful to be with you, and for us to sit here like we did all those years ago and chat."

"I'm pleased you two are enjoying yourselves because Seb and I aren't." Tina rolled her eyes before straddling the veranda railing.

"Why? What's wrong?" Victoria's fan slowed.

"The company books don't look too good. Uncle Dickie's investments, leases, and wharf fees aren't returning enough to keep Harbor Island profitable for more than five years. Unless we either cut staff or increase revenue, we'll be in serious trouble."

"Oh, dear." Cecilia lowered her fan.

"Are you sure? Dickie was always so careful." Victoria sounded worried.

Tina nodded. "We're sure. We've been over everything. We even spoke to Alan Rosenbaum yesterday, and he agreed with our findings. We need a strong business strategy to move this place forward. Fast." She slugged a long pull of iced tea and regarded the women.

"Well, this is easily fixed. I'll give back the million dollars Dickie left me."

"That's very generous of you, but you will not. That's not part of the deal. I'm sure Uncle Dickie knew things were getting tough before he died and even so, he left you that money. No. It's up to Seb and me to work this out."

"But I would rather give back the money than lose Harbor Island forever." Panic spread across Victoria's face in a flush of crimson.

"I know. And if push comes to shove, we'll *borrow* the money from you. But that's a last resort. I didn't tell you this to worry you. I just wanted to have your thoughts on the situation." She glanced sideways at Cecilia. "So, what do you think?"

"About?"

"About everything I just said."

Cecilia straightened and tapped an even tempo with her fan in the palm of her hand. "I don't like to stick my nose in, but since you asked. Dickie would never have left the island to you if he didn't think you could handle it. You need to stop looking at the negatives and start focusing on the positives."

Tina and Victoria regarded her with a frown.

"Stop looking at the liabilities you've inherited and start looking at the assets." She sipped her tea and batted her eyelashes over the glass rim.

"What? Sell off some assets?" Tina knew that wouldn't work.

"No." She paused. "What are the island's major assets?" Like a teacher prodding her student to think, she locked Tina in a steady gaze.

Tina tilted her head from side to side, waiting for the familiar crack of tendons. Tired or not, she knew Cecilia was onto something. She rubbed her neck and began. "Okay. Major assets . . . Well, this property, the shops in the town—"

"No." Cecilia sounded impatient. "Not man-made assets. Natural assets." The twinkle in her eyes caught Tina's attention and she leaned closer.

"Well, the major natural assets are the environment, the beach, the harbor. Everything that Uncle Dickie has protected and preserved, which is the entire ecosystem of the island."

"Correct." Cecilia nodded and waved her fan in the air.

"But what are you suggesting? That Tina and Seb sell off the natural assets?" The concern in Victoria's voice was unmistakable.

"Absolutely not. I'm suggesting they harness those assets as tourist attractions and charge people to see them." Triumphant, she leaned back in her chair.

Propped against a perpendicular veranda post, Tina gazed off into the distance. As dusk draped the island in its coppery shroud, she pondered Cecilia's suggestion. Her hand dragged across her chin before coming to rest on her mouth. *Focus on the positives.* With a slow nod, she turned back to the older woman. "Now, that's a good idea. We can increase revenue while still ensuring Uncle Dickie's legacy. We have enough staff already who can be trained to be custodians of the attractions. Under the right environmental protection strategy, we could turn this place into a tourist mecca, without causing any environmental damage."

"I have no doubt about it." Cecilia beamed.

"Based on the conditions of the will, you must have Alan Rosenbaum consult, but from what you're saying I think it would work." Victoria nodded her approval.

"I'll run it past Seb tomorrow and see what he thinks." Renewed hope rang in Tina's voice.

"Why don't you distill your ideas a bit more before presenting them to Sebastien?" cautioned Cecilia.

"I agree," said Victoria. "Mull it over for a couple of days. We all know Sebastien can be stubborn to the point of obstinacy. Get your ducks in a row, as the saying goes. If you want, we can help you." She cast a sideways glance at her friend. "I'd certainly like to think that the three of us saved the island without the need of a man." She sniggered.

"I didn't know you were such a feminist, Vickie," said Tina, surprised at her step-mom's suggestion to not include Sebastien yet.

"Trust me. There's a lot you don't know. So, do we agree? The three of us work on this for a few days and then once we've got it sorted, we'll meet with Sebastien and get it across the line."

"Suits me." Tina shrugged.

"And me," added Cecilia, flicking open her fan with an extravagant flourish.

"Done. Now, enough with the iced tea. Time for a glass of sav blanc to toast Harbor Island's Secret Board of Women." Victoria sprang from her chair and rushed into the cottage for the wine and glasses.

"I've never seen her like this." Tina shook her head, bemused at her step-mom's sudden empowerment.

"I have. Victoria was always very intuitive. She knew the best way to get around her father. He died before you joined the family. Percy was a tough, tyrannical man. He ran this place like a despot, expecting everyone to comply with his wishes, and pity help them if they didn't. Back then, I watched how Victoria responded to her father's unreasonable demands. Like her mother, she could find resolution and harmony without giving up her integrity. She's the ultimate negotiator." Cecilia's eyes clouded. "I have a feeling Sebastien has inherited some of Percy's traits, and Victoria's level of influence will be necessary to keep the status quo. Anyway, she knows that the best way to approach Sebastien is with her at the table. Like Dickie, she's campaigned for Harbor Island all her life. Despite everything, she won't see this island fail. She's a special woman."

"Indeed, she is."

CHAPTER TWENTY-TWO

"It's awfully kind of you to organize this party for us," shouted Tina over the amplified Hawaiian music coming from nearby speakers. Around her, store owners, staff, friends, and associates gathered on Harbor Island's beach for a dusk barbeque. The smoky smell of chargrilled meat wafted on the afternoon breeze tempting her taste buds, which had been liberally lubricated by wine from her bottomless glass. She teetered a little in the soft sand and realized the alcohol was making a beeline to her head.

"We wanted to throw an official welcome to you and Sebastien," said Marty Henderson, a smile creasing his face. Probably close to retirement age, Marty had not been blessed with height, strength or good looks. Short, rotund and with a face only his mother and wife could love, Marty was a stalwart supporter of Harbor Island and Uncle Dickie. Just breaching Tina's shoulder, he looked up at her with his best defining feature — his jaunty, genuine personality.

"It wasn't necessary, though." Tina gave a grateful smile.

"Of course, it was. We loved Dickie very much, and he was so generous to us when we arrived here all those years ago. That we've managed to keep the Local Store operating all this time is a credit to him."

Like Marty, his wife Pat lacked the physically attractive gene, but she shared her husband's genuineness and charitable spirit. "Besides, you and Seb are in charge now. We thought having an informal party where everyone mingles would be the perfect way to begin a new era. Cheers." Pat clinked her glass to the new owner, as did Marty. Each slugged another mouthful, and Tina moved closer to the tipsy threshold.

"Some more?" Jacob lifted the bottle of a crisp Napa Valley white to top up her glass, but she covered it with her hand.

"No thanks, Jacob. I need to eat something."

"They're dishing up food now if you want to get some." He nodded to the barbeque plate while replenishing the Hendersons' glasses. "I wouldn't wait too long, though. They swarm like locusts when free food is on." He chuckled and moved off in search of partygoers' empty glasses.

Tina wandered over to the service table with the Hendersons. "What's your take on how Harbor Island's been doing over the past year or so?"

"Well," said Marty, craning his neck up, "the Local Store has fared pretty well. There've been lots of day tourists—"

"I think the numbers are growing," interrupted Pat as they took their place in line.

"Really? I'll look into that with the Maui Tourist Bureau. They must be able to give me stats for the ferry transfers." She made a mental note to find out. "Do you think the private tourists are increasing as well?"

"Best to ask Melody and Veronica about that. The yachties usually go into the diner to eat. The girls keep good records from what I understand, so they should be able to tell you," said Pat, handing them each a plate.

Tina recalled Uncle Dickie telling her years ago that if you wanted to know what was going on, ask Pat Henderson. She knew every piece of gossip. She also knew if it were true or not. She was the white equivalent to the jungle grapevine. Tina stifled a smirk while they helped themselves to the buffet of steaks, sausages, a creamy ranch-style potato salad, and a tossed salad of innumerable leafy greens. Tucking a bread roll onto the side of her packed plate, she nodded toward the three empty chairs that Jacob hovered behind at a nearby rock. With their plates balanced precariously on their knees, they dived into their dinner. For a few minutes conversation lulled, broken only by murmurs of praise for the cooks. Tina's wooziness subsided with each bite, and her head began to clear.

"Who made this potato salad? It's to die for," she said, through a mouthful of creamy heaven.

"This one is Suzie's. You remember Suzie Lin, don't you?" Pat munched on the end of a burnt sausage. "The artist who owns the souvenir shop." She leaned in and whispered, "Silly Suzie we call her. She's as crazy as a loon." As Pat pursed her lips in a confidential manner, she received a nudge in the ribs from Marty.

"Stop that, Pat. Just because Suzie makes love potions and talks to the nature spirits doesn't mean she's mad. She's just a touch eccentric."

"A *touch* eccentric," shrilled Pat. "Really, Marty, the woman is crackers. I'm sure of it."

Tina cleared her throat. "Yes, I remember Suzie. And regardless of her eccentricities, she makes a great potato salad." She shoveled the last spoonful of deliciousness into her mouth before dabbing her lips with a serviette. She lowered her plate to the sand, more than contented with the local fare. Jacob appeared as if by magic to top up their glasses. Accepting only half a glass, she settled back and gazed out to the darkening horizon. Dotted along the water's edge, a row of kerosene fire torches were being lit. Their thick, damp wicks ignited with a flash of blue-and-orange flames, which quickly consumed the acrid smell of lamp oil. Within minutes the dozen lamps blazed and cast romantic shadows on the lapping waves.

"So, does Suzie have an opinion about the tourists coming to the island?" Tina sipped her wine, its crisp bite offsetting the fatty aftertaste of the potato salad.

"You'll have to ask her about that. But she did do a tarot card reading just before Dickie died and—"

"For goodness sake, Pat. Tina doesn't want to hear about mumbo-jumbo." Marty sounded exasperated.

"It's okay. Go ahead, Pat. What were you going to say?" In her job, Tina had spent enough time investigating stories to know not to discard any inconsequential information no matter how outlandish it seemed.

"Well." Pat dragged her chair closer. "She pulled the Death card and was most upset." Tina nodded for Pat to continue. "Poor Suzie still doesn't know whether it foretold Dickie's death or something about the island's death. She's been unnerved over it for weeks."

"Is she here tonight?" Tina scanned the partygoers on the beach.

"Oh, no. She didn't want to come out tonight. It's a new moon." Pat glanced upward at the moonless sky. "She's recharging herself and opening up to planetary energies." Waving her arms in an imaginary circle, she did a creditable impression of a shamanistic soothsayer.

Marty rolled his eyes and took a hefty slug of wine.

"Really?" Tina stifled a laugh. The behind-the-scenes drama of Harbor Island was more amusing than any reality television show.

"Yes. She's convinced there's something sinister afoot and it'll mean death to Harbor Island if someone doesn't find out what it is." Pat's vigorous head nodding drove her point home.

"All it is, is Suzie's latest conspiracy theory. She has a new one every few months, and this is the latest," Marty said with a huff.

"You're such a skeptic, Marty," slurred Pat, listing in her chair.

"Come on, Pat. I think we've taken up enough of Tina's time. She needs to mingle with the others. Time to say good night." Marty slipped his hand under Pat's elbow and guided her to her feet.

"Very well," she growled at her husband. "Good night, Tina. Good to have you here on the island. Dickie would have been so proud of you." Exhaling a heady mix of alcohol and chargrill over Tina's face, Pat swayed in the sand.

Tina jumped up, ready to block Pat's nosedive, but the store owner recovered like a self-righting canoe. Relieved and bemused, Tina shook Pat's hand. "Thank you both for going to all this effort. I'll pop down to the store and see you soon. Good night."

"Yes, see you soon." Pat staggered, more unsteady than before. With a gasp, Marty grabbed her and saved his wife from pitching face-first into the sand.

"Stop that," she scolded, slapping his hands away.

"I'm only trying to help," he pleaded.

With an indignant tilt of her chin, she lurched off. Doing his duty, Marty scampered beside her, safeguarding her unsteady steps. Above the splashing waves, Pat's voice could be heard chastising her poor husband for making her leave so soon.

Tina shook her head in amusement. She bent down, collected their dirty plates and glasses, and returned them to where the ladies were cleaning up.

"Thanks, everyone. Dinner was terrific." She shook hands, making sure she included them all.

Plenty of people still mingled and chatted on the beach. With their tongues loosened from alcohol, she decided to capitalize on the opportunity. She wandered from group to group, gathering information on how their businesses were going, how the island could be improved and any ideas they had for the future. Everyone agreed on the environmental protection of the island, but also voiced concerns about making more money. For Tina, it boiled down to greed versus green. Throughout the evening, one thought repeated itself over and over. *We must find a way to operate an economically successful business while keeping its impact within safe environmental boundaries.* It was like walking a tightrope.

With ideas whirring in her mind, Tina took her leave. She needed to find Seb, get home and write down her thoughts before going to bed. They'd arrived in the truck together this afternoon, and she'd seen him earlier in the evening, chatting and mingling, but where had he got to? The Chevy was still parked on The Esplanade, so he had to be here somewhere. As the new owners, he and Tina needed to keep a unified front, and he needed to keep her informed of his whereabouts.

She marched up the beach and the ambient light from the fire torches faded. Without the moon, sprawling patches of darkness littered the sand.

"Hey, Tina I've been trying to get a word with you all night." A figure pressed in beside her.

She flinched in fright before realizing who it was. *Damn.* "Oh hi, Rod." She forced a smile, inwardly hoping he would get the message that she didn't want to talk. "Well, I've been busy talking to everyone about the island. You know, getting their ideas."

"I have ideas, too, you know." He sounded petulant and hurt.

God, what is it with these men? They're like spoilt brats. She folded her arms and faced him. "Okay then, Rod. What are your ideas for the island? How do you think it could be run better?" She didn't care if she sounded like an officious bitch. She was tired, angry with Seb, and fed up with Rod's constant sexual inferences.

"Why don't you come back to the party, have a drink and we can talk about it there."

Her skin crawled up Harbor Hill all by itself. "Sorry, Rod. No can do. How about you go back to the party, have a drink, and I'll go home." She reconsidered her position and chose one of more diplomacy. "Listen, I'm tired. I'll pop in over the next day or so, and we can talk then. Good night." She shot him a lame smile, pivoted in the sand and continued her march up the beach.

"Okay. I was just trying to be friendly," he whined.

I bet you were.

As her legs pumped up the sand, her thoughts returned to Seb. She ground her teeth, her anger rising.

At a sound off to her right, her ears pricked. She stopped and listened. *Oh, no.* She glanced over her shoulder to check Rod wasn't following her, before creeping across the sand, then sliding into a crevice between two large boulders. Peering through the thin fissure, she spied a protected sandy cove, bathed in subtle starlight, and witnessed what she'd hoped wasn't happening. Seb had Melody pinned on her back, her legs pushed wide apart while he plunged into her with brutish force. Muffled rutting noises gasped from their throats. Tina looked away, biting back her rage. She pressed against the rock and gritted her teeth. Her head spun, and her stomach lurched. *Shit, shit, shit.*

She slithered back out from the crevice, did a quick reconnaissance and then hightailed it up the beach to the truck. Sliding into the driver's seat, she flipped the visor down and grabbed the keys. "He can bloody walk home," she spat, kicking over the engine. She snapped on the headlights and chucked a U-turn. "As if I don't have enough to worry about without throwing Seb's sexual appetite into the mix." The Chevy changed gear as she gunned it up the hill. She rubbed the heel of her hand between her brows, trying to expel the image of her brother and Melody screwing on the beach. *Argh . . .*

Incensed by her brother's stupidity, she mulled over what Pat had said about Silly Suzie's prophecy, about the death card. Next to Sebastien's sleazy sexual display, it claimed second-star billing on the cinema screen of her mind. The two images dovetailed together, and her stomach churned. "If Seb's reckless behavior brings about the death of Harbor Island, I'll kill him. I'll bloody kill him."

* * * *

On rising the following morning, Tina was surprised not to see any of the staff anywhere. Deducing they were all hungover, she requisitioned the truck and escaped the property so as not to face Sebastien. That showdown she wanted to keep for later. When she arrived in town, planning to have breakfast in the diner, it was closed. In fact, even now, one hour after their advertised opening hour of seven o'clock, the diner, the Local Store, and mechanics' shop were still shut. Harbor Island's esplanade felt more like a ghost town than a thriving visitor destination. Disappointed, she shook her head, and her jaw clenched tight. *These people need to muscle up.* Like most journalists, she'd hauled her sorry ass out of bed while nursing a blinding hangover when on assignment. But that's what you did. You had a job to do, and if you were dumb enough to wipe yourself out the night before, you still had to front up and get the job done. *Harbor Island will not succeed if these people don't take responsibility.*

By the time Suzie Lin opened her souvenir shop, Tina had paced the length of The Esplanade's pavement three times, her frustration growing. When the door cracked open, and its owner peered out, Tina huffed. Behind a pair of fine gold-rimmed round glasses, Suzie's dark eyes blinked, obviously startled to see a customer. A diminutive woman of about fifty, she wore ankle-length black silk trousers, topped with a blue mandarin-collared silk blouse printed in a delicate oriental design. Pinned with chopsticks, her glossy black hair coiled tight on top of her head, while her make-up free face shone in an even honey tone.

Tilting her head, she studied Tina closely. "Hello. Do I know you?"

"Good morning, Suzie. It's me, Tina Templeton. Dickie's niece."

Joy blossomed on Suzie's face, and she threw open the door. "Tina Templeton. I thought it was you, but you've cut your hair so short. Come in. Come in."

On stepping over the threshold, it was Tina's turn to blink. Mirroring the brightness of the shop's exterior, the four interior walls fought for attention. Each of three walls was painted in one color of the primary palette — red, yellow and green — while the fourth, in which the front door opened, dazzled white. She wondered if Suzie purposely painted it white to guide customers out of the shop, like heading to the light when someone dies. She muffled a giggle as she picked her way through the bric-a-brac. Glass cabinets displayed an assortment of cheap wares from across the world, including Chinese fans, Hawaiian shell jewelry, and hand-carved miniature Polynesian outrigger canoes. Clusters of crystals, beads, and volcanic rock waited for some eager customer to give them a new, cleaner home.

"Wow, Suzie, you certainly have a lot of giftware here." Tina tried her best to sound complimentary.

"Yes. It has taken me many years to put together this collection. There are some pieces I won't sell now because I have grown attached to them. But the art is for sale. I painted it all." With obvious pride, she waved her hand in a sweeping arc around the shop.

From floor to ceiling, different-sized canvases hung on the vivid walls, each tagged with the name of the piece and its retail price. Tina studied an oil painting of a landscape. "Is this a place on the island?"

"Yes. Every one of my paintings is from somewhere on Harbor Island."

Surprised by Suzie's skill as a painter, Tina wandered around the makeshift gallery. When one of the canvases caught her eye, she stopped. "If I'm not mistaken isn't this Rainbow Falls?"

"Yes, it is. You have a good memory, Tina."

"Uncle Dickie used to drive me out there a lot. It's a beautiful place. But how did you get out there to paint this?"

"Jim Fischer, Rod's father, used to take me out when he was alive. He was a good man. I miss his company." A veil of sadness fell over Suzie's face for an instant, but she shrugged it off.

"So, Jim had a vehicle?"

"Oh, yes. He had a rickety old truck. Didn't go very fast, but it got around enough for him to take me to special places to paint."

"What happened when Jim died? With the truck, I mean."

"Oh, Rod still has it. He uses it, I guess. But I don't have much to do with him." She screwed up her nose.

Tina decided to unravel that thread of information later. "Do you mind if we sit down, Suzie?"

"How rude of me, please sit." She offered her one of only two chairs tucked behind the counter in the shop. "I was just making some Chinese tea. Would you like some?"

"Yes. That would be lovely. Thank you."

In the far corner of the counter, Suzie dropped two tea bags in ceramic Chinese teacups. "I was terribly sad to hear about Dickie's death. I liked him. He helped me set up my new cottage business of selling love potions."

"Yes, Andrew told me all about it."

The kettle whistled, and Suzie poured the bubbling water into the cups. As the Chinese tea bag steeped, she offered Tina her cup.

"Thank you. This smells terrific. I'll just wait until it cools down a little." She breathed in the refreshing aroma and smiled.

"Now tell me, what really brings you down to see me?" A challenge lit her black eyes, and she sipped her steaming tea.

Thinking Suzie's mouth must be made of asbestos to tolerate such piping-hot water, Tina blinked and almost missed the question. "I, uh, I've been talking to everyone about how their business is going here on the island and if they had any ideas for improvement."

The woman's face blanched. "I knew it. Something is wrong, isn't it?"

"What on earth do you mean?"

"Everyone thinks I'm crazy, but I'm not. I see things others do not see."

"What? Like a clairvoyant?"

Suzie snorted. "Don't be silly. There's no such thing as clairvoyance."

But the tarot cards are spot on? Tina smirked at her tea.

"I see things at night, Tina. When everyone else is in bed, I see things out past the reef." Like an informant divulging secret information, Suzie edged her face closer. "I see them. Lights in the water. They've been there for the past year or so. Always in summer. They come and go, back and forth. I told Dickie about it a few weeks before he died. Poor Dickie."

"What do you think they are? UFOs?"

"Of course not. There're no such things as UFOs." She tutted loudly, rejecting Tina's ridiculous idea.

"What, then?" Unable to drink the scalding tea and with an empty stomach, Tina found her patience wearing thin.

"I don't know. That's what I told Dickie. I don't know, but the tarot cards have told me something is wrong here on Harbor Island."

And here we go with the tarot cards. Despite the heat of the tea, Tina lifted her cup to her lips, burning them on the rim. "Ouch." She returned the cup to the counter and sighed. "What do you mean something is wrong? Like what?"

Suzie huffed and puffed with obvious impatience. "I just told you, Tina. I. Don't. Know. I read and interpret the message of the tarot cards. It isn't written out for me word for word, you know."

"Of course not," Tina conceded. Trying to connect the dots of Suzie's rationale proved more difficult than she expected.

"But let me tell you this. It's got to do with the lights beyond the reef. That I'm sure of. Find out what those lights are doing, and you'll find your answer, and Harbor Island will be saved."

"Saved from what?"

"I. Don't. Know." Suzie dropped her cup on the counter with a loud whack.

"That's a mighty strong message, Suzie." Hairs on the back of Tina's neck bristled. Could Silly Suzie with all her idiosyncrasies actually be onto something?

"Well, Dickie didn't act fast enough and look what happened to him." She nailed Tina in a frosty stare.

"I'm not sure that's really the case," murmured Tina, tapping her foot.

"Mark the message of the tarot." Suzie wagged her finger. "Something is afoot here on the island which will be its undoing, and you must find out what it is."

"Any further ideas?" Tina's brows raised in a final query.

"Find out who and the what, and the why, when and where will follow." With her last piece of advice, Suzie swallowed the remainder of her tea. "Aren't you drinking your tea? Oh well." She collected Tina's cup and tipped it down the small sink.

Tina moaned as she watched her tea, which was now cool enough to drink, be thrown away. She'd been dismissed. She stood and managed an indulgent smile. "Thank you so much for talking to me, and I'll look into what you've said. I promise. And by the way, your potato salad last night was delicious." She strolled beside her to the shop's front door.

"Thank you. It was a special recipe given to me." Suzie grinned with obvious pride.

"By your mother?" asked Tina, delighted to participate in a more mundane conversation.

"Oh no. By the nature spirits who live at Rainbow Falls." As if overcome with transcendental bliss, her face luminesced, and she opened the door.

In one long stride, Tina cleared the threshold of the shop and said a quick goodbye. Feeling like she'd just stepped back through the looking glass, she shook off her encounter like a shaggy dog. *What a start to the day.* Barely eight-thirty and her brain had run a mental marathon. What the hell has been going on here? She stopped and stared out over the harbor. *What's with the lights at night, out past the reef?* She walked on, toying with the idea, while her stomach rumbled. *That bloody diner better be open for breakfast now.* Despite the allure of crispy bacon and fried eggs, she couldn't ignore the worry and dread squirming in her stomach. The mind-bending carousel ride she'd just taken with Silly Suzie haunted her thoughts. *Find out who and the what, and the why, when and where will follow.* The confrontation with Seb would have to wait. She had some serious investigative digging to do.

CHAPTER TWENTY-THREE

Melody floated around the diner like a love-struck teenager, obviously euphoric from last night's sexual escapade. Fortunately for her, Veronica served breakfast. Otherwise, she may have worn the brunt of Tina's bad mood, rather than the real instigator, Sebastien. On signing the tab, Tina decided to wander down to the wharf to digest a sensational meal. Based on what she'd just sampled, the diner was a gold mine waiting to be capitalized. Increasing tourist numbers would help the sisters repay their debt faster and get them established as a profitable business. Another tick for her green-before-greed plans.

Although she wanted to ponder her strategy longer, the summer's day brought back rich memories of long-gone, carefree times on Harbor Island. With the early-morning breeze blowing in across the harbor, her disposition brightened. Pausing on the pathway leading to the wharf, she dragged in the salty air. She tilted her head from side to side and cracked her neck until the last slither of tension drifted away on a passing puff of wind. In a happier mood, she walked at a steady clip onto the wharf and looked out to sea. The ferry from Lahaina arrived each day at ten o'clock. She could see it in the distance. Maybe that's what Suzie saw at night? Boat lights?

"Good morning," a chirpy voice greeted her.

She turned to face its owner. "Good morning, Rod. How are you on this beautiful day?"

"All the better for seeing you." He stepped forward, and she countered with a step back.

Pointing out to sea, she said, "Do you know if we get many boats cruising past here at night?"

"I've not seen many. Sometimes there're a few stray yachts traveling at night, but not often. Why do you ask?"

"Oh, I was just wondering. Did Uncle Dickie ever go out on the boat at night?"

"Not that I know of. He never asked me to help, if he did."

"But if he did, how would he have done it without your help?"

Rod shrugged. "Easy. The boathouse key is kept on a hook in the electric box on the wall nearest the wood pile. All he'd have to do is open up and go through the same process as we did the other day. As you saw, you launched the cruiser single-handedly with the remote."

"Who knows where the key is kept?"

"Most of the residents and staff, I guess." Again, he shrugged.

"But that's awfully lax security. Didn't Uncle Dickie mind?"

"Dickie always believed in trusting people. In all the years Dad and I have worked here, no one has ever taken the key."

Tina narrowed her gaze. "Still . . ."

"Do you want to change where the key lives? Happy to oblige if you want." Rod wore his eager puppy-dog expression.

"No. That's fine. There's plenty of time to review the operations of the island over the coming months. As they say, if it's not broken, don't fix it. Thanks, Rod." She flashed him a sunny grin, turned to leave and then stopped. "Do you still have that old truck of your father's?"

Confusion crinkled his brow. "Yes."

"It must be pretty old by now. Does it still work?"

"It chugs along."

"Good to hear. We might need your help with something in a day or so. Why not take it to Jacob and get him to give it a good overhaul. The company will pay."

"That's mighty generous of you. Thanks, I will."

"Good. Well, I'm off now. See you later." Tina gave him a beguiling smile before she marched back up the wharf. She felt his eyes boring into her, but she didn't care. She got what she wanted. A plan had hatched in her mind. One in which she couldn't risk Rod turning up unexpectedly to ruin it. Getting his truck into the mechanics meant she could keep an eye on his whereabouts.

* * * *

There was nothing for it except to confront it head-on. Tina jumped out of the Chevy and leaped up the stairs of the great pavilion in search of her brother.

She greeted Andrew, who was holding a meeting with the household staff. "Is Seb around?"

"Yes. He's in the office."

"Thanks." She threw him a wave and marched off. At least, the showdown would be in private. She glanced out to the gardens to check no groundsmen lingered near the office windows. On spying a couple, she detoured and shooed them off to another part of the property. The last thing she needed was for the jungle grapevine to get a whiff of the scandal.

She knocked once on the office door and then entered. He was alone. "Good morning, Seb. Got a minute?"

Swiveling in his chair, he greeted her with a subdued smile. "Where did you get to so early today?"

"I went down into town and had breakfast at the diner for a change." Sitting opposite him, she leaned back in the chair and crossed her legs.

"Good food?"

"Excellent."

"And the service?"

"Also excellent, but you already know that." Her lips tightened into a thin line.

"Excuse me?" Even under pressure, Sebastien's face remained a picture of innocent indifference.

"Please don't play dumb with me, Seb. You and Melody."

"I don't know what you're talking about."

"Let's cut to the chase. Last night, when I went looking for you to go home—"

"Yes, about that," Sebastien interrupted. "How dare you take the truck and leave me there to find my way home?"

"Cut the crap, Seb. I saw you screwing Melody on the beach." Sebastien's mouth opened and shut like a hungry goldfish. "Don't insult me by trying to deny it. I saw you. It's not something I'm likely to make up or forget." She shoved up from the chair. In one stride, she stood in front of him. She clamped her hands on the arms of his chair and lunged into his face. "I told you to keep it in your pants. But no, you had to seduce Melody and screw her on the beach at a party thrown in our honor. What is it with you, Seb? Do you have shit for brains?"

He erupted from the chair and faced off. "You know what, Tina? I don't give a shit what you think. I'll do what I like with whomever I like. It's none of your business."

"It is when you jeopardize Harbor Island by your actions."

He snorted and paced away. "How can screwing some little Hawaiian girl cause the island any harm?"

"You sexist, misogynistic pig. It's that very attitude that will bring this island to its knees." She jabbed her finger into his retreating shoulder.

He whirled on her, slapping at her hand like a fly. "Don't you dare speak to me like that. This island is rightfully mine. I have Reginald blood in my veins. You don't."

"Whether you like it or not, we're joint owners. Uncle Dickie made sure of that. And it's obvious I care more for this island than you do, even with all the Reginald blood in your veins."

"Just because you're some hot-shot journalist, you want everyone to bow and scrape to you. Well, I won't. You can't tell me what to do."

"I'm just trying to do the right thing for us, for the island." She dropped her pitch and tempered her delivery. "Seb, you can't do this. The damage is not worth the sexual gratification. Don't you see?"

Unmoved, he glowered. "All I see is what I've always had to put up with. A bossy bitch of an older half-sister who thinks she knows everything. Well, you don't. If I want to screw every girl on this island, I will. And you can't stop me." He shouldered past her and stormed from the office, slamming the door behind him.

Tina fumed, her hands balling into fists at her side. She tried to pace off her anger, but the office was too damn small. Instead, she growled at the ceiling and then dropped in her chair like a bag of cement. *Well, that went well.*

CHAPTER TWENTY-FOUR

"Andrew, can I see you for a moment, please?" Having spent the last couple of hours alone in the office considering her options, Tina decided to involve the only man she could really trust at that moment.

"Of course." He followed her through the great pavilion and into the grounds. Being past four o'clock, the staff had clocked off for the day, so Tina reasoned their *tête-à-tête* wouldn't be overheard.

"I know this sounds odd, but as we wander around, can you pretend we're chatting about the gardens. That way, if anyone is watching, they'd assume we're discussing plans for the grounds and landscaping."

Andrew's heavy-lidded eyes opened wide for just an instant before the respectful expression of a senior employee conversing with his employer graced his face. "Whatever you like."

"Good. Let's wander over to the orchids and discuss them."

Side by side they headed to the border gardens while maintaining their professional pretense.

"I'm not sure how to begin this, but in my job as an investigative journalist, I've developed a pretty good gut instinct over the years. And this is what I've learned: where there's smoke, there's usually fire." She cupped a delicate spray of white dendrobium blossom, and he leaned down to study it closer.

"I understand. It's the same for the Hawaiian people. Gossip is a wretched thing, but if there is one common denominator in the rumors, one must look at who that is."

"Exactly. The who is what I'm after." She linked his arm, leading him to the next group of orchids. "The common denominator is that there's something amiss here on Harbor Island. The Hendersons talked about it, some of the other store owners expressed their concerns, and Suzie Lin informed me this morning that she'd told Uncle Dickie about her suspicions of something being wrong before he died." Pointing toward a spectacular spray of raspberry-colored phalaenopsis orchids, she drew his attention to the plant.

"Yes, in fact, only a few days before Dickie died, he mentioned to me that he thought something odd was going on. But he didn't know what." Andrew nodded, looking at the flowers.

"Nobody knows what's wrong, or so they say. But you've just confirmed my hunch. If Uncle Dickie's suspicions were piqued, I must be on the right track. Andrew, I need your help."

Straightening up, he faced her. "Whatever you want, you can count on me."

She steered them toward a garden bursting with crotons and hibiscus on the other side of the great pavilion. Squeezing his hand, she stared long and hard at him. "I warn you, it might be dangerous. Are you up for it?"

"Of course," he replied without flinching. "Anything I can do to save Dickie's legacy, I'll do."

"But you cannot tell anyone. Not Sebastien, Vickie, Cecilia . . . no one. This must stay between you and me. Agreed?" She narrowed her gaze.

"Agreed."

"Right. Here's the plan." As Tina explained what she had in mind, she and Andrew circumnavigated the grounds, continuing their charade. By the time she guided him back to the driveway, early evening had dipped its mauve brush on the property, and the plan had been finalized.

* * * *

The timing couldn't be better. Above, the sky twinkled with the subtle luminescence of billions of stars. Deprived of moonlight, the night belonged to those seeking concealment — the perfect setting for illicit trysts, criminal behavior, and for Tina to execute her plan. As she huddled waiting for Andrew, her eyes scanned the beach and The Esplanade. Not a soul stirred. She hoped that included Silly Suzie.

"Tina, I'm here." Andrew's whispered voice sounded nearby.

"Here, Andrew." She craned her neck up a little and spotted him barely three feet away. "I've got the key. You ready?"

"Yes."

"Let's go."

Like a thief in the night and dressed in similar black attire, she scampered to the boathouse door, with Andrew close behind. She slid in the key, unlocked the door and slipped inside with her accomplice. "Did you bring the torches?"

"Yes." He handed her a torch, which she flicked on, keeping the beam pointed to the ground. Andrew did the same.

She shone her torch around the interior of the boathouse, and when convinced they were alone, she straightened. "Okay. Let's get going."

She leaped into *Harbor Island V* and retrieved the ignition key and remote control from the compartment next to the helm. As she got underway, she pulled on the captain's cap and offered Andrew a reassuring smile. Noiselessly, the barn doors swung open. The launching trolley engaged and within a couple of minutes, the stern was adrift in the water. Tina kicked over the engine. It burbled once and stopped. She gave it a little choke and turned the key again. Same response. "Shit. Come on," she cursed in a whisper. "Come on."

Andrew lifted his eyes to the heavens. "Dickie, a little help here, please."

By now, *Harbor Island V* had drifted further into the dark harbor without power or rudder. Tina gritted her teeth, pulled the choke further and turned the key once more. The engine kicked over with a cough. Tina opened the choke fully, giving it plenty of fuel. With a roar the boat came to life, the sound exploding into the night. Tina prayed no one heard it, but there was nothing she could do about it, except to have a plausible story ready as to why she took the cruiser out at this late hour. She exchanged a relieved smile with Andrew and steered into the harbor.

"Right." Her voice returned to normal speaking volume. "I'm not putting on our lights. I'm going to find the channel with the depth-finder and GPS like I did when we all went out with Rod." She noticed Andrew's face blanch. "Don't worry. I know what I'm doing."

"I hope so, Tina. I hope so." Perched in the first mate's chair beside her, he stared into the blackness before them.

In the dead of night, the sea and sky blended into a giant pot of black. With no horizon and no landmarks, *Harbor Island V* traveled blind into the harbor toward a reef through which only one channel permitted egress. The self-illuminating instrumentation panel glowed, its digital display mapping the ground and water beneath. Giving it her full concentration, Tina maneuvered slowly through the harbor, glancing up only occasionally. Buoyed by gentle lapping waves, the cruiser burbled into the dark silence.

"We're in the channel now. Steady as she goes." Without lifting her head, Tina steered the vessel via the instruments. A few tense moments passed in which she suspected Andrew held his breath, like her, praying not to hear coral scraping against the hull. Once she cleared the channel, she eased forward on the throttle.

"We're in deeper waters now." She blew out a breath and relaxed. "Lights on." She flicked the switch, and a far-reaching arc of light shone atop the ocean in front of them. "Now, let's see if we can find out what's going on around here. Hang on." She opened up the engines, breached the northern tip of the island and banked to the west. When they arrived at the back side of the island, she eased back on the throttle.

"So, what is it you think you're going to find out here?"

"I'm not sure, Andrew. Call it a hunch. With what you said about the decline in the turtle population, the strange lights Suzie's seen on the harbor at night and her crazy tarot card warning to Uncle Dickie about death, my journo's instinct tells me something odd is going on, and here is as good as any place to begin." Her voice was low and serious. "I'm switching off the guide lights now. You're going to have to be on watch. I need to keep my eyes on the instruments again and make sure I don't send us aground. Okay?"

"Okay." He nodded. "But what exactly am I looking for?"

"Other boats, lights ... anything that looks suspicious or out of place." Tina headed west and set a course one hundred feet offshore. Being on the open ocean at night, without guide lights, sent chills through her body. She prayed Uncle Dickie was watching over them. Onward she motored into the blackness, hopeful of safe passage.

"It's so dark out here, I can't see anything. Isn't this dangerous, motoring around without any lights?" Fear crept into Andrew's voice.

"Sure is. But it's the only way we can take someone by surprise."

"Or they can take us by surprise and run into us?"

"We're not in a major shipping channel, so I figure if anyone is out here at this time of night, they're probably lost or up to no good. Keep looking, Andrew." She sounded more confident than she felt.

A long breath escaped him as he strained to see through the windscreen. After a few protracted minutes of stressful silence, his arm shot up, his finger pointing to the shore about two hundred feet in the distance. "What's that?"

Tina pulled back on the throttle. Her eyes followed the direction in which he pointed. "What? What do you see?"

"I think there're lights ahead." He paused. "There. On the beach."

"I see them. I see them. Let's take a closer look." Controlling her desire to stick full throttle, Tina gained just enough speed not to be heard from the shore. Cloaked in darkness, *Harbor Island V* would be barely visible from the beach, but as Tina neared the spot where they'd seen the lights, she threw her cap on top of the digital display, sending the helm into total blackout.

"I'll just keep her in a tight circle until we figure out what's going on," she whispered, squinting toward landfall. "Can you see anything?"

"Yes. I think they're torches. About half a dozen people with torches."

"What the hell are they doing?"

"I hate to say it, but there's only one thing that would bring people out here at night."

Her brow creased. "What's that?"

"Sea turtles."

"You're kidding me?"

"It must be. I've heard rumor of turtle-egg-smuggling syndicates. They plunder the turtle nests to steal the eggs. Then they ship them off to Malaysia and other places that consider them to be delicacies. Big business from what I hear."

"That's terrible."

"They also grab the baby turtles when they've just hatched, sometimes by shining a light on the top side of the beach. The poor creatures think it's the full moon and they run toward it rather than out to the moon over the ocean. The thieves nab them by the thousands and ship them off to turtle farms in other countries, where once they've matured, they harvest them for their meat."

"Oh, Andrew, that's awful." She shuddered at the thought of the turtles' miserable fate at human hands.

"Yes. If this has been happening for a while, it would account for the change in their breeding habits."

"But these bastards are stealing from us. These turtles belong to Harbor Island. No wonder you've noticed your turtle numbers decreasing over these past years. Damn it. I'm going to stop this shit."

"But how? You can't go in there now. These guys are pirates and murderers." Andrew's strong hand clutched her wrist.

She clamped her mouth shut. She knew he was right. Going in all guns blazing could get them both killed. She reconsidered her options. "Don't worry. I'm not going in. I'm going to call in the cavalry." She flicked him an optimistic wink.

"I don't understand."

"The US Coast Guard. This is their jurisdiction. They can bust this turtle-egg-smuggling ring and put those guys' sorry asses in jail. Come on. Let's get out of here before I change my mind and take the law into my own hands."

"No, no. The US Coast Guard is a safer option. Let's go home."

Wheeling hard on the helm, she turned the cruiser and headed back, inwardly seething. *Bastards! How dare they steal from my island?* Recalling her conversation with Suzie, Tina had just found out *what* was going on and *where,* now she needed to know *who* was behind it.

CHAPTER TWENTY-FIVE

With its gauzy curtains hanging limply in the morning's stillness, the great pavilion bore a striking resemblance to a royal Persian tent. Its vaulted ceiling reached high to a central peak, and despite its vastness, a sense of privacy enveloped the immense space. As Tina crossed the pavilion, she paused for a moment. She'd still not come to terms with her massive inheritance. So much had happened since the reading of the will, she'd not had time to digest that this was her new future. Whether she wanted it or not, it had been thrust upon her.

"Where have you been?" called Victoria, signaling Tina to join her and Cecilia for breakfast.

"I've been busy chasing up a few things. Has Seb eaten?" The last thing she needed was an early-morning spat with him.

"Yes. He has the pouts at the moment. I assume you two had a fight over something?" Victoria slanted a brow as she scraped butter on her toast.

"Yeah. What's new?" Tina pulled out a chair. Trading in her frown for a smile, she turned to Cecilia. "And how are you this morning, Cecilia?"

"I'm wonderful, thank you, dear." Her green eyes glittered over the rim of her teacup.

During a few minutes of polite breakfast chit-chat, plates of poached eggs, pancakes, bacon and an assortment of pastries were served. Ravenous, Tina piled her plate and dug in.

"We've been thinking about our strategy to optimize the island's natural assets, and Cecilia and I have come up with a couple of ideas." In bright spirits, Victoria readied herself to explain.

Tina swallowed and waved her fork. "Vickie, now's not the time. We've got some serious business to attend to first." Her words landed with a thud, and the older women lowered their cutlery. "Sorry. I didn't mean to be rude, but there's more going on here than any of us expected." Through mouthfuls of food, Tina explained about last night's discovery.

"Who could possibly be doing this?" asked Victoria.

"That's what we have to find out. But I'm not taking any chances. That's why I'm calling the Coast Guard. I'm sure they'll be able to help." Swiping a piece of toast over her plate, she ensured she left no trace of food.

"Are you going to tell Sebastien about what you saw?"

"No. Not yet. We're not on very good terms, so I think I'll just follow this up by myself. Give him a couple of days to cool off. What do you think?"

Victoria exchanged a glance with Cecilia, who remained expressionless. "I guess so. I know he can be difficult, Tina, but he is your brother and part-owner of the island. He has a right to know."

"I know. Let me call the Coast Guard, see what they say. Then I'll tell Seb."

"Very well. But as soon as you talk to the Coast Guard, come and tell us." Victoria pushed her plate away. "This whole thing has put me off my breakfast."

"Don't worry about it, Vickie. I'm sure we'll get to the bottom of it. And when we do, pity help whoever is behind this."

"It reminds me of one of the clubs I performed in many years ago," said Cecilia, folding her napkin.

"How so?" Victoria propped her elbows on the table and sipped her coffee.

"For months the owner couldn't reconcile his alcohol stocktake. Because he wasn't there all the time, he had other people managing the club for him. He got his food and beverage manager, who was a long-time friend to do the weekly audit. But it kept coming up short. Eventually, the owner had no other option but to install hidden cameras, which he told no one about. And what did he find?"

"The food and beverage manager was ripping him off," Tina concluded.

"Exactly. As much as his friend pretended the alcohol must have been taken by the other staff, it was him all the time."

"But why does turtle-egg smuggling remind you of that episode at the club?" asked Victoria.

"Because it sounds like an inside job to me. Just like at the club. Someone who knows how the island operates is behind this." Cecilia reclined in her chair, looking pleased with herself.

"I think so too," added Tina, with a nod.

"Dickie would be mortified to know that someone he'd placed his trust in would turn against him like this." Disappointment rang in Victoria's voice.

"Don't worry yourself over it. At least we know what's happening. I'll call the Coast Guard and let you know. Okay?" Shoving back her chair, Tina rose and kissed her step- mom.

Concern drew Victoria's brows together. "Thank you, darling. But be careful. I don't want you taking any risks. I know how you can be."

"It'll be fine, Vickie. I'll see you both soon."

"We'll be up at the cottage. Victoria and I are doing a thousand-piece jigsaw puzzle together. It's terribly difficult." Cecilia rolled her eyes.

"What's it of?"

"Can you believe it? It's called the turtle guardian puzzle," said Cecilia.

"Two sea turtles and fish swimming through a brightly colored reef," added Victoria with a brittle smile.

"Where did you find that?" asked Tina.

"In Dickie's library." Victoria's voice hitched.

"He may not be with us in body, but it certainly appears that Dickie is still with us in spirit," said Cecilia, her eyes dancing from Tina to Victoria.

* * * *

Tap, tap, tap. Tina knocked at the cottage door and peered inside. "Vickie, Cecilia. Are you here?"

"Come in," called Cecilia, closing the back door behind her. "I was just in the bathhouse. Victoria had a couple of things to attend to. She'll be back shortly. Would you like tea or coffee?"

"I'd kill for a coffee, thanks." Wandering over to the kitchen table, Tina studied the half-finished jigsaw puzzle. "You're making progress on this. I hope it's a good omen for me and the real turtle situation."

"I'm sure you'll sort everything out. Let me make these, and we can sit on the veranda."

As Cecilia hustled up a couple of coffees, she moved with the efficiency and swiftness of someone much younger than her sixty-nine years. Although having known her for only a short time, Tina felt a growing affection for her. But there was something more. Aside from Cecilia being intelligent, successful and financially independent, she reminded Tina of a shamanic gypsy woman. She was a living, breathing dichotomy. Mystery swirled around her like the silk caftans she wore — illusive and graceful. It niggled at Tina, and she had to unravel that mystery. "So how long were you housekeeper here?"

"Probably about six months back in late 1973, early '74. Do you take milk and sugar?" She turned, and for an instant, Tina glimpsed the face of a young Cecilia Freemont, full of life and adventure, not yet changed by the passage of time.

"Just milk, thanks." Tina fiddled with the puzzle pieces, trying to find a fit. "Did you enjoy it here? When you were the housekeeper?"

"Very much. I was one of those well-educated, big-city hippie girls — full of feminist ideals and ready to change the world." Her mouth stretched wide in a nostalgic grin. "I was a drifter but coming here changed a lot of things for me." She walked forward, offering Tina a mug of piping coffee. "Let's sit outside for a while."

With mug in hand, Tina followed her host and folded into one of the rattan chairs. "Changed how?"

"I came to realize that life is too short not to give it your best shot. If you have a dream, you can't sit around waiting for it to come to you. You've got to go to it. No matter what." With a sly grin, Cecilia sipped her coffee and regarded Tina.

"And what was the dream you followed no matter what?"

"To be a professional singer."

"Vickie tells me you were a successful nightclub singer in America, playing the cabaret circuit."

"Yes. I was one of the lucky ones. My singing career supported me all my life." She glanced at the mug Tina held in her lap. "Is the coffee okay?"

"Oh, yes. I'm just letting it cool a little. I don't know how you drink it so hot." She blew across the steaming surface.

"I guess it's one of the benefits of living longer. You can take the heat better." Cecilia's eyes twinkled with unspoken meaning.

Tina steered the conversation back to what she wanted to know. "Did you ever get married? Have children?"

"I had many opportunities to get married, but I turned them all down. I wasn't going to tie myself to a man. And besides, I don't think I loved any one of them enough to marry them and have children."

Tina tilted her head. "So, you never fell in love?" A long silence hung between them, but neither broke the other's gaze.

Placing her empty mug on the side table, Cecilia folded her hands in her lap. "Yes, I fell in love once. But it wasn't meant to be." Like a cloud, the distant memory passed across her face, brushing it with a soft pink blush.

Suppressing the urge to barge in with the burning question she wanted to ask, Tina waited a beat. "That's a shame. Was he in love with you?"

"Yes, he was. At least, that's what he told me. But that was a long time ago."

"So, you never fell in love with anyone else all these years?"

"I loved other men, but not like that. There was a destiny to my first love that I never felt with anyone else again. I think it just wasn't our time. We went our separate ways, and we both achieved our dreams. It may not be the romantic happy-ever-after ending, but it is a happy ending. As they say, maybe in the next life." A bittersweet smile brightened her face. "Your coffee must be cool enough to drink now?"

"Yes, thanks." She sipped a few mouthfuls.

"And what about you, Tina? Do you want a romantic happy-ever-after ending or would you be satisfied with a happy ending?"

"Now that I've inherited Harbor Island with Seb, I doubt there'll be any time for me to consider a happy-ever-after. Besides, I've only just got divorced, so I'm off men for a while. I guess I'm like you in a lot of ways. I value my independence too much to give it away to a man."

"Maybe you haven't found the right man yet?"

"Maybe. But I'm not looking at the moment. There're too many other things to take care of." On finishing her coffee, she lowered her mug to the table.

"I remember a story about courage, told to me many years ago by a wonderful old Hawaiian man named Joseph. He spoke about the warriors diving off this high, jagged cliff called Black Rock to prove their manhood. At each stage of the pursuit, they had to overcome their fears: climbing the rock, standing on the ledge of the rock, leaping from the rock into the crashing sea below and escaping the fate of being dashed to pieces at the base of the rock. Joseph described the feeling of freedom when he dived off Black Rock as his soul taking flight, like a bird."

Tina frowned. "But what has that got to do with finding the right man?"

"When you find him, you'll have to overcome your fears and find the courage to leap. That's what love is all about, Tina, leaping into the unknown."

"But don't you regret not leaping with this man you loved so long ago?"

"Oh no, Tina, that's where you're wrong. We did leap. And I've never forgotten him or the feeling."

* * * *

"Where the hell have you been? I've been looking for you since yesterday afternoon." It was obvious Sebastien's mood had not improved since their argument, despite Tina giving him nearly twenty-four hours to cool off. Bellowing like a wounded bull, his voice bounced off the stainless-steel surfaces. Tina had just made a sandwich for lunch in the main kitchen when he'd taken her by surprise. Since calling the Coast Guard earlier in the morning, she'd done everything she could to stay out of his way, but her appetite had betrayed her. Startled by the new owners' altercation, the kitchen staff scattered, leaving Tina and Sebastien facing off alone in the vacuous kitchen.

"I'm sorry, Seb. I didn't know I had to report to you," she retorted, readying for another round.

"Well, if you expect me to keep you informed of what I'm doing, I expect the same in return." He splayed his massive hands on the counter and glowered. "So . . .?"

"*So . . .*" she hissed a sarcastic sneer. "I've been talking to some of the stakeholders and familiarizing myself with the overall operation. You know, a quick SWOT analysis: strengths, weaknesses, opportunities, and threats."

"And what did you discover?" His voice sounded less antagonistic.

"Not a lot yet, but over the next few days I'll have a report ready for us to go over if you like." A lurking half-smile twitched her lips, and she prayed it would be enough to temper his anger even more.

"Do you need me to do anything in particular? You know, to help?"

"Actually, would you mind meeting with Alan Rosenbaum and going through some of those figures with him. Get a clearer idea of the projected forecasts and risks? Why not go back to Maui for the weekend. Chill out away from this place. Then come back on Tuesday. What do you say?"

A salacious smile played at the corners of his mouth, and Tina knew she'd hit her mark. The chance for her brother to indulge his sexual persuasions away from Harbor Island would be too good to resist.

"You wouldn't mind if I took the weekend off?"

"No, of course not. I think we both need a break from work and from the island. I'll do some relaxing here while you're gone. You meet with Alan, and when you return on Tuesday, we'll start afresh. Get Jacob to motor you across in the cruiser. Andrew can give you a list of any supplies we need so you can bring them back with you." By now, she'd also convinced herself that it was a cracking plan. She smiled at Seb, and he responded in kind.

"Thanks. We could both use a break. I'll arrange everything, meet with Alan and see you back here Tuesday." Leaning forward, he brushed a desultory kiss on her cheek, turned and strode from the kitchen like a man on a mission. And Tina knew exactly what that mission was. For Sebastien to bed as many women as he could over the next few days. Feeling quite smug about her ingenious plan to get rid of him, she returned to her sandwich, tearing at the crust with zeal.

CHAPTER TWENTY-SIX

A knock on the door broke Tina's concentration. When she raised her head and saw Andrew, it became painfully obvious the toll Dickie's death, and subsequent events had taken on him. His greying hair seemed greyer, and his normally strong physique looked shrunken. Instead of a lighthearted, happy expression, exhaustion carved dark hollows under his eyes. Even the promise of a hot, summery Saturday had little impact on lifting his spirits. *He's the one who needs a break, not bloody Sebastien.*

"Yes, Andrew, what is it?"

"There's a Jack Holmes here to see you. He says he's from Honolulu."

"Jack Holmes?" She frowned. "Show him through, please. And, Andrew, take the rest of the weekend off. The staff know their rosters. They can manage without you. Go home and relax. Okay?"

"Thanks, I will. But you know where I am if you need me." Visibly relieved, he retreated from the office.

Into Andrew's place materialized a tall, animated, good-looking man in his early forties. Possessed of an uncompromising presence, he stepped forward with the confidence of a Shakespearean actor. His piercing dark eyes scrutinized her from his high-cheekboned face. Circumnavigating his inscrutable expression was a cap of thick black hair crested in a sharp widow's peak and a strong jaw roughened with dark bristle. Tina drew a breath. She wondered which was more compelling, the sheer force of will with which he entered the room or his drop-dead gorgeous looks. Before she had time to decide, a solid, well-proportioned hand thrust toward her.

"Morning, ma'am, I'm Captain Jack Holmes from the US Coast Guard." Even his rich, clipped voice added to his magnetic presence.

Gulping down her surprise that the Coast Guard enlisted such exemplary male specimens, she shook his hand. "Hello, Captain Holmes. I'm Tina Templeton, but I wasn't expecting anyone so soon. Do you have some ID?"

With a stiff smile, he dug out his wallet and flipped open his military ID, which she perused thoroughly.

"Thank you. Please have a seat." She flourished her hand to the vacant chair, into which he folded in one fluid movement.

"After your call yesterday, I decided it might be better if I shoot over in my civvies on the ferry. That way I'm not calling any attention to my being here."

"Yes, I understand." Though she didn't agree — Captain Jack Holmes would be hard-pressed not to call attention to himself no matter what he wore. Dressed in figure-hugging blue jeans, tan loafers, pale-blue polo shirt, and cream jacket, he couldn't be classed as a low-key visitor. In fact, he looked more like a wealthy playboy. *If he looks this good in his civvies, imagine what he looks like in uniform.* She chased the image away. She censored her naughty smile and said, "Would you like some coffee or tea?"

"No thanks, ma'am. But if you could talk me through what you saw on Thursday night, we'll get started with the formal investigation. As you know, the Coast Guard's role is not just to protect our borders, but to protect the marine environment as well. If what you say is true, and that's my job to find out, we have the power to enforce maritime law, arrest and detain these criminals until they come to trial."

"Well, Captain Holmes—"

"Please, call me Jack. It'll be less suspicious if people hear us talking." He slid his hand into his lightweight jacket and retrieved a brown leather-bound notebook and pen.

"Very well, Jack." Over the next hour, she provided him with everything she knew about Harbor Island's history, family, stakeholders, Origin Beach, Dickie's death and the terms and conditions of his will. In some cases, she didn't know the answers to the captain's questions, but nothing fazed him. When he back-tracked or side-barred topics, it reminded her of when she'd questioned informants for her stories. Being on the receiving end of his casual yet intense interrogation gave her more empathy for those who'd previously submitted to her grilling. Old school, he scribbled notes in his little notebook, flicking the lined pages as he went, with rarely a pause.

Eventually, he closed the notebook and tucked it back into his jacket. "Thank you, Miss Templeton—"

"Call me Tina," she interrupted.

"Thank you, Tina. You're a fine witness. Your attention to detail is impressive."

"Thanks. I'm an investigative journalist by profession, so I understand what you need — the facts, not supposition."

"Correct." He inclined his head. "You're not American, are you?"

"No, I'm Australian. My father and mother were Australian, but when Mum died, Dad married Victoria Reginald. My stepbrother and I grew up in Australia, but we holidayed here on Harbor Island. I've done a lot of traveling, so my accent is pretty muddled."

"Actually, it's real easy on the ear." For the first time since his arrival, his face relaxed. A lopsided smile broke its rugged symmetry, exposing a softer side to Captain Holmes. "Now, do you think we could take a walk around? I need to get a better understanding of the lay of the land, so to speak."

"Of course. I'm sure you'd like a coffee or tea by now?"

"Yes, I would. Thank you."

As Tina pushed up from her chair, he stood and stepped aside. Leading the way, she spared him a flirty glance, which he exchanged with an amused glint in his coal-black eyes.

* * * *

They strolled along The Esplanade, and Tina pointed out the various landmarks and shops, giving Jack as much information as she could.

"Over on the other side of the wharf is the boathouse." She lifted her arm, directing his attention.

"Yes. I noticed it when the ferry docked. That's where *Harbor Island V* is moored. Correct?"

"Yes. Do you want to see it?"

"It couldn't hurt. Let's wander over and check it out."

The breeze from the harbor swirled and wrapped them in a warm shawl of silence. Tina listened to the whispering waves as they rose and fell on the beach. The sound never failed to calm her. It reminded her of what was important in life and how transient everything was. When Jack turned his face to the harbor, she caught a glimpse of his love for the sea. It was refreshing to be near someone who understood.

"Have you been to Harbor Island before?" she asked, a dreamy tone in her voice.

"We tour the oceans around it, but I haven't actually been here. It lives up to its reputation, though. It really is one of the last places in Hawaii that hasn't been ruined by mindless progress."

"Yes. Thanks to Uncle Dickie."

"Sounds like he was a special man."

"He was." She stopped and caught Jack's arm. "Oh no. It's Rod Fischer. I told you about him — park ranger of sorts, does general construction and maintenance.

He's coming right toward us. How am I going to introduce you?"

"Just say hello, and I'll take care of the rest."

She gave him a nervous glance. But Jack just smiled. It was a wide-mouth, open smile that exposed a row of dazzling, well-formed teeth showcased against the backdrop of his sun-kissed, caramel-colored complexion. A shiver darted up from the base of Tina's skull. She looked him directly in the eye. Had she met him before? Her mind rifled through its files, searching for the memory, but she couldn't latch onto anything.

"Good morning, Tina," hollered Rod on his approach, his sinewy arm waving a welcome. Dressed in crumpled khaki cargo shorts and shirt, he eyed Jack's well-cut clothes with obvious envy, and the man who wore them, with suspicion.

Tina slowed the pace, allowing Rod to meet them. "Hi, Rod. This is Jack Holmes. Jack, this is Rod Fischer."

"Hi, Rod," effused Jack, thrusting his hand forward.

Rod hesitated a moment and then clasped the newcomer's hand with a pump. "Hi, Jack." Rod twitched and arched an eyebrow in her direction. Her lips tilted in a coy smile, but she remained mute, conceding to Jack. Unable to wait, Rod continued, "So, what brings you to Harbor Island, Jack?"

"Actually, I'm looking to buy a boat like *Harbor Island V*, and since she's for sale, I thought I'd pop over and check her out." He flashed an even bigger smile.

Confused, Rod frowned at Tina. "You didn't tell me you're selling the cruiser. Why would you do that? She's only new."

Her mind raced, but Jack had the answer. "It's not so much a straight-out sale, Rod. I have a cruiser about ten years older than yours, and I want to upgrade. Tina said she'd consider doing a swap-over with some cash for *Harbor Island V*. So here I am." Adding a jaunty tilt of his head, Jack played the part of a cashed-up buyer with aplomb.

A flicker of a smile graced Tina's lips. "Sorry, Rod. I didn't have a chance to come and tell you. But that's the situation. Why don't we go to the boathouse and take a look at her?" Stepping off, she set the pace while both men fell in beside her.

Keeping his voice low, Rod grumbled, "But what's the point of selling her? We need a decent boat. It doesn't make good business sense."

"Unfortunately, tough times call for tough decisions." She shrugged, and they walked on in silence.

On reaching the boathouse, Rod retrieved the key from its hiding place and opened up. "She's in here, Jack." Pouting, he stepped into the boathouse and switched on the lights.

"Wow, she's been well looked after." Jack wandered over to the vessel and caressed her like a well-loved pet.

"Yes, Rod does a terrific job of maintaining her." She gave Rod a grateful smile and watched, bemused as he puffed up his chest.

"Can we go aboard?" asked Jack.

"Sure," replied Rod, and then checked with Tina for confirmation.

"Of course."

Once on deck, she allowed Rod to give Jack the tour while she stood back and watched. No stranger to good-looking men, she was surprised at how Jack's presence set her heart to flutter. Fascinated by such an immediate visceral response, she studied the captain as he went about his mock inspection. Where Rod moved about the boat, Jack stalked it. Like some untamed predator, every step he took was calculated; every word he spoke loaded with inference; every look he gave scrutinized his quarry, which in this case, was Rod. Everything about Jack was on purpose and executed with purpose. Maybe that was what spoke to her on such a deep level. He was a man of intention and action.

Amid their conversation of boat specifications and performance, and on Jack's request, Rod switched on the batteries and returned to the helm. "Hey, what's this?" Concern echoed in his voice, and he nodded to Tina to join them.

"What?" Jack peered over Rod's shoulder at the instrument panel.

"The mileage is wrong." Studying the logbook in his hand, Rod pointed to the last figure on the column. "Here, I wrote it down when we took her out last time. But look at the mileage now." He pointed to the digital display.

"Maybe you wrote down the wrong number?" Tina suggested.

"No way. I'm very thorough when it comes to the boat."

"And you haven't taken her out since then?" Jack knew full well it had been Tina who'd taken out the boat on her secret mission.

"No, but someone else must have." Turning toward her, he said, "I'm sorry, Tina. Maybe we should have moved the key when you mentioned it. This has never happened before."

"Don't worry about it. At least, whoever took her out brought her back. And she's not damaged. We'll work out a new system with the key when we lock up today."

Relief flooded his face. "Thanks."

Space onboard boats came at a premium, but in a helm designed for two seated people, Tina found herself crushed next to Jack. Angling her shoulder, she claimed a little more room, but frisson still arced between them.

"Maybe we could take her out for a test drive tomorrow." Jack grinned at her.

"Of course. That would be fine."

"No need for you to trouble yourself tomorrow, Rod. I can handle the boat and from what Tina tells me, so can she. Thanks for the inspection, though."

Obviously unsettled at being told what to do by a stranger, Rod scowled and shot Tina a silent query while Jack disembarked.

"Yes, thanks, Rod. Jack and I will take her out tomorrow. I'll take the keys now and let you know after we come back where we'll keep them from now on." Holding her palm upward, she waited.

Rod dropped the keys into her hand and then set about completing his tasks. His silent displeasure ricocheted through the boathouse.

Once outside, Tina locked the door and pocketed the keys. "Rod, how's your truck going at the workshop?" She motioned for the two men to walk with her.

"Jacob's doing a terrific job. He reckons he'll be finished by Monday."

She raised her eyebrows. "Does he? That's quick. Mustn't have been much wrong with her, then?"

"No, not really. She just needed a good service, oil change, and tire rotation. Thanks for paying for it. It's really appreciated." He skipped a little two-step like an excited kid.

She laughed. "That's okay, Rod. We need another truck around here in case the Chevy suddenly dies. I figure if I can help keep yours in better condition, you won't mind helping us out if we need it sometime." On purpose, she squeezed his shoulder in gratitude.

He captured her hand before it could escape. "Geez, Tina. You know I'd do anything for the island and you."

Wiggling her fingers free, she extricated her hand with a tug. "Thanks. Now, Jack and I will leave you to it. I'll see you tomorrow or Monday."

Displaying his well-used hangdog look, he said, "Okay, see you then."

With a sunny smile, Tina strode off down The Esplanade with Jack beside her. Once out of earshot of Rod, Jack stopped. "Is there anywhere around here where I can get a good meal?"

"Sure. The diner up the road does food. I had breakfast there the other day, and I must say it was delicious. I'll be interested to know what you think of it." She nodded for him to follow her across the street.

"Terrific. I could eat a cow I'm so hungry," he joked. "Sorry. I hope you're not vegetarian?"

"No, I'm a carnivore." She laughed, matching his good humor.

"Glad to hear it. I wouldn't like to offend my leading witness."

Like a wild horse, an unrestrained thought galloped into her mind. The thrill of it raced through her body. There it was again — that unexplained feeling. She hoped she might mean more to him than just his leading witness.

CHAPTER TWENTY-SEVEN

"Well, you're correct. They do a damn fine burger and fries." Jack wiped his mouth, tossed the paper serviette onto his empty plate and sculled the last draft of his black coffee. "I'll get the check, and we'll be off."

"Off to where?" Tina gulped down the last of her lukewarm tea.

"Let's take a drive. Is the Chevy fueled up?"

"Yes."

"Good." He shoved out of his chair, and while he paid for lunch, she waited outside on the pavement.

"Oops, sorry. Oh, hello." A flush-faced and disheveled Suzie Lin swooped in, almost bowling Tina over.

"You look like you've run a marathon, Suzie."

"I'm running late opening my shop," she babbled, perspiration leaking from her pores.

Tina glanced at her watch. *Three hours late, in fact.* "But why so late?"

"It's those wretched lights in the harbor. They were there again last night." Eyes wide with excitement, Suzie's face glowed.

Jack slipped in beside Tina and cleared his throat. "Suzie, this is Jack Holmes. Jack, this is Suzie Lin, the owner of the souvenir shop I told you about, remember?" She paused for effect.

"Hi, Suzie." He offered his hand and a charming smile, both of which Suzie ignored.

"I don't shake hands with men I don't know. Who are you?"

"I'm a businessman from Honolulu."

Panic-stricken, Suzie grabbed Tina's forearm. "You're not selling Harbor Island, are you? Oh, don't do that. Dickie would never forgive you."

Tina held the store owner's shaking hands. "Calm down. I'm not selling the island. Please calm down. Take a deep breath." Demonstrating, she inhaled, and Suzie copied. "There. Now tell me about the lights you saw last night."

"Can he be trusted?" Her eyes raked Jack up and down.

"Yes, he can be trusted," reassured Tina with a soft laugh.

"Very well. Last night I was in my shop, painting a particularly lovely canvas until very late. When I finally finished, I came outside, and that's when I saw those damn lights again."

"Where?" asked Jack.

"Way out there. Beyond the reef. They kept going from one side to the other and back again." She waved her arm from right to left in a wide sweep.

Jack eased in behind her and gazed out to where she pointed. "Do you think they could have been boats? Small boats. Cruising from one side to the other and then they disappeared behind the cliffs at either end of the island?"

Narrowing her gaze across the ocean, Suzie twisted her lips. "Maybe."

"What else do you think they could have been?" asked Tina.

"Like I told you before, I. Don't. Know. But they were there all right. I kept watching them for ages. Back and forth. Back and forth." Inclining her head back, she glanced up over her shoulder at Jack. "You know, you could be right. They looked like they just kept going off and on, but maybe they were boats."

"How long did you watch them?" He slipped back beside Tina.

"Oh, maybe two hours. I got tired and had to go home." She shifted her gaze to Tina. "And that's why I'm so late now. I slept in. I must go and open the shop. Goodbye." Suzie pivoted and then stopped. Shuffling closer to Jack, she tilted back her head and squinted a long stare at his face. "Who are you? You're no businessman. Wait until I do a tarot card reading on you, my man. I'll find out who you are." She wagged a finger at him.

"Can we walk you to your shop?" he said, clearly unconcerned by her threat of exposure.

"If you like. It's just down here on the right." In small, brisk steps, she dashed off.

Jack hung back with Tina for a moment. "I see what you meant when you said everyone calls her Silly Suzie. She's eccentric all right."

"But why are we going to the shop?"

"You'll see."

By the time she and Jack arrived, the front door to the shop was flung open, and Suzie bustled around inside like an industrious beaver, preparing for her day's trading.

"Wonderful shop you have here. Original and artistic," said Jack, surveying the overstuffed shop.

Tina watched him amble around, inspecting the canvases and knick-knacks.

"Where's this painting that kept you up so late last night?" he asked while admiring a hand-woven placemat.

Suzie bustled to a nearby easel and carefully lifted the dust cover off the canvas. "I call it, *Grey day in the quarry.*"

Tina and Jack stepped closer to view the painting. Massive perpendicular cliffs of hewn grey rock loomed from the canvas. It had an almost 3D effect. The whole image was a monochromatic study in shades of grey, black and white. "Oh, Suzie, this is good. Really good."

Jack leaned in and sniffed. "Yes, it is. How much are you selling it for?"

Jittering like a bird on a wire, Suzie couldn't hide her anticipation of a possible sale. She raced to the counter and tapped away on an old calculator. While her attention focused on the math, Jack touched the canvas, testing the paint. It was then that Tina realized why he'd insisted on coming.

Rubbing his finger to thumb, he leaned over and whispered. "It's still wet. She may be crazy, but she's no liar."

"Three hundred dollars," exclaimed Suzie in a loud voice.

"I'll take it."

"Cash," she added.

"Done." He strode to the counter, folded off three one-hundred bills and handed them over.

"You'll have to wait a day or two until it dries." She slipped the money into her trouser pocket.

"That'll be just fine. I'll pop over and collect it when I'm ready to go. Thank you, Suzie." He struck out his hand and this time it was accepted.

"Thank you, Jack Holmes, whoever you are." A glint flickered in her dark eyes.

* * * *

The Chevy roared to life, and Tina shot a dutiful glance at her handsome passenger. "Where to, Captain Jack?"

"Do you know how to get to this quarry Suzie painted?" He was all business once more.

"I think so. It's been a long time, but it's hard to get lost around here as there aren't many roads to choose from." She edged the Chevy onto The Esplanade and drove past the row of shops, then veered up the hill behind the boathouse.

"Aside from Rod and yourself, who else owns vehicles on the island?" He pulled out his notebook and pen, poised to take more notes.

"That I couldn't say for sure. I didn't see any paperwork on it anywhere. But Andrew might know."

"Good. I want to meet Andrew officially as well. He's been here the longest and probably has his ear to the ground better than most. You're sure he can be trusted?"

"Absolutely."

"And if someone wanted to get a vehicle on the island, how could they do it?"

"Only by barge, I expect. There's no other way. And I think Uncle Dickie would have had to approve it."

"Now, it'll be up to you and Sebastien to approve it. Correct?"

"Yes." She nodded, acknowledging yet another of her growing responsibilities.

A scattering of modest local houses dotted the landscape as they headed further inland on the dirt road. Climbing up the ranges, the Chevy found its stride in being given a good run.

"When was the last time you came out here?" Jack asked.

"Years ago."

"Is the road used much normally?"

"I don't think so. I mean, it's only the residents who use it, and I doubt they'd be many of them with vehicles. Why?"

"If the road isn't used much, you'd have to wonder why it's in such good condition. It looks like it's regularly graded."

She hadn't noticed, but he was right. The road's smooth surface belied how much rain fell in the wet season. No potholes or storm-water channels interrupted the truck's progress. "You're right." She tossed him a frown. "Why would Rod keep this road in such good condition if no one was really using it?"

"That's what I intend to find out. How long does it usually take to get to the quarry?"

"From memory, normally about forty to sixty minutes depending on the road."

He pulled back his jacket sleeve to check his watch. "We left town about ten minutes ago. Let's see how long it takes."

Skirting along the back ridge, Tina recalled driving this way with Uncle Dickie. Not much had changed. A web of untouched jungle clung to the mountain face on their left and plummeted into a deep ravine on their right. Shades from lush emerald, through mint, to tree-frog green crawled over the dark volcanic rock, determined to reclaim everything else since it couldn't devour the road. Like a giant brown serpent snaking through the ranges, the dirt road wound onward into darker, wilder territory. Neither she or Jack spoke. She wondered if the primitive beauty of this place touched him as much as it did her.

She slowed down. "We're here. The quarry is just around the next corner."

"Okay." He checked his watch and nodded. "Thirty minutes on a good road." Wariness settled on his face. "Go slow." He reached behind his back and pulled out a pistol. She jolted. "It's okay, just a precautionary measure in case we surprise anyone." His lips pulled in a grim line.

From experience in the field, she knew trouble could be waiting for them, but to see him cock his weapon sent icy shivers down her spine. She slowed to a crawl and rounded the corner. In front of them, a vast angular wall of salt-and-pepper monoliths reached skywards. The ancient jungle embraced the old quarry, its tendrils caressing the rock's hewn face as it attempted to soothe its harsh edges. She brought the Chevy to a halt.

"Looks pretty much like Suzie painted it. You wait here. I'll get out and have a look around." His hand pulled down on the door latch.

"Wrong thing to say to an investigative journalist." Her mouth puckered. Jack frowned. "Telling me to wait here," she explained. She opened her door and jumped down at the same time as him.

With his gun lowered to his side, he took the lead and light-footed ahead on a quick reconnaissance. After a few minutes, he called out, "Doesn't look like anyone else is here," and he holstered his weapon.

Branching off on foot, Tina surveyed the old quarry and its surrounds. She understood the importance that mining would have had to the sustainability of the island long ago, but to see the destructive footprint it left on the land made her sad and angry. The sooner the jungle reclaimed it, the better. Let nature cover the eyesore until it vanished forever. Behind her, she heard Jack's footsteps crunch on loose gravel, and she cast a quick glance back in his direction.

"Shit." She stumbled, buckling to her hands and knees.

"Are you all right?" He dashed to where she dropped.

"Yes," she spat, angry at her clumsiness. "I should watch where I'm walking." Rolling onto her bottom, she rubbed her knees. Fortunately, she'd worn cotton trousers and not shorts, otherwise her knees would have been as grazed as her palms.

"Here, let me look." With a surprisingly tender touch, he clasped her hands and inspected the damage. "Not too bad. Antiseptic will do the trick. You don't want infection here in the tropics."

"I know. I know." She winced. "How stupid am I, tripping over a damn—" When her eyes spied the culprit, she gasped. "Oh, God. Look." Her shaky finger pointed to not an oval-shaped rock, but an empty sea turtle shell semi-covered by moss.

Crouching over the shell, he peered inside. "There're knife marks on the internal walls of the shell. Someone's gouged out the turtle's body." He growled in disgust.

Pity pricked her heart when she thought of the terrible death inflicted on the gentle creature. "But what is it doing all the way out here in the quarry? They surely couldn't have hauled a live turtle from Origin Beach to here, just to kill it?"

"No. They probably killed it at the beach, took the meat and dumped the shell here." He raised his head and scanned the base of the quarry. "Sorry, but this time you do have to wait here. I'm going to look around a bit more and see what else I can find."

She had no other choice but to stay where she was. Her palms stung, and her wrists ached. She'd be more hindrance than help to him in this condition. She cursed herself for appearing so inept and awkward. Before long, the sound of crunching gravel signaled his return.

He dropped down on one knee beside her. "There're more turtle shells over there to the right." He pointed to a small clearing on the far side of the quarry. "Assholes!"

"Oh, that's awful." She shook her head, thinking how devastated Uncle Dickie would be if he were still alive.

"Come on. I'll help you up." He reached down and slipped his shoulder in under hers, heaving her upward.

"I'm fine. I can walk." She stumbled a little before finding her balance.

"You sure?"

"Of course." She glued a brave smile to her face, although her knees screamed.

"All right. I'll grab this shell as evidence. I don't want to disturb anything else in case these guys discover we've been here. I noticed you've got a tarp in the back of the truck we can cover it with. When we get back to the property, we'll sort out what to do with it then." Lugging the bone-and-cartilage casing onto his shoulder, he steadied it and paced to the truck. By the time he loaded and covered it, Tina arrived, and he helped her into the passenger seat. "I'll drive. You just sit there and relax." Reaching across her, he clipped in her seatbelt.

When he withdrew, the musky smell of his aftershave lingered under her nose. At least there was an upside to tripping over. She locked eyes with him and exchanged a smile. "Thanks, Jack."

The open skin of her palms smarted, demanding attention. On many occasions, she'd witnessed how a simple scratch in the tropics could turn septic in no time. Bloated purple fingers and toes from coral scratches were the worst, sometimes taking weeks to heal. Although healthy and strong, Tina knew she needed to disinfect and bandage her hands as soon as possible. She also made a mental note to put a first-aid kit containing A-grade disinfectant and gauze bandages in the Chevy.

With Jack behind the wheel, the truck rumbled to life. "Right. Off we go."

Obviously not wanting to leave any telltale signs of their presence, he backed away without throwing up any gravel or dirt. In his safe hands, Tina reclined in the seat, willing her hands to stop throbbing. They didn't. But for the first time since arriving on Harbor Island three weeks ago, she felt like she wasn't alone in shouldering the escalating problems she'd inherited.

CHAPTER TWENTY-EIGHT

Despite her burning palms and sore knees, she enjoyed the trip back home. With Jack at the wheel, she admired not only the stunning scenery but delighted in the intelligent company. "Were you serious about taking *Harbor Island V* out tomorrow?"

"Absolutely. I brought an overnight bag with me. Andrew was kind enough to stow it in the kitchen on my arrival this morning."

"Just like the boy scouts?" she teased.

"Yeah. Just like the boy scouts. Always prepared." He laughed. She liked the way it sounded. Deep and rich, like melted chocolate. She was thrilled his visit would be extended.

By late afternoon they drove into the property, and since the staff had clocked off for the day, no one witnessed their arrival. Jack checked their turtle shell cargo, securing the tarp over it firmly, before returning the truck keys to Tina.

"Come on. I'll take you to the guest quarters." She led the way, going via the kitchen to collect his bag.

"Amazing property you and your brother have inherited," he said as they strolled out the kitchen's rear door.

"When I was young and spent my school holidays here, I called it my happy place. There was always something wonderful to do — swimming, hiking, gardening, and boating with Uncle Dickie — like one of those idyllic, secret places in children's storybooks. That's what Harbor Island was to me." She sighed heavily. "And now, I'm responsible for keeping it that way."

"With your brother."

"Yes, but I don't think Seb sees it the same as I do. For me, Uncle Dickie left Harbor Island under our stewardship to protect and improve. But for Seb, I think he sees it as his future cash cow."

"So, he's the greed before the green?"

She turned to face him. *Had he really said that?*

"What? What did I say?" Polite panic touched his face.

"That phrase you used. My vision for this place is the green before the greed. It's odd that you used the same turn of phrase." Before he responded, Tina brushed it off and continued along the pathway. His chance remark was not something she had time to think about. Still ... When they reached the end of the pathway, she opened the wood grain door and smiled. "Here we are." Once inside the bungalow, she gave him a quick tour of the amenities.

"Very nice." He dropped his kit bag on the bed.

"Thanks. Harbor Island is special, but then again, I'm biased."

"I don't think you're biased. It is special, including this bungalow. The US Coast Guard rarely gets quarters like this." He strode across the room and out through the sliding patio glass doors on the other side. "The gardens are super. It must take a hell of a lot of staff to maintain this place."

"It does. But the gardens were always Uncle Dickie's passion." She edged in beside him while he admired the orchids.

He bent over and reached for the spray of waxy pink flowers, allowing them to droop in his palm. "I love orchids, but I don't have the time in my job to tend to them. But if I did, these would be my first choice in the garden." He lowered his hand, and the spray of flowers nodded under their own weight once more. With the same care, he lifted Tina's hands and inspected her inflamed palms. "You better go and tend to these."

Feeling a blush as pink as the orchids flash up her neck, she withdrew her hands. "You're right. I'll see you back in the kitchen at five o'clock. I'll arrange for Vickie, Andrew, and Cecilia to join us for dinner in the great pavilion. I can introduce you then."

"Okay. I'll see you at five." His face opened in a smile.

Tina thought it was as lovely as the orchids. She waited a moment, expecting him to say more, but he didn't. Like a hypnotist, his gaze never faltered, his dark eyes penetrating her subconscious. She tried not to, but she blinked first. "See you then." She eased past him and headed for the door.

"Tina?" His warm, velvety voice tapped on her shoulder.

"Yes?" She turned.

"I'm glad I took this case."

"I'm glad you did too." Before another hot flush betrayed her, she left Captain Jack Holmes to freshen up.

As she hurried away, she found herself thinking things she shouldn't. Unexpected, erotic images filled her mind. Skin-on-skin contact with Jack's muscled body as it pressed hard against hers in a steamy shower. The hungry urgency of hands lathering each other with swathes of silky soap, exploring private places. Running from the lust that ricocheted real-time in her body, she fled along the pathway, into her bungalow and slammed the door behind her. Too loud, but she didn't care. A breath trembled between her lips. Gripped by the escalating fantasy, her chest heaved, and her groin burned. Try as she might to ignore it by rationalizing that she'd sworn off men, it didn't work. She strode into her bathroom to take a shower. But despite how cold she turned the tap, she couldn't dislodge the image of making love to Jack Holmes or the insistence of her reawakened desire.

* * * *

With Sebastien away, inviting Victoria, Andrew, and Cecilia to dine with her proved easy. The promise of a convivial atmosphere with no sibling rivalry meant everyone arrived on time, ready for an amicable evening.

"We haven't seen you all day." Victoria pressed a soft kiss to Tina's cheek.

"I've been busy working on a couple of things."

"And how's it going?" asked Cecilia, looking her elegant, gypsy best in a white cotton caftan, strewn with rainbow crystals.

"Pretty good."

"Drinks, ladies?" Andrew poured glasses of white wine and handed one to each.

As Tina reached for hers, Victoria grabbed her hands. "Darling, whatever have you done to yourself?" She inspected her stepdaughter's iodine-stained palms, which also sported a couple of plasters.

"It's nothing. I fell over today and grazed them. I'm fine. Really I am."

Victoria frowned and twisted her mouth in displeasure, but said no more.

"Cheers," interjected Andrew in a cheery voice, saluting his glass to the women.

"Cheers," came the chorus.

"So, have you called the Coast Guard yet about what you and Andrew saw on Thursday night?" asked Victoria, sipping her wine.

"In fact, I did."

"And?" asked Cecilia.

Tina lowered her glass and gave each of them a quick glance. "It seems the US Coast Guard is one of the few organizations in the world that act swiftly." Puzzled expressions greeted her. "I'd like to introduce US Coast Guard Captain Jack Holmes from Honolulu." Flourishing an arm toward the partition at the back of the great pavilion, she presented her surprise guest like a game-show hostess.

On cue, Jack appeared and strode toward them. Along with the others, Tina drew a breath. Impressive even in casual blue jeans, white shirt, and blue blazer, he marched up to the group, the epitome of military bearing and authority. "Good evening, everyone," he said, coming to a sharp halt.

"Jack, this is Andrew, whom you met this morning," said Tina.

Andrew's mouth stretched in a sly smile. "Good to meet you, Captain." He offered his hand, which Jack grasped in a hearty shake.

"Sorry about the subterfuge this morning, Andrew. Call me Jack."

"This is my stepmother, Victoria Templeton, Uncle Dickie's sister."

Jack transferred his attention to Victoria and offered his hand. "Pleasure to meet you, Mrs. Templeton."

She blinked twice and hesitated.

"Vickie, are you all right?" asked Tina.

"Yes, yes. So sorry. Lovely to meet you, Jack." She shook his hand.

"And finally, this is Cecilia Freemont." When Tina turned to Cecilia, she noticed the same dazed expression pass across her face. "Are you all right, Cecilia?"

"Yes, my dear. I'm sorry." She lifted her delicate hand toward Jack. "A pleasure to meet you, Captain."

"And you, Ms. Freemont." He shook her hand gently.

"Can I get you a drink, Jack?" offered Andrew.

"A Bud would be terrific if you have one?"

"Budweiser it is," obliged Andrew, returning to the bar.

In the few moments it took to retrieve Jack's beer, Tina and Jack traded strained smiles with Victoria and Cecilia. Tina gave a puzzled frown to one woman and then the other. *What on earth is going on with these two?* But she daren't put them on the spot about their odd behavior. Later — it would have to wait until later.

"Here you go, Jack." Andrew handed him the beer.

"Thanks. Cheers, everyone," he said, before tugging a long draft from the bottle.

"Well, Tina, it's time to fill us in on all the details," prodded Cecilia.

"Maybe it's best if I leave Jack to explain what happened today and where to from here." She relinquished the floor. While they listened to the captain's comprehensive account of the day's events, she glanced at the others. The same emotions she'd felt throughout the day were mirrored on their faces: respect for Jack's obvious expertise and commitment to his job, horror at their gruesome discovery at the quarry, and relief that they weren't alone in having to deal with this serious and dangerous problem.

"Tomorrow, Tina and I are going to run *Harbor Island V* out to Origin Beach to take a look around. There's foul play at work here. I'm sure of it. My job will be to find whoever is behind it."

"Do you have any ideas who it could be yet?" Victoria stared hard at the captain, her anger obvious.

"No, ma'am. Not yet. But rest assured, I will find them. Excuse me for swearing, ladies, but these assholes are environmental criminals and as an animal lover myself, I hate the thought of what's going on."

"Animal lover you say," interjected Cecilia, her eyes bright with interest. "Any favorites?"

"I love dogs, ma'am. I can't have one, because I'm not around enough to care for it properly. But nothing beats a dog — loyal, protective, loving and vigilant."

"Funny you should say that." Cecilia turned to Victoria and smiled. "Remember Lucy, Dickie's golden retriever? She was such a good companion to me when you were both at college."

"Yes, I do. She was a wonderful dog. Dickie adored her." Victoria exchanged a wistful look with Cecilia.

"I left Harbor Island not long after we found her abandoned on the beach. How long did Lucy live, Andrew?"

"She lived well into old age. Broke Dickie's heart when she finally died. He had other dogs after her, but none of them meant as much as Lucy." His eyes moistened at the sweet memory.

Cecilia reached across and clasped his hand. "I know. Lucy was a special dog."

"That's why I love dogs," added Jack. "They have the power to touch your heart forever."

"Dinner is served, Miss Tina." The soft voice of Harbor Island's head cook interrupted their conversation.

"Thank you, Matthew. Everyone, let's sit down." With a sweep of her arm, Tina gestured toward the table. When Victoria and Cecilia moved ahead, she tried to overhear their whispered conversation but failed. Nevertheless, she noticed they engaged in an excited exchange with askance glances at Jack. Their eyes twinkled, and their lashes fluttered. Maybe like her, the older women were a little besotted by the handsome captain.

* * * *

By the time they'd consumed a delicious dinner of baked fish, vegetables and salads washed down with bottles of crisp white wine, the night ended on a high note with everyone laughing and chatting like long-time friends. Watching Jack interact throughout the evening endeared him even more to Tina. Aside from being easy on the eye, his sense of duty to his work reminded her of her commitment to her job. Workaholic was the term often used to describe their Type A personalities, but she took that as a compliment, not a criticism. Something she felt sure Jack did also. Being around a man who possessed a strong work ethic added to her rapidly growing affection for the Coast Guard Captain.

As they strolled back to the bungalows together, she ventured into more personal territory. "You say because of your job you don't have time to garden or care for a dog, so what do you have time for?"

"Not a lot. I've had a couple of serious relationships, but nothing really stuck. I guess I'm too tied to my work. At least, that's what all the previous women in my life have said. Sure, I love my work, but the irony is I do want to settle down and have a family of my own. Finding the right partner and the timing hasn't been right yet. But I better get to it soon."

"Why's that?"

"I'm nearly forty-three, so time is running out if I want to marry and have kids while I'm still young enough to enjoy them. What about you?"

"I was married for seven years, but that didn't work. We divorced about a year ago."

"Oh, I'm sorry to hear that."

"No big deal." She shrugged. "Uncle Dickie never wanted me to marry David in the first place. I should have listened to him. Fortunately, David and I never had any kids, so it made the breakup a lot easier."

"Do you want children?"

"To be honest, I never thought of it until recently. Inheriting Harbor Island has changed my thinking on many things, and having children is one of them. Who am I going to leave my share of Harbor Island to when I die? Without children, Uncle Dickie's legacy could end up anywhere. But if I want to have a family, I better start thinking about it seriously. At thirty-eight my clock is ticking." She slowed to a stop. "This is my bungalow." She faced him, not wanting to leave. Talking to Jack felt familiar and comfortable.

"I admire what you're doing here. Keeping your uncle's legacy alive won't be easy."

"No, it won't," she admitted. "But my life has never been about doing it easy. Uncle Dickie used to call me his 'go-to' girl. Go to Tina, and she'll sort it out. I think that's why he left Harbor Island to me and Seb."

"So, are you going to move here to live?"

"I don't know." She sighed. "But the longer I'm here, it seems the more I'm needed. This place requires constant management, and it's not Andrew's job. Unless I keep on top of what's happening on the island, the risk of things going wrong increases. I'm sure you understand?"

He nodded. "Yes, it's the curse of leadership."

"Even if I wanted to go back to Australia, I just don't know if I can without jeopardizing the island." Vocalizing this thought made it real for Tina. She had arrived wanting to make a change in her life, and here it was. Her past happy place would become her new home, whether she was ready for it or not. If she was to honor Uncle Dickie's legacy properly, there was no other option but for her to move here. She dragged her hand across her chin and shuddered at the thought of such a monumental change. But she also felt exhilarated by the opportunity. "But my main focus at the moment is to stop whatever is happening at Origin Beach, establish a sustainable tourism strategy to increase revenue and get Harbor Island into long-term profitability."

"Not much time left for love and children in that program." He gave a short, sharp laugh.

"No, I guess not. But if you want something bad enough, you make time."

"Agreed." Jack gazed into her eyes.

A shiver of nervous excitement prickled her skin. This time she would not blink first. But she did. "Well, good night, Jack. After breakfast, we'll take out the boat."

"That's the plan." He nodded, his dark eyes twinkling. "Good night, Tina."

She opened her door, stepped inside and closed it softly behind her. With her back pressed against it, she listened for his exiting footsteps. Nothing. But in his job, he was a master of stealth, so he could either still be there or have left without a sound. She remained against the door wondering how in just one day, this man could have made such an impact on her. Not the ditsy type to be swept away by handsome men, she felt elated in his presence, valued in his company, and respected for who she was as a person. Jack Holmes possessed the unique ability of making a woman feel important, not because she was of the "fairer" sex, but because she was a worthwhile human being.

CHAPTER TWENTY-NINE

Sunday morning dawned with the same grand promise Tina remembered from her childhood summer holidays. The atmosphere sparkled so pure and clear, she could see for miles out to sea without a single haze shimmer. Likewise, the water's clarity provided uninterrupted views to the treasure chest of brilliant coral at the bottom of the harbor. In true nautical fashion, Tina dressed in white shorts and boat shoes offset by her blue-and-white striped singlet top. Over the past few weeks, her skin had shed its insipid shade of alabaster white, the result of spending long hours in offices, studios, and planes. Now it glowed, deepened into a golden bronze from the sun's caress. All the running around the island had removed those few stubborn kilos she'd struggled to budge, leaving her muscles trimmed and defined.

At last, her body had returned to its natural lean, athletic shape. She felt good in her own skin for the first time in ages. Behind the helm, she skippered *Harbor Island V* with confidence, despite the periodic bite from her wounded palms. Life on Harbor Island suited her.

Standing beside her, Jack looked as handsome and in command as she imagined he would. With his navy shorts, shoes and white T-shirt, he made her perfect bookend. The thought delighted her more than she wanted to admit.

"You handle this boat damn good. You're quite the skipper." He beamed at her.

"Thanks. That means a lot coming from a US Coast Guard Captain." She exchanged a smile to match his.

Steering through the channel, she set course. Canary-yellow sunlight melted over the cruiser, and *Harbor Island V* sliced through the morning waves with ease. It breached the northernmost corner of land and arced west in double quick time, capitalizing on the perfect boating conditions. Rushing in through the side windows, the wind played in the cabin, teasing Tina's naked neck, arms, and legs. How she longed to be going on a relaxing Sunday run, rather than on the business of finding sea turtle smugglers. Nevertheless, one day when all this was over, she resolved to enjoy the island, like she used to. Take some time out and unwind.

Navigating the back coast of the island, she slowed and motored parallel with the sweeping curve of the shore. "Just up ahead on your left is Origin Beach. There." She pointed.

Jack retrieved his binoculars and gazed toward the stretch of beach. "I see the turtle tracks. The next full moon is the tenth of June, so the eggs will be hatching soon. If we want to save the baby turtles, we need to work out how this ring is operating before then."

"Do you see anything else?"

"Not yet. The jungle behind the beach looks impenetrable." He dropped his binoculars. "There must be another way to get in and out. Otherwise, we wouldn't have found all those adult turtle shells in the quarry."

"As I said, the only way is through the jungle behind the quarry, but I don't know how they do it. You're right, the jungle is impenetrable." She shook her head, disappointed.

"Okay. I've seen enough. Let's keep going and circumnavigate the island. I'm interested to see what's beyond Origin Beach in case they're coming in that way."

"Right." She pushed forward on the throttle, picking up speed.

Further along, massive cliffs sheered the shoreline, drawing a thin line of sandy beach at their base. "No way they can come in there," said Jack, gazing through his binoculars.

In less than twenty minutes, the cruiser passed the western point of the island. Before them, an ocean of cobalt blue stretched into the distance with no other land in sight. With the binoculars still jammed to his eyes, he surveyed the endless watery landscape. "Slow down and check your course."

She pulled back on the throttle and punched in her coordinates.

"Out there." Jack dropped the binoculars and pointed. Tina looked in the direction but couldn't see anything. "Here, I'll skipper. You stand up and look through these." Handing her the binoculars, he traded places. She stared through them into the infinite sea of blue.

"What am I looking for?" Her brow furrowed.

"It's a ship. Look harder."

After a few moments, she spied a tiny black spot blinking on the ocean swell. "I see something, but I can't say it's a ship."

"Trust me. It is." He stayed on course toward the speck in the distance.

Lowering the binoculars, she slid into the first mate's chair in the helm. "What does it mean?"

"The illegal sea turtle trade also includes the hatchlings. During the hatching season when tens of thousands of baby turtles dash to the beach at night, these gangs gather up as many turtles as they can. They dump them into water chambers in their tenders, and when they're full, they ferry them to their main fishing vessel waiting offshore. They offload the baby turtles into big under-deck tanks then return to the beach for more live cargo. Once the fishing vessel's tanks are full, they ship them back to whichever countries pay the highest price for turtles."

"And you think that spot out there is the main fishing ship?"

"Yes, I do. And I think they've got tender vessels with water chambers in which they load the hatchlings from the beach and then relay them back to the main ship night after night. That would account for the lights Suzie sees in the harbor at times."

"But what are they doing on the harbor side of the island? Surely, they'd keep as low a profile as possible and stay on this side of the island?"

"You'd think so. I couldn't tell you why they ventured into waters where they could be seen, but my gut tells me their operation revolves around nabbing the hatchlings and that ship out there is part of it. We won't go too much further, but I do want to take a closer look. Here, you take the helm."

Once more they exchanged places, and Tina kept a steady course. Jack adjusted the binoculars to his vision and gazed hard into the distance. "Pull back a little. Now veer south as if you're a vessel that lost course for a while. I don't want them getting suspicious and if we go any closer, they will."

"How's that?" she asked, setting the prescribed course.

"Good." He moved toward the back of the cabin and gazed out. "It's a fishing vessel all right. I bet they anchor out there and come closer to Origin Beach each night. I'd stake my job on it." With binoculars by his side, he strode back inside. "Okay. Let's go back to the harbor."

Pushing hard on the throttle, she steered for home. "What now?"

"If I'm right, it means there has to be a way they get their tender boats through the shore-break reef and onto Origin Beach. And I've got find a way to get there on foot. Are you sure there's no other way I can get to Origin Beach aside from through the quarry?"

"Well, there's Rainbow Falls."

"Tell me."

"Rainbow Falls is a waterfall cut into a hundred-foot sheer cliff face, surrounded by jungle. You get to it along the same road as we took for the quarry, but not as far out."

"Can you drive me there when we get back?"

"Sure. But I don't know what you expect to find. The terrain is just as difficult as the quarry."

"Tina, I've got to find a way onto Origin Beach without being seen. And the only way is through the jungle. I need to do reconnaissance, so I can plan the mission. On foot is the only way."

"Okay. But I'm coming with you."

"Not this time, I'm afraid. You can drive me there, but you'll have to wait in the truck until I return. Too dangerous." A non-negotiable expression creased his brow.

"But you might need some help," she persisted, hoping to change his mind.

"Thanks for the offer, but unlikely," snorted Jack. "As a captain in the US Coast Guard, I'm well equipped for these types of solo missions."

"I'm sure you are." She flashed a sarcastic grin and wondered if he was well equipped in other ways.

* * * *

"How was it?" On their return to dry dock, Rod stood waiting and offered his hand to Tina as she disembarked.

"Terrific, thanks, Rod." She jumped down from the cruiser without his assistance.

"I think we might have ourselves a deal," added Jack, reverting to his alias of prospective boat buyer. "It's a mighty fine cruiser. You've done a good job maintaining her, Rod."

"Thanks," he replied, tenderly stroking the hull. "I'll be sorry to see her go, though."

"Never mind. Some hard decisions need to be made, and this is one of them." At a brisk pace, Tina led the way out of the boatshed, locked the door and pocketed the keys. "So, what's on your agenda for today, Rod?"

"Not much. Since the truck is in the shop, I'm kind of trapped here in town."

"What do you usually do on your day off?" Jack's nonchalant, chatty manner accompanied them from the boathouse.

"Maybe go for a drive to Rainbow Falls or over the back ridge. Not much. Just hang out mostly."

"Tina drove me out that way yesterday, and the road's in great shape. You do a terrific job with its maintenance," enthused Jack.

Rod grinned. "Yeah, well what can I say? I like living here on the island, and I want to keep my job. Besides, what else is a guy supposed to do if he can't find a girl." He directed a lame smile at Tina, who huffed loudly.

"You intend living here for the rest of your life, then?" Jack reeled back Rod's attention.

"Maybe. Who Knows?" He shrugged. "One day I hope to have enough money to work for myself, travel, and buy a decent home."

Thrusting his hand forward, Jack shook his hand. "Well, I wish you luck."

"Ah . . . Thanks. That's right kind of you." Rod's brow wrinkled.

"All the best in the future." Jack pivoted and guided Tina beside him to walk to the truck. Glancing back, she smiled goodbye at Rod, who stood wide-eyed and blinking.

* * * *

By the time they arrived at Rainbow Falls, the sun had arced west of noon. Steering the Chevy from the dirt road onto the grassed plateau surrounding the lagoon, Tina pulled to a slow stop and switched off the engine. The early-afternoon light refracted in the waterfall mist and tiny rainbows danced in the spray.

"Now, I understand why it's called Rainbow Falls." Jack peered through the windscreen. "Spectacular."

"Yes. Uncle Dickie used to bring me out here for picnics and get quite misty-eyed. He never told me why, but he said it held special memories for him. If you like, I'll show you around before you go trekking off through the jungle." Twisting her lips in a wry smile, she tried once more to change his mind.

"Sure, show me around if you like, but you're still not coming." Jack leaped out onto the spongy grass.

Out-smarted, Tina slid from the cabin. If his smile wasn't so damn charming, she could have maintained her offended pout. "All right. Follow me. This is the way to get to the waterfalls. Or at least it used to be. If you try going around the other side of the lagoon, you'll get trapped under that ledge." She pointed to the low-lying rock outcrop on the opposite side.

As they traipsed closer toward the falls, the ground became sodden and slippery. The relentless sound of crashing water drowned out any chance of talking, so basic sign language became the means of communication. Doused in the falls' chilly spray, they scrambled across uneven, slick boulders. Tina paused. She glanced back and watched Jack as he rooted around in the nearby jungle, looking for any signs of recent passage. Obviously finding none, he nodded for her to move on. She crawled over another mossy boulder before stepping gingerly onto the slippery ledge behind the falls. Sure-footed, he stepped in beside her. With their backs up against the rear rock face, they gazed out through millions of gallons of water, thundering into the lagoon.

"Rainbow Falls," she mouthed and lifted her arms high. By now, she was as wet as if she'd swum in the lagoon. But she didn't care. She enjoyed the adventure, particularly since Jack looked equally wet and bedraggled.

He pointed two fingers at his eyes, telling her he was going to look around. Careful not to slip, she followed him as he investigated the cliff face behind the falls. He moved to the opposite side and peered under the ledge. When he turned around, his face lit with surprise. He cocked his head for her to follow. He slithered under the ledge and out of sight, and she shadowed him. With his guiding hand, she found her footing until she was standing upright in a man-size cave.

"I never knew this was here," she gasped, her voice now audible.

"Unless you went looking for it, it's easy to miss." Shining his torch, he circumnavigated the cave's walls. "Look." The beam of light disappeared.

"A tunnel? But how?"

"That's what I'm going to find out. You're going back to the truck. Pretend you've come out to Rainbow Falls for a quiet Sunday afternoon by yourself. That's your story just in case someone turns up. You cannot be seen anywhere near here. Okay?"

With a heavy sigh, she nodded in compliance. "But how will I know if you're all right?"

"I'll be fine. If I'm not back in two hours, call the Coast Guard." He chuckled at his joke and tweaked her chin. Lowering his voice, he added, "I mean it, Tina. Do not follow me. I'll be back soon." Then he strode off out of sight down the tunnel.

"Be careful," she called but figured he was already out of earshot. She exited the cave and pulled herself back under the outcrop. Once more on the ledge behind the falls, she crossed to the other side and scrambled around the lagoon to wait near the Chevy as instructed.

What on earth am I going to do for two hours? With no other option, she rummaged in the rear cargo tray of the truck. Grabbing the tarp, she gave it a good shake and laid it on the grass. She and Jack had hidden the turtle shell before leaving this morning. Stripping down to her underwear, she hung her wet clothes over the sides of the truck to dry. On the tarp, she stretched out like a starfish and allowed the sun to work its magic. Thoughts of Suzie Lin's nature spirits played in her mind, and she closed her eyes. She imagined cheeky, dancing sprites skipping around the lagoon, darting in and out of the water, laughing and singing. Perhaps Suzie wasn't so crazy. *Surely, being this relaxed was a good thing?* And as Rainbow Falls roared, Tina drifted into silence.

* * * *

Dinner had been an understated affair in Hill Cottage. Wanting to ensure their conversation would not be overheard by staff, Tina had catered with assorted sandwiches and a fruit platter. Nothing fancy, but chased down with some good wine and coffee, it had been more than adequate.

Now with the table cleared, Jack unfurled a large piece of paper onto it. While Tina, Victoria, Cecilia, and Andrew remained seated, he stood in command. "Okay, this is how they're doing it."

He ran his finger over his make-shift map. "There's a tunnel from Rainbow Falls that starts here and leads about half a mile or so through the rock. It comes out here." He drew the tunnel line and marked the end-point with an *X*. "It opens up into a small sandy cove only a few hundred yards west from Origin Beach, which is here." Another *X* marked the spot. "Tina and I didn't see it when we cruised around the island this morning. But now that I know where it is, I could spot it from the ocean. The tunnel entrance is just above the high-tide mark. There're footprints everywhere on the beach, which means lots of recent activity."

"Do you think the tunnel's been there for a long time?" asked Andrew.

"By the look of it, it's not recent. Maybe it had been covered over by the jungle before now. I'm not sure. But it certainly has made the smuggler's job a hell of a lot easier."

"How does the operation work?" Andrew asked, studying the map closely.

"I suspect its three-fold." Jack marked the relevant points. "First, there's the international arm, which has the large tanker offshore that we saw today way out at sea. Attached to the tanker are some smaller tender vessels that come ashore into this sandy cove. I suspect the ground crew collects the hatchlings, which go into the water tanks onboard the tenders and are then transported back to the tanker. Or they collect the eggs and transport them back on the tenders."

"But what about the empty shells of the adult turtles you found at the quarry?" Cecilia asked.

"That's the second part of the operation. The crew is taking adult turtles, unfortunately, the females when they come to Origin Beach to nest. They slaughter them after they've laid their eggs, extract the meat and probably Cryovac and refrigerate it onboard the tanker. Turtle meat is considered a delicacy in many countries, so they can get top dollar for it."

"But the shells you found were in the quarry. Why take them all the way from the beach, through the tunnel to Rainbow Falls and then transport them to the quarry?" Victoria's finger pointed out their route on Jack's map.

"This is the third part of the operation. The shells would be too obvious if they left them at the falls. It's a more popular spot for people to visit than the quarry. I'm certain there's a Harbor Island local who's hiding the shells at the quarry because he or she thinks they won't be found there."

"What?" said Victoria. Shock, anger, and disappointment clouded everyone's expression.

"Any idea who?" asked Cecilia.

"Not yet, but to get the shells to the quarry, they must have their own vehicle. So that narrows the suspects considerably. Andrew, you need to give me the names of everyone on Harbor Island who has a vehicle or who has had one recently or who has access to one. Can you do that?"

"Of course."

"Terrific. Now whoever the local is, they know the island well. In fact, they could well be the mastermind behind the entire operation. So, they're no idiot."

Murmurs raced around the cottage table as they discussed who might have the intelligence and cunning to pull off such an abominable campaign.

"So where to now?" Tina leaned forward in her chair, her eyes ablaze. Watching Captain Jack Holmes in his official capacity excited her on so many levels.

"Tomorrow I go back to Honolulu and make my report. Then when I've got everything sorted, I'll let you know when the Coast Guard will be here to catch these guys."

"Great." She tried to sound enthusiastic at nailing the bad guys, but her disappointment at Jack's departure crept into her voice.

"Will you lead the Coast Guard operation?" quizzed Cecilia, a slight blush coloring her cheeks.

"Yes. More than likely, ma'am."

"Wonderful. It means we'll have the pleasure of your company again." She slanted a glance at Tina, who grinned and looked away.

Jack folded the map and tucked it into his vest pocket. "Now, if you'll excuse me, I think I'll turn in for the night and get a start on my report."

Tina sprang to her feet. "Do you want me to walk you back?" She winced at her skittish schoolgirl enthusiasm.

"No. That won't be necessary. Are you able to drive me to the wharf tomorrow?"

She reined in her eagerness. "Of course. Do you want to take the ferry back or do you want to leave earlier and go back on the cruiser?"

"The ferry is how I arrived, so I'll go back the same way."

"Okay. Breakfast at eight, then?"

"Perfect. Good night, everyone."

A chorus of good nights followed Jack to the door.

"Wait up. I'll come too and get those names for you," called Andrew, who after a brief farewell joined Jack on the veranda. The two men strolled down the stairs toward the jungle corridor. By the time their voices disappeared into the night, Tina stood at the sink washing the dishes.

"Well, well, well. He certainly is something, isn't he?"

Spinning around, Tina narrowed her gaze on Cecilia. Perched next to Victoria, she wore a cheeky smile to match her friend's.

"Cut it out, you two. I admit, he's very handsome, intelligent, obviously good at his job and physically fit." She resumed washing.

"And single!" chimed Victoria.

"Vickie, stop it." Wiping the suds from her hands on a towel, Tina walked back to the table. She exchanged Victoria's naughty smile with a serious frown. "As if I have time to think about a relationship with all this going on." She waved her arm in a wide sweep indicating her Harbor Island responsibilities.

"Nonsense. He's a mirror image of you. Strong, determined, passionate, smart and the list goes on. Has he made any advances?" asked Victoria, her eyes dancing with glee.

"No, he hasn't," chided Tina. "And if he had, I certainly wouldn't be telling you two busybodies." As her lips twisted into a smirk, she knuckled her hands on her hips.

"Well, Tina, take it from an old woman. Don't leave your run too late. There's magic between you two. I can feel it." Cecilia's jewel-green eyes locked on her.

"I agree," said Victoria. "There's something about Captain Jack Holmes. Don't you think?"

"Seriously. I have no idea what you two are on about. By the sound of it, it's you two who have a crush on Jack. I'm off to bed. Good night." Turning on her heel, she strode from Hill Cottage, head held high. She tried to ignore the good-natured laughter chasing after her. But the truth of it was they were right. She'd fallen for the handsome captain in the couple of days he'd been on Harbor Island. Now on the eve of his departure, she found herself hoping he would return.

* * * *

"Here she comes." Watching the ferry cut through the channel into the harbor, Tina shaded her eyes from the morning glare. "It'll be a much slower trip back than if I took you in the cruiser." She shot him a quick sideways glance.

"And not nearly as pleasant." Hidden behind his reflective sunglasses, Jack's dark eyes were unreadable, but the charming smile lifting the corners of his mouth reassured her. Bending down, he collected his overnight bag and his recent purchase from Suzie Lin. "Thanks for getting the painting for me this morning."

"Do you think you'll actually hang it?"

"No. I bought it as evidence. It proves Suzie had been painting in her shop until late, like she said." He paused, as if working out what to say next. Although lots of noise and activity filled the wharf, she only heard the awkward silence between them. "Tina?"

"Yes." She faced him with too much anticipation.

"I'll call you as soon as I've got everything organized. I don't want to pre-empt our strike on this one. We get one hit at nailing these guys and getting the evidence to prove what they're doing. It might take me a week or so. But I'll do everything in my power to put an end to this as soon as possible."

"Thank you. I understand." Although she'd hoped for a more intimate conversation, she appreciated how committed he was to her plight. "I'll be here."

He leaned closer, brushing his cheek against hers. "I'm counting on it."

Her face flamed from his touch, and the skin on the back of neck tingled. Before she could speak, he pivoted and headed toward the gangplank to board the ferry. She wanted nothing more than to throw herself after him, wrap her arms around his neck and never let him go. But that wasn't who she was. She was an independent woman. One who lived life on her terms, unaccustomed to compromise or episodes of unrestrained emotion. Yet despite her rationalizations, as she watched him board the ferry, she hungered for more.

When you find him, you will have to overcome your fears and find the courage to leap. That's what love is all about, Tina, leaping into the unknown. Cecilia's words rushed into her mind, unbidden yet timely. Deep in her core, something stirred. For the first time in her life, Tina sensed the inexplicable truth of loving someone — more than all else.

CHAPTER THIRTY

By Tuesday morning, the promised SWOT analysis report lay printed on the office desk awaiting Sebastien's return. Since Jack's departure, Tina had thrown herself into work, determined to focus on Harbor Island's future rather than her own. Nodding in satisfaction, she knew the report had merit. Her eco-tourism plan of naturalist-guided activities including reef-snorkeling tours, turtle-nesting habitat excursions on Origin Beach and hiking expeditions to Rainbow Falls had the potential of generating significant revenue while honoring Uncle Dickie's green legacy.

She glanced at her watch. *Seb will be here soon.* Deciding to present her report in the best possible manner, she went in search of Matthew to arrange some coffee and sandwiches. Within thirty minutes, refreshments were laid, and she readied herself in the great pavilion as the sound of crunching gravel signaled the Chevy's arrival.

"Hey, Tina, how goes it?" Sebastien's warm voice greeted her before he stepped through the curtains. She spun around, and her welcoming smile vanished. "This is Gary Crowther." With a sweep of his arm, Seb stepped aside to present a lean, bespectacled young man topped with rust-brown hair. A thin-lipped smile creased the stranger's horsy-looking face as he approached, extending his hand in welcome.

"Sebastien has told me so much about you. It's a pleasure to finally meet you."

Open-mouthed, she accepted his handshake and shot a silent query to Sebastien.

"Gary is an architect. He's a professional associate of Alan Rosenbaum. I've been telling Gary about Harbor Island and what we plan on doing here."

"And what are we doing here?" Tina's reedy voice sliced with a sharp edge.

"Well, we have to come up with a plan to bring in revenue. And what better way to do it than build a resort right along The Esplanade?" Triumph spread across his face. Tina seethed.

"But, Seb, we haven't reviewed the SWOT analysis yet. Only then can we make our decisions for the future welfare of the island. I doubt a resort is something Uncle Dickie would have approved of at all." Daggers flew from her eyes, finding their mark.

Sebastien stiffened. "Harbor Island no longer belongs to Uncle Dickie. We have a responsibility to make this island profitable, and a resort is a sure thing. Gary has graciously accepted my invitation to inspect possible locations and sketch up some ideas."

Due to the architect's presence, the impending battle between sister and brother stalled, giving Tina a moment to regroup. "Gary, won't you sit down and have some refreshments. There's coffee and sandwiches, so please help yourself." Smiling sweetly at her guest, she motioned him to a chair. "Seb, can I see you for a moment, please." Minus the smile, her face burned hot with barely concealed indignation. She snapped a turn and marched to the back of the great pavilion, into the office and closed the door behind them.

"What on earth do you think you're doing? I sent you off to Maui for a few days' R and R, and you return with some foolish idea of building a resort on Harbor Island."

"Hey, you're not my boss. You didn't send me anywhere."

"Sorry, my mistake," she hissed through clenched teeth. "But what gives you the right to tell some architect about our problems and drag him over here to sketch up plans for something we are definitely not building. Have you gone mad? Uncle Dickie would be rolling over in his grave."

Throwing his hands in the air, Sebastien paced the small room. "I am so sick and tired of hearing his name, Uncle Dickie this, Uncle Dickie that. He's dead, Tina. D.E.A.D." He leaned into her face, spitting each syllable.

"I. Know. That," she spat back. "But we have an obligation to his legacy." She heaved a ragged breath. "Listen, we need to work together to find a solution here. Not be at each other's throats. You shouldn't have brought Gary here without at least talking to me first."

"Don't care. He's here now, and I'm going to show him around." He made for the door.

"I'm warning you, Seb, we are joint owners of Harbor Island, but if you cross me, by God I will find a way—"

He wheeled back and lunged at her. "Find a way to what? Get rid of me? Buy me out?" She pursed her lips. "You may be an investigative journalist, but you have nothing on me. And you never will." He sneered.

"Really? You'd be surprised what I have on you, Sebastien Templeton." Even though his recoil was only slight, she knew she'd hit a nerve. "And since this place is about to go bankrupt if we can't agree on a future strategy, I figure I could buy you out. Something is better than nothing." She thrust her face closer, teeth gnashing.

Only the sound of the office door opening broke the stalemate. "Whatever is going on in here?" Victoria stood glaring in the doorway, her hands on her hips. "You sound like a pair of squabbling cats."

"It's Tina. She's so unreasonable."

"Me. What about you? Bringing over an architect to build—"

"Stop it. Both of you. For goodness sake, you cannot continue behaving like this. You are grown adults, joint owners of this magnificent estate and still you can't find common ground." Both offenders opened their mouths to speak, but Victoria raised her hand in protest. "I'm not in the least interested in your opinions. I am only interested in the legacy of Harbor Island. Handed down for centuries through the Reginald family, to my father, Percy and then my brother, Dickie. You have a duty to your generation of Templetons to overcome your differences. Sort it out, or otherwise, I will. Mark my words, I will use the money Dickie left me to buy this place if you two can't get over your differences." She nailed each of them in a scathing stare and stormed off like the grand dame of the island.

Hands clenched, Tina glowered at Sebastien. He glowered back. On a sharp exhale, she said, "What about this for a compromise." The last word tasted bitter. "Since your architect has come all this way, show him around. He can sketch up some ideas. However, my report demonstrates another, greener way of making the island profitable without the investment required for a resort. When Gary leaves, we can discuss both ideas together. Agreed?" She thrust her hand forward to seal the deal.

"Agreed." Sebastien huffed and gave her hand a single, adversarial pump.

* * * *

"I don't know what I'm going to do, really I don't." Tina's brow knitted tight, and she wondered if the crease lines would ever disappear. Across from her on Hill Cottage's verandah sat Cecilia looking a picture of calm. "Seb's down there now, on The Esplanade, showing that bloody architect where he wants to build a resort. All the locals will see them and wonder what's going on. Knowing Seb he'll tell them, and that'll be the end of it. Everyone will think we're going to oust them from their businesses. Oh, God, I knew it would be hard working with him, but not this hard." Spearing her fingers through her hair for the hundredth time in the last couple of hours, she slumped.

"Why are you telling me all this and not Victoria?" asked Cecilia.

"Because I know what she'll say." She told her of Victoria's threat to buy back the island. "Not that a million dollars would be enough money for Seb to give up his share. God knows I've tried, but he's just not willing to see any other way than turning Harbor Island into a cash cow. Not only that, when it all comes down to it, blood is blood. Seb is *her son*, whereas I'm only her stepdaughter."

"So, you're scared she'll take his side, choose him over you, and the resort will go ahead?"

"Maybe. I don't think she would, but when push comes to shove in these types of family matters, blood is thicker than water, you know."

"But what about the blood between Victoria and Dickie?"

"You'd know more about that than me. You lived here, even if it was only for a short time. And you've been friends with Vickie for years. What do you think?" She locked eyes with the older woman.

"I can't be sure, but I think Victoria would do her very best to keep the legacy of her brother alive."

"Even if it meant alienating her son?"

"That I couldn't answer, but maybe." Cecilia reclined in her chair, thoughtful. "Tina, may I ask you something?"

"Sure."

"What is it between you and Sebastien that causes all this tension?"

A long silence stretched between them before Tina decided to confide in her. "I'll tell you, but you must promise not to say anything to Vickie. All right?"

"Very well," agreed Cecilia.

"Seb got into some shady dealings on a development project in Australia a few years ago. Dad told me about it just before he died. He asked me to keep an eye on Seb, just in case he needed help, which I did through my sources. It seems Seb got himself out of it."

"I see. Does Sebastien know your father told you?"

"I honestly don't know. But I know Seb is prone to mix with the wrong crowd when it comes to money and financing his ideas. That's why I'm so worried about his plans for Harbor Island."

"I can understand how that would cause a stalemate between you, particularly if he's been dishonest before."

"Plus, there is the condition Uncle Dickie placed in his will about losing the inheritance if any criminal activity is discovered. All of it places me in an untenable position. I can't tell Vickie about Seb's prior dealings, as I promised Dad I wouldn't. But it makes me look like a right bitch at times. Based on what I know of Seb's history, I'm worried what he might do here." She paced the veranda in long, stiff strides. "And I don't want Vickie using her inheritance to try to sort out this issue with Seb and me. I've got to find a way out of this myself."

"I think you're getting ahead of yourself. Why not wait until the architect has left this afternoon and meet with Seb with your plan, as agreed. Victoria and I will be there for moral support if you like. Once you have this meeting and see how Seb responds, then you can decide the next step."

"I guess you're right. But I hate not being in control."

"I noticed." One of her sculpted brows arched high in amusement.

Tina sagged into the chair. "You're right. There's nothing I can do until I give Seb the chance to consider my proposal. And if he remains committed to his plan—"

"And you remain committed to yours—" interjected Cecilia.

"I'll have to find another way."

"Take it from someone who has lived nearly seventy years, my dear. Although things may look bleak, waiting around the next corner is a solution you haven't even considered."

"I hope you're right." She reached over and gave Cecilia's hand an affectionate pat.

"Have you heard from Captain Holmes today?"

"No." Tina sighed. *Another situation I can't control.* "He said he'd call me sometime this week with what's happening."

Cecilia inclined her head, a lazy smile gracing her kind face.

"What? What is it?"

"Oh, nothing. I just think you and the handsome captain would make a dashing couple."

"Maybe we would, but I don't have time for love and romance at the moment."

"That's a pity. He makes a good guardian."

Indignant, Tina scowled. "I don't need a guardian, thank you very much."

"No, I know that. But the island needs another one to stand beside you." Cecilia's face lit with delight.

"Ha-ha. You're very crafty, Cecilia Freemont." Tina stood to leave. "By the way, how did you go with that jigsaw puzzle?"

"You mean the turtle *guardian*." She emphasized the last word, which Tina acknowledged with a thin smirk. "Victoria and I finished it yesterday."

"Well, it must be time to find something else to occupy your time. Another puzzle, maybe?"

Cecilia pushed up from her chair. "I have plenty to occupy me, my dear. Island life is always full of secrets and simmering emotions."

Tina's face hardened with suspicion. "And that's what I'm afraid of." She kissed Cecilia's blushing cheek. "Thanks for listening to me and for your advice. I'll see you later."

"Don't worry so much. I'm sure everything will work out just as Dickie wanted it."

"We'll see." She turned and strode down the veranda stairs. Behind her, she thought Cecilia said something else, but she didn't turn back. Yet she could have sworn she heard her talking to someone else. With no time to follow that train of thought down the rabbit hole, she marched on to prepare for another round with her brother.

* * * *

Grim-faced, Sebastien sat through Tina's stirring half-hour presentation of her eco-tourism plan. Obviously galled that she'd also invited Victoria and Cecilia, he remained mute throughout. Now, as he read the proposal in more detail, a strained silence hung thick in the office. He closed the binder and folded his hands on top. "So, you think that running reef-snorkeling tours, turtle-nesting habitat excursions and hiking expeditions to Rainbow Falls has the potential of making this island profitable?"

"I do." She nodded. "It also protects the legacy of Harbor Island and supports the local community."

"Mother? What do you think?" Seb cast an enquiring look at Victoria.

"To be honest, Sebastien, I think the eco-plan has real merit."

Tina's heart hammered in her chest as she watched Sebastien twirl the diamond ring on his pinkie finger. Like a thundercloud, his mood darkened. She stiffened and dragged her hand across her chin.

"As joint owners of Harbor Island," he nodded curtly at Tina, "our job is to make this business profitable. In my opinion, snorkeling, turtles and hiking will not." Oxygen sucked from her lungs as Tina's temper flared. "We need a solid, ongoing revenue stream which we could achieve from a resort—"

"Do you have any idea how much capital it would take to build a resort?" interrupted Tina, reproach rising in her voice.

"I do. And I've spoken to Alan Rosenbaum about finding investors to fund it."

"Does Alan think building a resort on Harbor Island is a good idea?" Victoria's brows lifted in surprise.

"Well, he hasn't really voiced an opinion per se, but he's told me he has a pool of cashed-up investors looking for projects at the moment."

"Honestly, Seb, you can't be serious. This resort idea of yours is too risky. Resorts are notorious for never returning the revenue invested in them in the first place, let alone being profitable." Tina managed to keep an even tone, but her temper strained at the leash. "We've inherited a virtual goldmine of natural assets here, and you want to rip them up and pave paradise?"

"It's called progress, and without progress making money is hard." His tone was stubborn and sarcastic.

Tina glanced at Victoria, who remained inscrutable. She was on her own. She steadied herself on a deep inhale and changed tack. "All right, Seb. Since we're at loggerheads on how best to move forward with Harbor Island, what do you suggest we do?"

He frowned and looked at his mother.

In a measured voice, she said, "You know how I feel about Harbor Island, Sebastien. About the Reginald family, who worked long and hard for centuries to keep this island as unspoiled as possible."

Watching Sebastien's fingers savagely twist his pinkie finger ring, Tina knew a showdown was imminent, and she readied herself for the strike.

"I really think you should reconsider Tina's eco-plan. Give it—"

But before Victoria finished, he launched from his chair, baring his fangs. "So, what am I supposed to do? Be pussy-whipped into something I don't want any part of?" His words dripped with contempt and menace.

"Well, that's not going to happen. I've got Reginald blood in my veins, and I won't be told what to do by women." He glared at each of them.

Victoria visibly bristled, and dark flints flashed in her eyes. "The Reginald blood that flows through your veins, Sebastien, reminds me too much of my father. He was an arrogant, selfish man, and I pray to God you've not inherited his wicked ways."

Sebastien growled, low and dangerous. "Despite what you think, I will not be told what to do by you or her." He shot daggers at Tina.

"Sebastien, stop this at once. Your father and I have raised you to be a better man than this."

"My father is dead. I am the man now. And things are going to change around here whether you like it or not."

Tina swallowed hard as she watched Victoria's eyes pool with tears. Sebastien held his ground, unwilling to concede. She had to do something. She was through being bulldozed by her brother or trying to talk sense into him. And she certainly couldn't stand by and watch him treat Victoria so badly. What could she do? Her mind raced with alternatives until one blinding idea popped into her head, and she knew it was her only choice. To save Uncle Dickie's legacy, a sacrifice was needed. She squared her shoulders, lowered her voice and staked her power position in the conversation. In a well-modulated, considered voice, she said, "Okay, Seb, let me make you an offer."

He blinked, distrust warping his features.

Tina sidled in front of him until they stood chest to chest. "What do you think Harbor Island is worth in its current state and based on our projected forecast for the next five years?"

He scowled and grumbled, "Anywhere between six and eight million dollars."

Her chest tightened. "Right, let's split it down the middle. Make it seven million dollars. I'll buy out your share of Harbor Island for three and a half million dollars. I'll give you a ten percent deposit within ninety days and the balance ninety days after that. That will give me time to divest my assets in Australia. I'll take on Harbor Island as the sole owner and protect Uncle Dickie's legacy, while you get to resume your life in Australia, all cashed-up." She heard Vickie and Cecilia gasp for breath, but ignored them. Her nails bit into her palms. She dared not unclench her hands as they'd belie her confident exterior with their trembling. Facing off, she fixed him in an unwavering stare. *What have I done? All my money, my unit, everything.*

"Tina, don't . . ."

Without breaking eye contact with Sebastien, Tina whispered, "It's okay, Vickie."

"Sebastien, you cannot take your sister's offer. Uncle Dickie left Harbor Is—"

"I am so sick of hearing about Uncle Dickie." A sinister growl rumbled from his chest like an erupting volcano. He wheeled on his mother. His face contorted into a predatory mask as he leaned in close to her. "Your brother was nothing but a freak! A namby-pamby, cock-sucking—"

The force of the slap rang through the office. Sebastien recoiled, his cheek blazing red.

"How dare you speak about your uncle like that?" Victoria straightened, full of fury. "Your father is rolling over in his grave right this very minute. Get out. Get out!" She snapped her arm in the direction of the door.

Sebastien sneered and turned to Tina. Thrusting out his hand, he hissed, "Three and a half million dollars. You've got yourself a deal. You can have this godforsaken place. Good luck. You're going to need it." Elbowing past her, he stalked from the office without a glance at his mother. *Whack.* He slammed the door with such ferocity the small office trembled like a frightened child.

"Oh, Tina, what have you done? All that money." Victoria rushed over and hugged her.

"It'll be fine, Vickie. Really. We'll work it out." She wrapped her stepmother in a tight embrace, rubbing circles on her back. With the tension leaving her body, Tina exhaled long and slow. Only then did she manage a look at Cecilia, who remained quietly seated in the back corner of the office. "Well?"

"Percy Reginald would have been very proud of his grandson today. He made as big an ass of himself as his grandfather did when he was alive." The wry amusement in her voice broke the tension.

Victoria reached out, beckoning Cecilia into the circle. "Unfortunately, you're right. My dear son has too much misogynist Reginald blood in his veins and not enough Templeton tolerance. Better he leaves Harbor Island. I'll let him cool down and then talk to him. Make peace before he goes. He is my son, and I love him."

"Dickie's legacy is now yours alone, Tina. How do you feel?" Cecilia gazed up at her.

"Aside from millions of dollars poorer, I feel relieved. Now, I can get on with making this my happy place again."

CHAPTER THIRTY-ONE

Exhausted from the week's work, Tina took a break on one of the Adirondack chairs under the fragrant plumeria tree. What with the breeze playing nature's lullaby in the branches and the afternoon's warm caress, she fell into a deep sleep with no recollection of doing so. The insistence of Andrew's soft voice stirred her. "Excuse me, Tina. Excuse me. Tina, wake up."

Groggy, she dragged herself from the void of peace and blinked up into his face. "Yes, Andrew, what is it?"

"It's Captain Holmes. He's on the phone."

At the mere mention of Jack's name, her spirits lifted, and she sprang to her feet. "Thank you, Andrew." Rushing to the office, she groomed her hair as if expecting to see him.

She closed the office door behind her, slipped into the chair and snugged the phone to her ear. "Jack. It's good to hear from you." She sounded breathless and far too keen, but she didn't care. It had been a grueling week.

"Hey, Tina, are you okay?" His velvety voice drizzled over her like warm honey, and she melted. She needed someone to talk to, to share her troubles with, and most of all someone who understood the weight of leadership.

"I'm fine. Just overworked and overtired. A lot has happened since you were last here."

"Tell me. I've got time."

She sighed. "To cut a long story short, Seb and I had a major falling out. Vickie and Cecilia were there. He wouldn't budge from building a resort, and I wouldn't budge from protecting Uncle Dickie's legacy—"

"I remember, the green before the greed." In her mind's eye, she could see his face soften in approval. His empathy strengthened her spirit.

"Anyway, I offered to buy out Seb's share of Harbor Island for three and a half million dollars, and he accepted."

A long whistle sounded down the phone. "That's a lot of money."

"It's basically everything I have, but I couldn't see any other way out. He left a couple of days ago. It was a bit uncomfortable, but I think everything will settle down. We all made up, sort of, and the lawyer is drawing up the agreement, so it'll be official when I sell everything back home in ninety days. Seb's gone back to Australia, and I'm staying here. Forever, it seems." She smiled. Though still a little rattled by the speed at which everything had happened, she was happy with her decision.

"Leave you alone for a few days, and the world spins off its axis." He chuckled an easy laugh, and she responded in kind. "From a purely selfish point of view, I like that you're staying."

"Really?" Her cheeks heated. *Thank goodness he can't see me.*

"Absolutely." The moment stretched like pulled toffee between them, sweet and delicious.

"Anyway, I've been doing the work of at least a dozen people, getting on top of everything, but enough about me. Tell me what's happening with our Origin Beach mission."

"Well, the full moon is next Thursday, the tenth. So, Operation Origin will commence on Tuesday the eighth. As soon as we see any action on the beach or the water, we'll swing in and arrest them. I'd like to come over to the island earlier to do a little recon. On the Monday-morning ferry, if that's okay?"

"Yes, of course." She'd prefer him to come tomorrow and stay all weekend. *God, I'm not only tired, but I'm also needy.*

"Terrific. You get some rest on the weekend. I have no doubt next week will be just as grueling, especially if you want to catch these guys with us."

"You mean I can come with you? With the Coast Guard?"

"Yes, but only on my conditions, and one of those is to get some rest over the weekend. Okay?"

"Aye, aye, Captain." She all but saluted with delight. "Thanks, Jack. I needed a pep talk. I'll get some rest this weekend and pick you up Monday morning at the wharf."

"I look forward to it. See you then."

She waited for him to hang up, but the line remained open.

"Tina?"

"Yes, Jack?"

"Despite how difficult all of this has been for you, I'm really glad you're staying."

"Me too. Thanks." A soft sigh escaped her lips, and her heart skipped a beat.

"See you Monday."

"Bye, Jack."

* * * *

The reward of well-deserved R and R paid remarkable dividends. Up bright and early on Monday morning, Tina leaned into her bathroom mirror, looking for the dark circles that had rimmed her eyes only the week before. She couldn't see them. *That's better.* She dressed hurriedly in white cargo pants, matching T-shirt and loafers. After scrunching some product into her hair, she couldn't decide whether she'd chosen such a vivid outfit because she didn't want Jack to miss her standing on the wharf or if she was celebrating her shining new role as soon-to-be sole owner of the island. Either way, Jack's arrival played a major part in her happiness.

By the time she dashed into the great pavilion, breakfast was being served.

"You look lovely, Tina," complimented Cecilia. "All aglow for Jack's arrival, I see?"

"I guess so." She reached for a piece of toast and scraped on a lick of butter.

"Aren't you going to join us for breakfast?" Victoria indicated a chair.

"No thanks. I want to get to town. See some of the shop owners before Jack arrives. I'll see you both later." With toast in hand, she turned to leave.

"Now, that's a young woman about to leap into the unknown," teased Cecilia.

"I heard that," called Tina through a mouthful of toast.

"Whatever do you mean?" asked Victoria.

By the time she jumped in the truck, Tina knew Cecilia was retelling the story of Black Rock and what she'd told her about falling in love. With a big, fat grin splitting her face, she steered around the turning circle, gravel crunching under the wheels. *Bloody matchmakers, that's what those two are.* But as she drove up the driveway, another thought tickled her fancy as to why she'd chosen white today. Maybe on some unconscious level, she'd decided to sacrifice herself to love, to leap into the unknown and hope Jack would join her. *God, now they've got me thinking like that, too.*

* * * *

"Hey, Tina." With a wave of his arm, Jack strode down the wharf toward her, duffel bag slung on his shoulder.

"Hi, Jack." Her stomach performed a pancake flip.

As he stepped in, his spare arm encircled her waist in a quick, tight squeeze. "It's good to see you." He beamed. Without sunglasses, the dark depths of his eyes fixed her with simmering intention.

"And you too." She exchanged his intimate look and hesitated wondering, hoping. But the moment passed. "The truck's just over here. Didn't you bring your uniform?" She bit her lip. Her inner desire to see him in his captain's uniform had leaped from her mouth before she could stop it. *God, I sound so lame.*

"It's in here." He tugged at his bag. "I thought carrying a suit bag would look too suspicious. If it's okay with you, can I unpack first?"

"Sure. Everything's ready for you back at the property. Jump in."

Once inside the cabin, she glanced across at him. He looked right at home, reclining on the seat, with his long legs stretched into the foot compartment. She liked that he fitted so well, not just in the Chevy, but into everything to do with Harbor Island.

"What's been happening around here, aside from the fight with your brother, his departure and you becoming the sole owner of Harbor Island?" He mocked her with a lift of his brow.

"What? Isn't that enough?" she teased.

"Knowing you and how this place runs, I suspect there's more to tell."

"Well, Andrew's been keeping a watchful eye on Rod Fischer but has nothing to report. After he got his truck back from the shop, Rod's kept a low profile and not driven it anywhere except around town. So, I'm not sure he's your inside man for all this turtle business."

"Maybe, maybe not. What else?"

"I spoke to Silly Suzie this morning, but she hasn't seen any lights on the harbor since the last time when you were here. And aside from that, everything seems to be going along as normal."

"Do you know if Rod's been out in the cruiser?"

"No way. The keys are with me all the time now."

"Well, I know that tanker is still at sea. We received reports of its location, so that's a sign something is afoot.

By tomorrow night, it'll all be over. We'll get these assholes before they know we're even there."

"Sounds good to me. So, what do you want to do after you unpack?"

"I'd like to go out to Rainbow Falls again. Take another look around. How about you arrange a picnic lunch? We can use that as a cover. 'Boat owner takes prospective buyer to Rainbow Falls to negotiate a higher sale price.'" Gesturing air quotes on the last sentence, Jack laughed, his eyes crinkling in the corners.

"Or maybe ... 'Prospective buyer seduces boat owner at Rainbow Falls to negotiate a lower price.'" She shot him a wicked grin with a matching wink.

"Now that's a cover story I'd be keen to execute." His voice was dark chocolate.

Blindsided by his directness, her skin danced a merry jig. His fleeting yet penetrating glance left little doubt in her mind of Jack's readiness to explore something more between them. Her heart skipped a beat. The Chevy's cabin temperature rose as a current of energy sparked between them. Harbor Island just got a whole lot happier. Without a word, she returned her gaze to the road.

* * * *

After a quick reconnaissance through the tunnel to Origin Beach, Jack joined her for a leisurely picnic lunch. Delicate chicken sandwiches followed by an assortment of cheeses and tropical fruit satisfied their appetite. But there remained another appetite neither of them broached. A warm, tingling sensation cloaked her skin. Perhaps it was from the heat of the afternoon sun or the buzz from the white wine. More likely, it was from sharing this intimate time with Jack, particularly in such a romantic setting.

Listening to him talk, Tina reclined on the picnic rug, propped on her elbow. The rich timbre of his voice soothed her, and her eyelids drooped. Further lulled by the sound of the falls thundering on the other side of the lagoon, she drifted between past and present. Fond memories of Uncle Dickie and the times they'd spent picnicking at Rainbow Falls flooded back to her. This ghost from the past brought with him a kaleidoscope of loving images, inspiring adventures, and grand promises. Gently, Jack's voice encroached as the ghost faded. Happiness swelled her chest. With a deep sigh, she lay back on the rug and drifted. The touch of Jack's fingers brushing her cheek broke her silent reverie. Her eyes fluttered open to be captured in his dark, passionate gaze. "Are you trying to seduce me, Captain Holmes?"

"Only if you let me, Miss Templeton."

"I'm not sure we should mix business with pleasure. Isn't that against Coast Guard rules?" The thrill of anticipation darted up her spine as his fingers caressed her ear.

"I'm not on duty at the moment, so this is pure pleasure."

"Well, as long as we're not breaking any rules." She closed her eyes and invited him in with the parting of her lips.

When he grazed her mouth with his own, she breathed him in. His soft mouth claimed her, welcoming her tongue to dance with his. He tasted of wine, warmth, and want; of someone she had waited for and had now found. He crushed her closer, his kiss at once, rough and tender. Like the vines in the surrounding jungle, she clung to him, nourishing herself. Eventually, he withdrew the gift of his mouth but held her in a mesmerizing gaze. "The moment I walked into your office, I knew I was in trouble. Never have I fallen this fast or this hard. And never have I bared my heart on my sleeve like this."

"Oh, Jack—" Silenced by his finger pressing to her lips, she waited.

"I don't want you to say anything. I want you to think about what I've said. And if you feel like me, that there could be a real chance at a future for us together, let me know. Otherwise, after tomorrow, I'll walk away and not bother you again. But if you want me to stay, I will do my utmost to make you happy, so we can build a life together."

She blinked away the tears welling in her eyes. Tracing her thumb along his rugged jaw, she swallowed hard. "I'll think about what you said and whether I feel the same as you. But what if I make the wrong decision?"

"From what I've seen to date, you make damn good decisions, particularly under pressure."

"And do you intend putting me under more pressure?" she purred.

"Only if you let me."

Reaching up, she pulled him closer, and whispered, "Permission granted, Captain." Then she pressed her lips to his, eager to once more taste the promise of another unexpected future.

CHAPTER THIRTY-TWO

By the time Operation Origin finally got underway, her senses reeled. Aside from Jack's personal advances at Rainbow Falls, the past twenty-four hours had been filled with the planning and preparation for tonight's mission, which was further exacerbated by Tina's poor performance in front of Victoria and Cecilia that her relationship with the handsome captain was purely platonic. When he reappeared after tonight's dinner dressed in his blue combat uniform complete with flak jacket, helmet, and accessories, her last-ditch attempt at composure failed miserably. Jack Holmes, Captain in the US Coast Guard, had hooked her line and sinker.

"Are you ready?" He pulled on his black gloves with a sharp snap.

"As I'll ever be." Adrenaline surged through her body, and she suspected it was not only because of the mission but because of how sexy Jack looked.

"She will be safe, won't she?" With concern spreading over her face, Victoria rose from the couch on which she'd taken up residence after dinner.

"Absolutely. She's not getting off *Harbor Island V.* She'll be waiting out at sea, near the Coast Guard cutter *Stockdale*, while the teams go ashore."

"And you must be careful too, Jack." Cecilia looked up into his face, anxiety settling on hers.

"Of course, I'll be safe. I've been doing these types of operations for years. Don't worry. Both Tina and I will be home before you know it, the turtles will be safe, and the smugglers locked up." With a grim smile, he turned toward Andrew. "You stay close to Officers O'Neal and Collins just as we discussed. They're in town waiting for you. They've got eyes on Rod, and they might need your local knowledge. Just do what they tell you. Got it?"

"Yes, Captain. You won't get any heroics out of me." Andrew gave a weak smile to accompany his worried expression.

"Don't fret, Andrew. You'll be fine." Tina shrugged on her black parker and cap.

"Right. Let's go." After a few hasty farewells, Tina, Jack, and Andrew piled into the Chevy and drove off.

"Pity the full moon is in two days' time. There's so much damn light everywhere, but it's the perfect time to catch these guys because of the hatching. Anyway, keep your head down, Andrew. I doubt there'll be any trouble in town, and O'Neal and Collins are armed, so you won't be in any danger."

"Don't worry about me. If Rod is involved, he doesn't have the guts to take on armed Coast Guard officers. That's for sure." Growing confidence crept over Andrew's face.

"Good for you." Tina gave his shoulder a playful punch.

Within a few minutes, Jack pulled the truck to a stop at the far end of The Esplanade. "There they are. Over there." He pointed to two fellows dressed in civvies loitering near a pandanus tree.

"I see them." Andrew nodded and opened the door. "I'll see you both back at the property when this is all over. Go save the turtles, for Dickie's sake."

"Thanks. We will." Tina squeezed his hand as he slid from the cabin. "You've got the spare key for the Chevy in case you need it?"

"In my pocket." He tapped his trousers. "I know where you're parking it. So, if we need it, I'll make sure it's there for when you get back." With a nod goodbye, he hurried over to meet the officers, and they faded into the shadows.

"Now it's just us." Jack eased the Chevy onward. Once hidden behind the boathouse, he switched off the engine and glanced at his watch. "The cutter will be making its way to our rendezvous point. We better get a move on."

Beside him, Tina scurried to the boathouse and unlocked the door. Once inside, they leaped onto *Harbor Island V* and set to. In no time, the cruiser slid into the water, and she set a course out of the harbor to meet the *Stockdale*. Moonlight skipped and slanted off the waves as if playing hide-and-seek. Lit with a carpet of distant stars, the night sky twinkled, reminding her of the childhood nursery rhyme — *How I wonder what you are.*

"Beautiful night," said Jack, standing at her shoulder as they motored out beyond the reef.

"Certainly is." Her voice sounded wistful. "Tell me, are all your team as fearless as you?" She inclined her head upward to meet his piercing stare.

"I'm not fearless. We're trained to go into tough situations and get the job done." He brushed off her compliment with a self-effacing smile and shifted his gaze out to sea.

"So, if this sort of adrenaline-pumping stuff doesn't scare you, what does?"

"Not knowing."

"Not knowing what?"

"Who I am."

"But you're Jack Holmes, a captain in the US Coast Guard."

"That's my professional title, but . . ." He leaned forward, eyes narrowing. "Look, the *Stockdale*. There."

The dazzling white cutter with its distinctive blue-and-red bow stripe floated like a beacon on the waves.

"How do you ever accomplish covert operations with a ship that glows in the dark," she quipped, steering toward the waiting ship.

"That's why we have shore teams and boarding teams. The ASIS patrol vessels have the speed and stealth needed to get in and out fast. Now, you know the plan. You'll wait here near the *Stockdale* while we go ashore." Across the waves, a dark shape sped toward them. "That's my team now." Moving to the aft of the cruiser, he leaned over as the ASIS pulled alongside. While he exchanged rapid words with his crew, Tina peered through the wheelhouse window, studying the boat pitching beside her. She estimated it to be only about twenty feet in length, and although it looked sturdy enough, she reminded herself it was still just an inflatable boat. *Not much between them and the deep blue sea.* With four crew already kitted up onboard, only one seat remained for Jack.

"See you when it's done." With a cocky grin and tilt of his head, he slipped over the side.

She watched his team salute their captain and deliver the vessel to his command. He then stepped behind the wheel. Giving her a polite smile, he pulled hard on the wheel and with a strong thrust of throttle cleared *Harbor Island V.* As the cruiser bobbed in the ASIS's wake, another three vessels appeared, racing behind Jack's lead. All headed to the sandy cove near Origin Beach.

Positioned in the northern ocean, miles from Harbor Island so as not to be seen, the *Stockdale* and the cruiser waited. Even with night-vision binoculars, Tina couldn't see any lights coming from the direction of Origin Beach. Like a bored child, she fidgeted and paced, her impatience growing. She hated missing out on the action. On assignment, she never stayed behind. She was always in the thick of it. She'd agreed with Jack to remain here, but patience was not one of her strong suits. Checking her watch, she figured fifteen minutes had passed since they'd left. She didn't want to jeopardize the mission, so she decided to give them another fifteen minutes and then she'd motor a little closer to see what was happening.

On slow throttle, she burbled away from the *Stockdale.* With all navigation lights and communication channels switched off and instrumentation dimmed, she left the safety of the Coast Guard cutter and crossed the northern channel. Butterflies stirred in her gut with a warning that her impetuous behavior could have serious repercussions. But she ignored it. Harbor Island belonged to her, and she had every right to know what was going on. Being careful to not get too close, she motored out some distance from the reef, desperate for any sign of movement. On the beach, the sand gleamed like a silver platter under the wash of moonlight, but she could see no sign of movement. Perhaps the smugglers had already got their payload and left?

Easing a little closer, she traveled alongside the reef in a westerly direction. She remembered the location of the sandy cove from Jack's map, so she headed toward there. Then all hell broke loose. Random lights, shouting voices, men scrambling after each other fleeing up the beach, shots fired. Adrenaline squirted into her stomach as she watched the dangerous drama unfolding onshore. She drank it all in, at once worried for Jack and relieved that the smugglers were finally getting what they deserved. Suddenly, the sound of scraping hull snapped back her attention. *God, I'm on the bloody reef.* Heart in mouth, she thrust the throttle into reverse and slowly edged the cruiser back. Her vessel was in distress. She had no other option but to switch on the boat's lights, communication channels, and instrumentation. Knowing that the cruiser now shone as bright as a lighthouse beacon, she groaned. But she needed all her senses. Motoring blind was no longer an option. More scraping made her wince, but she held steady.

"Come on. Come on."

Like a wounded animal, the hull yelped as the coral bit into the timber. Beads of sweat burst from her skin. Still, the hull squealed. Time stretched as the reef clung a little longer to *Harbor Island V.*

"Come on, let go." The highest in the set of ocean waves came to her rescue. With a final howl, the reef cast off the cruiser like an intruder. Picking up speed to deeper waters, Tina sighed and dragged her hand across her chin. "Shit. That was close." Just as she turned the cruiser around, she sighted an ASIS speeding toward her, and her heart sank. "I'm in for it now." Within minutes, the vessel pulled alongside, and Jack rafted it to the cruiser. By the time he leaped onto the aft deck, she stood ready to apologize.

"What don't you understand about obeying orders?" His voice boomed through the night's silence, broadsiding her.

"I'm sorry, but—"

"There are no buts, Tina. It was a very simple directive. Stay near the *Stockdale*." Disappointment flashed in his dark eyes.

"But I didn't hamper the mission, did I?" she pleaded, her voice thin. "You still caught them, didn't you?"

"Yes, we did, but that's not the point. I only allowed you to come because I trusted you would do as instructed. You could have blown the entire mission. Worse, you could have found yourself shipwrecked. I thought you were smarter than that." He snapped an about-face to disembark.

"Jack, wait. I'm sorry. You're right." She reached for his arm.

Wheeling around, he scowled. "Now is not the time. I have teams on the beach making arrests and other teams about to board the tanker. I need to get back and finish this. You go home. I'll leave with the *Stockdale* tonight."

"Jack, no." Her mind reeled, trying to find a way to make him stay. "But what about your things at home?"

"I'll organize to collect them once I've processed these guys and finished my report. I'll call you sometime this week." He swung over the side and untied the ASIS. Staring up at her, he shook his head. "Damn it, Tina."

His jaw clenched as if biting down on something hard to swallow.

Flooded by tears, her eyes blinked faster. Too stunned to speak, she stood rigid, heat flashing her cheeks. The moment froze between them. *Oh, God, what have I done?*

He shoved away from the cruiser's hull with such force it sent both vessels in opposite directions.

"Jack, please . . ." Leaning over the side, she reached after him. But he was already gone. Tearing through the waves, the ASIS carried him back to Origin Beach. Back to what he promised he would do. And she couldn't even keep a simple promise of staying near the *Stockdale*.

Harbor Island V listed in the ocean in the same way she did, alone and unmanned. Dragging her hand across her chin, she strode back into the wheelhouse and took charge of the cruiser. Tears burned tracks down her cheeks. With no other option, she set a course for the harbor. "Shit," she said aloud through gritted teeth. "Shit. Shit. Shit." And as she cursed herself, the realization of what she'd just lost in Jack Holmes hit her with such force she clutched her stomach.

CHAPTER THIRTY-THREE

Since returning alone on Tuesday night, Tina had not heard from Jack. After a sleepless night, she'd spent an uncomfortable, rather than jubilant breakfast with Victoria, Cecilia, and Andrew. She'd done her best to explain what had transpired with Operation Origin, based on the little she knew. Andrew fleshed out the story with his news that Rod Fischer never strayed from his house that night, leaving Officers O'Neal and Collins little to do before being collected early the next day. Tina's confession of how she'd disobeyed Jack's orders and why he hadn't returned with her shocked everyone. Although genuine, their sympathy was edged with disapproval, as if each of them wanted to tell her what a fool she'd been. That the risk she'd taken was unwarranted, and she was too pig-headed for her own good. But no one reprimanded her poor decision making. Without Sebastien around, Tina was left to defend against a cold war rather than a knock-down, drag-'em-out fight. She realized she preferred the latter.

"It's been five days, Cecilia, and I still haven't heard from him. What do you think I should do?" Before pacing yet another length of Hill Cottage's veranda, she paused for the older woman's counsel.

"Well, you could always contact him."

Tina screwed up her face. "What would I say? Hi, I'm the idiot who couldn't keep her promise?"

"No. Make him an offer he simply can't refuse." She smirked.

"I have no idea what you're talking about."

"I overheard someone talking in the diner the other day about World Sea Turtle Day on June sixteenth. Why not do some sort of celebration and invite Captain

Holmes over as the guest of honor for saving Harbor Island's sea turtle population? He can't possibly refuse."

Tina narrowed her eyes, considering Cecilia's suggestion. "That's not a bad idea. I'll look into it. Thanks, Cecilia. You're the best." She leaned down and pressed a grateful kiss to her cheek.

"Think nothing of it, my dear. I don't like to see young love thwarted."

No longer listening, Tina galloped down the stairs, leaving Cecilia calling out her goodbye.

* * * *

"Hello, Tina. What can I do for you?" Jack's voice sounded brusque as if she'd disturbed him from serious business, or maybe he still didn't want to talk to her.

Deciding not to revisit the past, she ventured forward in a bright, bubbly manner. "Jack, as a thank-you to you and the Coast Guard, the island's stakeholders would like to honor you with a World Sea Turtle Day celebration on the harbor. I'm hoping you and your key crew members are free next Wednesday to join us." A tense silence stretched down the phone. She pursed her lips so as not to fill it with inane comments.

"That's not necessary. It's all part of the job."

She could have been mistaken, but had his voice softened slightly? "Please, Jack. Let us say thank you for everything you've done."

"Next Wednesday you say. What time?"

"Would day or evening suit you better?"

"Probably the evening. But the *Stockdale* has gone back to Honolulu with the crew. It's only me here in Lahaina finishing off the reports with the local police."

Tina's heart leaped. "I could send Jacob over in the cruiser to collect you if you like on Wednesday. What time?" She held her breath while another pause tugged at the conversation.

"What about five o'clock?"

"Terrific. Jacob will collect you from Lahaina Harbor at five." In a quieter voice, she added, "I've had your clothes laundered and packed, so they're ready to be collected."

"That wasn't necessary, but thanks. I'll pick them up on Wednesday. By then, I'll be able to give you and the stakeholders a full report on the operation."

"Everyone is keen to hear the outcome. Thanks, Jack. I'm looking forward to seeing you on Wednesday."

"Thanks, Tina. See you then."

The line went dead. All in all, she thought it went well. There was no antagonism, blame or simpering apologies. *Very mature, in fact.* Nevertheless, she wondered if she would be able to be as equally mature when she came face to face with him in a few days' time.

* * * *

Reminiscent of the welcome party thrown for her and Seb when they first arrived, the locals chipped in to help with the World Sea Turtle Day celebration down on the harbor. Lights festooned The Esplanade, torch lamps flamed along the shoreline, brightly clothed tables groaned under the homemade food, and ice buckets chilled too many bottles of wine, while a barbeque sizzled in readiness to char everything to a crisp. Aside from cooling the workers' damp skin, the afternoon breeze carried the Hawaiian music coming from the old beach speakers down toward the harbor.

Standing on the wharf, Tina gazed back at the celebration taking shape. A warm glow filled her heart. Despite the past months' difficulties, Harbor Island had reclaimed the spot in her heart as her happy place.

"Hey, Tina, who's this surprise guest that's coming over for World Sea Turtle Day?" Brushing up against her, Rod reminded her of a tomcat on the prowl.

She moved aside. "As I wrote in the island newsletter, it's a surprise. So, you'll just have to wait and see."

He scratched his sandpaper chin. "Anyway, I thought you should be the first to know. I'm leaving Harbor Island. I'm finally going to travel like I always wanted to." His smug expression made her cringe.

"Really? When are you leaving?"

"Tomorrow." He grinned.

"That was quick." But she was pleased he was leaving. The sooner, the better.

"Well, after meeting that guy who's going to buy the cruiser, Jack's his name, right?" She nodded. "Well, I thought, what's the point of hanging around here? May as well go see the world while I can."

"Where are you off to first?"

"Not sure." He shrugged. "I'll get to Honolulu and grab a flight that takes my fancy. Just go where the wind takes me, I guess." Another cringe-worthy smug grin.

Tina shuddered but was saved by the sight of *Harbor Island V* navigating through the channel, making its way toward the wharf. She saw Jack sitting in the first mate's chair beside Jacob, and her breath quickened.

"Hey, isn't that Jack with Jacob?" Rod craned his neck, eyes squinting toward the advancing cruiser.

"Yes, it is." She did her best to keep her tone light and breezy, but Rod's revelation and his simpering behavior unsettled her.

"Hi, Tina," hollered Jack from the aft deck, his usual disarming smile stretched wide on his face. "Hey, Rod, come and help us tie off, man." He waved him over to where Jacob eased in beside the wharf. In a flash, Jack leaped out of the cruiser and kissed Tina on the cheek. "Thanks for inviting me to this shindig, Tina." He grabbed Rod's hand and pumped. "How are you doing, Rod?"

Before Rod's mouth formed an answer, two uniformed policemen leaped from the cruiser onto the wharf, handcuffs at the ready.

"What the . . .?" Rod stumbled as Jack forced him into a rear wrist lock.

As one of the officers grappled Rod's hands and cuffed him, the other read him his Miranda rights. "Rod Fischer, you're under arrest for your involvement in the illegal sea turtle trade. You have the right to remain silent. Anything you say, can and will be held against you in a court of law . . ." And as the officer continued to Miranda him, Jack guided Tina aside.

Eyes wide, she stared at him. "From what Andrew told us, Rod didn't have anything to do with the smuggling. He didn't make a move all night during Operation Origin."

"Not that night, he didn't, but he was most definitely the local mastermind of the turtle smuggling. By the time we hauled the smugglers off the beach and the tanker, and took them back to Maui, they spilled their guts about Rod. He was the one who made the contact in the first place. Putting the turtles up for the highest bidding pirates to come and collect without any threat of being discovered. All he had to do was keep the road maintained in case the smugglers needed another escape route, be on call during their night-time operations and collect a handsome return for his troubles."

"Bastard," she hissed, nailing Rod in a death stare.

"One thing I've learned in all these years is there's no honor among thieves. They'll rat each other out as quick as look at you."

"But why didn't you come and get him earlier?"

"The police have been watching his movements and his bank account. When they saw a large transfer of funds today, they knew he was on the move. They've been biding their time, getting everything in place, so when they swooped, they had enough evidence to arrest and convict him."

"Unbelievable. I can't thank you enough, Jack. Really I can't. You've been right all along. Rod, the smugglers, everything." She wanted to throw her arms around his neck and kiss him.

"Do you think so?" His voice sounded rich and throaty as his fingers intertwined with hers.

"Yes. I'm sorry about the other night."

"Forget it. I'm sorry too. I overreacted. You're not one of my crew. I had no right treating you that way. I was just so concerned you'd got into trouble on the reef and—"

She pressed his lips closed with her finger. "No. It was my fault. I acted irresponsibly. You were only doing your job. Forgive me." He nodded, and she removed her finger. "Besides, I haven't had a chance to answer your question yet."

"What question is that?"

"The one you asked me at Rainbow Falls. If I felt the same way as you, and if I thought we had a real chance at a life together."

"And?" Anticipation brightened his face.

"I do, Jack. I think we do. I'm hoping you still do as well." She held her breath.

"Oh, darling, of course, I do." He squeezed her close, and she felt every ounce of air escape her. She clung tight to him and secretly pledged never to let her pride or stubbornness ruin her future again.

* * * *

By the time Jacob delivered the police officers and Rod to Maui and returned a second time to Harbor Island, the beach party was in full swing.

"Thanks, Jacob." Tina hugged him.

"My pleasure. I never really trusted Rod. And I never liked that he had access to the cruiser when Dickie was alive."

"Well, from now on it'll be just you and me with keys to the boathouse. *Harbor Island V* is now officially under your care and maintenance."

"Thanks." His face beamed.

"It's probably time to introduce Jack," Andrew whispered in her ear. "Before the party gets too messy." He laughed, and Tina thought how wonderful it was to see Andrew happy again.

She jumped onto a makeshift rostrum of wooden crates and hushed the crowd milling on the beach. "As you know, today is World Sea Turtle Day. I'd like to introduce Captain Jack Holmes from the US Coast Guard, who arrested the sea turtle smugglers from Origin Beach. If it hadn't been for Jack, Harbor Island would have seen its turtle population decimated." She stepped down, nodding to Jack to take her place.

Loud applause welcomed him, and he bounded onto the rostrum in one effortless leap.

Suzie Lin's high-pitched voice interrupted the applause. "I knew you weren't a businessman looking to buy the cruiser." Everyone gawked at her while she wagged her finger at Jack.

"Suzie, hush now." Nearby, Pat listed from too much wine, but Marty saved her from further embarrassment.

"You hush yourself, Pat Henderson," Suzie snapped. "I knew he wasn't a businessman because the cards told me so and the cards never lie."

Good-natured laughter broke out.

"Those cards of yours are pretty damn good, then," began Jack, a twinkle in his eye. "Everyone, it was Suzie who helped us in the first place. She saw lights going to-and-fro in the harbor at odd times in the night."

Heads turned toward Suzie who puffed up with pride. "I told you," she said to Pat Henderson, who rolled her eyes. Back to Jack, she asked, "Did you find out what they were?"

"Seems the local water police had heard a rumor about pirates or smugglers in these parts and sent out a couple of night patrols. That's what you saw, Suzie."

"See. I'm not silly after all." More laughter rang out.

"Indeed, you're not. But the water police never strayed too far. It wasn't until Tina contacted the Coast Guard, and we got involved that we discovered what was happening. The local police have just arrested someone you all know. Rod Fischer." Amazed gasps and murmurs filtered through the crowd. "He masterminded the entire smuggling operation. So, it seems we've got them all. The Harbor Island sea turtle population is safe, and I have no doubt will recover over the coming seasons." A raucous cheer filled the night, and he stepped down.

"Oh, Jack . . ." With her arms slung around his neck, Tina gazed into his dark eyes.

"All's well that ends well." The lyrical voice of Cecilia Freemont interrupted the kiss Tina intended to press to his lips.

Jack smiled. "Yes, it is. Good to see you, Cecilia. And you too, Victoria." He nodded to both women.

"So, now that everything is over, will you still visit us?" asked Victoria.

Threading her arm through his, Tina exchanged a mischievous smile with him. "Captain?"

"If you ladies don't mind," he stared at Cecilia and Victoria, "I'd like to do more than visit. I'd like to spend as much of my free time here as I can. I've fallen pretty hard for Harbor Island" — his fingers twined with Tina's, their gazes fused — "and for its new owner."

"Marvelous," chimed Cecilia.

"I certainly have no objections," added Victoria.

"Neither do I." Despite the gawking onlookers, Tina melted into his arms and surrendered to their public kiss.

* * * *

Cradled in Jack's arms, Tina couldn't think of any place she'd rather be. "I can't believe it's been over three months since we first met."

"It feels like we've known each other forever, but at the same time, it feels like only yesterday." He kissed the top of her head.

"I know." Snuggling back into his chest, she molded into his body. Anchored close to shore, inside the Origin Beach reef, the cruiser bobbed on the gentle waves. Tina loved how deserted the beach appeared, knowing that next season it would be covered with turtle tracks, without human interference.

"This is the way to enjoy a Sunday — a picnic lunch on the boat by ourselves. Plenty of sun, love and . . ." He rolled her onto his lap and kissed her, long and tender.

"Mmm, I agree." She traced her fingers along his jaw, and a slow burn lit her groin.

"So, what are we going to do, Tina?"

"What would you like to do?" she purred, eager at the thought of making love on the aft deck.

"No, not that." He grinned, shaking his head. "I'm being serious. You've just about settled everything with Sebastien. Your eco-tourism plan is underway, which by early indications will succeed. Cecilia has taken up permanent residence in Hill Cottage, and your stepmother flies between Australia and here to help if you need her. But what about me? I just can't keep coming over here whenever I can."

"What do you mean?"

"I love you, Tina. You know that. I want us to wake up next to each other, every day. Not just once or twice a week. I want us to build a real life together. To have children who will one day inherit Harbor Island and continue your and Dickie's legacy."

She straightened. "But, Jack, what are you saying? What about your captaincy?"

"I've already completed twenty years of service with the Coast Guard. I could retire now with good benefits. Then, we could manage Harbor Island together."

Her breath hitched.

"Tina, will you marry me?" In an instant, he kneeled on the deck and produced a velvet ring box from his pocket. On opening the lid, a brilliant-cut solitaire diamond twinkled up at her like a lost puppy, begging to be taken home. "I know this is fast. But we did say when we first met that we're both nearing our expiration date if we want to settle down and have a family."

"Oh, Jack. I can't ask you to give up your career to be with me."

"You're not. It's my choice, much like when you gave up your journalism career for Harbor Island."

"But—"

"Tina, this whole place, you, the island, everything has got me under its spell. I knew it from the moment I landed here and met you. This is where I belong, with you on Harbor Island. It's my destiny. Please say yes."

Through misty eyes, she stared at his handsome, sincere face. Uncle Dickie had always said she needed an intelligent, ambitious man. *Jack most certainly was that.* But marriage? She'd given up her career, her life, everything to own Harbor Island and protect Uncle Dickie's legacy. And now Jack wanted to be a permanent part of that. What was there to think about? "Yes, Jack. I'd love to marry you."

"Oh, darling, my darling Tina." He pulled the ring from its box and slipped it onto her finger. "I will do everything I can to make you happy, to make us both happy."

The facets of the diamond danced like firecrackers in the sun. She touched his cheek with her left hand, at once admiring him and the circle of his commitment. "I know you will and so will I. This will be our happy place together." She cupped his face and crushed her lips to his, her heart hammering a happy beat. Like the young male warriors diving off Black Rock, she had leaped into the unknown without being dashed to pieces. She had faced her fears and been triumphant.

CHAPTER THIRTY-FOUR

"Cecilia, are you home?"

"Yes, come in, my dear."

"No, you come out here." With a quiet giggle, Tina glanced down at Jack, who was hiding near the bottom of the stairs at Hill Cottage.

"What is it?" Drifting through the doorway, Cecilia stepped onto the veranda.

"Since Jack and I are getting married soon, and you're going to be here alone while we're on our honeymoon, we thought you might need a bit more company."

"Nonsense. You're only going for a couple of weeks. I have Andrew and the staff. Anyway, I like my own company, and I'm very happy here at Hill Cottage." With a sharp nod, she made it clear she didn't need any help.

Jack jumped up from his hiding place. "So, you won't be needing this, then?" In his arms squirmed a fluffy ball with four gangly legs.

Cecilia squealed, and at the same time, the puppy barked a happy hello. "Oh, Jack. A golden retriever puppy. For me?" She rushed toward the stairs, arms outstretched.

He strode up and gave her the puppy. "Yes, she is."

"She?" Bright-eyed, Cecilia turned to Tina, who nodded.

"We remembered how much you and Uncle Dickie loved Lucy all those years ago. We figured since you're staying here forever, you need another Lucy. And here she is."

The furry bundle licked Cecilia's face as she buried her head into its coat. "Oh, she's lovely. Lucy, my own sweet Lucy." With teary eyes, she looked from Tina to Jack. "Thank you, darlings, what a wonderful surprise."

Reaching down, Tina retrieved a cardboard box. "Here's her lead, some dog food, a couple of bowls, and other bits and pieces."

"Oh, how wonderful. Hand me Lucy's lead, please. We'll take her for a walk."

Lucy spun in circles on the deck as Cecilia tried to latch the lead to her collar. "She's going to be a handful, isn't she?" She giggled like a young girl. Finally securing the dog, she led Lucy down the stairs with Tina and Jack flanking the happy couple. "I can't thank you enough. Lucy's such a happy little puppy. Look at her."

Lucy's head shoved into a low-hanging flower blossom for an almighty sniff, before dropping to the ground in search of the next odorous adventure.

"I knew you'd love her." Tina squeezed Cecilia's spare hand. "And you can bring her to the wedding as well."

"Really?"

"Yes, she can sit beside you, Victoria and mom in the front row, just as long as you keep her tied to the chair. We don't want her running off during the ceremony or dragging you across the lawn." Jack boomed a mighty chortle. Startled, the puppy turned and barked as if wanting in on the joke.

"Lucy, behave. It looks like I have my work cut out for me to get you ready for the wedding." Cecilia leaned down to stroke the puppy's head. In return, she received a love-struck look and a doggy smile. Cecilia straightened and turned to Jack. "How is your mother? Will she be well enough to come to the wedding?"

"The doctors think so. Her heart rhythm is back to normal, so they've given her the all clear at this stage."

"Good news." She turned to Tina. "And I can't wait for Victoria to arrive either. I've missed her over these past couple of months."

"Me too. It seems like ages since we were all together."

Tugging on Lucy's lead a little, Cecilia did an about-face. "Come on, Lucy. Back we go."

Jack stepped in beside Tina, clasping her hand, while Cecilia and Lucy ambled beside them. "When do you leave the Coast Guard, Jack?"

"Just before the wedding. I've got a week to vacate my service accommodation and bring my things here. I'm really looking forward to finally living here on the island and to helping Tina manage the place."

"Nothing like having a man around to help out, eh?" teased Cecilia with a sideways glance at Tina.

"I have plenty of men to help out, thank you very much."

"Yes, but Jack's different. He's here for the long haul, aren't you?"

"Absolutely. I'll be here long after you and . . . I'm sorry, I didn't mean—"

"Don't apologize for telling the truth. You and Tina will be here long after Lucy and I die. I just pray I'll be here long enough to see you start a family of your own."

"I'm sure you will. We won't be wasting any time with that," quipped Jack with a wink.

Tina explained, "I'll be forty in a couple of years, so I don't have too much time up my sleeve. We've talked about having a couple of kids, so once we're married, we intend to start straight away."

"That's wonderful news. I do love hearing about the future you plan together. Come upstairs with Lucy and me. I'll make some sandwiches for lunch." Cecilia's green eyes flashed at them. "Please?"

Exchanging a look, Tina and Jack nodded.

"Okay. As long as it isn't too much trouble." He offered his hand to guide Cecilia up the stairs.

"For you two, nothing is too much trouble. Come along now."

Watching them climb the stairs in front of her, Tina paused. How fortunate she was to have Cecilia in her life. Like a best friend and a second mother, she'd given her good advice yet allowed her to make her own decisions. And she adored Jack. Now with Lucy as part of the family, Harbor Island grew happier by the day.

* * * *

The late-afternoon wind gusted along the sidewalk, whipping the clothes and hair of the people standing outside Honolulu airport. Unseasonably cool, it sent a chill up Tina's arms. Tinged with regret, she and Victoria lingered saying goodbye to Jack, whose gaunt face and slumped shoulders showed his anguish. Tina's heart ached for her normally confident captain. "Won't you come back with us tonight, Jack? Take a break for a day or two."

"I can't, darling. There's too much to do."

"But I don't want to leave you alone. Not now."

"Tina, you have to go back and finish the wedding arrangements."

"We could postpone it if you like."

"No. We're getting married as planned." He managed a weak smile and drew her closer. "Thanks for being with me today for Mom's funeral. And you too, Victoria. Thanks for flying in earlier to be here."

"That's quite all right, Jack. Although I never met Elspeth, she must have been a good woman to have raised a son like you." She leaned over and pressed a sympathetic kiss to his cheek.

"Your plane to Kahului is leaving soon. You better check in. I'll finish everything here and see you in a few days. I love you, darling." Wrapping Tina in a tight hug, he buried his face into her neck and clutched her closer. "I can't wait for us to be married."

She pulled free of his embrace and touched her lips to his. "And I love you, too. I'll be waiting for you. Goodbye, darling." She hooked her arm into Victoria's, and they headed into the terminal. She cast a final glance back over her shoulder and flashed him a sweet smile before he turned and strode away. "Oh, God, I feel so sorry for him. This is so awful."

"I know, darling, but these things happen in life," said Victoria, in a pragmatic tone.

"But he has no one now. His father died five years ago and now his mother. He'll have no family at our wedding."

"He'll have you, and that's all that matters."

"I guess." She clutched Victoria's hand harder. "Thank goodness I still have you, Vickie."

"Yes. Just you, me and Sebastien left in our family."

"How is Seb?"

"Actually, he seems to have settled down a little. He reminds me so much of my father. When he gets his own way, he's a pleasure to be around. But heaven help anyone who tries to tell him differently on anything. Then he turns into a tyrant."

"You don't have to tell me. At best, Seb and I tolerate each other in small doses."

"He really wanted to make it to the wedding, but I think he needs a little more time away from Harbor Island."

"I understand. Let the dust settle. To tell you the truth, I'm sort of relieved he's not coming. That way there can be no upsets on the day."

"You're probably right." Victoria patted Tina's hand as they weaved through the throng of people. "I'm so excited to be seeing Cecilia again. I've missed her."

"And she's missed you. It'll be great to have some time together again, just the three of us before Jack arrives." Tina slanted a loving smile at her step-mom.

"Yes, it will."

A sense of happy urgency ushered them to the gate. It was good to be going home.

CHAPTER THIRTY-FIVE

Standing on the steps of the great pavilion, Tina gazed out toward the harbor. Just on sunset, the sky burned with sweeping patterns of orange clouds through which intermittent fading patches of blue marked the last of the day. An eerie purplish hue colored the ocean. Its waves pitched themselves onto the beach, like a lover unwilling to leave. The unerring rhythm of the island sustained her, just as it had always done since she was a child. It had been three days since Elspeth's funeral, yet the world kept turning, day into night and tide upon tide. It was nature's disregard for human affairs and emotions which reminded Tina that the circle of life was endless, yet perfectly complete. Very soon, she would share this eternal magic with someone she loved and who loved her in return.

Horn beeping, Jacob eased the Chevy into the turning circle, bringing it to a stop on the gravel sweep in front of her. Rushing down the stairs, she flew to open the passenger door. "Happy birthday, Jack." As he slid from the cabin, she threw herself into his arms and peppered his face in kisses. "Come in, darling. Victoria and Cecilia can't wait to see you. We've got cake and champagne waiting."

A ghost of a smile passed his lips. He took her hand. "Let's go in."

Beside him, she strode up the stairs, butterflies circling in her stomach. "Jack, what's wrong?"

"I'll explain everything when we're inside."

After effusive happy-birthday welcomes from Victoria and Cecilia, Jack turned serious. "Can we all sit at the table? I've got something to say."

Trading confused looks, Tina, Victoria, and Cecilia moved to where he indicated at the dining table. At the head, he lowered himself into the carver chair; Tina sat to his right, Victoria next to her and Cecilia to his left. The atmosphere crackled with tense anticipation. No one spoke as they settled into their places.

"As you know, my mother just died. Being the only child, I was left to go through her things, and I found this." From his jacket pocket, he pulled out a frayed, yellowed packet. To avoid damaging the old envelope, Jack carefully fingered out a piece of equally ancient paper, folded into thirds. Tina looked at the two older women, who sat rigid and wide-eyed. "Does anyone know what this is?" Taking his time, he looked at Tina, but she shook her head. He shifted to Victoria, and she shrugged. Then, he locked his intense gaze on Cecilia, who lowered her eyes. "Let me read it to you. I'll abbreviate its contents." He cleared his throat. "Application having been made on the thirtieth day of October 1974, to me the Director of State Children Department by Robert John Holmes and Elspeth Carol Holmes, resident at 25 Noah Street, Honolulu, to adopt Richard, an infant of the male sex, aged three weeks, an American citizen, the child of CiCi Freemont—"

"What?" The shock tore a gasp from Tina's throat.

Jack lowered the paper and turned to Cecilia. "Is this you, Cecilia? Are you the CiCi Freemont in this adoption order?"

"Yes, Jack. I am."

"Oh, dear." Victoria's hand stroked her throat.

Cecilia dropped her head, avoiding Jack's gaze. The curtains in the great pavilion hung motionless. Not a breath of air stirred. Not a sound penetrated the vacuous space. Only the deafening beat of Tina's heart confirmed she was awake. She dared not move or speak for fear that the frozen tableau of the four of them would shatter into a million pieces.

After a moment, Cecilia straightened and met Jack's blistering stare with a blast of glittering green. "I named you Richard after your father, Dickie Reginald." Her words landed with a thud.

"Oh, God, Uncle Dickie?" Tina sagged.

"Go on." With features carved from stone, Jack remained inscrutable. Ramrod straight, each hand clenched on the table, he looked a tower of tormented emotions.

"Your father and I had had one wild, impetuous moment long ago. I was twenty-five, and he was eighteen, struggling with his sexuality. We both loved each other in only the way young love can: all-consuming, passionate and completely. After that one time, we both knew our love was doomed. Dickie's preference was for men, but our love for each other remained unalterable. When I found out I was pregnant, I left Harbor Island, for everyone's sake."

"Did Uncle Dickie know?" interrupted Tina.

"No. I never told him because he would have wanted to marry me, to do the right thing, even if it ruined his life in the process." She sighed. "No, Dickie never knew—"

"But I did," interjected Victoria. "Cecilia confided in me back then. Together, we found her a place in Honolulu to stay and give birth to her baby. If my father had found out, he would have disinherited Dickie immediately, and Harbor Island, the greatest love of Dickie's life beside Cecilia, would have been lost forever."

"So instead you chose to lose me?" An edge of bitterness sharpened Jack's voice.

"I made the only choice I could at the time, Jack. I loved Dickie very much, but Harbor Island's legacy was far more important than our doomed love. I was twenty-six years old and cast out by my own parents for wanting to be a singer. I wasn't financially able to raise you on my own. With all my heart, I believed you would have better opportunities in a stable family with both a father and a mother. And look at who you've become. Captain Jack

Holmes." She beamed proudly at him. "It was 1974, Jack. Things were a lot different then. There was little future for an unwed mother and her illegitimate child."

"Didn't your parents ever tell you that you were adopted, Jack?" asked Victoria, her voice soft and sympathetic.

"They did, but they never told me anything more than that. And this is the first time I've seen this adoption order. When I saw the name CiCi Freemont, I remembered Tina telling me about Cecilia's stage name."

"And that's why you two did a double-take when you first saw Jack, isn't it?" Tina leaned forward, scrutinizing Victoria and Cecilia. "You saw some of Uncle Dickie's features in his face. I thought there was something familiar about him as well, particularly when he smiled, but I couldn't work out why. Now, I understand."

"You're right. Cecilia and I recognized Dickie in Jack the moment you introduced us. We've talked about it since, but we agreed to let sleeping dogs lie, as they say."

Cecilia cast him a gentle smile. "When I first met you, Jack, you reminded me so much of Dickie. Not just because of your good looks, but the way you carried yourself, your mannerisms and your sense of duty. The more time I spent with you, the more bells rang in my head, and I knew." A glint of tears shone in her eyes. "I just knew that you were our son."

"You have Reginald and Freemont blood in your veins, Jack. You were conceived here, and you belong on Harbor Island. I have a feeling that's why you fell in love with the island and with Tina," added Victoria, a touch of whimsy in her voice.

"Forty-five years ago, Dickie and I set this destiny into motion. A destiny you couldn't deny." Cecilia looked him straight in the eyes as she placed her hand on his.

Watching biological mother and son connect consciously for the first time, Tina stiffened. Either the encounter would end in an explosion of hateful emotions and bitter resentment or transmute into something miraculous.

"Jack . . ." Victoria drew his attention. "You are the rightful heir to Harbor Island, except Dickie didn't know you existed. You have every right to contest the will if you choose." She paused for effect. "However, I don't think that's what you want. Together, you and Tina can achieve great things here. Then your children will continue the Reginald line and your legacy."

In a thundercloud of emotion, Jack shoved up from the chair. "Damn it. Why couldn't all this stay a secret? For God's sake, Tina and I are getting married. How could I contest the will? What sort of asshole would try and take his fiancée's inheritance away from her?"

"But, Jack . . ." Tina sprang up and rushed to his side.

"Think about it, Tina. Once this comes out people will wonder why I'm *not* contesting the will. Then the rumor mill will start, and everyone will whisper behind our backs. In the end, they'll think I'm no better than a cowardly gold digger, trying to weasel in on your inheritance, rather than being man enough to contest it myself."

"But it isn't true? Who cares what people think?" urged Tina.

"Not me usually, but there's a helluva lot at stake here. You, me, Harbor Island, the respect of the staff."

"But, Jack, who needs to know?" It was Cecilia's gentle voice that galvanized everyone's attention.

He paused, looking down at her. "What do you mean? You can't keep this a secret."

"Why not?" she asked with a shrug.

"We kept it a secret until now. Just because you and Tina know about this, doesn't mean it has to become public knowledge," added Victoria, agreeing with her friend.

"Are you serious?" He wheeled to face her. "Don't you want everyone to know I carry Reginald blood? That the estate is actually being handed down through the bona fide bloodline?"

"No. I'm more interested in you and Tina starting your married life together, without the burden of public opinion. That's why Cecilia and I were willing never to broach the possibility of you being her son."

"That's right. Victoria and I would have taken the secret to our graves. And we still can."

"Me too, darling." Tina slinked an arm around his waist and gave him a squeeze.

He broke free of her reassurance and paced back and forth with his thoughts. With an aching heart, Tina looked on, while he wrestled with his emotions. She glanced sideways at Victoria and Cecilia who shook their heads to let him be, so she slipped back into her chair and waited. Time stood still while Jack grappled with his world turned upside down. Tina knew he agonized over each possibility, trying to make sense of a situation he'd had no control over. Eventually, the mask of misery began to fade from his face, and his pace slowed. He returned to his chair, folded his arms on the table and eyeballed each woman in turn. "So, you're suggesting we keep the current status quo. I'm ex-Captain Jack Holmes marrying Tina Templeton, the rightful heir to and owner of Harbor Island, and we live happily ever after?"

"Correct," said Cecilia and Victoria in unison.

He tilted his head toward Victoria. "Are you sure it'll never bother you that no one will ever know my true ancestry?"

She shrugged. "No. Does it bother you?"

"Maybe it will when we have kids. I don't know—"

"Well, it'll be your decision, with Tina of course, if you want to tell them your ancestry when they're old enough to understand."

He turned to Cecilia and clasped her hands. "And what about you? How do you feel about keeping this a secret?"

"Oh, Jack, I've lived with you in my heart every day for all these years. Now, I get to live with you on Harbor Island, like mother and son. I can never replace your mother who raised and cared for you, but if you let me, I can be a pseudo mother and grandmother to you, Tina and your children. What's the difference if the rest of the world knows or not? I've found you, and I couldn't be happier."

A calm hush fell in the great pavilion. Like a deserted church, after confession has been heard and the parishioners gone, nothing remained but quiet serenity.

Jack stared off into the distance for some moments, while the women waited. Tina reached out and laced her fingers through his hand. She felt so sorry for him. She knew what it was like to lose both parents. To feel like it was just you, without a mother or a father. Here was Jack, with both his parents gone, now finding out that his biological mother sat across the table from him and that Uncle Dickie was his father; that his ancestry gave him the legal right to the island. Her head reeled with the news. She couldn't imagine how he felt, but she prayed he'd make the right choice.

His chest heaved. "I remember when I was at school, I was all fired up about bad things happening in the world perpetrated by bad people. My football coach, Mr. Harrison sat me down and asked me what I was going to do with my life. At the time, I told him I wasn't sure. He looked me square in the eye and said, 'Jack, if you don't like the world around you, get out there and build a new one.' And I did, by joining the Coast Guard. And now, I have another new world to build with Tina." He gazed at her and his mouth loosened into a soft smile. "Harbor Island. No matter how I got here, whether it was fate, love or sheer dumb luck, I'm here. And nobody but the four of us in this room needs to know the history of how it all began." He paused. His mouth widened in his winning smile. The same signature smile he'd inherited from his father. Decision made.

Tears spilled from Cecilia's eyes. "Happy birthday, my darling Jack. Never did I think I would spend one of your birthdays with you, my wonderful son. How lucky am I." Rising from her chair, she slipped in beside him and kissed his cheek. "I know Dickie would be so very proud of you, as I am."

"Thank you, Cecilia. I'm sure we'll spend lots of time together talking about him. He sounds like a remarkable man."

"Yes, your father was."

"Happy birthday, Jack," added Victoria, "and I wish you many more."

He scratched his neck and grinned. "I'll say this only once and never again . . . Thanks, Aunty Vickie." He chuckled and gave her a mischievous wink. She reached out and squeezed his hand.

"Despite these revelations, you'll always be Captain Jack Holmes to me. Happy birthday, my love." Tina pulled his face to hers and planted a wet kiss to his lips.

Jack slapped his hands on the table and looked around the great pavilion. "Now, where's that birthday cake and champagne."

* * * *

A Hawaiian spring wedding in the grounds of the Templeton Residence drew people from near and far. Even the local press ferried over to watch former award-winning Australian investigative journalist Tina Templeton marry ex-US Coast Guard Captain Jack Holmes.

The tireless work of the groundsmen resulted in the gardens resembling a lavish movie set. A couple of days before the ceremony, all the flowers, especially the dendrobium and phalaenopsis orchids bloomed en masse. When Tina picked a few on the morning of her wedding day, she assuaged some of her guilt because there were so many. *Sorry, Uncle Dickie, but I don't think you'd mind my picking them for my wedding bouquet. After all, Jack is your son.* As she snipped the weighty stems, she sensed her uncle's loving presence and approval. Everywhere she looked, everything was under control, everything was perfect. Resplendent grass formed an even green carpet on which the newly built gazebo perched ready for the ceremony, while thousands of vivid plumeria flowers lined a center aisle flanked by neat rows of white timber chairs adorned with white satin ribbons and bows. The staff flitted around adding finishing touches. There was nothing for her to do but get married.

In Hill Cottage, Tina wrangled a floral crown trailing a long, layered veil onto her head. Dressed in a fitted ivory silk sheath, satin slippers and holding a bouquet of orchids and straggling jungle vine, she looked like a medieval princess.

"Oh, darling, you're beautiful." Victoria patted tears from her eyes.

"Simply perfect," said Cecilia. "Now, I have something for you, my dear." Scurrying to the wardrobe, she returned with a small wooden box. "Many years ago, when I left the island, I told your grandmother, Leilani, I was pregnant with Dickie's child."

Victoria gasped. "You never told me Mother knew."

"Sorry, my dear friend, I promised her I wouldn't." She turned to Tina. "When I was leaving, Leilani gave me money to help me through. And she gave me something else." From the box, she lifted a fine gold necklace on which hung a large, deep lime-green stone. "This is peridot. I think it was mined from the quarry here long ago. It's worth quite a lot. I expect she thought that if I needed money, I could pawn it. But I could never do that. You must have it, Tina, on your wedding day. I know that's what Leilani would have wanted." Stretching in front of her, Cecilia pulled the necklace around Tina's throat and fastened it.

"It's gorgeous on you," said Victoria, staring in admiration.

"Yes, it is. Congratulations, my dear. I wish you and Jack the future Dickie and I missed out on." Cecilia kissed her on both cheeks.

"Thank you, Cecilia." Her fingers fidgeted with the stone. "It's very generous of you. I'll treasure it always." She paused. "Now, we best get moving. You two go first. And once I hear you singing, I'll do the big reveal."

Victoria and Cecilia chatted like schoolgirls as they hurried down the stairs from Hill Cottage and down the jungle corridor to the main property. With her veil held high by two housemaids, Tina stepped at a slower pace until she finally began her long walk toward the gardens flanking the great pavilion. The housemaids scurried like mice, rearranging her veil behind her, and then fled to join the staff watching the ceremony.

As Tina came into full view of the guests, the sultry, jazz tones of cabaret singer CiCi Freemont rang out. Singing *a capella*, her voice rose loud and pure. "That old black magic has me in its spell, that old black magic that I know so well . . ."

Unable to squelch the sheer joy bubbling up inside her, Tina trembled, her bouquet of Uncle Dickie's favorite orchids dancing in her hands. She'd been right all along. Harbor Island was her happy place.

END OF PART TWO

PART THREE

2027

CECILIA

CHAPTER THIRTY-SIX

"Come on, you two. Time to wash up for dinner." The shrill tones in her voice left no doubt as to Tina's annoyance.

"But, Mom, can't we stay a little longer with Nanny CiCi?" At the age of seven, Richard Holmes was unmistakably a Reginald. Possessing the dark, exotic looks of his great-grandmother, Leilani, he was a handsome young boy. Though what pleased Cecilia most was that Richard had inherited a strong sense of duty to care for others, just like his grandfather and father. Beyond proud, she knew he'd carry on Dickie's and Jack's legacy into the future.

"Please, Mommy, I want to stay with Nanny CiCi and Lucy a little longer." Christine, on the other hand, carried most of Tina's genes. Even at four, she was tall, blonde and stubborn, often crossing swords with her mother. Her nickname of daddy's princess proved most apt as she often played Tina and Jack off against each other with innocent finesse. *She's a smart one, that one.*

"Now, children, you must do what your mother tells you. And poor Lucy is getting tired. Don't forget she's getting old, just like your Nanny CiCi." She opened her arms, and the children rushed in for a farewell cuddle.

"I'm sorry, Cecilia, have they been too boisterous?" With an apologetic smile, Tina mounted the stairs of Hill Cottage to greet Cecilia with a kiss.

"Of course not, my dear. They've been perfect angels." She exchanged a wink with both children, who giggled.

"Okay. Time to leave Nanny CiCi alone and do as your mother says." With unquestionable authority, Jack's towering frame appeared at the bottom of the stairs. "Say your goodbyes. It's time for dinner."

Richard and Christine pouted and clung to Cecilia.

"Do you want to join us tonight for dinner? I can get one of the staff to help you down to the great pavilion if you like?" Tina stroked Cecilia's hand.

"Please, Nanny CiCi," pleaded Richard and Christine.

"Not tonight, my dears." She kissed their flushed cheeks. "I'm feeling a little tired. I think I'll just have some sandwiches sent up. If you could do that for me, please, Tina?"

"Of course."

Having joined his family on the veranda, Jack leaned in and whispered so no one could hear. "Are you okay, Mother?"

Lifting her eyes, she exchanged his worried expression with a loving smile. "Of course, I am, Jack. Now, you take the children. After dinner, maybe you'll bring me ice-cream so we can all have some together. How's that?"

Much whooping and jumping from the children meant the trade-off of leaving now for having ice-cream afterward met with their approval.

"We'll see you after dinner, then." Tina leaned over and kissed her once more.

"Bye, Nanny CiCi. Bye, Lucy." Richard and Christine kissed one of Cecilia's cheeks each and hugged Lucy in turn. Scrambling to take their mother's hand, they skipped down the stairs.

Lingering, Jack stroked her arms. "We'll all come up for ice-cream after dinner. Okay?"

"That would be wonderful. Now off you go."

"See you soon." He bent down and kissed her cheek.

Reaching up, she cupped his face in her hands. "You have made me so very proud, Jack. You and Tina have transformed Harbor Island into something far greater than your father and I could have ever done. And Richard and Christine are simply wonderful children. I love you, my darling son."

"And I love you, too, Mother." With tears pricking his eyes, he turned away and followed his family.

"Come, Lucy, sit beside me." With a slight limp, the old dog waddled over to drop down beside the rattan chair. Straining to stroke her head, Cecilia reached down, her fingertips just touching. "Oh, Lucy what a time we've had, eh, girl?" The dog lifted its face, now peppered with greying hair. "Despite everything, Harbor Island has kept its secrets and flourished. You've been my best friend through all these years, Lucy." With a shallow exhale, she closed her eyes.

"And what about me, CiCi? Wasn't I your best friend?"

The cheeky tone of a familiar voice stirred her. On opening her eyes, she blinked. There, in front of her stood Dickie, his trademark smile lighting his face. Young, handsome and radiant, he shone like a heavenly angel.

"Of course, you were, Dickie. Always." Brightened by his presence, she returned his loving smile.

"Do you remember what you told me, CiCi?" He tilted his head.

"What was that, my darling?"

"That if you were the right one for me, I would find you, and we would be together."

"Yes, I remember now."

"Well, here I am." His hands opened wide, sending his aura into effervescing, golden shafts of light. "We have done our duty. We have fulfilled our destinies. The time has come for us to finally be together. I've missed you, CiCi."

"I've missed you, too, Dickie."

"Are you ready, my love?"

"Oh yes, my darling. I'm ready." Weightless, she rose from her chair and placed her hand delicately in his. Instantly, she transformed from an old lady into the impetuous young woman of twenty-five who had first arrived on Harbor Island.

"I have always loved you, CiCi."
"And I, you, my darling Dickie."

Whimpering, Lucy gazed out into space. Inclining her head from side to side, she watched an inexplicable reunion take place. Confused, the old dog turned her head to lick the limp and lifeless hand of her owner. In the distance, another fiery sunset streaked across the delphinium blue skies, while happy gulls squawked over the harbor as they headed home for the evening. At last, everyone had found their home, their happy place.

THE END

BEHIND THE SCENES

I remember vividly when the idea for this book came to me. My husband and I were out in our boat on the Broadwater on the Gold Coast in Australia. It was one of those magnificent boating days — calm, sultry and cloudless. Having just completed *Retribution*, I'd been waiting on the inspiration for my next book. Nothing yet had beamed in. As someone who is willing to wait for inspiration rather than forcing my creativity, I was enjoying a couple of weeks off from my writing schedule.

While we were relaxing on the Broadwater and lapping up the beautiful weather, an old Huon pine cruiser drove past us. Like a bolt out of the blue, *Island of Secrets* landed in my consciousness. The story arrived well-formed, with characters I immediately visualized.

I'd visited Hawaii a couple of years earlier, and Maui, with its volcanic geography, lush vegetation, and captivating sea life lived up to its name of the Magic Isle. It was the ideal location for *Island of Secrets*.

Immersing myself in the island's history, I grabbed a copy of James A. Michener's epic tale, *Hawaii*. In discovering how the missionaries came to the islands and their impact on the indigenous population and culture, I gained a deeper insight into this special place. An insight I've woven into Part One of *Island of Secrets*.

Told across forty years, the story begins in the heady 1970s. Having been a teenager during this time, I drew on my experience, as well as researching this amazing decade. The early 1970s saw the world undergo exponential change. With a sense of freedom coursing through our veins, we viewed the planet's evolution with passionate optimism, seeking out opportunities to make the world a better place. It was an empowering time of enthusiasm, peace protests, and free love, all bubbling forth from the post-civil and equal-rights era and the women's liberation movement. With this as her backdrop, Cecilia launches into her big adventure. And like many young women of that time, she is fired in the kiln of life. In Part Two, we meet her again. Now in her late sixties, she is matured and polished, but her essence and loyalties remain the same. She becomes the reflection character for Tina, who must deal with her own personal and environmental issues to save the legacy of Harbor Island.

At its heart, *Island of Secrets* examines the lives of not just Cecilia and Tina, but all the empowered women — Leilani, Victoria, Beatrice, Loretta, Silly Suzie et al. Women from different times and cultures who face similar challenges and find the courage and strength to overcome them. It is an exploration of how we view the fundamentals of life. Is it love or money that motivates us? Where does loyalty lie in the equation? What moves us to make the decisions we do? And no matter the dilemma we face, there comes a time when we must acknowledge that love is the ultimate answer.

I hoped you've enjoyed reading *Island of Secrets* as much as I did writing it. If you have, please consider leaving an honest review on the retailer's site and/or on Goodreads.

Sign up for my no spam newsletter at:

https://rebrand.ly/dd-newsletter

AUTHOR BIOGRAPHY

For readers of contemporary fiction, Diane Demetre is a fresh, passionate voice in storytelling. She is an award-winning author of genre-busting romance novels with a twist. Her dramatic flair, sense of place and evocative style create an entertaining escape for her readers. Diane's works feature empowered heroines who live life to the fullest on their terms, much like the author herself.

Winner of Romance Writers of Australia Emerald Pro Award Best Unpublished Manuscript 2017, *Retribution* is a masterful creation of insightful suspense.

Winner of Luminosity Publishing Readers' Choice Awards Best Books and Best Covers 2015 and 2016, the Dance of Love series are stand-alone titles filled with erotic adventures set in exotic locations. *Dancing Queen* was voted Luminosity Publishing's Best Book and Best Cover for 2015, while *Tiny Dancer* and *Dance to a Gypsy Beat* were voted Best Book and Best Cover for 2016.

Connect with Diane

https://dianedemetre.com/

ALSO BY DIANE DEMETRE

Dance of Love series:

Dancing Queen – Book One

Tiny Dancer – Book Two

Dance to a Gypsy Beat – Book Three

Romantic Suspense:

Retribution

DIANE DEMETRE

LUMINOSITY
PUBLISHING